Gateway

GATEWAY

This book is a work of fiction. The characters, places, incidents, and dialogue are the product of the author's imagination and are not to be construed as real, or if real, are used fictitiously. Any resemblance to actual events, locales, or persons, either living or dead, is purely coincidental.

For more information, to inquire about rights to this or other works, or to purchase copies for special educational, business, or sales promotional uses please write to:

The Zharmae Publishing Press, L.L.C.
5638 Lake Murray Blvd, Suite 217
La Mesa, California 91942
www.zharmae.com

FIRST EDITION

Printed in the United States of America

ISBN:978-1-937365-59-2

10 9 8 7 6 5 4 3 2 1

Gateway

Brian Dorsey

Spokane | Seattle | Portland
San Francisco | Los Angeles | La Mesa

Gateway is dedicated to the memory of Tyler Ammon, my daughter Em's best friend. Tyler's father (Jeff Ammon, LT, USN) was killed in action in Afghanistan in 2008 and a few months later, Tyler was diagnosed with cancer. Following a long and brave struggle, Tyler lost his battle in 2010. In a way that only military families can understand, the Ammon family is our family, and neither Jeff nor Tyler will be forgotten.

In addition to the lead character carrying Tyler's name, 10% of the author's first-year profits will be donated to Relay for Life so that Tyler's fight can go on until a cure is found. For more information go to: http://www.relayforlife.org/. To donate directly in Tyler's name, donate to Bubba's Bunch at North Mason Relay for Life.

. . .

Gateway

Prelude

The concussion from another explosion felt like a punch to his gut.

"Captain Martin," yelled Major Tyler Lucius Stone over the comms circuit.

"Almost…there," panted Captain Emily Martin, her voice strained from running at a full sprint. "45 seconds."

"You've got twenty," shouted Stone over the sound of gunfire.

"Roger—move your asses!" Stone could hear Martin yell to her men before her comms cut out.

A round impacted on the boulder beside Stone, peppering him with splintered fragments of rock. Wincing, Stone quickly raised his rifle and drew a bead on the first Terillian that came into view. Three rounds thundered from his rifle, and his opponent crumpled to the ground.

"Are they in position yet?" asked Lt. Hauser. "Team two is ready."

"Stand—"

Another grenade exploded nearby, showering Stone and his men with splinters, leaves, and dark, gritty sand. "Standby," he yelled into the comms circuit.

Returning fire, Stone quickly surveyed the situation. His team of four was pinned down, no doubt, just as Stone had planned. A platoon of Terillian Scout Rangers had his men cornered at the base of a rock formation and were advancing rapidly—too rapidly. In their haste to make prisoners or trophies of the vaunted Humana Elite Guard, they had lost their situational awareness. While the Terillians quickly advanced, Stone's other men had flanked them and were almost in position to spring their trap.

"In position," shouted Martin over the comms circuit. "Standing by."

"All units, open fire!" ordered Stone.

The already chaotic scene erupted with a crescendo of gunfire as both flanks of the Terillian troops melted away.

In a few seconds it was over.

His ears still ringing from the explosions and gunfire, Stone slowly rose from cover to survey the field. As he stood up, clumps of dirt and debris fell off his uniform and a small cloud of dust rose around him as he shook off the remaining fragments of rock, earth, and vegetation that had covered him during the firefight.

The concentrated fire from Stone's men was effective; the small underbrush to his front had been mowed down as if a giant scythe had cleared the area of everything living. Strewn among the jagged stumps and scattered leafs were the bodies of several Terillians.

A motion of Stone's hand directed the rest of his team to rise and check for survivors.

"They walked right into that one, sir," a nearby private boasted to Stone as they walked toward the center of the carnage.

Stone looked down at his ammunition counter. *20 remaining* was displayed. A little longer and they would have been throwing rocks at the Terillians.

"Easy day, Private," smiled Stone. It wasn't really that easy but he figured he didn't need to let the new guy know just how close it had been.

"Major," came a voice from behind Stone.

He turned to meet the sound. Captain Martin saluted as she wiped a long line of dirt from her left cheek with her other hand.

"Sir," she reported. "Thirty-four Ters engaged, Thirty-four kills."

"Our casualties?" asked Stone.

"One KIA—Lt. Vena, the First Family kid, and three wounded, none serious," she replied.

"Vena," repeated Stone.

"Yeah, that black sheep kid from the Vena Family. The one whose daddy made him join to clear his name after that whole relationship-with-one-of-us-commoners thing," chimed Martin.

Stone knew Vena's name all too well. He had protested his assignment from the beginning. If Vena had not been from a First Family, there was no way he would have been in the Guard. His combat skills were marginal. His aptitude was always overridden by his pride, and he barely made it through the Guard initiation. In fact, Stone had thought Vena's father planned for exactly this outcome. A dead son with military honors might have sounded better to the Vena family than one who loved a commoner.

"I know who Vena is," replied Stone sternly.

"Of course, sir," yielded Martin with a nod. "I've called for a pickup, and we will have Vena and our wounded out of here in five minutes. I'll have a team check the Ters for intel as well."

"Very well, Captain."

"Sir," replied Martin as she saluted once again and turned to carry out her duties.

"Emily," exclaimed Stone as Martin started to walk away.

"Yes, sir," replied Martin and she stopped and spun back toward Stone. As she turned, her auburn red hair, tied up in a tight ponytail, brushed lightly across her face. At just under 177 cm, a sculpted athletic build, smooth olive-colored skin, and brilliant blue eyes, Captain Emily Martin could rival any First Family heiress with her beauty. But she was too good a soldier to care about such things.

"Anything else, sir?" she asked.

"Good job getting into position back there. I can always count on you to save my bacon at the last minute."

"If I had been there any sooner it would have been boring," she smiled. "And I hate boring. Besides, as soon as we're all done here, we're off for rest-and-freakin'-relaxation for the next four weeks," she said as she put her finger up to her head like a pistol. "Shoot me now," she joked as she turned and stepped over a dead Terillian.

Chapter 1

Major Tyler Lucius Stone smoothed the long, thick sleeves of his heavy uniform as the shuttle drifted toward the orbiting station. Running his hand down the crisp sleeve of his pressed tunic, Stone noticed the army of lint brazenly advancing across his uniform. While meticulously plucking the invading particles from his sleeve, he felt the coarse fabric of his uniform against his calloused fingers. The rigid cloth immediately reminded him of the unyielding and often frustrating idiots at High Command. Both, dress uniforms and armchair generals, were a pain in the ass, but at least the uniforms didn't get anyone killed.

He missed his fatigues. Humani combat fatigues were designed to feel like a second skin, but dress uniforms retained the coarse, unventilated, and undeniably uncomfortable feel—all in the name of tradition. Every time Stone was forced to wear his dress uniform, it only intensified his hatred of the "military geniuses" that made all of the decisions without a clue of how they would impact him and his men.

"Major Stone," reported the shuttle pilot over the intercom, "we will arrive at Gateway Station in approximately ten minutes."

"Very well, Lieutenant," he replied. "How about you do the inspection and I will fly the shuttle back."

"Say again, sir?" asked the pilot.

"Nothing, Lieutenant," said Stone with a small chuckle. Stone dreaded the administrative and political aspects of his R&R assignment. As a member of the Elite Guard he was much more at home in battle dress, loaded down with ammunition and covered with the dirt and grime of the field.

Rest and relaxation...what a joke, Stone thought as he shifted his attention to a second wave of lint that had assaulted his trousers. He let out a grunt of frustration.

We can travel across star systems but can't come up with a lint-free dress uniform? Stone thought.

The endless inspections, glad-handing, and political niceties were more stressful than a recon mission deep into the Dark Zone. This inspection was the third of the week: a visit to the Gateway control center. Militarily speaking, the Gateway station was probably the most important outpost on the far edge of the Xen Empire. Its strategic position and the station's proximity to Alpha Humana also made it perfect fodder for inspection teams. The need for periodic inspection was real, but why the hell did he have to wear his dress uniform? Chalk another one up for the uniform regulations and the ability of something as innocuous as lint to ruin his day.

"Standby for final approach," reported the pilot.

Stone naturally shifted his center of gravity as the shuttle banked to make its approach. As he did, he looked out the window toward Alpha Humana. He had spent less than half of his "rest and relaxation" at home. Such was the fate of a soldier. And one he gladly accepted, especially when the alternative was dealing with the First Family politics of his fiancée, Lady Astra Varus, and her father, Senator Dominotra Varus. Despite her beauty and intelligence, Stone felt his engagement more a matter of duty to his family because of the social and political rewards it would bring his black sheep branch of the Lucius family.

The jolt of the magnetic mooring lines alerted Stone that the shuttle had arrived. Stone quickly removed a few more pieces of lint, although it was a lost cause. Smoothing out his sleeve one last time, Stone readied himself for a day of tedious inspection and political posturing.

The shuttle door opened. Stone squinted as his eyes adjusted to the white brightness of the compartment. Quickly focusing, Stone surveyed the scene in front of him. The passageway leading to the hangar deck was immaculate. As the passage to the station's quarterdeck was the first thing visiting politicians and flag officers saw, it was constantly being shined, buffed, and sparkled. Clean beyond any practical purpose and ornately decorated with unit awards, military statues, and hand-woven bunting, the ostentatious display seemed a waste to Stone. As he stepped from the hatch of the shuttle, Stone was greeted by the Gateway Station Executive and the security officer.

"Welcome aboard, Major Tyler Lucius Stone," reported the security officer. "I am Captain Nathanial Li."

A well-dressed colonel stood next to Li, impatiently awaiting Li's introduction.

"Allow me to introduce our Executive, Colonel Cataline Tacitus, patriarch of the Tacitus family," said Li. Cataline was of average height and build, with a remarkably unforgettable face. Despite his natural plainness, Cataline displayed all the accoutrement of his wealth and power. His hair was well groomed and starting to gray, giving his mane a distinguished salt-and-pepper look. His boots and belt, while within regulation, were clearly designed specifically for him and probably more expensive than Stone's entire wardrobe.

In typical First Family fashion, Cataline stood like a statue awaiting the appropriate response between members of elite families.

"Colonel Cataline Tacitus," replied Stone. "I am Major Tyler Lucius Stone. I am honored to make your acquaintance."

Although he hated such political uselessness, Stone ended his greeting with a slight bow to indicate the position of a patriarch of a First Family.

"Greetings, Major Lucius Stone," replied Cataline in all of his self-ingratiating majesty. "How are things on Alpha Humana?"

"Well, Colonel—"

"I have heard," interrupted Cataline before Stone could reply, "of your recent engagement to Lady Astra Varus. It is quite the talk among the First Families. Senator Dominotra Varus must be happy to add your family's illustrious military reputation to the Varus political sphere."

Cataline paused. "And it definitely won't damage your family's standing, given the indiscretions of your ancestor, Lady Julia Lucius."

Stone's disdain for Cataline was growing quickly.

"I try to avoid politics, Colonel," replied Stone calmly. "I, like my ancestors, bring honor to the family through military service."

The Cataline gave a sardonic smile in understanding of Stone's implied slight. "Yes, of course," replied Cataline. "Enough about Humani gossip; we should commence the inspection."

"Yes," added Captain Li. Stone could tell Li was happy to break the tension between the two senior officers and get to work.

"We are always happy to have the Elite Guard help ensure our security measures are sound," added Li.

"No need to blow smoke up my ass," replied Stone. "Inspections are universally despised except for the administrative idiots at the command level."

Stone did not fail to catch Cataline's shocked reaction to his all-too-truthful reply.

"Regardless, Major," interrupted Cataline, allowing his annoyance to show. "Occasional inspections are a key indicator of efficiency and morale."

"Of course, Colonel," replied Stone, "but if you train only to pass inspections, you find your command's efficiency and morale impacted by constantly trying to meet random checklists and metrics that don't really prepare the men for combat...but I guess non-combatant commands have a different...let's call it...perspective on things."

Stone cast a knowing smile toward Li, who was trying not to show too much enjoyment at the not-so-subtle jab at his pompous commander.

Stone continued. "I figured I would review the command-directed security checklist, walk through a security drill, and inspect the records. That should give me enough comments to validate my visit. What do you think, Captain?"

"As you wish, Major," replied Captain Li, returning Stone's smile.

"So goes the Humana military machine in all its bureaucratic glory," said Stone. "Let's get this over with and let you get back to work."

"Major Stone," huffed the irritated Cataline"I hope it is your intention to give us a thorough inspection."

"Always, Colonel," replied Stone. "The Guard is glad to be of assistance."

Stone could play the game too, even though he hated it.

***

Captain Li led the way as he, Cataline, and Stone toured the control room. The room was full of the normal activity one would expect in a control center for a station tasked with controlling the defense grid for an entire section of the Xen Empire. The green hue from display panels illuminated the individual workstations of the dimly lit room. At the center of the room a massive holographic display screen provided a real-time update of overall satellite grid status as well as other data points ordered up by the watch commander.

"This is the hub of the station, Major Stone," stated Li. "Since the signing of the Peace Accords with the Terillian Confederation over 150 years ago, Gateway Station has controlled the satellite grid that monitors and controls access to the Dark Zone as established in the Accords."

"Captain," interrupted Cataline, "the correct term is Neutral Quadrant. Remember, formality is the first sign of a professional officer."

Before Captain Li could correct himself, Stone interjected. "That's all right, Captain. For those of us who have been there," he said with a cold glance toward Cataline, "the Dark Zone describes it pretty damn well."

Stone had spent the better part of his adult life playing the deadly game of cat and mouse with Terillian Scout Rangers in the undeclared war that had continued between the two sides since the Accords. This clandestine war, combined with piracy and slave trade, the growth of petty warlords, and the utter isolation of the planets in the pseudo-demilitarized zone had utterly devastated what were once vibrant worlds.

Captain Li looked toward Cataline. The colonel's face had turned a dark shade of red with both embarrassment and anger. Li tried in vain to contain a smile as he continued the brief.

"The *Neutral Quadrant* defense grid provides three major functions. First, neutrino sensors monitor for radiation levels to alert us to the presence of large warships or transports performing jumps. Second, directional lasers track the speed of any vessel larger than a corvette and emit electromagnetic pulses to disrupt magnetic fields generated by large warships for trans-system jumps. Finally, the satellite data is linked directly to Alpha Humana command to provide real-time early warning capabilities and provide data bursts to our allies in the Xen Empire via electron spin shift-heavy matter transmissions of data."

"This station," added Cataline, attempting to regain his composure, "provides assurance of Terillian compliance with the Peace Accords, and furthermore—"

"Thank you, Colonel Tacitus," interjected Stone. "Captain, let's take a look at your latest security bulletins.". He had no desire to hear the colonel enter into a political speech. He knew the purpose and function of Gateway Station.

"Very well," replied Li as he directed Cataline and Stone out of the control room and to the communications center.

***

"I understand," Stone retorted, holding a stack of security documents in his hand, "but Command Security has prepared a new bulletin to update the instruction. Does your Information Officer review the security notice reports daily?"

"He does, but I—"

Li was again interrupted by Cataline.

"We will have him report to you and discuss the message traffic on the new requirement. Sergeant!" shouted Cataline. "Get Lieutenant Riepan up here."

While one of the several sergeants at the back of the line scurried off to find the lieutenant, Stone glared at Cataline.

"I usually see the officers responsible for each area present at their stations during inspections," Stone said to Li.

"Sir..." Li paused to give a quick glance toward Cataline. "We, uh—"

"Major Stone," interrupted Cataline proudly, "do you not think senior officers should represent the station for high priority visits?"

Stone took a long breath, displaying his frustration. "Present, yes. But senior officers rarely have the in-depth knowledge of programs to adequately represent their commands."

Stone paused again to let the comment hit home. "That is, after all, why we have junior officer and senior enlisted. Is it not, Colonel?"

"Major Stone," Cataline fumed, "I do not think—"

"I am sorry, sir," interrupted Li. "I felt I could adequately support Colonel Cataline, so I—"

"That's fine, Li," said Stone, stopping him in mid-sentence. "Being a junior officer, it *is* your responsibility to provide backup to your seniors, *regardless* of the circumstances."

Satisfied he had made his point, Stone continued, "Never mind about Lieutenant Riepan."

"Major, I would still like to provide you with the—"

"That will not be necessary, *Mister* Tacitus."

"Very well, Major Lucius-Stone," replied Cataline, his anger evident.

Stone knew his failure to address Cataline by his rank was a breach in military and social etiquette, particularly for a dishonored offshoot of the Lucius family such as his, but Stone knew that Cataline, however much it infuriated him, would not press the issue.

"I am sure Captain Li will resolve the issue," continued Cataline as he shot a burning glance in Li's direction.

As the inspection continued, Stone could feel the high, tight collar of his dress uniform suffocating him. While Captain Li read off the combat ratings of his Emergency Response Team, all Stone could think of was how the double-breasted tunic felt like sandpaper against his chest, the tight collar choked him, and how ridiculous the ceremonial Elite Guard sash looked. If it were up to his fiancée he would wear the cumbersome and cartoonish ceremonial dress everywhere. Finally, he could take no more. Running his fingers inside the collar of his uniform, he spoke.

"I have seen enough records, Captain," he said with a sigh—part from relief and part boredom. "Let's take a look at your protocols for workers."

"That was not on your scheduled agenda." said Cataline.

It pleased Stone to throw the political oaf off-step. That's what he had hoped for with the request. After all, if he had to wear that damn uncomfortable uniform, he could at least share his pain with that jackass Cataline.

"Perhaps tomorrow we could review the protocols," continued Cataline. "If your inspection included worker access processes, it should have been written in your precept message."

"I plan to complete the inspection tonight, *Colonel Tacitus*," said Stone. "And, as per the precepts, my mandate is to 'verify security measures are adequate to the level commensurate with the tactical importance of the station.' I believe that brings worker access under my purview. After all," Stone continued, "the Gateway Station is the front line defense against an attack by the Terillian barbarians, were they to attack through the Neutral Quadrant."

"I am sure we can meet your needs, Major," interjected Captain Li.

Stone could tell he was not alone in his feelings regarding Cataline. Li had a light sheen of sweat collecting on his face, and his face was still red from Cataline's earlier statements. All Li needed was some pompous ass from one of Alpha Humana's First Families to ruin his reputation.

"The shift turnover begins in an hour," continued Li. "That would be the best time to view our practices."

"Captain, I'm not sure that turnover is the most prudent time," replied Cataline, showing obvious, almost unnecessary, concern.

"One hour it is, Captain," said Stone bluntly.

What was the Colonel's problem? Stone wondered. Li's suggestion of observing the turnover was not only valid but showed that he had faith in both his men and the process. Stone assumed Cataline was probably just worrying about looking bad to his buddies at High Command.

***

The turnover of maintenance workers and support personnel was organized chaos. Four thousand military personnel were billeted to the station, who only left for furloughs and leave, but the civilians were a different story. Three shifts of exactly eight hundred and thirty-four personnel transited through the civilian portal of Gateway station daily.

Stone, Li, Cataline, and a line of junior officers and sergeants as recorders monitored the streams of workers as they passed through the checkpoint. Security chips were displayed, retinal scans verified that the correct person had the correct chip, and locator pins were issued to track movement throughout the station.

"Do you have any questions regarding the process?" asked Li as they observed the turnover.

"Seems to be well organized, Captain," commented Stone.

"Thank you, sir. If there are any discrepancies, the turnstiles are shut down and all personnel already through report to assembly room seven," reported Li.

Stone noticed the lights fade as the power grid transferred. After a few seconds, full power returned to the lighting and the terminal processors. The anomaly was not missed by Li either.

"That's odd," stated Li. "I will have one of my teams check the power grid and reactor control center."

"Not necessary, Captain," directed Cataline. "I authorized transfer station shifting to support maintenance on the executive levels."

Li's face again grew red and his head quickly swung in the direction of Cataline.

"Colonel Tacitus…sir…power grid shifts during turnover is a bad idea," stated Li, looking embarrassed by the position in which Cataline had placed him. "These tasks should occur during non-peak hours, as is our practice."

"That had been our *normal* practice, Captain," sneered Cataline. "But several key officers and officials have complained that shifts reset their environmental controls and it takes hours to reach homeostasis again. For this reason I have authorized any work that may affect executive levels of the station to be performed during the first shift to allow time for stabilization of environmental controls before leadership retires for the evening."

"Environmental controls," barked Stone. "You mean air conditioning and hologram programming."

Stone was floored. Cataline was allowing major shifts in the station's power grid in the *middle* of shift turnover security procedures so he and a few other select elite wouldn't have to have the temperature of their staterooms vary by a degree or interrupt viewing of home videos of themselves with their mistresses and Recreation Girls. This was definitely going in the report. "Colonel," Stone added, "I *highly recommend* you return to your normal practice of grid shifts regardless of what areas are affected."

Li was staring blankly at Cataline when Stone turned toward him. "You obviously were not aware of this change in policy, Captain?" Stone asked Li.

"No, sir," commented Li, still locking his gaze on Cataline. "If I had known, I could have had portable power stations connected to mitigate the gaps."

Li was cut short by the Station's general announcing system. "Colonel Tacitus, your presence is requested in the Information Center. Colonel Tacitus, your presence is requested in the Information Center."

Li's communicator sounded next. "Captain Li, this is the security watch officer, Lieutenant Mosa. I am receiving reports that our network has been compromised and we're seeing brief losses of input signals from satellite grids X76 and B7 through 10. I have informed Fleet Command and High Command watch officers. Recommend setting condition Alpha and manning all security stations."

"Do it. I am on the way," Li commanded into the communicator as he started moving toward the nearest elevator. "Tell High

Command to scramble Alert Package Delta in response to possible degradation of Gateway function. Recommend the Gateway fleet set wartime cruising watch stations."

"Son of a bitch," shouted Li as he and Stone ran toward the elevator, closely followed by Cataline. "If we lose the Gateway, the Terillians could be orbiting Alpha Humana within the month."

"I will report to the communications room to make a report to High Command after I am finished in the Information Center," said Cataline as he struggled to keep up with Stone and Li. "Captain..." puffed Cataline. "...Li, I place you in charge of tactical decisions...keep me informed while I contact Command."

Cataline slowed his pace as the two healthier men drew farther away.

As Stone and Li entered the elevator to the security branch, they heard Li's orders being carried out throughout the station.

ALL NON-MILITARY PERSONNEL REPORT TO ASSEMBLY AREA SEVEN. ALL OFF-WATCH PERSONNEL REPORT TO YOUR MUSTER STATIONS. NOW SET CONDITION ALPHA. MAN ALL SECURITY STATIONS. ALL PILOTS REPORT TO READY ROOMS. THIS IS NOT A DRILL. THIS IS NOT A DRILL.

It would be a long time before Stone would have to worry about inspections and lint again.

Chapter 2

As the Gateway virus continued to deteriorate the operation of the satellites, the Xen Empire had begun to mobilize. Being the closest Xen Alliance planet to the Gateway, all Alpha Humana fleets were en route to the Gateway boundary, and reserve units had been called into action. There was little doubt that the enemy was mobilizing as well.

Stone stood in the corner of the crowded and muggy briefing room. Flat-panel displays projected data about Sierra 7. Environmental conditions, natural hazards, and climate information flashed across the screens. Stone did not need to review data slides; this would not be his battalion's first trip to Sierra 7, or "The

Wilderness" as the planet was called to those who had been there and survived. The nickname came from a lack of large civilized settlements and the abundance of various flora and fauna—a large portion of which were poisonous, aggressive, or just plain deadly.

The Intel Officer began the briefing.

"Sierra 7 has a variety of deadly indigenous animals of both reptilian and mammalian species..."

As the Intel Officer droned on, Stone struggled to focus.

"Blah, blah, blah," whispered Captain Emily Martin as she leaned toward Stone.

Martin continued to talk over the brief. "We're finally gonna stop dicking around with the Ters and all this jackass can talk about is little fuzzy tree monkeys...seriously."

"Captain, please?" asked a transport pilot feverishly trying to take notes.

"You actually have to get out of your environmentally controlled *cock*-pit for any of this to matter," she shot back. "Just shut up and take your little notes...actually, I'll give you a hand..."

Martin snatched the notebook out of the pilot's hand and wrote a note:

1. Drop off the Guard and get my pansy-ass back to the ship

2. Watch some movies, jerk off, watch some more movies, sleep

3. Pick up the Guard

4. Repeat

"There ya go, pumpkin," smiled Martin as she handed the pad back to the embarrassed pilot. "That's ALL you need to know about this mission."

Stone cracked a little smile. Captain Martin was known throughout the Guard for her aggressiveness, skill, and her inability to control her mouth-brain interface. In addition to her less than politically-correct attitude, Martin had several things working against her. First of all she was a woman, and a beautiful one at that. As one of only four women, and the only officer, in the Elite Guard, she was always under a microscope. She had to be smarter and better than the men she was rated against—which she was. Second, she was from a family that had only risen to middling status in the last few generations. When she should have been trying to "marry up" to a higher family, she was crawling through the mud and muck on remote, desolate planets. Despite all of this, she had struggled to gain a reputation as a brave and dependable officer—a reputation she was not afraid to defend with her fists or sword if need be.

Stone leaned in toward Martin.

"Those little fuzzy monkeys are tasty though," he whispered.

Martin smiled as they turned their attention back to the briefing.

"…The Red Moss fields are visually stunning but pose several dangers. Bright red moss covers the ground for miles, broken by dark-blue pools of water from underground springs. The only trees are Orchid trees with black bark and bright white-pedaled leaves, which constantly fall and replenish themselves. The falling petals rapidly decay on the moss and provide nutrients to both the moss and Orchid trees…"

"Shoot me now," mouthed Martin to Stone.

Stone made a motion toward the briefing screen in a halfhearted attempt to show concern for what the Intel Officer was saying.

"…Several animals inhabit the fields as well. Albino primates about half a meter tall live in the orchid trees…"

Martin laughed out loud, forcing the Intel Officer to pause and regain his composure.

"…The red fields also provide excellent cover for Red Moss vipers. They blend in almost perfectly with the moss and their venom is potent enough to bring down a sable tiger, or a man…"

"Ugh," added an exasperated Martin as she lightly, repetitively banged the back of her head off the bulkhead.

"Shhh!" directed a combat system officer in Martin's direction.

Martin stood straight from her position leaning against the bulkhead and smiled at the complaining officer. Slowly, she raised her right fist and extended her middle finger to the officer. Leisurely shifting her smile to a scowl, she returned to her reclined position against the bulkhead.

Martin turned her head back toward Stone. "This is just a freakin' show for higher-ups who are finally getting their chance at playing soldier. I guess now they are realizing they might actually have to do something for once in their privileged careers. Sooner or later these jackasses are gonna get someone killed."

***

A light fog crept over the gently flowing river. An occasional flickering reflection of light off the water hinted that the first sun was beginning to rise. The harmonic chirp of a bird could be heard over the light bubbling of the water as it passed over the rocks protruding from the stream. A tiger wasp lay resting on a large leaf, soaking up the first rays of sunlight. In a flash, the wasp disappeared as it became breakfast for the striped dragon lizard on the log below. The lizard, having filled its belly, took its turn in the cyclic flashes of sunlight.

Behind the lizard there was a small disturbance in the water. A head slowly broke through the surface, then a torso. The lizard vanished into the undergrowth with a flash of its red tail as first one, then two, and finally dozens of Guard soldiers slowly emerged from the water.

The first wave quickly exited the water and took up defensive positions. Others rapidly stowed their water respirators and vanished into the undergrowth to take up positions as point and flankers.

Stone, water dripping from his camouflaged face, took a deep breath of fresh air. He and his men had been breathing recycled air through their water respirators for over an hour and the damp, clean air felt refreshing. After a quick second to enjoy the moment, Stone called for his company commanders over his communicator.

Once they were assembled, Stone gave his orders.

"Captain Tacitus and Alpha Company have already established a defensive position anchored on the opposite bank. Bravo Company will reconnoiter to the North, Charlie to the South, and I will accompany Captain Desro with Delta and move west. If anyone makes contact or retrieves intel, relay back to Alpha who will then relay back to REGCOM for pulse data transfer to Red Fleet. Rendezvous time will be 1400 in fifteen days. We have support from 2nd Battalion at REGCOM via Hawk attack ships if needed. Follow your instincts and don't forget Terillian Scout troops aren't the only deadly things out there."

"Aye, sir," replied Captain Martin of Bravo Company as she tucked the digital map into her pocket. "It's good to be back in action," she added as she turned to rejoin her company.

"Hey, Emily," called out Charlie Company Commander Hugh Jackson as he squatted next to Stone. Leaning on his rife, Jackson was tall and muscular with a shaved head and an out-of-regulation thick black goatee covering his square jawline.

"Bet my company gets more Ters than yours," taunted Jackson as he looked up toward Martin, eagerly awaiting her reply.

Stone subconsciously stepped away from Jackson as Martin stopped, exhaled, and turned once again to face him.

"Maybe you can find some Ters in the mud," she said as she gave Jackson a shove with her boot, sending him backwards into a large puddle of mud.

"Damn it!" cursed Jackson as he looked up at Martin.

"Oh, wait, one more thing," said Martin as she displayed her middle finger to Jackson.

She turned back to Stone. "Sorry for that, sir, but…"

"Happy hunting, Emily," interjected Stone.

"Happy hunting, sir," said Martin with a smile.

She gave a quick salute and ran off to join her company.

Stone had high hopes for this mission. His men were well trained and ready to get to work, and he was confident of his company commanders as well. Captain Arilius Tacitus was his senior officer and most likely would take Stone's place should promotion or death create the vacancy.

Arilius was the ideal soldier. He was tall, powerful, formal, and proud. He was also a relative of Cataline Tacitus, so there would be no roadblocks to his career progression. His family name, rugged looks, perfectly cut dark black hair, and caramel-colored skin, inherited from his mother's line, also made him one of the most eligible bachelors among First Family daughters.

Although Stone despised most of the "chosen ones," as Martin called members of the First Families, Arilius had proven himself to be a skilled officer, having saved Stone's bacon more than once.

Jackson, still cleaning the mud off his face, had spilled his share of blood for his people as well. Jackson had lost his right hand to a Terillian major and his left eye to a Brackien raider; both had been genetically reconstructed. He had also lost two wives to his love of Montar wine and Recreation Girls. Unfortunately, Captain Emily Martin had been his first wife, and when she caught him with the Recreation Girls he had to have his left eye reconstructed a second time, along with half of his teeth. Stone knew he could always count on Jackson, not only for his abilities in the field but also to lighten the mood when things got too serious.

Captain Venarus Desro had served well as a platoon commander and had been promoted when Captain Colter was killed by a Red Moss viper during the battalion's last visit to Sierra 7. Desro was pale, tall, and wiry, with his light-brown hair cut high and close. Despite his stature, however, his body always seemed to be tightly coiled, ready to spring into action.

Similar to Stone, Desro had connections to a First Family, but his line had long ago been wiped from the Venarus lineage.

Desro had done little to help his status by taking a barmaid for a bride. Stone remembered feeling sorry for Lana, his wife, at the last regimental banquet. The enlisted wives would not speak to her because she had married an officer and the majority of officers' wives were elitist social climbers always trying to prove their superiority. She had held up well, though, and eventually became good friends with Captain Martin—their mutual hatred for snotty, over-privileged bitches being a common bond.

Confident, but cautious of the mission, Stone took up a position beside Desro as his men fanned into the wilderness.

***

A week had passed since the battalion had dispersed to conduct reconnaissance operations, and Stone was pleased. No contact reports had been received from the other companies and things were going well in Delta. The company had been in the moss fields for a day and a half, and there had been no major problems. Aside from the headaches caused by the toxic red moss and the bites from blood beetles, things were almost going too well.

The company was deployed in its normal formation. Second platoon, under Lieutenant Alister Lowstreet, was assigned to the scout patrol operating a thousand meters ahead of the main body.

"Any reports from the other companies?" Stone asked Delta Company's communications officer.

"Nothing other than required checks, sir," the young lieutenant replied.

As he moved along in the formation, Stone strained his eyes to focus. Orchid petals drifted slowly to the ground as they were partially suspended in air by the constant gentle breeze blowing over the red moss fields. As the petals floated toward the red moss below, the scene reminded Stone of the mid-winter snowfall in the Northern Hills of Alpha Humana. Stone had warned his men, as he always did, about becoming complacent in the visually stunning environment, but he often found himself being lulled by its deceitful beauty. *Hopefully the scout platoon is more focused than I am,* Stone thought.

"Contact two hundred meters ahead," came through the comm link into Lieutenant Lowstreet's earpiece.

"Terillian patrol; squad size, approaching from 025."

"Roger. 2nd squad, take position for ambush," responded Lowstreet, after activating the command frequency so the Desro and Stone would hear his platoon's comms.

2nd Squad took up positions quickly and quietly. In a matter of seconds they had blended into the landscape completely.

***

Lying prone near the trunk of an orchid tree, Lowstreet steeled himself as the noxious spores from the red moss burned his nostrils and throat. His position gave a perfect vantage from which to watch the approaching Terillians. After freezing momentarily to allow a viper to slither over his rifle, he slowly shouldered his weapon and brought the scope to his eye. Through the white haze of the orchid blossoms Lowstreet saw the Terillian patrol gradually materialize. He gently rubbed his index and middle fingers against his thumb and then placed his finger in the trigger guard and listened over the comms circuit.

"Last man," was whispered over the circuit, telling Lowstreet that it was now his call.

Lowstreet selected his target, breathed out his stabilizing breath, and passed the word, "Fire. Fire. Fire."

With the third order, the field erupted with the sound of gunfire. Out of the corner of his eye, Lowstreet saw a tiger break across the field for cover in a dense copse of orchid trees. He had apparently been lying in wait and had been startled by the Elite Guard, depriving him of a meal.

Quickly returning his attention to the kill zone, Lowstreet was pleased with his squad's work. It was over in an instant. The patrol had disintegrated in the precision attack before the echoes of the first gunshot died away, replaced only by the screeching of the orchid monkeys.

Lowstreet slowly rose from his position and finally let out the deep cough against the burning moss spores that he had been holding back. Having cleared his throat, Lowstreet moved toward the dead Terillians.

"Delta command, 2nd squad," reported Lowstreet, "All clear, twelve engaged, twelve neutralized. No casualties."

***

"Roger 2, on the way," replied Stone as he quickly made his way to the ambush position, arriving in just a few seconds.

"Regulars," stated Stone, his jaw clinched slightly and his brow furrowed in thought as he viewed the fallen Terillians.

"These are the first regulars I have seen," confessed Lowstreet. "They seem less savvy than the Scout Rangers we usually encounter."

"Less savvy, yes, but they make up for that in numbers," sighed Stone. "Regular troops are like roaches: where there's one, there are thousands."

"It looks like there must be a significant Terillian operation underway on Sierra 7," said Desro.

"Significant and close," replied Stone. "This patrol is lightly provisioned. They are probably no more than two days from a base of operations."

Stone was concerned. Lowstreet's confession about never having seen a Regular was no surprise. Very few soldiers had encountered regular troops. Stone himself had only seen Terillian Infantry three times in his eighteen years of service, each time much closer to the Terillian side of the Dark Zone. Regular troops on patrol meant that at least a full regiment, probably more, was nearby. With that many

Terillian troops in the area, a company-sized reconnaissance was much too large and would soon be discovered.

"We must withdraw to the river and consolidate our forces," said Desro.

"I concur," answered Stone. "Inform REGCOM and get the company back as quick as you can."

"Will you not be returning with the company, sir?"

"I want to obtain more intelligence first. I will take Lieutenant Lowstreet and Sergeant Kilgore and recon the enemy position. Inform the Colonel I will contact REGCOM with extraction data in the next ninety-six hours."

***

Having shed the rest of the company, the trio made good progress. Once out of the fields they made their way up the gently sloping forests toward the Silent Plateau above. The Plateau was a wasteland of volcanic rock that covered a long-dormant volcano. Stone hoped that from this vantage he could survey the vast plains below as well as gain intelligence on the status of Slocum City, the first in a series of trading villages that dotted the seemingly endless plains leading to the Great Ocean.

Underneath these plains lay substantial amounts of Uranium, Cobalt, and Titanium—all of which were important to both Alpha Humana and Terillian military and industrial pursuits. The series of villages created an economic tie between the ore mines and the black market traders and slavers. Miners would bring their ore into trading villages where they traded for mining equipment, luxuries, and slaves.

As the men neared the Plateau, the soft undergrowth of pine needles and the pleasant smell of evergreens began to mix with scattered lava rocks and an occasional whiff of sulfur.

"We're getting close," said Kilgore as he wrinkled his nose against the now pungent smell of sulfur.

"That's the problem with this planet," replied Lowstreet. "It stinks."

It was not long until the cool, refreshing forest scene completed faded away into a landscape of jacked rock, sulfur springs, and acid fumes. Lifeless and deserted, it would be a long, miserable trek across the Silent Plateau.

***

After a few exhausting hours, the men reached the peak.

"I'm going to see if I can get a look at the plains from those rocks," whispered Stone. "We should be able to see the lights from Slocum City from up there," he said, pointing to a large outcropping.

Lieutenant Lowstreet and Sergeant Kilgore supported Stone as he started his climb up the rock formation. He moved quickly but quietly; too much noise would attract the Terillian patrols Stone was sure were nearby. The smell of volcanic sulfur filled Stone's nose and he tasted the chalky bitterness of the dust he created as he climbed. *I hate this freakin' planet,* he thought.

Near the top, Stone slowly pivoted his body to look between two large rectangular rocks perched at the peak of the stone formation. As the plains slowly came into sight through his night vision scope, what he saw nearly caused him to lose his footing.

Dozens of transports, Alpha attack craft, and heavy hover tanks dotted the landscape. The Terillians had turned the plains into an immense military camp.

Stone had seen enough, and he quickly retreated down the rock to his companions.

"Anything?" asked Sergeant Kilgore as Stone reached the bottom.

"The Terillians are on Sierra 7 and in force. At least a brigade," replied Stone as he wiped his charcoal-covered hands against his trousers. "They have either violated the treaty by allowing transport carriers through their side of the Gateway or this operation has been underway for some time."

"Looks like we're going to have a real war to fight after all these years," replied Lowstreet, his face showing a mixture of excitement and concern for the unknown future that lay ahead.

"That's up to the Forum and the Xen Alliance to determine," said Stone. He was trying to be stoic but he knew the lieutenant was right. "Either way we need to get this information back to REGCOM. Let's get the hell out of here and make our way back down the opposite slope. From there we can call for extraction."

Chapter 3

Stone leaned against a large evergreen trunk while Lowstreet contacted REGCOM. As he felt the sticky sap of the tree tug against his fatigues, for the first time in the mission he took a second to contemplate his physical condition. Although they had been out of the red moss fields for a few days, the blood beetle bites still stung and irritated his skin. The sulfur from the Silent Plateau had immediately taken the place of the red moss spores in causing his throat and nose to feel raw. Now the sap of the evergreens had provided the perfect glue to combine the pine needles and volcanic dust into a prickly-sandy mixture that coated his face and hands.

It's still better than wearing that damn dress uniform, Stone thought as he let out a slight chuckle.

"What is it, sir?" asked Lowstreet, who had just reached Stone to give him a report.

"Nothing, Lieutenant," replied Stone. "But we do have a great job, don't we?"

"Yes, sir," replied Lowstreet.

Stone chuckled again. "What's our status, Lowstreet?"

"Yes, sir. REGCOM has been contacted with the intel and extraction is to occur near the base of the volcano at 0800," reported Lowstreet.

"Roger, Lieutenant," replied Stone. "All we have to do now is to stay quiet and unnoticed for the night. We'll set up a two-hour watch rotation and head out at 0600."

"Sounds good, sir," said Kilgore, who had been lounging nearby. "I'll take the first watch."

As Kilgore moved off to take up a defensive position, Stone found a small log that was just the right size to pass for a pillow. Finding a good spot to lie down, he leaned his rifle against a nearby tree, removed his sword, and settled in for a quick nap. The log was actually more comfortable than he had anticipated and he quickly drifted off, holding his pistol over his chest.

***

"Wake up, sir," whispered Sergeant Kilgore. "We've got company." It was not his words but Kilgore's hand shaking his shoulders that brought Stone out of his slumber.

"What is it, Sergeant?"

"There is a group of slavers setting up camp about 500 meters down the slope. Looks like they have collected some captives."

Stone despised slavers and black marketeers in general. It was known in most of the higher social circles that these immoral and lawless acts were perpetrated daily in the Dark Zone, but for the most part it was overlooked. Stone knew this complacent stance was partially due to the economic gains reaped by wealthy Humani from their secret patronage of the black market. Over the last few decades the activity of the slavers had increased and become more violent. Most of the remote settlements in the Dark Zone, even small towns and cities, were under constant fear of raids. On most occasions, however, slavers avoided Xen troops and in turn the Xen paid little attention to them. The Terillians, however, seemed to engage the slavers almost as often as they did Xen troops. Stone always assumed this was an attempt to limit Xen profits from the illicit trade economy.

"Lieutenant Lowstreet has been observing for the last hour and recommends we move clear of them and inform REGCOM of a new extraction site," said Kilgore as he subconsciously grasped his rapier.

"Take me to him," whispered Stone as he locked his sword into place and gripped his rifle.

The two men made their way to Lieutenant Lowstreet without a sound. Positioned behind a large felled tree and some heavy undergrowth, Lowstreet signaled to Stone and Kilgore that there were five slavers and approximately eight captives.

Moving quickly, Stone shifted his glance from the ground to Lowstreet's position as he and Kilgore quietly made his way to the lieutenant.

"Looks like it's mostly women, probably for the Plains brothels," whispered Lowstreet. "There's a clear path over there for us to move around them," he added as he pointed toward a small slope covered with heavy undergrowth.

"I'm going to take a closer look," said Stone.

"But sir," whispered Lowstreet, "we need to get to our pickup."

"I understand, Lieutenant. You and Kilgore maintain your positions here while I move in a little closer," ordered Stone quietly.

"Yes, sir," replied Lowstreet faithfully.

Lowstreet signaled to Kilgore and the two slowly moved into good locations to provide cover fire if required.

Stone carefully made his way down the slope. Again alternating between the ground below his feet and the slaver's position, he carefully moved forward, remaining close to good cover and monitoring the slaver's movements. Moving methodically but quickly, Stone covered the ground swiftly. In a few seconds Stone was in position, kneeling in a growth of heavy laurel and briars a few meters from the slavers' camp. Ignoring the thorns puncturing his skin, he scanned the area. From his position he was able to get a good view of the captives. Six women and two children were locked in a large hover wagon. As Stone examined the group more closely, one of them stood out. She had black hair that fell to the middle of her back, and although she was wearing the clothes of a subsistence farmer from one of the many settlements surrounding the Red Moss fields, something was not right. She seemed too...healthy. Also, while the others huddled together and were outwardly shaken by their ordeal, she sat alone, looking straight ahead. Her face did not show fear or anxiousness. Instead, she exuded a dogged determination that made her conspicuously different from the other captives.

Stone shifted his observations to the slavers. Two large men sat by the fire. Through the flashes of light created by the crackling fire, Stone could see that both wore a mixture of Xen and civilian clothing. In the orange hue of the fire, he could also see that each slaver had a top-of-the-line assault rifle at their side. Paying more attention to the cheap wine they were drinking than their captives, they laughed loudly as they passed a bottle back and forth.

Stone's attention was drawn to a noise behind the hovercraft. At first they were indistinguishable, but eventually he recognized the sound of voices. Slightly shifting his position and sucking in a deep breath as a thorn tore at his skin, he focused on the voices.

Three dark shadows silhouetted the dimly lit hovercraft and slowly grew taller as the men came into view. Three additional slavers slowly made their way from behind the ground rover that towed the hover wagon. Stone could see one of them walking with an obvious limp.

"I can't believe you let that farmer wench get the best of you," the largest of the three said to the limping man.

"Maybe we should sell you to the brothel and have her work with us," quipped the other, clearly taking joy in his companion's pain.

"Screw you both," said the injured slaver. "That cow attacked me while I was trying to gather up the children. I was obviously distracted."

"So it only takes a few children and a woman to overpower you," joked the large one. "That's enough. I shouldn't have wasted my time with the little brats anyway. This one looks a lot more...sturdy."

As the slaver spoke, he smiled and licked his lips like he was about to dig into a steak. He slowly reached his hand into the cage, rubbing the woman's thigh.

"She's definitely of better stock than the typical broken-down bitches we see around here," he said.

Stone's attention returned to the woman's face; her determination remained. As the slaver moved his hand over her thigh, the woman took a deep breath as if she was trying to gain control of her emotions. The slaver's hand moved up her thigh, between her legs.

"Maybe we should—"

In a rapid motion, the woman quickly grabbed his hand and twisted. Stone could hear ligaments popping from his position as she snapped two of the slaver's fingers backward.

The slaver let out a scream and fell back away from the cage grabbing his hand.

"She got you again!" shouted one of his companions.

The injured man held his hand in front of his face. His middle and index finger were mangled and disfigured from the woman's attack. Reaching inside his jacket, he pulled out a neural-inhibitor and injected his hand. The painkiller worked quickly; after a few seconds the slaver inhaled deeply and snapped his fingers back into their joints.

"That bitch is going to pay," he said, as he grabbed a stun stick and garrote rod from the hover wagon.

"Come here, bitch!" yelled the slaver as he made his way back to the cage. "It's time this beast was tamed."

The woman tried to scoot to the back of the cage but could not escape the reach of the slaver. He quickly struck her with the stun stick and before she could recover he slid the rope over her neck and tightened it by pulling the excess through the rod.

"Get her out," he ordered to the other slavers.

"I guess Lor is going to break her in before we sell her," laughed the largest of the slavers.

The remainder of the captives quickly scrambled to the opposite side of the cage and cowered in fear as the slavers opened the door and yanked the woman onto the forest undergrowth. She let out a large, deep groan as she crashed into the ground on her side. The woman attempted to gain her footing but the slaver pinned her to the ground, the garrote rod driving her neck and head into the forest ground.

"Lay her on that rock over there," shouted one of them.

Still pinned to the ground, the woman was dragged face-first across the camp. Along the way she struggled, kicking her feet in an attempt to find something to anchor her body against.

"Remember, don't kill her. Her coding makes her worth twice as much," added one of the slavers.

She struggled fiercely but it was useless. Every attempt at movement only tightened the garrote. Her grunts were barely audible over the slavers' laughter.

"That's it boys, right here," shouted the large slaver as the attackers forced the woman to a large rock about waist high only a few steps away from Stone's hiding place.

Stone instinctively removed the safety from his assault rifle but soon thought better of it. If he did act, better to make as little noise as possible. Slowly putting his rifle down, he unsheathed his sword.

"Get her head," directed Lor to the large slaver. "Tal, hold her shoulders down," he said to the other.

Stone was at a crossroads. He had placed himself and his men in a bad situation. He knew things like this happened in the Dark Zone, but never before had it occurred at arm's reach. No honorable soldier should allow this to happen. On the other hand, if there was gunfire Terillian patrols might hear and endanger their extraction.

As Stone tried to come to terms with his morals and his mission, the slaver pulled the woman's trousers to the ground and began to unbutton his own. The woman turned her head against the force of the slaver holding her and looked directly toward Stone's position, as if she knew he was there. Her face was bruised and caked in dirt and pine needles.

His eyes fell upon hers. There was no fear, only that same determination. Her eyes made the decision for him. This would not happen to her.

"It's time to tame this shrew," boasted Lor. "Don't worry sweetheart. I'll keep you intact for transport to Venato."

He reached for her waist, but before the slaver could touch her Stone sprung from the darkness. His sword was swift and found its mark, cutting the would-be rapist from his collar bone to the opposite shoulder. As he fell Stone quickly spun around, plunging his sword into the largest slaver just below his neck. The startled third attacker reached for his sidearm but was too slow. As he raised his weapon, Stone's sword swept downward. The man let out a screech as his hand, still holding the pistol, fell to the ground. Another quick movement laid the man's chest open. Blood sprayed from his wound and covered the woman as she rolled off the rock.

Their senses deadened by alcohol and surprised by the suddenness of the attack, two men beside the fire had just begun to bring their weapons to bear at Stone when automatic gunfire bursts from behind him knocked the first slaver to the ground before he could fully stand.

Falling to the ground in recoil from the explosion of noise, he quickly looked toward the source.

The woman, still bound by her hands, had taken a rifle from the first of Stone's victims. She held the weapon to her shoulder and was aiming the heavy rifle with one hand tied tightly to the other. Another burst exploded from the rifle. Stone turned back to see the final slaver jerk violently and crumple over backwards as the rounds from her rifle impacted his torso.

Stone quickly jumped to his feet. Raising his sword, Stone looked toward the woman. He saw the barrel of her weapon now leveled in his direction. He froze for a second as he followed the barrel into her deep green eyes.

She lowered her head slightly and pulled the trigger.

Click.

The magazine was empty.

Before Stone could react, the woman dropped her weapon and vanished into the wilderness.

Kilgore and Lowstreet quickly covered the ground from their concealed position to the camp. Stone was standing by the captives on the hovercraft when they arrived.

"Are you all right, sir?" asked Lowstreet.

"I'm fine. Go get that woman."

With the order the two men raced into the darkness, leaving Stone alone with the captives and his thoughts.

As he looked over the traumatized captives, he tried to figure out what was different about that woman. He had willingly, however morally warranted it was, endangered his mission and his men for her and would now have to pick up the pieces. The disheveled group in the cage was no threat. They would be released to find their way back home. His main concern turned toward the threat of nearby patrols and his fear that the gunfire would draw them in. Then there was that damn woman.

***

"Where did she go?" panted Lowstreet as he rushed through the underbrush.

"She couldn't have gone too damn far," replied Kilgore. "Over there," he said as he saw movement.

Lowstreet led the way, leaping over logs and ducking under branches in his pursuit. Suddenly, he felt a blow to his chest and his feet leave the ground. Struggling to catch his breath after impacting the forest floor, he reached for his rifle. Just as he gripped the stock, he felt the pressure of a foot on his hand followed instantly by the crashing pain of another boot to the side of his head. Recoiling from the blow, he rose to his knees and looked toward his attacker. As he glanced up he saw the woman coming at him again. She swung toward his head with her knee, but this time he was able to block her attack. Grasping the woman's leg he rose up, lifting her off the ground and driving her back into the forest undergrowth.

"Bitch!" exclaimed Lowstreet as he attempted to land a blow to her jaw, but was blocked. A powerful combination of fist and elbow to his ribcage halted his attack.

Following the punch to his ribs, Lowstreet felt the woman's legs wrap around him and roll him onto his back. Now on the defensive, Lowstreet tried to pry his arms underneath the woman's but she brought her forehead down hard against his nose. His head instantly grew heavy and his vision blurred. Before he could recover, Lowstreet felt the pressure on his body shift as she repositioned.

Lowstreet felt his neck tighten as she placed her knee over his throat and brought her full weight down on him.

Lowstreet felt himself losing consciousness when suddenly the weight was removed from his throat and he felt the woman's body go limp on top of his. Looking over the woman lying on top of him, Lowstreet saw Kilgore standing over him, holding the rifle he had just used to knock the woman unconscious.

"Are you okay, L.T.?" asked Kilgore as he rolled the woman off Lowstreet's bruised body.

"I think so," answered Lowstreet as he spit blood from his mouth. "I think she broke my…." A wince of pain verified that his nose had been broken. "What the hell was that?"

"I don't know, sir, but I need to find out what they have been feeding this girl. She was kicking your ass."

Still clearing the cobwebs from his head, Lowstreet wasn't in the mood for Kilgore's typical ribbing. "We need to get her back to the major."

Kilgore smiled. "No problem, sir. I'll keep an eye on her for you to make sure you're safe."

***

Stone had released the captives and was inspecting the hover wagon when he heard his men returning. Kilgore came first, pulling the woman by her upper arm, her wrists still bound by the slaver's ropes. Lowstreet followed, his rifle held on the woman. As the light from the campfire illuminated his face, a large welt was visible on Lowstreet's face and dried blood caked his deformed nose.

“That was not easy,” exclaimed Kilgore. “This little farmer girl is a bad-ass. She can fight.”

“She broke my damn nose,” mumbled Lowstreet.

“That’s because she’s not a farmer,” said Stone in a matter-of-fact manner, having come to his own realization. “Bring her over here.”

Stone stared into the woman’s eyes as Kilgore led her to him. The determination had been replaced with anger. Returning Stone’s gaze, her deep green eyes burned through him, distracting him from his thoughts.

“You’re quite a handful,” said Stone. “A little too much of a handful to be a farmer or herder.”

As he spoke, he placed his hand behind her neck and slowly moved her hair aside. She resisted but he placed more force on the back of her head, driving it toward the ground. There it was on the back of her neck: the telltale tattoo of a circle with four arrows forming a cross in the center.

“What’s your rank, Terillian?” demanded Stone.

The woman coolly returned Stone’s glare but remained silent.

“You’re kidding me!” blurted Kilgore. “She’s a damn Scout Ranger!”

“Guess I don’t feel as bad about having my ass kicked now,” declared Lowstreet.

“What are you doing here and how did you allow slavers to capture you?” inquired Stone.

“Captain Mori Skye, Scout Rangers. And my mission is classified.”

"An officer," said Kilgore, even more surprised.

"Which battalion?" asked Stone.

"Classified."

"I risked my life to save your...well, to save you," stumbled Stone. "You should consider yourself lucky to be my prisoner."

The woman's eyes burned with green waves of anger. "Save me! You destroyed my mission. How can I..."

She quickly stopped when realized she had said too much.

"You are telling me you planned to be captured and raped by filthy slavers?" asked a surprised Stone. He was almost as shocked that she had given up any information as that she had intentionally allowed herself to become a prisoner of the slavers.

The Terillian's glare moved away from Stone and she slowly lowered her head, hiding her face from his view.

"Not all missions are desirable," she replied, "but they must be done nonetheless."

The woman looked back up into Stone's eyes and continued.

"I'm sure you have done things in the line of duty that have been unpleasant even to you—although Xen puppets such as you Hanmani have no conscience or morals."

Hanmani seemed to be some sort of slang for Alpha Humana in the Terillian language. Stone had heard the term before from other Terillian prisoners, but when she said it he felt his body tense with anger and his skin grow hot.

"We are not puppets," shot back Stone, his jaw clinching tight and his fists subconsciously tightening. "We're a well ordered and peaceful people who *must again* defend ourselves against Terillian aggression."

"Aggression!" barked Mori.

She lunged toward Stone, but Kilgore's grip was firm. Pulling against Kilgore's grasp, she continued.

"Your fleets are concentrating at the Gateway. Slavers, no doubt backed by Xen funding, are raiding our space and your operations around the Navato Asteroid Belt are clearly in violation of the Peace Accords, and you have the audacity to call us aggressors?"

Stone knew this was an obvious lie. Although he had no doubt there was some funding of the slavers by wealthy families, it was not systematic and the Navato Asteroid Belt was a wasteland. He had never been there nor heard of any operations by the Guard in the area. Either way, it was the virus at the Gateway that had ignited the new hostilities.

"We're concentrating because your spies have attacked our Gateway!" he replied, still angered at her more than he should be.

"The Gateway is damaged?" asked Mori, seemingly surprised by the news.

"You know it was," Stone snapped back at her.

Now it was Stone who had to stop himself from giving too much information. This woman had him on edge and he wasn't thinking clearly. He had to control his emotions.

"There are no operations in progress in the Navato area," Stone continued. "That is just more Terillian propaganda to support your invasion of the Dark Zone."

"Invasion? You have got to be kidding me. Just another lie. We know you have been operating there for years. Or maybe your Xennite masters haven't told you everything."

"Major, its 0745, 15 minutes until extraction," interrupted Lowstreet. "We should move now."

The woman had completely thrown Stone off his game. He had allowed his emotions to boil to the surface and had almost lost track of time. At least Lowstreet still had his head on straight.

"Enough questions," said Stone. "We will let the intelligence specialists deal with you. Besides, we need to go and you're coming with us. Kilgore, take her with you."

As Kilgore gave a tug to her arm, the unmistakable *whiz* of gunfire flew past his head, impacting with a thud in the tree behind him.

"Contact left!" shouted Kilgore as he grabbed the woman's arm and dove to the ground.

Stone and Lowstreet took defensive positions as the gunfire grew more intense. Rounds began to impact all around them.

"On the ridge!" yelled Kilgore.

He leveled his rifle and fired a burst. About fifty meters away a Terillian infantryman fell dead.

"They're regulars," exclaimed Stone as he returned fire. "A lot of them."

"We need to get the hell out of here!" shouted Kilgore. "Let's get that Scout and get...Where the hell did she go?"

Stone turned to the see his captive disappear into the woods. So much for his prisoner—now it was a matter of survival.

"Set up defensive fire and withdraw by increments!" Stone ordered over the gunfire.

With precision only elite forces were capable of, the three men began their running gun battle. One man would retreat a few meters and then stop to provide fire for the others, who in turn stopped to cover the latter. If they had been facing Scout Rangers they would have been in trouble, but the regular troops were slowed by the accurate and rapid fire of the trio. The deadly race continued for three kilometers, until the group reached the extraction point.

Racing across the open ground, Stone and his team dove into a dry creek bed.

"Where's our pickup?" panted Lowstreet, still winded from the running fight. "I'm out of ammunition."

"Me too," replied Kilgore.

Stone checked his rifle. *8 rounds remaining* read across his weapon's status menu. Once the Terillians realized they were out of ammunition, they would assault en masse. Their escape route was littered with Terillian dead but the numbers were still in the Terillians' favor. By Stone's guess there were probably a hundred or more regulars still in pursuit.

"If we can draw them in closer," shouted Stone over the incoming gunfire, "we can at least take a lot more of them with us."

Just as Stone had expected, the Terillians began to emerge from the woods and rush toward Stone and his men.

"It's been an honor to serve with you men," said Stone, feeling the weight of his decision to engage the slavers—especially to save an enemy.

"The honor is ours," replied Kilgore. "A good soldier does not let the helpless suffer. You did what you had to do with the slavers. You had no way of knowing she was Terillian, let alone a Scout Ranger. At least I can go to oblivion with the look on Lieutenant's face when she dropped him to the ground ingrained in my mind."

"Glad I could make your passage into nothingness a pleasant one," replied Lowstreet as he placed his hand on Kilgore's shoulder.

Stone dropped his empty assault rifle to the dusty creek bed and drew his sword. He gripped the handle with the determination of someone both resigned to and willing to accept the hand fate had dealt. He looked toward his men. Lowstreet stood with his sword at his side, staring toward the enemy. Kilgore held his sidearm in one hand and his rapier in the other. At least he would die among brave men.

"It sounds like they are close now, gentlemen," said Stone. "Shall we greet them?"

Stone felt the dry, coarse dirt in his hand as he pulled himself out of the creek bed to face the enemy. As he looked onward, scores of Terillian infantry were only a hundred meters away, ready to sweep the three away in one huge wave. The men readied their weapons as the Terillians came closer.

Stone's mouth felt dry. He had faced death many times, but this felt different. Although he had learned to control fear, he didn't need to this time; it was a natural calm, accepting of the inevitable.

Fifty meters…

"I'll take the twenty in the middle," joked an uneasy Kilgore.

Stone looked toward Lowstreet, who gave a quick chuckle at Kilgore's joke, but was obviously preparing himself mentally for his death.

Forty meters…

Stone, digging his back heel into the ground, picked his first targets and braced for the force of the onslaught. At least if this was the end, he would die well and among brave men. Almost unconsciously, he started to recite the Guard Oath out loud.

"*I will stand strong in the face of danger, for my comrades will do the same*

I will be unafraid of death for death comes but once and cowardice is forever"

Lowstreet joined in.

"*I will go close against the enemy, for my will is stronger than his*

I will show courage, for it is the one possession that cannot be taken"

Thirty meters….

Kilgore's deep voice added to the chorus, almost drowning out the growing noise of the oncoming horde.

"I will die with pride, for I am fighting for my lineage and my people

I will face death with joy, for I will become immortal—my shining glory never forgotten"

Suddenly the ground in front of them opened up and the air exploded with the thunderous sound of gunfire. Instinctively, the three fell prone as the Terillian assault collapsed under a solid wall of destruction. For what seemed like an eternity the air was filled with the constant roar of gunfire, punctuated by loud thuds from concussion grenades.

As quickly as it had begun, it ended.

As he rose from his prone position, Stone's ears were still recovering from the unexpected explosion of sound when the dust began to clear in front of him.

Stone could hear dull, muffled voices shouting as the ringing slowly dissipated.

"What the hell was that?" asked Kilgore, himself yelling as result of temporary shock to his hearing.

Stone looked over the devastation. Dead Terillians covered the ground in front of them as if a giant blade had cut them down. In the foreground, Stone saw scattered breaks in the ground from which he could see the heads and upper torsos jutting out. As he regained his focus, he saw a figure emerge out of the ground not ten meters in front of him.

Then another. And another.

As the first figure moved toward Stone, he recognized the unmistakable walk. The long, red hair bouncing back and forth in a ponytail was a dead giveaway too.

It was Captain Emily Martin and a platoon of her men.

"Captain Martin!" shouted Stone. "You could have let us know you were there before."

"No time, sir," smiled Emily. "Besides, we wouldn't have been able to get all of them if I hadn't let them get out in the open."

"Where's the transport?" asked Lowstreet.

"Had it dip behind the clump of trees about four kilometers away along with the Hawk gunship in case we needed it," reported Martin proudly.

"Good job, Captain," acknowledged Stone. "Now let's get the transport back and get out of here so we can get the cruiser out of orbit. This planet is crawling with Ters."

***

As the troops buckled up in the transport for the return to the cruiser, Stone saw Sergeant Kilgore smiling at Martin.

"What the hell are you looking at, Sergeant?" she demanded.

"Nothing, ma'am. Just wanted to let you know that we may have found some competition for you down there in the Wilderness," answered Kilgore, his smile growing as he glanced over at Lowstreet, who instantly began to blush.

"What are you talking about?" she asked again, looking a little more irritated.

"Well, ma'am, you're no longer the only female to kick L.T.'s ass, and this one was only a farmer," blurted Kilgore as he erupted into laughter at his own personal joke.

While the veteran Kilgore tormented Lowstreet and irritated Martin, Stone contemplated the success of the mission. He had uncovered a major Terillian operation and solid evidence of a violation of the Accords. His men had performed well, too. Stone only wished he could say the same for himself. He had lost the focus of his mission and placed Kilgore's and Lowstreet's lives in unnecessary danger. He still could not put his finger on what had driven him to investigate the slavers, and was equally unsettled about how the Terillian woman had distracted him.

Either way, they had made it back with valuable intelligence and, with the timely help of Martin, racked up a substantial body count. He could not focus too much on the past. There would be many more missions to come.

Chapter 4

Sitting in his stateroom onboard the cruiser *Areilia*, Major Stone stared at the blank data screen in front of him. Stone hated paperwork of any kind and fitness reports were by far the most frustrating. Taking a sip of whiskey as he opened up the regimental record database, he prepared himself for the hours of tedium ahead of him.

"More elitist First Family shit," he said to himself as he opened up the first record. Emily Martin had perfect scores of ten in tactical skill, leadership, fitness testing, loyalty, and combat performance. Unfortunately, due to her family's status she could only receive a score of five in last category—suitability for major command. Even more frustrating, the final category was worth 20 points, skewing the entire fitness report.

A yellow light illuminated at his desk, alerting him that someone was requesting to enter. Stone activated the door mechanism.

"Come in," he shouted with his back to the entrance.

"Major Stone, do you have a moment?" asked Captain Arilius Tacitus.

Stone motioned for Arilius to enter. "Have a seat, Captain."

As Arilius pulled a chair to Stone's desk, the major pulled another glass from his top drawer and poured a drink for the captain. Stone looked up toward his second in command.

"How are things going, Captain?"

Arilius took the glass and, after a healthy drink, spoke.

"Morale and efficiency are high throughout the battalion. Have you heard anything regarding our next mission?"

"So you came to get some information?" smiled Stone. "Not getting anything from your well-placed relatives?"

"They are always telling me things," said Arilius dryly. "Unfortunately they are not military men and have no idea what is important and what is not. Besides they are too busy trying to elevate their position as all of Alpha Humana jumps on the war bandwagon. New regiments and brigades are being formed daily. Uncle Herodices informed me that two battle groups from the Dorans arrived at the Gateway and are conducting independent operations at the edge of the Dark Zone."

"So you do get some good intel from your connections," replied Stone as he held his glass to his lips.

"Some," smiled Arilius as he took another drink.

"Things are moving fast," replied Stone. "It's only been a few weeks since the Sierra 7 mission and the whole planet is ratcheting up for war."

After a slight pause and another drink he continued. "I understand the need for rapid mobilization but we're going to pay for it in the short term. New recruits are undisciplined and have no idea what they are in for. And new units mean new commanders. These positions won't just be filled by career officers but political appointees as well." Stone paused again, lowered his drink slightly, and smiled at Arilius. "No offense to the political elite."

"None taken," said Arilius. "Most of them are idiots and political dandies."

"They will cost lives but I fear it is inevitable in the political-military structure of Humana society. Hell, I wouldn't be surprised if Astra's father tried to obtain a field grade commission for one of his teenage nephews."

"Maybe," said Arilius with a wry smile.

"Don't tell me he already has," replied Stone as he allowed his glass to overflow slightly. "Damn it," he laughed. "Look what you've made me do."

"You can't blame me for what the Varus family does," replied Arilius, his grin growing larger.

"You definitely know something."

"I know nothing about Dominotra's nephews," answered Arilius, still holding his playful smirk.

Arilius took another drink and swallowed loudly followed by a satisfying "Ahhh."

"Enough about Varus family politics," he continued. "I'm sure you will soon have your fill of that. Have you caught the new media links? They are really focusing on Terillian belief in primitive religion as a foundation for their aggressive nature. One report made links between their religious zeal and the illogical beliefs of our ancestors during the religious wars."

"Zealots or not," replied Stone. "The Scout Rangers are more than competent warriors."

"Speaking of warriors," smiled Arilius, "I also saw another presentation on Agrippa Lucius Stone and the battle of Echo 10."

"It figures they would bring him up."

"Well your great-great-grandfather was one of the heroes of the last war. And you seem to have fared pretty well carrying such a common name."

"I guess he went a long way to make up for my ancestor marrying a commoner," replied Stone, a little irritated.

Arilius realized he may have said too much. "Regardless, the Stone name seems to be on the comeback."

"Enough to be a political tool for the Senator Dominotra Varus," said Stone as he threw back another drink. "And besides, it's more about the Lucius family *erasing* the Stone part of my line. It's like every one of my ancestors since Martin Stone have been trying to bring honor to the Stone name in order to have it absorbed by the Lucius—and now Varus—families."

"It is a good move for them," said Arilius in a matter-of-fact manner. "The Varus family has always been powerful and influential, but they are not warriors. Dominotra knows that is what has kept his family out of the ProConsul's chair."

"I guess that's where I come in—a decorated warrior from a line of warriors," Stone replied as he held his glass up in a toast to no one.

"It will add military credentials to the Varus name. I'm sure Dominotra envisions his grandson sitting as ProConsul."

"A Stone sitting as ProConsul—I don't think I'll live to see that."

"Not a Stone," said Arilius, "a Lucius-Varus."

"True. Stones can defend the planet, they just can't rule it."

"Pretty much. But I don't think you have much to complain about, sir. With all the political bullshit comes the Lady Astra."

A reminiscent smile replaced the frustration that had been growing on Stone's face.

"I guess you have a point there. Even though she can be a handful."

"I'm sure she can," laughed Arilius. "But what a pretty handful."

"Astra is ambitious and can be an overbearing...but she is intelligent, exciting, and one of the most beautiful women on the planet. I guess if you had to have baggage, it might as well be pretty baggage."

"Pretty, indeed."

"And a challenge," smiled Stone as he took another sip, "And you know how I like a challenge."

Their discussion was cut short by the ship's announcing circuit. "*Major Stone, your presence is requested in Colonel Hastings's stateroom.*"

"I guess it's last call," said Stone, just before polishing off the rest of the whiskey in his glass.

"Enjoy your chat with the colonel," smiled Arilius.

Stone looked puzzled. "You know something, don't you?"

"I know nothing, Major," replied Arilius as he sipped his whiskey. "You shouldn't keep the colonel waiting. I'm sure it's important."

***

Standing outside Colonel Hastings's office, Stone wondered why he had been called at such an hour. Rumors spread like viruses in the fleets and he had at least ten outlandish stories running through his head when the light outside Hastings's door turned from red to green, signaling he could enter.

"Request to enter, sir!"

"Come in, Stone. Have a seat."

As he sat in front of Hastings's desk, he noticed stacks of personnel files on his desk and flat screens displaying officer profiles. He also noticed the harried look on Hastings's face as he spoke.

"Now that we're in a *real* war, as the politicians call it," said Hastings, still shuffling papers and scrolling through data screens, "we have been directed to make significant changes to the structure of our special forces."

"What do you mean, Colonel?" asked Stone, realizing he was squirming in the chair that had suddenly become very uncomfortable.

"The Elite Guard is to be temporarily reduced to one regiment. Our brilliant leaders in the Forum and High Command feel that, as we move to a more conventional war, the role of clandestine operations will be diminished and that our experience will be of better use if spread throughout our rapidly growing ranks."

"How is it to be done? Who is staying?"

"The majority of field grade officers will be transferred to regular units. Our captains will be split between regular units and staff duty to support new commanders. Our junior officers will be detailed to new regiments to create scout reconnaissance units embedded at the regimental level. Our enlisted will be transferred to training commands, offered temporary commissions—if their family standing warrants—or act as senior enlisted advisors to new officers."

"Which regiment is staying?" asked Stone again. He was trying not to be disrespectful or seem anxious, but was failing miserably.

"The 1st will remain intact."

A wave of relief flowed over Stone. He would stay with his men.

"Except for you," continued Hastings.

Stone felt his stomach tighten. "But Colonel—"

"It's not my decision, Major. You can thank your political connections for your good fortune."

"Good fortune, sir?" said Stone, rising from his chair. "How is losing my command good fortune?"

"You may be losing your battalion, Stone, but you are gaining a regiment."

"A regiment? I can't command a regiment as a major. It's—"

"I know, not in accordance with regulations. That's probably why your soon-to-be father-in-law somehow obtained a colonelcy for you."

"A colonelcy? I don't..."

"Well, it's done, and you will be given a standing unit," stated Hastings, with what Stone realized was a bit of jealousy. Hastings had served in the Guard for thirty-five years and was still one of the best soldiers in the unit. His family status was not much better than Stone's, however, and he was the first in his family to gain true military honors. In one giant leap, Stone had jumped past the rank of Senior Major and straight to Colonel. Furthermore, he was to be given a standing unit, not one of the mobs of new recruits.

"Which unit, sir?"

"The 25th Air Assault. Not a bad unit; they actually have some limited combat experience. They took part in putting down that revolt of miners on Alpha Satellite 12 about five years ago. They weren't facing Scout Rangers, but at least they know what it feels like to be shot at."

"Sir, I am grateful for the opportunity, but can I—"

"No, you cannot turn down the assignment," blurted Hastings. "The political wheels are turning and they are taking you to high places, son. You're a Colonel of the Line now and I'm sure with your talent and your new family's connections I'll soon be saluting you."

Hastings paused in what Stone interpreted as a moment of reflection on what could have been. Stone knew Hastings should be a general, but it would never happen.

Hastings continued.

"Your orders are prepared and a transport is ready to take you to the Twenty-Fifth's headquarters back on Alpha Humana. I have temporarily assigned you an aide until you can pick one from your unit. He will be waiting for you outside your quarters with your uniforms."

"Sir, I don't know what to say," stammered Stone. "I didn't ask for this."

"Don't worry, Colonel," replied Hastings in a calming voice. "Just keep in mind the slings and arrows of the battlefield are usually much easier to avoid than the intrigue of politics. Watch your backside on the field and at home. Good luck, Colonel Stone."

Chapter 5

The transport shuttle doors opened and Colonel Stone stepped out, followed closely—a little too closely—by his aide.

"Sir, you are scheduled for a 0800 intelligence briefing at Alpha Humana Command tomorrow. There is a 0900 fitting for your ceremonial uniform. At 1100 you have an informal meeting with media link interviewers. They have provided a list of questions and preferred answers based on a Forum subcommittee finding of most preferred public responses. At 1300..."

Stone was sure Hastings would get a laugh out of this. He was convinced Hastings had "assigned" him this hyperactive puppy dog of an aide just to spite him.

“Lieutenant, stop talking for just a second,” pleaded Stone as the two walked toward the commons area of the docking station. “It sounds like my schedule is already full; maybe there is enough time for a head call—”

“Actually, sir,” said the fidgety lieutenant, “your—”

“You’re kidding me, right?” interrupted Stone, ready to run himself through with his own sword.

“I have your time for the rest of the day, Colonel,” echoed a familiar voice from just around the corner.

Turning the corner, a smile came to Stone’s face; it was Lady Astra Varus. She was standing next to her father, flanked on both sides by Senate guards. Stone paused to take in the vision that was the Lady Astra Varus. “Definitely pretty baggage,” he said under his breath.

Her long blonde hair was immaculately done and cascaded in shimmering waves down to her waist. She wore a black dress that was cut to show enough cleavage to tease, but not flaunt, with a split just above her waist to show her firm, flat stomach. As the dress flowed down her body it again was strategically split to show her outer thighs and then her calves. She was so beautiful he almost forgot the required greetings.

“Senator Dominotra Varus,” recovered Stone, “I humbly request to embrace your enchanting daughter.”

“You have my blessings and continued approval, Colonel Tyler Lucius Stone,” replied Varus, his taught, pencil-thin face slightly wrinkled from forming a plastic smile only a politician could make.

"We are pleased to see you well and welcome your overdue promotion to Colonel of the Line."

Stone hated these shows. Even the social elite never really spoke this way unless they thought someone was watching. As it was a commons area and both Dominotra and Astra were political beings, there was sure to be a media recorder nearby.

"As always, Senator," continued Stone. "I am honored by your kindness and patronage."

Dominotra replied with a slight nod of his head.

With that, it was done. At least he could now touch his fiancée.

As Stone placed his arms around Astra's thin waist, she pulled him in close. A chill of excitement and surprise washed over his body. This was the first time she had held him in a familiar manner in public. Until this point, when they embraced in public she had draped her arms around his neck briefly and then moved her hand to meet his, always using her left hand to signify she was still *legally* available.

She then stood on her toes, bringing her lips to his ear. Before she spoke she let a slow, hot breath flow over his neck, sending chills down his spine.

"I have missed you, Colonel," she whispered, still holding the embrace. "With your promotion, father has been so pleased that he has agreed to allow you to claim your marital rights at your discretion."

She paused again to allow another breath to tickle his neck, moving the sensation to another area of his body.

Stone mentally paused for a second as he thought about the awkward conversation that would have been between a *normal* father and daughter, but the feeling of Astra's body against his soon refocused his attention.

"Your aide has cleared your schedule for the next several hours at my request. Perhaps you would like to see your new quarters," Astra said softly in his ear.

She slowly pulled away and slid her *right* hand down to his and began to walk along with him.

"Father, I wish to escort the Colonel to his new quarters and ensure he gets settled," she said as she lightly squeezed his hand.

"Very well, Astra. I shall expect you at dinner tomorrow. Perhaps the Colonel's schedule will allow him to attend."

Stone knew it would. Dominotra and Astra were probably on the fifth revision to *his* schedule but now was not the time to be concerned about such matters. He was about to consummate his engagement to one of the most attractive, powerful, and sought-after women on the planet. Well worth the pain of a stuffy dinner.

As the two walked down the corridors, they were greeted by almost everyone that passed. It was either "Good day, Colonel" or "My Lady" or some other acknowledgement of Stone's rank or Astra's social status. After a few moments, Astra stopped by a security door outside Stone's new quarters.

"I've taken the liberty to add myself to your access list," smiled Astra as she entered her identification code into the access panel.

As the door opened and Stone looked at his quarters, he was stunned. The entranceway led to a large room with a massive desk made from what appeared to be extinct Perilian wood.

Two guards snapped to attention as the couple entered the room. "Be gone," ordered Astra with a wave of her hand as she moved into the room. The two guards quickly scurried out of the room and took up position just outside.

"The quarters are amazing," mumbled Stone as he took it all in.

Marble covered the floors. Inlaid in the marble were bronzed depictions of Humani military might and political authority. Representations of Senatorial processions and famous battles were stamped in the shining metal. Columns had been placed in the entranceway to the room housing his desk. The columns, while providing no support, again were stylized. The column to the right was etched with the Lucius family crest and the left with that of the Varus family. Above the entrance to his office was etched the Elite Guard Oath:

I will stand strong in the face of danger, for my comrades will do the same

I will be unafraid of death for death comes but once and cowardice is forever

I will go close against the enemy, for my will is stronger than his

I will show courage, for it is the one possession that cannot be taken

I will die with pride, for I am fighting for my lineage and my people

I will face death with joy, for I will become immortal—my shining glory never forgotten

As he read the oath, Stone was taken back to the first time he had pledged the words, during his marking ceremony when he became a member of the Guard so many years ago, and his close call on Sierra 7 with Lowstreet and Kilgore. The words had become a part of his life, his ethos—just as they had for any member of the Guard.

"Let me show you more, Ty," said Astra as she pulled him through the room.

"To the right are the paintings depicting the arrival of the first Xennite ship on Alpha Humana, battle scenes from the First Terillian War, and a portrait of your ancestor, Colonel Agrippa Lucius Stone, the hero of the Battle of Echo 10."

"These are wonderful recreations," said Stone.

"They are not recreations," replied Astra as she slowly rubbed her hand over Stone's forearm. "My father acquired the originals at my request. For you."

Stone again was stunned. One of these paintings was worth more than a year's salary for a colonel.

"I don't know what to say. They are wonderful."

Astra raised her hand to Stone's cheek and pulled him to her for a quick but enticing kiss.

"You're going to be a restored and senior member of the Lucius family and your quarters should reflect not only your family's military heritage but your new social status as well," said Astra as she directed him toward the opposite wall. "That's why I have placed your family crest and all of your decorations and awards on this wall."

Stone wasn't sure how she had gotten all of these items together but he had long since quit trying to put any limits on Astra's ability to get what she wanted.

"This is really great," he remarked, the shock still showing on his face.

"That's just the beginning," she replied as she walked toward his desk with one hand tugging his shirt just above his navel.

Walking behind the desk, she selected one of the buttons on a touch screen embedded in the desktop.

"Here we go," she said as she pressed on the screen.

As the button was pressed, the wall directly behind the desk opened up to display a view of the entire city of Mt. Castra. He walked to the window and looked out over the stunning city with Astra's arms clasped around his waist from behind.

"Beautiful, isn't it?" said Astra.

Directly across from his room was the Forum, home to the Senate. Its lighted marble walkways and massive columns made an impressive backdrop to the Procession Field. It was here where the Senate announced the election of the ProConsul and major political functions were held. Between the Procession Field and the Forum stood the Eternal Flame. The Eternal Flame was a two-story marble foundation supporting a massive flame that had burned since the Forum first voted to go to war with the Terillians almost 200 years ago. The flame symbolized never-ending vigilance and the enduring power of the Alpha Humana society.

To the right, monolithic buildings rose majestically to the sky. Lit by random lights from hundreds of rooms within, they almost sparkled against the night sky. Between the buildings sped hundreds of hover vehicles of all types. The hoverways, sometimes ten deep, had always mesmerized Stone. Somewhere in the chaos of the bustling traffic was an inherent order that made it work. For Stone, it symbolized Humana society. He could not help but feel pride in his people. With the help of the Xen allies, they had risen from the verge of extinction to again be a thriving and formidable civilization.

Centurion Centralous was to the left. The nerve center for Alpha Humana's military and home to High Command. The darkness of the fortified portion of the city was in stark contrast with the rest of the view. Stone laughed to himself—most of the people inside the building weren't that bright either.

"The world is ours, Ty," said Astra as she turned Stone to face her.

He could feel the pressure of her body against his as she pulled him close.

"And I am yours," she whispered in his ear.

Slowly, seductively, Astra stepped backwards toward the desk, both hands around his waist. When she reached the desk she slid her behind on top of the desk and slowly pulled Stone between her legs, first slowly caressing his face and then moving her hands down his chest, unbuttoning his tunic as she went.

"It's time you take what is yours, Colonel," she demanded, unclasping his belt and dropping his trousers to the floor while her feet teased the back of his legs just above his knees.

"As you wish, Lady Astra," he replied as he began to remove his tunic.

"Wait." She paused, moving her hands slowly from his chest to the collar devices depicting the new rank on his tunic.

"Leave your shirt on, Colonel," she pleaded.

"As you wish."

He conceded and lowered his head to give her a long, passionate kiss. As they kissed, she slowly wrapped her legs around his waist and guided him to his prize.

Maybe being a colonel wasn't going to be too bad after all.

***

"I hate dress uniforms," Stone confessed to Astra as they made their way down the carpeted hallway to the dinner.

"I don't understand, Tyler. You are so impressive in your dress uniform," replied Astra.

Astra was stunning as usual. She wore a strapless forest-green dress that fell to the floor. This dress, just like all of Astra's, was specifically designed for her to tastefully display her physical beauty. Around her neck was the Varus family engagement necklace. Encrusted with huge diamonds and emeralds, it had been flown from the Varus estate to Mt. Castra under heavy guard specifically for the dinner. Her hair was tightly bound and pulled back behind her head, highlighting her flawless facial features.

“Thank you, dear,” replied Stone, “but regular army uniform regulations require me to wear full medals. In the Guard I at least only had to wear miniatures.”

“You should be proud of your medals, darling,” said Astra. “You *are* the most decorated officer on active duty.”

“That’s exactly the problem. I’m wearing ten pounds of cadmium medals on my chest and I sound like a damn wind chime in a hurricane.”

“That just lets everyone know they’re in the presence of a hero.” Astra smiled slightly.

“Yes, dear,” replied Stone, realizing Astra was growing irritated with his complaints. He subconsciously raised his hand to his neck as that familiar itchy feeling around the collar and wristbands began to set in.

Astra gripped Stone’s hand. “We are nearing the receiving line. Make sure you remember the etiquette,” she warned with a smile.

Turning the corner, Stone saw the line of politicians, generals, and admirals waiting to meet him and his new fiancée. His stomach grumbled from hunger and the absurdity of formal dinners. As they neared the line, a captain stepped forward to begin the ceremonial introductions.

“Colonel Tyler Lucius Stone and the Lady Astra Varus,” said Stone to the young captain.

The captain seemed worried. Stone actually saw a bead of sweat run down the man’s forehead and his face turned red.

After an uncomfortable pause, the captain spoke softly so no one but Stone and Astra could hear.

"Colonel Lucius, ah…Stone, sir, I…"

Astra interrupted.

"Captain, did my father's staff inform you of our arrival and 'introduction?'" she asked coldly.

"Yes, milady"

"Well," replied Astra in a quiet but cold tone that seemed to tear straight through the nervous captain, "I suggest you do not keep us waiting any longer."

"Yes, Ma-lady," answered the captain as he turned toward the receiving line.

"Colonel Tyler Lucius of the 25th Air Assault Regiment, and his fiancée the Lady Astra Varus," announced the captain as they approached the first greeter in the receiving line.

"Lucius," Stone whispered to Astra. His common name had been omitted. Although technically of aristocratic lineage, his branch of the family had been barred from using their ancestral name in formal settings.

"The Lucius family has agreed to restore your lineage to full status within the family structure," smiled Astra. "You no longer need to carry that common name."

"Another present from your father?" asked Stone flatly.

Astra answered only with a smile.

Stone had no doubt that only a few generations ago a Varus family member would have needed to bathe if someone with a common name like Stone had so much as touched them. Politics definitely made strange bedfellows.

Stone trudged his way through the receiving line, acting out the usual pleasantries. First he would be congratulated on his promotion or the jangling rows of medals displayed on his uniform. Next came the declarations of Astra's beauty and ramblings about the stir the engagement had caused throughout the social elite.

This theme played out all along the receiving line as he moved past magistrates, senators, two major generals, and three fleet admirals. Finally he and Astra had run the gauntlet of distinguished attendees and made their way to their table.

"I love these events," exclaimed Astra as Stone pulled her chair out for her to sit.

"Seems like a lot of pomp and circumstance for a decent dinner," he whispered in her ear, giving her just a taste of how much he despised these "functions."

"It's not about the food, Tyler," she snapped back. "Stop complaining. It's about being seen and mingling with the *right* people."

"And who are the *wrong* people?" said Stone under his breath.

Astra smiled and put her hand on Stone's knee.

"I'm only looking out for our best interests," she said quietly, speaking through her smile. "Other than Arilius Tacitus the rest of your captains will never rise above the rank of major. I just want to make sure they don't weigh you down, especially that...woman, Martin. It's scandalous that a woman, especially one as attractive as

Martin, would lower herself to military service when she should be—"

"Marrying up," replied Stone, his voice rising above the current volume of their conversation.

"Please lower your voice," demanded Astra under her breath. "And, yes," she replied. "But I can tell it isn't the time for this discussion."

"Or the place," he replied.

"Very true, Tyler," said Astra. "Rest assured, Tyler, you will get used to these functions and grow to enjoy them. Besides, I'm sure you will find everything worth the effort."

As she spoke, Astra slowly ran her hand up Stone's thigh to remind him that food wasn't the only thing he had to look forward to as long as he behaved and played his role.

Stone suddenly realized he had neglected introductions.

"Gentlemen," he squeaked, as Astra's hand gave one last squeeze, catching him off-guard.

"Colonel," replied Colonel Romanari Vatarus.

Vatarus was a well-respected officer and middle son of one of the First Families. His wife, Lady Vespa Vatarus-Brutii, was the daughter of Senator Germanicus Brutii, the Varus family's major political rival. As such, Vespa and Astra hated each other.

"Lady Vespa, I am glad to see you could attend," said Astra, her pitch slightly elevated to show that she was still being civil even though she would rather gouge her rival's eyes out.

"It is only my duty as a faithful *wife,*" quipped Vespa. "It sounds like you may soon understand what those duties entail, Lady Astra. Besides, your father does throw such quaint little dinners."

Astra paused to take a drink of her wine and then swallowed hard.

"I'm sure my *father* is honored by your attendance and we are pleased you approve of our *little* gathering."

Romanari Vatarus gave a quick glance at both ladies and then turned to Stone with a smile on his face.

"At least it will be entertaining, eh, Colonel Lucius? Dinner and a show."

Stone could not help but let out a laugh. Romanari had been at this game for a while and was still able to laugh at the ridiculousness of it all. As a middle son, he was not burdened by the duties of a future patriarch and enjoyed the freedom that it allowed him.

Stone was not as lucky. The laugh brought a quick kick on the shin by Astra and a look that he was sure would stop a sable tiger in its tracks. Seeing that Stone had gotten himself into trouble, Romanari changed the topic.

"Let me introduce you to the other regimental commander, Colonel Casius Neo."

"Welcome Colonel Stone, ah, Lucius," stammered Colonel Neo.

In his haste to rise and greet Stone the young colonel clumsily bumped the table, nearly causing his glass to topple over. Awkwardly grabbing for the drink, he quickly steadied the glass and took a deep breath before continuing. "I look forward to learning from both you and Colonel Vatarus...and, oh, excuse me, may I introduce you to my quest, the Lady Ophelia Tacitus."

A cousin of Captain Tacitus and niece of Cataline Tacitus, the "Lady" Ophelia could not have been more than seventeen or eighteen. She seemed as infatuated with the grandeur of the event as Stone was irritated by it. Her family had prepped her well for the evening, however, and she was ready with the appropriate greetings.

"Greetings, Colonel Lucius, your presence brings great honor to an already distinguished table," she said, slightly bowing her head in the direction of Romanari Vatarus.

"Your grace is much appreciated at our table," noted Astra, casting a quick, icy glance at Vespa. "You do your escort much honor, Lady Ophelia."

With that Astra turned her gaze toward Neo. As she stared, she made a quick motion with her hand reminding the timid, delicate flower of a colonel to sit.

Casius Neo was just the type of officer that had come to power during a rapid mobilization. A member of a First Family, his great-uncle had been a Senator and his father a regional magistrate. Although he had served in the military for five years before the mobilization, Neo's military experience had been limited to staff and administrative duties at High Command. When the war drums began to beat, his great uncle pulled some strings and had him transferred into a line regiment as Senior Major of the 34th Heavy Assault Battalion.

Conveniently, the regiment's colonel soon retired amidst rumors of inappropriate behavior with a servant of the Neo family and misappropriations of funds from the regimental budget. This paved the way for the promotion of Neo and, without a doubt in Stone's mind, needless deaths of his men in future battles.

As Stone was sizing up the guests at his table and trying to stay positive about the evening, the appetizers arrived.

Neo, trying his best to regain his composure, turned to Stone.

"Colonel Stone," said Neo as he leaned back to allow the servant to place an appetizer on the table, "it must be nice to have your line once again associated with the Lucius family."

Astra choked slightly on the grape she had just placed in her mouth.

Vatarus let out a cough, clearly meant as a warning to Neo that he had made a social blunder.

Vespa sat quietly, smiling at the discomfort she knew Astra must be feeling.

Stone, slightly taken aback, looked blankly at Neo. As he did, he saw Ophelia nervously turn her head slightly toward Neo and give him a cautious, warning look with her eyes and a slight shake of her head.

"Um, I..." Neo stumbled.

"I'm sure he is," interrupted Astra, doing what she did best. "The Lucius family is honored to be able to restore Tyler's branch of the family to their lineage. After all, his line has provided us with some of our most honored heroes. From Colonel Agrippa Lucius Stone down to Tyler himself, the line has served our society with bravery and won the *right* to reclaim the Lucius name."

Stone saw Astra give a slight glance to Vespa, as she knew she had recovered quickly and robbed her adversary of the opportunity to see her squirm. Stone was impressed with Astra's ability to think on her feet and a little humbled by her acknowledgement of his ancestor's service.

"You are correct, of course," added Vespa, conceding Astra's victory.

"To the restoration of the Lucius line," joined Ophelia quickly. As she stood to give the toast, she used her right hand to guide Neo to stand as well.

"To Colonel Tyler Lucius," added Neo.

Stone remained seated and gave a nod of appreciation as the rest of the table rose to join the toast.

As they returned to their seats, Vatarus leaned toward Neo.

"I think the battlefield may be less complicated than this dinner. If only you could enlist the Lady Ophelia into your regiment."

Neo returned a smile of relief to Vatarus.

"Oh my!" gasped Ophelia in a playful response. "Could you see a lady of a First Family in fatigues in the muck and mire?"

"I most certainly could not," replied Stone with a duplicitous smile.

The dinner continued in the same manner, a little awkward and occasionally comical.

As the dinner concluded, the quests retired to the ballroom to engage in more "strategic" mingling.

Astra was in her element. She quickly flitted from one group to another, graciously accepting compliments and giving them when required, all the while with her new toy in tow. Her conversations were tactical works of art. Never too complex or controversial, even though she had the political wit to talk most senators into a corner, she was the epitome of social grace.

Stone had just found his own mental quiet place and had begun to grow numb to the glad-handing when Astra dragged him into a small group of high-ranking officers speaking with her father.

"Colonel Lucius!" proclaimed Dominotra in a loud voice as the couple came near, obviously feeling the wine. "Let me introduce you to your new Brigadier."

As Senator Varus stepped out of the small circle, Stone's new commander came into view.

It was Cataline Tacitus! And he was a Brigadier!

"I have been looking forward to having you under *my* command, Colonel," said Cataline, soaking up the shock painted across Stone's face.

Stone was certain that Cataline's negligence with security procedures had something to do with the Gateway virus. In his mind, Cataline's body should be decomposing in the crucifixion fields with the other traitors and murderers.

Dominotra saw the tension and spoke.

"Following the Terillian attack on Gateway Station and given our rapid mobilization, General Tacitus has been assigned a position commiserate with his experience and his family's status. I am sure with such leadership, the 2nd Brigade, 2nd Division will soon be ranked among the most famous of our people's illustrious history."

Stone felt Astra's hand squeezing his fingers white. A quick glanced at her father's face showed his growing concern about Stone's response. Feeling the pressure of Astra's grip and Dominotra's stare, he held his eyes on Cataline. A few seconds passed that seemed an eternity.

"Congratulations on your promotion, General." Stone almost choked on the words.

"And yours as well, Colonel," replied Cataline, his mouth curling upward in a contented smile. "We will have to discuss my plans for the regiment, Colonel. I am anxious to hear your recommendations."

Recommendations! In his mind he had already knocked the pompous ass unconscious. The 25th was *Stone's* regiment and that paper-pushing, over-bred, elitist son of a bitch would have nothing to do with how he commanded *his* regiment. Stone, still aware of Astra's death grip on his hand, took a deep breath.

"I will have to get settled in first. Perhaps in a few weeks I can come to your headquarters and brief you—"

"I think it would be better, and more appropriate, if I were to visit your headquarters," interrupted Cataline. "Perhaps I could do a quick inspection."

Stone felt his dinner start to work its way back up his throat. Sooner or later he would have his day with Cataline. Politics be damned.

"As you wish, General," Stone replied in a slow, tempered voice, trying not to explode. "I shall have my executive set up the details with your staff. Please forgive me, but I am still getting settled to my quarters and I believe my fiancée has promised me a tour of the city."

"Beg my forgiveness, General," interrupted Astra coming to Stone's aid. "I am a woman and only desire to spend time with my fiancé as he has been so often away in service of the people. Please indulge a lady's request."

"Of course, Lady Astra," smiled Cataline. "I would be remiss if I did not allow you time with the Colonel before he is called away to service yet again."

"Gentlemen," said Stone as he turned and made his way toward the exit with Astra at his side.

As soon as they cleared the hall, Astra let loose.

"What the *hell* was that about, Tyler?"

"I can't believe that bastard is my Brigadier," Stone snapped back. "You should have told me. That arrogant prick has no place commanding a brigade."

"Do not forget your place, Tyler," snarled Astra as she looked up toward Stone, her fury evident. "Cataline Tacitus is the patriarch of the Tacitus family and is *entitled* by birth to command. He is—"

Stone's glare caused Astra to pause. He looked at her with an intense but vacant stare, as if she no longer existed as a person.

"Lady Varus," said Stone in a slow, cold, and calm manner, overtly displaying the explosion of anger that lay just below his quiet tone.

"I am aware of the requirements of this society. I have been fighting—" He firmly grasped her wrist. "—and *killing* for it for almost two decades."

He continued to hold her wrist firm and his eyes locked onto hers. He could see her grow uncomfortable with his glare.

"You have several admirable qualities," he continued, "and I am on the whole honored to make you my wife. You think me less a man because of my aversion to silly parlor games and political intrigues. The importance of these political games is not lost on me, nor is their importance to your family's honor. And don't think I don't understand how important this is to my family's status. But, unlike you, I don't live in the vacuum of the ballrooms and dining halls of Alpha Humana. I am a warrior of the Elite Guard. This colonel's uniform doesn't change that, just as it doesn't remove the markings placed upon my chest when I took my oath to serve my people so many years ago. I will do what I have to when it comes to politics, but this isn't about politics. That man is not fit to command and I say that not as a member of a damn First Family, but as a soldier who has seen battle and knows the true measure of honor, and it's not in a name, Astra."

He took a short pause.

For once, Astra said nothing.

Stone could see she was unsettled. "Don't challenge me again in matters *you* know nothing about," he warned.

Stone released his grip and Astra quickly stepped away from him. He could tell he had truly frightened her.

"I meant no disrespect, Ty," she retreated. "I know little of military matters as you say. Of these things I know only what a woman is told by men who know better. I was only trying to ensure that social dogma was adhered to. Openly challenging a First Family patriarch without irrefutable evidence would be political suicide. I only mean to protect you in the manner in which *I* am well versed. Please forgive me."

Astra continued in her efforts to soothe Stone. "We can learn of each other's worlds, Ty, and better complement one another. I am sure after we are wed and get to know each other in more social settings we shall not have problems such as these," she said as she eased toward him and gave him a hug, not unlike a scolded dog returning to its master.

Stone slowly began to regain his composure. He realized he had actually frightened Astra, an emotion Stone was sure she had rarely, if ever, felt. He also knew that Astra thought herself to be of better blood than him and when angered she was not afraid to at least imply that point. It was a price that Stone was willing to pay, however, for the sake of his family—just another duty he had to perform for his family and his people.

He knew that Astra was right, politically speaking. Cataline would stay his commander and there was little anyone, even the

Varus family, could do about it. But maybe he had shown her enough of a glimpse of the monster that he kept dormant when in the company of normal people to make her think twice about unleashing her social superiority on him again—at least for a while.

"Perhaps we should let the matter go and I will attempt to handle my issues with *the general* on my own."

Astra gave a quick glance up toward Stone. He saw a hint of trepidation in her eyes.

"On your own?"

"I mean I will not make my problems with him public fodder."

"You see, Ty, we are already beginning to understand each other," said Astra with a sigh of relief as she took his hand. "Let us put this nasty event behind us."

As they walked down the passageway to his quarters, Stone began to wonder just who had won their little argument. He couldn't ponder the question too long; he had to meet his new regiment tomorrow and figure out how to work with his new commander without killing him.

***

The next evening Stone sat at the desk in his quarters waiting for his key subordinates to arrive. The 25th had just returned from training maneuvers and had been granted two days' liberty, so Stone had delayed officially assuming command until after the break to allow the men some time to wind down. While his men were enjoying a well-earned break, Stone had called his senior officers in to get a gauge on what he had to work with. As his people geared up for war, the Humani military swelled quickly and the data links had not been fully updated with new officer billets, so Stone would have to get to know his principal officers face to face.

First to enter the room was Senior Major Barilus Bruni. Stone had heard a little about Barilus through the grapevine. He apparently had a solid record and led a company as a captain during the mining uprising.

The Senior Major entered the room.

Bruni represented himself well in person as well. Close to two meters tall, his well-groomed, dark mustache showed a peppering of grey, hinting at his age. A scar from a bullet wound on his left cheek indicated his combat experience.

"Greetings, Colonel Lucius—"

"Come in, Bruni," interrupted Stone. "If we have to go through the formalities of introduction, the meeting will take a week. Besides, political niceties do little good in the field."

"Very well, sir," smiled Bruni. "I am here to answer any questions you have."

"So, Major," asked Stone, "what is your assessment of the unit?"

"Honestly, we are in pretty good shape, sir. Although clearly not up to par with a Guard unit," added Bruni.

"I understand, Major," replied Stone, accepting the compliment. "Please continue."

"Of course, sir," Bruni continued. "We performed very well in our last exercise, scoring especially high in insertion methods and battalion coordination. We were also evaluated as above average in marksmanship."

"What's your assessment of the exercise parameters?" asked Stone, attempting to dig a little deeper.

Bruni paused.

"Parameters, sir?" he asked.

"Yes. Did the exercise provide an adequate opportunity to both train and evaluate the

unit?"

"Well, sir," started Bruni, "these exercises are designed by High Command to fully—"

"I don't want the political answer, Major," interrupted Stone. "Give it to me straight."

"No B.S.?"

"No B.S."

"Well in that case, I would say it was hard to properly gauge our performance."

"Why is that?" asked Stone.

"The parameters, sir. They didn't really challenge our initial tactical plan. The insertion was not adequately resisted and follow-on logistical support was never interdicted."

"I see, Major."

"I have more, sir," replied Bruni. He had been given the opportunity to speak his mind and would make the most of it. "Furthermore, our ammunition supply was effectively endless, our wounded were allowed to return to our ranks following each day's scenario, and our opposing forces were two new regiments; they actually placed themselves in a crossfire situation in one scenario where they would have inflicted more damage on each other than us."

"So it was a typical High Command exercise," said Stone with a smile on his face.

"Pretty much, sir. All flash and no substance. That is not to say we did not perform well, we just were not pressed in a manner to fully evaluate our combat readiness against anything other than an armed mob."

"Fair enough, Major," said Stone. He liked Bruni's honesty regarding the status of the unit. He seemed to be a man he could work, and hopefully go into combat, with.

"Who else have you brought with you, Bruni?" continued Stone.

"I have brought both battalion commanders, the captain who has been serving as our staff and intelligence officer, and the commander of our recon platoon."

"Let's bring them in and see what we've got," replied Stone.

Major Victor Gates entered the room and reported. Stone was instantly impressed by Gates, who looked every bit the professional.

"According to your record," stated Stone, "you have reached terminal rank due to your commoner status but have stayed in the service and apparently"—Stone paused as he flipped through Gates's record—"have ranked well even against your First Family counterpart, Major Atticus Vatarus. That either speaks volumes about your abilities or Vatarus's incompetence."

"I like to think my record speaks for itself, Colonel," replied Gates. "And I am honored to be ranked alongside an officer as fine as Major Vatarus."

"Well said, Major," replied Stone. "Let's bring Vatarus in."

Atticus Vatarus strode into the room like he was on parade. "Colonel Lucius, sir, Major Atticus Vatarus of the Vatarus family has the pleasure of making your acquaintance and honor of serving under your command."

Atticus, first cousin to Colonel Romanari Vatarus, was definitely of noble birth and he wanted everyone to know it. His uniform, personally tailored, fit like a glove. He wore the ornate ring that designated him as a graduate of the elite Xenus Military Academy. Even the hilt of his traditional officer sword was decorated with gold-inlaid braiding. Stone rose from his seat to greet Vatarus.

"Shall we dispense with the formalities and speak freely, Major?" asked Stone, trying to gauge his all-too-proper major.

"Aye, sir," replied Vatarus. "Pleasantries aside, I am pleased that command of this regiment did not fall to some whelp whose Senator-father has finagled some backroom deal that will get me or my men killed due to his incompetence. You may be in command because of your political affiliations, but I do not doubt your ability to command."

Stone was taken aback. He had not expected such a frank statement from a rising star in the Vatarus family. Not only had Atticus Vatarus commented on the same fears Stone had regarding political appointments but he had mentioned concern for his men. He was still obviously arrogant but maybe he could back it up with his actions. Hopefully Vatarus would work out as well.

"I can promise I will lead this regiment to the best of my ability, Major Atticus Vatarus," replied Stone in the formal way, with which Vatarus was obviously pleased.

"I believe my staff officer is next, Major Bruni?" asked Stone.

"Yes, sir. Your staff officer is a direct transfer from the Guard."

Stone's interest was piqued. The idea of another Guard officer in the unit brought a smile to his face. He assumed it was one of the captains from 2nd regiment. Perhaps Captain Nelson. Stone had heard good things about him. As the door opened and his chief staff officer entered, the all too familiar walk and bouncing red hair was unmistakable.

"Emily!" exclaimed Stone forgetting himself.

Quickly regaining his composure, he continued, "Captain Martin, what a pleasant surprise. I had thought the 1st regiment was to—"

"When I found out where you were going, sir," interrupted Martin, to the obvious chagrin of Vatarus, "I requested a transfer and Colonel Hastings approved it, so here I am to cover your ass again."

"More like she requested a transfer ten times until Hastings got sick of saying no!" blurted a lieutenant as he burst into the room.

It was Jackson, another of Stone's former captains, which confused Stone almost as much as the series of undignified introductions, which clearly annoyed Vatarus.

"What are you doing here, Jackson?" asked Stone.

"Well I figured Emily wouldn't know what to do without me so I had to come along and keep an eye on her keeping an eye on you."

"That's Captain Martin, Lieu-ten-ant," snapped Martin, her face turning red with a mixture of embarrassment and anger. "You have lost the right to call me Emily both by your loose morals and now by your rank. Only a fool would request a demotion but I could always count on you to make the wrong decision."

Martin turned away from Jackson.

"Colonel Stone, may I present your Recon platoon commander, Lieu-ten-ant Jackson."

It was getting late and if he didn't break up the meeting, he was sure Martin would end up kicking Jackson's ass and Vatarus's head would explode from the lack of formality in which she did it. It was definitely an interesting group of officers.

"Well, Gentlemen, and Captain Martin, I think that will be enough for tonight. I truly look forward to working with you all. You are all released for the remainder of the liberty. I will see you all at 0700 in two days."

"Aye, sir," the group replied almost in unison.

"Good to work with you again, Major. I mean, Colonel," said Jackson, who had waited as the others left. "Thanks for breaking up the group hug early. I am getting my new recon platoon together for some extra individual combat training. They're pretty ragged right now."

"You had better get to work then, Jackson," replied Stone. "Time is probably not on our side."

"Aye, sir," he replied as he saluted and headed out the door to catch up to the others.

Chapter 6

The brigade gymnasium was empty by normal standards. A group of fifty young men stood in a circle with Hugh Jackson in the center. The men seemed physically fit and in all outward appearances looked like excellent stock for a recon patrol. As Jackson called them out one by one, however, he methodically dismantled their airs of confidence and made a mockery of their individual combat skills.

Jackson's booming voice yelling instructions and insults at his upstart platoon filled the massive confines of the near-empty gym, but they were not alone. A few soldiers were working out in the gravity room to improve their stamina, while others ran laps around the gigantic indoor field.

And there was Captain Emily Martin.

Standing outside the virtual combat course, Martin secured her sword inside its scabbard and pulled down the edges of the tight high-performance shirt that hugged her toned body like a second skin. It was great for workouts but rode up a little, exposing a portion of a set of abs any Humani male would be proud to display. She usually ran the course at night, as there were fewer distractions. When she worked the course during normal hours, she tended to draw a crowd. There were the random males that made a sport of watching attractive women work up a sweat, and then there were the competitors and the admirers of her skill.

Martin had mastered the virtual combat course as a cadet under Stone's tutelage. By the time she was a junior lieutenant she had set the course record—for males as well as females. Now it was her therapy and a way to continue to challenge herself. She had broken her own record four times.

"Ready, Captain?" asked the course master. "Same as usual?"

"Yep, Master-Guns. Remove all the safeties and go live fire."

Normally the course, which included randomly generated and fully automated IA combatants with full sensors to rate their survival status, was set so that the IAs would provide a laser-generated signal for hits and a small electrical charge with each one to remind the competitor they had taken a hit. With the safeties removed, some carried edged weapons and the laser markers were replaced with rubber cased bullets.

"Going for a record today, Captain Martin?" asked the old Fleet Marine Master Gunnery Sergeant.

"Every day, Guns."

Martin rechecked her sword and put her audio clip to her ears. As the powerful beat of the fast-paced music began to pulse through her body she looked over toward the course master, rubbed the palms of her taped hands together, and nodded.

As the light above her head shifted to green, she sprang into action. At a full sprint in a flash, she dove over an obstacle, drawing her sword while airborne. Landing into a roll, she rose and landed a kill shot on the first IA. A second target immediately sprung up behind her, swinging a sword. Emily dropped to the ground in a split, landing a fist to the inner knee of the IA. As the IA buckled she brought her sword upward.

"Kill" registered from the IA's voice communicator.

Martin continued her rush across the course as rubber bullets impacted all around her. Jumping over and sliding under obstacles, she was a blur. The powerful music filled her head and her sword flashed like lightning, taking out one IA after another. Reaching the last few meters of the course she was mid-stride over an obstacle when an IA sprung up immediately in her path. Without hesitation, she pressed off the obstacle with her right foot and threw her left on top of the IA's shoulder. Stepping over the IA she spun mid-air, landing a strike across the back of the IA.

"Kill."

Hitting the deck at a full run, she sprinted the remaining few paces to the end of the course and past the electronic tag signaling the end of her run.

Emily stood at the end of the course glistening with sweat. Panting slightly from the exertion but recovering quickly, she removed the audio clip, started to pull the tape from her hands, and waited on her score.

"Not too bad, Captain," said the Gunnery Sergeant.

"What's the total?"

"807. Another record."

"Damn," said Martin. "I thought it would be a little higher."

"That's two points higher than your best record and thirty-five more than the highest ranking mortal."

"Yeah, I know," she conceded. "810 sounds a lot better than 807 though."

"Maybe next time."

"Definitely next time. Set me up for same time tomorrow, Guns."

"Aye, Ma'am."

In the background Martin could hear Jackson tormenting his trainees, drawing her attention to her ex-husband as he worked with his men. After returning a salute from the Marine course master she walked over to watch the training.

***

"Corporal Hansen, you're next," said Jackson as he waved for the young man to enter the training ring.

The corporal stepped forward. No more than twenty-one, he was a mountain of a man.

"Okay, meat," taunted Jackson, "take me out."

The corporal lunged at Jackson, who quickly tied the large man up in a knot.

Jackson tightened his grip and the massive corporal grunted as he tried in vain to break free.

"Come on, Corporal," joked Jackson. "You all fight like women. Maybe we should ask some girl from Nero Street to come down and challenge me."

"What about me, Lieutenant?" asked Martin. "Will I do?"

"Oh, Captain Martin," said Jackson. He released the corporal from his grip and rose to greet his ex-wife.

"Captain Martin, I did not realize we were in the company of a senior officer." Looking over toward his trainees he bellowed the order, "Attention!"

As the trainees stood tall and erect, Jackson saluted with a smile.

"Of course when I speak of a woman, I did not mean you, ma'am."

Martin leered at Jackson.

"Of course not, Lieutenant, I am well aware of what you call a woman."

"Well, ma'am, there are women and then there are *women*," replied Jackson.

"You are definitely right. How about an advanced lesson for your trainees?"

Jackson looked over toward his men. There was no way out. Unsure of the outcome, he leaned in to Martin.

"If you had wanted to get close to me, I can think of many better ways to…"

Before he could finish, Jackson felt his leg moving upward as Martin swept his leg out from under him and pushed him onto his back. As he fell, she spun him on his side and locked her arms through his. Jackson's men gathered around them in a circle.

"Nice, Emily," said Jackson. "Let's tussle."

Jackson kicked his legs in the air and spun free of Martin's hold. Jumping back to his feet, the two former Elite Guard officers circled each other.

They came together again. Jackson caught Martin's right leg as she kicked at his ribcage.

As he did, he felt Martin grab his free hand.

"A little spent from the course?" asked Jackson as he strengthened his grip on Martin's leg.

"Maybe, but it shouldn't keep me from kicking your ass…again."

Jackson felt Martin's weight shift as she went airborne, swinging her other foot into the air and crashing against his head.

Jackson stumbled backwards as Martin completed her spin and landed facing him.

"Nice," chuckled Jackson as he spit out one of his teeth. "I guess we're really gonna do this?"

"Come on!" demanded Martin as the mesmerized trainees watched the show.

The two collided once more. After rolling on the ground, Jackson felt Martin's arms locked around his neck and her legs tightened around his torso.

Jackson's arms were free, however, and he landed several powerful blows with his elbow to her ribs. The last of the blows inflicted enough damage to cause Martin to loosen her grip with her legs. Jackson capitalized and grabbed Martin's ankle in a submission hold. Struggling for his breath, Jackson gave Martin a warning.

"If you don't let go…" He fought for more air. "…I will break your ankle."

"Break it, then," she grumbled in his ear. "If you have the balls."

Jackson increased the pressure to show Martin he could do it. As he did, he could hear her groan against the pain in her ankle, but she only squeezed more tightly around Jackson's neck.

Jackson felt his head begin to grow heavy.

"*Captain Martin, your presence is requested at regimental headquarters,*" echoed through the gymnasium.

Seeing his opportunity to save face, Jackson gave a light tap to Martin's calf in quiet submission so that his men would not see.

Jackson felt a rush of blood flow to his head as Martin released her hold. Jackson slowly stood, but remained bent over with his hands on his knees. After taking a few precious breaths he looked over toward Martin, who stepped toward him with an obvious limp.

"We will have to continue this *training* later, Lieutenant," said Martin, still working her ankle in small circles as she stood next to him.

"Yes, Ma'am," replied Jackson, giving her a slight smile as he saluted. Returning the salute, Martin quickly turned to report to headquarters.

Jackson returned his attention to his men and stated in a thundering voice, "That was an example of how to combat a skilled warrior. Remember, no matter how good you think you are, someone else is probably better..."

Jackson gave a quick glance toward Martin, who was almost at the exit. He knew she had heard his compliment and wanted to see her response.

Jackson saw Martin pause for a second, as if she was going to turn around. But she continued on, the limp now gone, and her red ponytail bouncing.

***

While Martin and Jackson were working out their tensions, Stone lay asleep with Astra curled up next him. Astra had acquired the suite of rooms next to his quarters, allowing her to spend nights with him and then return to her room through an adjoining door she had ordered constructed during the renovation of Stone's quarters. This way she would have a place to prepare herself each day without having her servants and their gossip-hungry ears traipsing through Stone's quarters.

Stone was awakened by the high-pitched tone of his door opening. As he was gathering his senses, Captain Martin burst into room.

"Colonel Stone, I...excuse me," she paused as she saw Astra sitting up next to him, pulling the covers over her body to protect her modesty.

"What are you doing in here, Captain?" demanded Astra.

"Forgive me, sir and aahh...Lady Astra. I have urgent news concerning the regiment. I did not expect you to have...company."

"Whatever *it* is, Captain, I am sure it can wait until morning," replied Astra coldly. "And I would remind you that you should address your commanding officer as Colonel Lucius...*not* Stone."

"I am sorry, Ma-Lady, but it cannot wait. I must speak to Colonel *Lucius.* Now," replied Martin, allowing her feelings toward Astra to show a little.

Stone could see Astra preparing to release a torrent upon Martin.

"It's okay, Captain," he said, turning back toward Astra. "It is obviously an important *military* matter."

He was trying to hint at their earlier conversation.

Astra apparently understood.

"Very well then," she pouted, as her eyes shot flames at Martin.

Stone rose to get dressed, quickly jumping into the dress trousers that were lying on a chair nearby. He soon found a shirt and began to pull it over his head.

Used to seeing Stone's body due to the close quarters of Guard service, Martin failed to avert her gaze as Stone pulled the shirt over his very developed chest and toned stomach.

"Perhaps in the future your *staff* could show a little more discretion and contact you via comm link first. We can't just let *anyone* come and go as they please," declared Astra coldly.

"You are correct, Lady Astra," replied Martin with a glare. "It was my mistake for not thinking of the colonel's new…situation."

Stone could feel the tension between the two.

"We can talk in my office," he said quickly, wanting to separate the two.

Stone escorted Martin out of the bedroom, leaving Astra to stew about their uninvited guest.

"What is it, Emily?" he asked as they walked into his office. "It's a little odd to be calling at this hour."

"We have been activated, sir. Intelligence has shown evidence that the former renegade Nero has been negotiating with the Terillians."

"The same Navarus Nero that masterminded an attempted assassination of former Proconsul Aurelius Maximillus?" asked a surprised Stone.

"Yes, sir. Nero and his followers are believed to have conquered a group of small villages on Juliet 3 where he set himself up as dictator."

"I know about that, Captain," replied Stone. "When I was a captain, we did some work in the area and there had even been talk of a punitive mission. But it was deemed that the forces it would have taken to pursue him were not worth the effort and he was allowed to become just another Dark Zone warlord."

"He has done quite well for himself since then," added Martin. "Over the last ten years he has consolidated power on Juliet 3. With close to five thousand men under arms and a small fleet of combat aircraft, Nero has created a formidable little empire on Juliet 3."

The new tactical importance of Juliet 3 suddenly hit Stone. Its relative proximity to important supply lines of planets trading with Alpha Humana and its suitability as a possible base of operations for the Terillians made the planet a valuable target for both sides.

"What are the details?" asked Stone.

"We don't have a lot, sir. High Command received word from agents operating on the planet that Terillian emissaries have been seen dining with Nero in recent weeks. They have decided that they cannot allow Juliet 3 to fall into Terillian hands."

"I agree. That would significantly impact our trade in the Dark Zone at the very least."

"Yes, sir. High Command has recalled all of 2nd Brigade. We're to have the regiment standing by at 1200 in two days to meet transports from the *Lucius Pantelus Varuk*. Once onboard, General Tacitus will to have more information but it seems clear we will finally be entering the Dark Zone in force."

"It seems so, Captain," Stone replied. "Draft the necessary orders and ensure every member is contacted immediately with the recall order."

Martin hustled out of Stone's quarters to prepare the regiment for deployment. Stone had hoped to get to know his officers and work with the regiment a little more before they went into combat, especially since he had absolutely no faith in his own superior.

Chapter 7

On the 3rd day of the 11th lunar cycle, 4785 Alpha Humana years, two Humani battle groups entered the Neutral Quadrant for the first time in over 150 years. The force, under command of Admiral Bruti Plutarch, included the battle cruisers *Lucius Pantelus Varuk* and *Arilius Gaes Prime*; orbital destroyers *Redoubt, Intrepid, Courageous,* and *Defiant*; five fast cruisers; and several *Tiger* class battle frigates. It was this group of warships that would fire the opening salvos of a Second Tero-Xennite war.

Colonels Stone, Vatarus, and Neo sat in General Tacitus's stateroom waiting for him to enter. As the door swung open Cataline's aide, a little weasel of a man, called attention to the group.

They had barely begun to rise when the general entered. Most flag officers would have the room take their seats immediately as they entered. But not Cataline Tacitus. He arrogantly strode across the room to the front of the group. After a brief pause to savor the power that came with flag rank, he spoke.

"Please, at ease, men. Have a seat," he said, trying to pretend he did not love having the entire room stand for him.

He turned on a data screen and continued. "We're currently bringing auxiliary reactors online to support our jump to the Juliet system. We should plan on beginning offensive operations in less than seventy-two hours."

"Sir, I have reviewed the terrain and have some recommendations for landing zones," added Stone as he started to rise to show his proposed sites.

"Recommendations will not be necessary, Mr. Stone," interrupted Cataline, motioning for Stone to return to his seat. "I have conferred with High Command and we have agreed on the landing zones."

Stone looked over at Vatarus, who was visibly surprised at Cataline's rebuff of Stone.

"General Tacitus," spoke Vatarus. "Perhaps Colonel Lucius's experience in these—"

"Silence!" shouted Cataline. "I am in command of this brigade and once a decision is made it will be your duty to follow my orders. Is that understood?"

Cataline was looking at Vatarus, but everyone understood the explosion was probably meant for Stone.

"Yes, sir," replied Vatarus as he leaned back into his chair, still openly annoyed.

"As I was saying," continued Cataline, "the first brigade, consisting of the 5th Air Assault, 52nd Heavy Infantry, and 158th Mt. Castra Reserve Militia, will land in the plains to the west of Nero Two. They will be commanded by General Casius Brakus, but I will maintain tactical command of the overall expedition."

Cataline shifted the screen to a new location. "Colonel Vatarus, you will deploy in the mountains about halfway between Nero Two and Narus City. Your mission will be to prevent reinforcement of any forces General Brakus encounters. To facilitate this, you will receive additional hawk attack ships from the 25th and will have tactical control of 2nd and 3rd squadrons from the compliment onboard *Lucius*."

Stone's anger boiled just under the surface. Cataline was already depleting Stone's force and he did not yet know what mission he would be given.

"The plan is to have Vatarus hold the mountains and then have General Brakus move eastward to link up with Vatarus's troops and move on Narus City. It is believed this will be an adequate display of power to sway many of Nero's lieutenants. Once outside Narus City, I will join the force and commence negotiations with Nero to sign a treaty of amicability and support."

"You will not be commanding from the planet?" asked Vatarus.

"No, Colonel, I believe the operation can best be monitored and directed from a central location."

Stone's face grew red. He knew Cataline to be arrogant and incompetent; now he knew he was a coward as well.

"Colonel Neo."

"Yes, sir," squeaked the young colonel.

"Your regiment will remain onboard to support General Brakus if needed or to assist in holding the mountains as the situation develops."

"What will the 25th be doing?" asked Stone no longer able to hold his tongue.

"Well, Colonel," replied Cataline, "Intelligence believes that a large portion of Nero's manpower is concentrated near the city of Lady Lunari. It is thought that a recent forced migration of a few nearby villages has resulted in small but violent domestic uprising. He has perhaps 1000 of his men in this area to restore order. It will be your assignment to make a forced landing in the farmlands near the city and demonstrate in the area to hold his forces there. Keeping those forces stagnant or delaying their response to the main landing should guarantee our success."

"Sir, Lady Lunari is over 1000 miles from the main force. If I become heavily engaged, particularly with limited numbers of hawk attack ships, what unit will provide support?"

"We do not believe support will be needed for your portion of the operation. High Command is confident in the intelligence."

Stone's anger boiled hot. High Command could be confident from their bunkers on Alpha Humana. To make matters worse, the spies employed by Xen Intelligence were almost never completely accurate and sometimes switched their alliances based on who paid the most.

"Sir, if Nero has been negotiating with the Terillians, how do we know that there are not already Terillian troops on J3? It seems that if there are Terillians on the planet—"

"Colonel," interrupted Cataline, "I do not have time for second guessing of orders put forth by High Command and myself. This mission will take place. Do you understand, Colonel?"

"Sir, I understand. I am only concerned with the ability for my unit to be supported should we—"

"Enough, Colonel! I would not have expected such timidity from you. If you do not have the stomach to command a regiment then I shall find someone who does. We are far from the protection of your adopted family, Mr. Stone, a fact you may have forgotten."

Stone rose from his chair, his hand involuntarily moving toward his sword. He could not believe this coward was challenging his honor. He felt the monster inside him come to life.

"General, I have served faithfully in more combat missions than any officer involved in this operation. Furthermore, I am not the one that should be worried about the distance from the political powers at home. Do not forget, sir, I am no longer Elite Guard and as such am now authorized to claim the right of proporia combata. If you truly question my honor, you can face me in single combat and in my victory I'll take both your life and all of your property, leaving nothing for your lineage." Stone stared coldly into Cataline's eyes. "Remember this before you question my honor again."

Cataline paused as he contemplated Stone's not-so-idle threat. He grew slightly pale as Stone's words began to sink into his mind.

"I meant no challenge to your honor, Colonel. That does not change the fact that I am your commanding officer and you have been assigned your mission. Do you wish to carry it out?"

"Whether I wish to or not does not matter. I will perform my duty. If there is nothing else, General, I would like to return to my men and prepare for our mission."

Cataline stood silent. After a few seconds, Stone excused himself from the table and left to prepare for a mission he knew to be a mistake. As he made his way to his quarters, he spoke out loud to himself. "Sketchy intelligence, inexperienced troops and commanders, not to mention a renegade warlord thrown in—not the best way to start a war."

***

The officer's lounge onboard *Lucius* was packed. With over four hundred officers from ship's crew, 350 aviators, and 250 infantry officers, the lounge was never short of patrons. Each clique usually stuck to themselves, especially the 150 Corner lounge where only officers from First Families had access.

Although the military band was playing stylized versions of the military tunes that had become all the rage on Alpha Humana, they could barely be heard over the low roar of countless conversations common at military functions. Oaths regarding upcoming military exploits, stories of beautiful women, and other tall tales and boasting were lively, ubiquitous, and generally more fancy than fact.

Martin sat at the table with some other captains from the 25th and Major Gates. While they chuckled, laughed, and made jokes about the pilots, she pretended to listen but was already mentally preparing for the mission, especially the landing.

"Where's Jackson?" asked one of the captains. "I figured he would have been the first one here."

"How should I know where Lieutenant Jackson spends his leisure time?" replied Martin, even though she knew exactly where he was. She had been watching him for the last twenty minutes.

"Oh, there he is," said another captain at the table as he pointed to a table near the bar.

Jackson was sitting with two "ladies" from the recreation division. The girls were intently listening to Jackson, who was no doubt telling tales of past missions.

"He seems to be doing pretty well for himself," laughed one of captains.

"If you can call that doing well," interrupted Martin, showing her disdain for both Jackson and the two women he had enthralled in conversation.

The recreation divisions were a new invention in the fleet. Comprised of only the best looking young women in the fleet, they were detailed from their enlisted billets and eager civilian volunteers to act as hostesses, and sometimes more, in the officer's lounges of capital ships. Volunteers came forward in droves. The opportunity for women from common or even middling families to interact with and possibly snare a husband from a good family was great incentive.

Back at Martin's table, the conversation turned to their new commander.

"I hear our new CO is a hard-ass," said one.

"Yeah, but I heard he was a political appointee too," said another.

"No, he used to be Elite Guard and was promoted with the reorganization," added a third.

"That doesn't matter, he has the lineage of a First Family and is marrying the Lady Astra, Senator Varus's eldest daughter."

"Talk about hitting the jackpot."

"A colonelcy, a beautiful wife, and a First Family—talk about luck."

"It's not luck," interrupted Martin, no longer able to keep quiet. "He's earned everything he's got and more. As for his engagement...I quit trying to figure out First Family politics years ago."

"You seem a little sensitive about the subject, Emily," joked the officer sitting across from her. "I know you are from the Guard, but maybe you and the colonel know each other *a little better* than that?"

Martin's face grew red. "Screw you, Nathan."

"He was...is my commanding officer," replied Martin. "That is all."

The table could tell the topic of discussion was getting a little uncomfortable. After a few seconds of silence Major Gates spoke. "I think we need some more drinks."

"I'll get 'em," volunteered Martin, eager to get away from the table for a bit.

As she stood from the table and walked toward the bar, she made eye contact with Jackson. By this time he had one of the girls on his lap and the other whispering something in his ear. Jackson raised his drink to Martin in celebration of his future conquest. She turned away as if he didn't even exist.

"Bastard," she mumbled to herself after she turned away from Jackson and headed to the bar.

At the bar Martin pushed her way to the front and grabbed the bartender's attention. Sometimes being beautiful had its advantages.

"What can I get you, ma'am?" smiled the man behind the bar.

"Five shots of whiskey."

"No problem, Captain," said the man, smiling again.

It took only a few seconds and irritated everyone who had been waiting much longer for their drinks, but the man quickly returned with the whiskey for Martin.

"Here you go, ma'am."

"How much?" asked Martin.

"These drinks are on me," said a voice from behind her. "Put it on my tab."

Martin could feel a body pressing up against hers. She slowly turned around to see whose ass she was going to kick. Her eyes landed squarely on the well-developed chest of a tall major. She looked at his nametag…"Gius."

Shit. A First Family asshole, she thought to herself.

Martin looked to his left where two other men, one from the Venari family and another Gius, probably the tall man's younger brother, stood.

"Can I help you, Major?" asked Martin staring up at him, her contempt obvious.

"Oh, excuse me, Captain…what is it…Martin?" said the man with a dry smile as he obviously was more interested in Martin's chest than her nametag. "You looked like a Recreation Girl from behind. I didn't realize you were an officer."

"Well I am an officer, Major, sorry to disappoint you."

"Oh," he replied as he looked over her body, "you definitely don't disappoint. I am Markus Gius of the Gius family…"

Blah, blah, blah, thought Martin as he spoke.

"…Perhaps you would like to join me in the 150 Corner for some drinks."

Emily's stomach turned at the thought.

"No thanks, Major. I am an officer, not a—"

"I know, Captain," said the man as he leaned in and put his hand on her back. "Still, you are nice to look at…maybe we could meet up later and…"

Martin felt the drinks she had already had start to come back up her throat.

"Major, let me go…this is your only warning."

The major's face grew red with anger.

"I am Major Markus Gius, a son of a First Family. If I ask for your company, I will have it."

As he spoke he moved his hand down to her behind and pulled her tighter.

Martin allowed him to pull her closer.

"Major," she whispered in his ear.

"Yes, honey."

"I warned you."

With that she wrenched his arm behind his back, grabbed the back of his head and slammed it into the bar, breaking his nose. The man's two companions started to move toward her but before they could take a step, Martin's sword was holding them at bay.

Her arm locked around Gius's head and, forcing him against the bar, she leaned in.

"I warned you, Major. I am not one of those foolish little whores looking for a husband. I am a Line Captain and member of the Elite Guard. Perhaps you should take your broken nose as a lesson in manners and be done with it. You First Family pigs don't own everything, despite what you think. If you want to continue this discussion, I shall take it as a sign of disrespect and challenge you to proporia combata for the insult."

"Excuse me for my rash actions, Captain…I meant no disrespect," replied Gius submissively, coming to the sudden realization that she was a Guard officer.

"Go back to your kind, Major."

The once proud-looking First Family officer nodded and headed back to the 150 Corner with his followers in tow.

Martin turned back toward the bartender.

"How much for the drinks?"

"On the house, Ma'am," smiled the man behind the bar.

Returning to the table, Martin distributed the drinks and took her seat.

"So what are we talking about now?" she asked.

"Uh…nothing, Emily," mumbled one of the captains, having seen her handle the three men. "Why don't you tell us about our new CO?"

***

The men at Martin's table were not the only ones to see her little scuffle. Jackson and his new "friends" had seen it all as well.

"How outlandish!" said the girl on Jackson's lap. "What horrible behavior for a lady."

"Yes," said the other. "Obviously she comes from poor bloodlines."

"Get up," said Jackson dryly.

"What, honey?" replied the girl.

"I said get off of me!" ordered Jackson as he lifted the girl off of him and pushed the other aside.

"What's wrong, honey?" said the second girl.

"Go find another ladder to climb," answered Jackson as he walked away from the two and over to Martin's table.

"My I join you?" he asked.

Major Gates, as the senior officer, motioned for him to sit.

"Thank you, sir," he said as he sat across from Martin. "How are you doing, Captain Martin?" he asked.

"Good, Lieutenant, and you?"

"Better now," he smiled as he joined the conversation.

***

After several hours the group at the table began to break up. Martin, Jackson, and one of the captains remained.

"You're alright, newbie," said Jackson. "You've been able to hang with two Guard officers drink for drink…well almost."

"Th…That's right," slurred the drunk captain, "Y-You g-guys…"

The captain stopped in mid-sentence trying to form his next thought.

"Almost is right," smiled Martin. "I think you should call it a night, Captain Yang," she added as she reached over to steady the wobbling captain.

"I th…think…right," mumbled the captain as he slowly, clumsily rose from the table with the aid of Martin.

After attempting to right the empty bottle he had knocked over in the process of standing, the captain cupped the overturned bottle then raised his hands and motioned for the bottle to not move.

"G—good evennn," he took a deep breath, "nning," said the captain as he turned, stumbled, and began to stagger out of the bar.

"He's gonna be hurting tomorrow," laughed Jackson. "No way he's making officer call."

Martin let out a sigh and turned toward Jackson.

"Well, Lieutenant," she said, "I guess I will let you get to your evening, uh, activities."

As she rose, she felt Jackson put his hand on her forearm.

"Don't be ridiculous, Emily. Sit for a while," he asked. "I won't bite...well, I might," he added with a cocky look on his face.

Martin hesitated. She had done this before with Jackson, and always after a few drinks. She had had more than enough to drink. She was afraid of what might happen if she stayed, and at the same time hoped that it might.

After a few seconds Martin shook her head slightly, took another deep breath, and ran her hands through her hair.

"Fine," sighed Martin. "But don't expect this to be a repeat of that night on Port Royal. I won't make that mistake again, regardless of how much I've had to drink."

"Seriously, Em," said Jackson in a calming voice. "No tricks. Just have a seat."

Martin took a long look at Jackson. *I am going to regret this*, she thought as she sat down again.

"What do you want to talk about, Hugh?" she asked as she took another drink, looking for an excuse to make a bad decision. "How you were all cozied up with those trampy Recreation Girls? How you purposely took a demotion? Your *incessant* lack of military bearing?"

"I admit I am a jackass, Em," replied Jackson, "but I don't want to talk about that right now."

Martin had given up on the glass and was drinking straight from the bottle now.

"Maybe I do, Hugh," she snapped back. "Do you know what it's like to have to see you constantly…your philandering, your jokes and taunting?" She paused. "That's bullshit and you know it."

"Em, I didn—"

"I'm not done," Martin stopped Jackson mid-word.

She took another drink from the bottle.

"I took this assignment to get away from you. And you followed me!" Martin continued, raising her voice.

"Wait," interrupted Jackson. "I didn't follow you here, Emily. I came for the same reason you did. You know we would follow him wherever he goes, no questions."

Martin, rapidly feeling the effects of the alcohol, could see that Jackson was telling the truth—but she knew that already.

"You…" Martin paused, her emotions and intoxication getting the best of her. "You get in my head and mix things up for me. Nobody else does that and it makes me less of a soldier. I know you're not good for me, but I can't get away from you, and neither one of us will leave him. So the only thing I can do is to be a bitch and push you away from me."

"I don't make it easy, Em. I know," said Jackson, putting his hand out toward hers. "I know I'm nothing but trouble for you. Why do you think I do half the things I do? Regardless of what I feel, I know I will mess things up and I won't do that…again."

Martin took another drink and bowed her head slightly, trying to sort out her emotions. *Damn him*, she thought.

"I hate that you can do this to me," said Martin as she scooted closer to Jackson and put her right hand on his thigh.

Martin felt Jackson remove her hand from his thigh and place both of them on the table. "I'm sorry, Em," said Jackson softly. "I would love for tonight to end just like that night in Port Royal, but you're right, it's not fair. And I don't want to hurt you anymore…that's what I wanted to talk to you about."

Martin felt a lump in throat and a tear start to well up in her right eye. At least she had been able to count on Jackson for good sex that she usually regretted the next day, but apparently he was going to screw that up too.

"Hugh," pleaded Martin as she moved her hand over his forearm gently, "it's okay, I know what I'm…"

Martin again felt Jackson place her hand back with the other. As she looked at Jackson, she could tell he had no designs on her affection but his eyes gave away his feelings.

"Emily," said Jackson as Martin felt his hands cover hers. "I am putting in for a transfer after this mission."

"No," she replied. She hated how much Jackson could tear her up inside as soon as she left an opening.

"You're right, Em. I only get in your way and cause trouble for you. I just needed to tell you to be careful."

"What do you mean?" asked Martin. "You know my combat record…"

"I don't mean that," interjected Jackson. "Hell, you're the best soldier I have ever seen. I am talking about being close to Stone as his political star rises."

"You know I don't give a damn about politics," she replied, accepting that she would not spend the night with Jackson but confused about his concern.

"You might not. And we both know the Colonel only does what he feels is his social duty. Even if he hates it, he'll do what he must to restore his family name. He feels he's carrying the weight of his entire lineage on his back. But the Colonel's fiancé…"

"Oh, the Lady Astra," added Martin as she rolled her eyes.

"That's right, Emily," answered Jackson.

As he continued, Martin felt his grip on her hands tighten. "And don't underestimate her. She is as talented in politics as you are at warfare. She will not like how close you and the Colonel are and *will* try to find a reason to get rid of you. One way or another."

"The Colonel won't allow it," shot back Martin.

"It might not be up to him, Emily. With this war going public, you have to exist just as much in her environment as our own. Just be careful."

"I'll be fine," she said confidently.

"It's not just you, Emily."

Martin felt a rush of anticipation as Jackson leaned in close.

"Your father—"

"Don't," said Martin quickly, almost yelling. "You don't get to talk about—"

"Stop," said Jackson boldly.

Martin froze. She saw the seriousness on his face and conceded. No one else, except maybe Stone or her father long ago, could silence her in such a way.

"You know how these First Families are, Em. If she decided to get you out of the picture, the *Lady* Astra will not be above using your father as leverage. And you and I both know she has the power to do just about anything she wants to."

"I fucking hate them," replied Martin. The tear that had started to form was now running down her cheek. "They ruin people's lives and don't give it a second thought."

"It might be better for both of us to leave," blurted Jackson.

"But you said you needed to be away from me?" asked Martin, her emotions in turmoil.

Jackson's concern, her emotional roller-coaster ride, and a few more minutes of the whiskey flowing through her veins again stirred up the old feelings.

"Can you promise to not hurt me again?" she asked, almost pleading.

Martin saw that he loved her—that she knew. Staring into his eyes, she saw Jackson start to answer, then pause.

"Emily," he replied as Martin felt him release his hold her hands and sit back in his chair. "You know I'm no good. And I can't make you a promise like that, no matter how much I want to."

Martin felt sick. Of course he was right. She knew that for them, love was not enough. Their careers, Jackson's lack of control, and

Martin's need for structure made any chance of true happiness for them impossible. Struggling to regain control over her emotions and the alcohol in her system, she sat up straight in her chair.

"So we do what we always do," said Martin, struggling to be strong with the only man other than her father that she had allowed to see her weak. Martin looked for a response from Jackson. He looked as emotionally wrecked as Martin felt. After a long pause he spoke.

"Well, Emily. Keep an eye out for Astra because she'll have both of hers on you."

As Jackson spoke, Martin saw his attitude shift from one of caring and concern to the carefree Jackson everyone else knew.

"Thanks for the advice," she said, helping him end their painful conversation.

"No problem, Emily...uh...Captain," interrupted Jackson, a smile coming to his face as he rose from the table and placed his hand on her shoulder, giving her a gentle, caring squeeze.

Martin looked up toward Jackson who gave her a telling smile and then glanced over to the pool of Recreation Girls.

"It was nice talking, but I need to take advantage of this target-rich environment before it's too late," added Jackson as he removed his hand from her shoulder and gave her a hearty slap on the back.

"See ya at quarters...well, maybe," he added as he headed off toward the eager group of women.

Martin watched him walk over to the waiting stable of social climbers and easy women and wrap his arms around the waist of the two blondes.

"Shit," said Martin as she turned back to her bottle. "That was a close one," she added as she took a long drink.

Chapter 8

The peaceful quiet of space was interrupted by the explosion of metallic noise as massive spaceships decelerated following their jump to Juliet 3. As the fleet reached orbital speed, the bridge of the *Lucius Pantelus Varuk* came alive with activity.

"Jump location verified accurate," reported the navigator.

"Very well," acknowledged the ship's captain, with Admiral Nevarus Sequentius standing at his side.

"All weapons systems and sensors operational," reported the Combat Center Watch Officer.

"Very well."

“Combat air patrol package delta launch confirmed,” announced the Air Combat Coordinator. “Twenty-five condor fighters off-ship and comms checks verified.”

“Captain, sensors have detected the presence of both increased neutrino levels and concentrated metals,” reported the Combat Center Watch Officer.

“How old?” demanded the captain as he hurried over to the data screen.

“How many concentrations?” he continued as he bit his lower lip and clenched his jaw.

“Is there a problem, Admiral?” asked the nearby Cataline, not understanding the reason for concern.

“Possibly,” replied a frustrated Sequentius. “The neutrino levels could have been residual radiation from reactors onboard a large spacecraft and the concentrated metals could be byproducts of the magnetic concentration process from their jumps.”

“Five concentration sites, sir. Sensors have analyzed data and determined them to be too small to support any jump activity within the last two weeks. According to the computer there’s a 75 percent probability the increased magnetic signature is due to a recent asteroid,” reported the Watch Officer.

“What about the neutrino levels?”

“Barely above background levels, sir. Tracking sensors report no spacecraft other than ours in this sector.”

“Very well, Ensign,” replied the captain. “Inform engineering to maintain auxiliary reactors online just in case someone pops up.

Admiral, the *Lucius* battle group is prepared to support assault operations."

"Very well, Captain. The *Arilius* has reported ready status as well."

With that, Admiral Sequentius turned to General Tacitus.

"You may begin your assault, General."

***

Inside the Raven troop carrier, Stone looked across the hangar to Martin. He had known her since she was a teenage cadet training with his platoon for her combat certification, and she had always fascinated him.

"I am amazed how excited you look before a mission," confessed Stone.

"Are you kidding, it's better than sex...and much more satisfying," she said sarcastically as she glanced toward Jackson, who was setting a few seats down the line.

Not knowing what she had said, Jackson smiled and gave a thumbs-up.

Stone could only laugh.

As Stone watched, Martin started fiddling with her hair, which hung down to her shoulders. After a few seconds of restless twisting and twirling she bunched her hair into the familiar ponytail he had grown accustomed to seeing her wear in the field.

As she finished tying off her hair she glanced at Stone, her face beaming like a child opening a birthday present. Stone knew her excitement was not a manifestation of apprehension or fear. Captain

Emily Martin was one of the few people who served not only out of a sense of duty; she truly loved what she did.

"Ready to get back into the field, sir?" she asked while loading an extended clip into her rifle and verifying her weapons status menu. "I've had enough R & R to last the rest of my life."

"Probably not as ready as you, Captain," he smiled back.

Their discussion was cut short by the transport's intercom.

Raven squadron 3, this is Air Combat Control, execute Lima Seven. Launch all aircraft.

"Back in the saddle," she smiled as she rubbed her hands together.

With the order the transport lifted off from the hangar bay and lunged out the bay doors into space. As the transports rendezvoused and began their descent to the planet, Martin spoke again.

"This is the smoothest ride I have ever had in a combat transport," she said.

"You've got to be kidding me," said a nearby young lieutenant fighting to keep his breakfast down.

"We're used to a very different insertion technique," replied Stone as he placed his hand on the young man's should to steady him.

"Wha...What do you mea...mean?" asked the pale lieutenant.

Martin was more than happy to answer.

"The dead stick or silent insertion," she shouted over the humming of the shuttle propulsion system. "To limit electronic emissions for clandestine missions, the transports initiate a short impulse burst for the correct trajectory. After that, you just sorta fall through the atmosphere like a meteorite."

Martin made zooming grandiose hand gestures as she continued to educate, and taunt, the young lieutenant.

"All sensors and navigation equipment are secured until a few hundred meters from the ground when the transports come alive, engage reverse thrusters, and pull massive gravitational forces coming to a stop a meter or two from the ground."

Martin made a violent jerking motion to demonstrate the g-force of such an insertion.

It was more than the lieutenant could take. As he lost his breakfast all over his shoes, Martin looked toward Stone and smiled.

Stone knew there was nothing subtle about this mission. They were coming in sensors at full power and guns blazing. There would be no question about their arrival.

Looking out the viewing window during the slower-than-usual descent, Stone was amazed by the spectacle unfolding as he watched. He could see dozens of transports in their pre-assigned assault routes heading toward the planet. As he looked further back he could see the massive battle cruisers and orbital destroyers drifting along, protected by swarms of condor fighters.

Stand by for entering the atmosphere.

Just as he turned away from the viewing window he saw the hawk assault craft and condor fighters speeding past the transports to provide support for the incoming transports. If only there were more.

Stone feared the stripping of his assault craft would severely hamper his efforts and endanger his men.

"STAND BY FOR INSERTION" was passed through the transport as the blackness of space transformed into the blue skies of Juliet 3. The rumble of the transport told Stone they were making the final banking turn before disembarking. A loud buzzing horn actuated as the compartment light shifted from white to red and the intercom spoke again.

"TEN SECONDS. 9, 8, 7…"

"I love this part," shouted Martin over the roar of the thrusters as she gripped her rifle.

Stone looked down toward Martin's feet; her toes were tapping up and down with anticipation.

"3, 2, 1…"

The transport impacted the ground, safety harnesses released, and the doors instantly dropped. The sound of thruster engaging was deafening and the flash of sunlight from Juliet 3's two suns was bright as Stone exited the transport. Rushing out of the open doors, the first thing he saw as the glare from the sunlight faded was Martin racing toward a small embankment running along an irrigation ditch. He quickly followed.

Leaping over the embankment and taking up a position next to Martin, Stone began to survey the area. In front of him was an open field of waist-high amber-colored wheat. The wind generated from the transports' engines caused rippling waves to pass over the large field, reminding Stone of waves on a turbulent sea. Beyond the field a slight rocky rise gave way to dense forest. Just north of Stone's position was a modest farm with a storage building and a few small buildings. Behind the farm a gentle slope led to a wooded knoll that jutted out from the flat landscape around it. To the east lay broken fields in various levels of harvest. They extended to the horizon. South of his position was more broken and rocky ground leading to two large hills, both densely wooded.

But nothing else. No defensive positions, no enemy troops, not even civilian farmers.

"Where are they at?" asked Martin as she peered through her optical magnifier toward the opposite side of the wheat field. "We should have come under fire before we even hit the deck."

"I don't know. Let's get a status from Vatarus and Gates."

Martin was right. Stone had expected to take casualties before the first transport hit the deck.

"Bravo one, Bravo two, this is Romeo Charlie, report status," ordered Martin over the comms channel.

"Romeo Charlie, this is Bravo One, status to follow: All Ravens on deck, no casualties, no hostile contacts, over."

"Romeo Charlie, this is Bravo Two, status to follow: All Ravens on deck, no casualties, no hostile contacts. It's like we landed in a cemetery, over."

Things were going very well, almost too well. Stone grew even more unsettled by the cemetery comment Senior Major Bruni had added to his report. Either the enemy had left the area, which meant they would cause problems for the main force or they were waiting for something. Either outcome was bad.

"All right, Captain," ordered Stone as he continued to scan the landscape. "Once they have their perimeters set up, have Vatarus, Gates, Bruni, and Jackson meet us in that farmhouse to our right."

"Aye, sir," answered Martin, quickly turning her attention to barking orders to the staff contingent under her command.

***

The war counsel assembled in a rundown farmhouse in the center of the 25th defenses. Senior Major Bruni was sitting at a small, creaky wooden table in the center of the room reviewing logistics data cards. Gates squatted by the entrance drawing circles on the dusty floor with his knife. Jackson appeared dead to the world, asleep in a hand-woven chair by a heating duct. Vatarus and Martin stood on the porch in front of the house arguing the uniform regulations regarding Martin's now infamous ponytail.

"Good evening, sir. Shall we get started," she said eagerly as Stone approached, happy to end the annoying argument with Vatarus.

"Attention on deck!" shouted Martin as she entered the small room in front of Stone.

As he entered the room, Stone saw Martin give a quick kick to Jackson's chair to wake him. The group gathered around the table as Bruni finished preparing the digital map. When he was ready, he nodded to Stone.

"Well, gentlemen, what's our status?" asked Stone.

"Sir, we have had no contact with Nero's men," replied Vatarus.

"The few farmers we have questioned have given us nothing," added Bruni.

"On one hand," said Gates, "we should be glad our landing wasn't opposed. On the other it's a little odd for Nero to have let an entire regiment land without putting up a fight."

Gates was right. The whole situation was uncomfortable to Stone. He was reminded of the calm on the central plains of Alpha Humana as the thunderclouds quietly but inevitably rolled over the landscape.

"What is our current position?" asked Stone.

Barilus manipulated the controls on the digital map and a hologram of the terrain illuminated above the table. He began to speak.

"Major Gates has taken up positions along this ridge just north of here. 2nd Battalion links up with the 1st near this wheat field and their line extends into the rocky terrain south of here and up those two small wooded hills over there."

Turning from the hologram, Bruni pointed out the window to show the two rocky outcroppings rising from the fields outside.

"Our positions have good logistics and communications lines as well," added Gates.

"When do you expect to move, sir?" asked Vatarus.

"Not yet, Major," replied Stone as he turned toward Jackson. "Lieutenant, I want you to take your men and set up sensors and sonic mines 360 degrees around our lines. You can start immediately"

"Yes, sir," said Jackson as he hurried out of the room to carry out his mission.

"I want our lines to be solid before we begin any forays toward the city. I agree with Gates; let's make sure if Nero has any surprises we will have a few of our own for him."

"Shall I inform General Tacitus that we will remain within our current lines?" asked Bruni.

"Contact the general and tell him we have conducted an unopposed landing and will begin operations in the area. If our landing wasn't obvious enough to get Nero's attention then us stumbling around the countryside isn't going to make much of a difference."

Stone looked across the table at his senior commanders. He could see the apprehension on their faces. "Let's get back to the men and keep them alert," he ordered.

***

In the hills west of Stone's lines, a Terillian captain stepped into the bunker entrance where Nero was talking with a Major General Nathan Windsong, commander of 2nd Division,

Terillian Light Infantry. Both men were leaning over a hologram terrain, which highlighted the area where Stone's men had landed. The area around Stone's position was dotted with markers indicating Terillian units.

"The Hanmani forces have set up a small perimeter half a day from the city of Lady Lunari. It looks to be of about regiment strength," reported the captain.

"Very well, Captain," replied the general as he looked up from the hologram. "Inform General Lighthorse in sector five to commence operations against the main force. I will be en route with additional forces within the hour. General Nero, I will leave a brigade under General Fallingrock to augment your brigade."

"Yes, General," replied Nero, still getting used to his new Terillian rank. "What are your directions for the Xen regiment here?"

"Destroy them," he replied.

***

Colonel Stone paced back and forth, one hand on his sidearm holster and the other resting on his sword. The heat radiating off the ground added a murky haze to the sea of wheat gently waving in the warm breeze. He knew the enemy was out there somewhere.

"Sir?" asked an unusually apprehensive Martin.

"Tell him again," said an exasperated Stone. "I recommend withdrawing from our current location to support the main force."

"Yes, sir," Martin replied and walked over to the communications station to contact *Lucius* and Cataline's staff.

As Martin turned away another captain stepped beside Stone, who was still inspecting the terrain for signs of enemy movement.

"What do you think, sir?" asked the captain.

"We have been on the ground most of the day and made no contact. Either there are no enemy forces nearby or if they are nearby, they are waiting for us to move out to spring a trap, or they aren't too worried about our isolated regiment. If the latter is the case, the main force would need all of the support they could get."

"Colonel!" shouted Martin as she ran toward Stone.

"What is it, Captain?"

A look of frustration came over her face. "Command orders you to press on toward the city. They have met more resistance than expected, including Terillian regulars, and they are hoping our position will draw some forces away from them."

"Regulars?" said Stone. *Cataline and those idiots at High Command have dropped us into a trap*, thought Stone.

Stone paused for a moment of contemplation. Martin and the small group of officers around him waited in anticipation of his next order.

Stone stepped toward Martin. Putting his hand on her shoulder, he looked into her eyes with determination. "Captain, order Major Gates to select a company to respond to breaks in the lines when they occur and have Major Vatarus ensure he has good secondary and tertiary defensive positions; those hills will be our best location to hold them off. They will be coming soon."

"Sir, how do you know?" asked the young captain.

Captain Martin interrupted again. "Sir, our sensors are detecting motion from the west, east, and south. Lieutenant Jackson is reporting engagement with a Terillian Scout Ranger squad to the South as well."

"Get those hawks in the air, Captain," Stone ordered Martin. "And contact the *Lucius* and request condor air cover."

In the distance, gunfire could be heard-probably Jackson's recon patrols. Stone looked across the hazy fields to the west and the sloping hills beyond. They would be coming soon.

"Incoming Terillian Alphas from the west and south!" shouted Martin, receiving a report from the comms center through her repeater.

Gunfire could now be heard from the north, growing in volume. Stone's worst fears were materializing before him. Isolated and low on air support, enemy troops were coming out of the woodwork.

"Major Gates reports contact with irregulars," reported Martin.

Scanning the horizon, Stone soon saw the small, fast-moving dots just above the treetops on the sloping hill. He looked back over his shoulder as his woeful number of hawks lifted off and flew overhead to engage the enemy, their thrusters temporarily drowning out the gunfire in the distance. The heat and wind from the thrusters washed over Stone's body and blew up tiny tornadoes of dust. As the dust subsided, Stone watched the small force of hawks streak across the field in front of him on a collision course with the enemy aircraft.

The three anti-aircraft stations he was allotted by Cataline began to open fire as Terillian attack ships raced toward his position. There were a lot of them…a lot. As they grew closer, he saw the flashes from their tungsten Gatling guns. The ground in front of him immediately erupted from their exploding shells. Fragments of dirt and metal pelted Stone's body as he dove to the ground. The sound of the enemy aircraft was deafening as they passed over his position. Rising to one knee, Stone shouted to Martin through the cloud of dust that still covered the area.

"Martin, I need those condors."

"Roger, sir," came a reply as pieces of rubble and earth still fell to the ground around her.

Stone rose and surveyed the damage from the strafing run. The young captain, or what was left of him, lay in a pile of wrecked flesh to his left. Stone took a deep breath…there would be more.

"At least it was quick," said Martin as she looked at the remains of the captain and shook her head.

Leaning in toward Stone so he could hear her over the noise of the battlefield, Martin shouted, "*Lucius* reports they have released 3 condors for cover!"

"Three!" yelled Stone over the sounds of anti-aircraft gunfire and the roar of attack craft, both friend and foe, overhead.

"Admiral Sequentius wants to hold most of his condors near the fleet. He is now concerned that the magnetic concentrations were actually from Terillian Battleships. He wants to keep his condors close in case fighters from the planet engage the fleet."

Stone felt his heart drop.

"There were magnetic concentrations when we arrived and they still chose to continue with the mission?" he asked, shocked that ground commanders had not been informed. "There were probably more than enough Terillians on Juliet 3 to not only destroy our regiment but possibly the whole force?"

"Colonel, over there!" shouted Martin.

Stone looked toward the south and Major Vatarus's battalion. The rocky terrain below his lines came alive with movement. Like swarming insects, hundreds of Terillians poured over the broken, rocky ground. These pests had deadly stingers, however. The attack was about to begin in earnest.

Stone turned back to Martin. "We need to get fire on that position now!" as shouted while pointing toward the Terillian soldiers rushing toward them.

The thud of artillery fire on the two small hills was heard instantly as his order was carried out. In seconds the swarming mass of enemy troops was dotted with bright flashes as the artillery rounds exploded amongst them. The rapid percussion of large caliber automatic weapons from the five hover tanks under Stone's command soon joined the chorus. Red tracers made their way toward the Terillians. Like angry hornets, they tore through anything in their path.

Despite the deadly fire, the Terillians kept coming. Before long, Stone could clearly make out the tracers cutting swatches from the sea of humanity about to crash into his position.

Finally, at about eight hundred meters, they were in range of small arms.

Stone looked toward Martin and nodded.

"Light 'em up!" she ordered.

The rattle of hundreds of automatic rifles created a constant percussion of noise against the thuds and explosions of larger weapons. The concentration of fire created what looked like a solid wall of death as metal tore into the advancing enemy.

Hundreds fell.

To Stone's surprise, a Terillian emerged from the rippling web of tracers, then another, and another. Unbelievably, some had survived the onslaught and kept coming. Soon they crossed Stone's lines.

Fortunately, the devastating fire had taken a toll on the enemy's numbers and the few that reached his lines were soon beat back and started to retreat back across the fields littered with their dead and injured.

A cheer went up across Stone's lines as the Terillians retreated. An excited soldier turned toward Stone.

"We've defeated them, sir!" he shouted.

Stone looked across the field, the battle was only a few minutes old and hundreds lay dead in front of him.

"No, Corporal," replied Stone. "That was the first wave, they were just letting us know they were out there. There will be more. Look back toward the ridge," continued Stone as he pointed back across the field where a dozens of Terillian hover tanks were massing.

"Damn," replied the young soldier as he gripped his rifle, noticeably shaken.

Placing his hand on the man's shoulder, Stone spoke.

"The day is young, Corporal. Remember you fight for our people...they will need our best today."

***

Throughout the afternoon wave after wave crashed against Stone's positions. Moving all along his line was Stone, reinforcing weakened areas, strengthening morale, and supporting shaken officers. Standing at the crest of the tallest hill in his line as the sun began to set, he received the latest update from Martin.

"Major Gates has been killed by a Terillian attack craft while trying to rally Lieutenant Savoy's platoon. Major Bruni has taken direct command of Gates's battalion but he is slowly giving up ground under repeated attacks. We're making the Ters pay for each meter, sir, but were slowly being forced back in all areas."

"What's the status of our air support?" asked Stone.

"All of our hawks are out of commission and the three condors the *Lucius* sent have been chased out of the sky by a squadron of Foxtrots."

"Do you have any good news, Captain?"

"Well," replied Martin, "our northern lines have been forced into a thin enclave a few hundred meters from the base of the two hills held by Major Vatarus so at least you won't have to run so far between units." Martin gave a quick smile to Stone; the situation was bad, but they had both been in bad situations before.

"Always the optimist," he replied. "Let's check in with Vatarus."

As the two ran toward the crest of the largest hill, they passed wrecked hover tanks, discarded and damaged weapons, and the dead and wounded. Quickly making their way to the top of the hill, they soon saw Vatarus, who was directing a nearby heavy gun position.

"How are you holding up, Major?" asked Stone.

"Could be—" Vatarus winced as a medic repositioned his blood-soaked left arm to apply a dressing. "Could be better. We have held off three major assaults. The last was hand to hand but we held those bastards off."

"What is your status, Major?" inquired Martin.

"We're holding our current positions," he replied while the medic applied coagulant gels to his arm. "We have 240 killed or severely wounded, thirty-five missing or unaccounted for with 225 still under arms. Our ammunition is at 25 percent."

"Bruni is a little worse off," added Martin. "He has about two hundred men and is about the same for ammo."

"It looks like we're facing at least a brigade to the south, sir," grunted Vatarus as the medic injected a nerve suppressor into his mangled arm. "I think they will make their final push soon."

Stone looked over the field as the last rays of sunlight passed over the hills from where the Terillian hordes had been launching their relentless attacks. The pastures and farmland in front of his lines were now charred and smoking with hundreds, maybe thousands of Terillian dead littering the desolate wasteland. As he pondered the destruction, Martin's voice brought Stone back.

"If they attack in force in more than one position we will be overrun," said Martin.

Stone struggled to decide his next move. The weight of command weighed heavily on him.

"What's your plan, sir?" asked Vatarus.

"Surrender is not an option," interjected Stone. "No Xen unit has ever surrendered in recorded history."

"We can't retreat either," added Vatarus. "We have no control of the airspace and if we make a run for it we would be swept from the field by Ter Alpha aircraft and hover tanks."

Martin raised her hand to inform Stone and Vatarus she was receiving a report from Bruni.

"Sir, Bruni reports troops massing near his positions."

Suddenly two Terillian attack craft soared over their position, their Gatling guns spewing death as they passed.

The group dove for cover in their battlement as the earth exploded all around them in a swirling mass of dirt, metal, and flesh.

As the dust settled from the strafing run, Stone gathered himself and rose from the ground looking for the others.

"Are you all right, sir?" asked Martin, sitting up on her knees to dust of the debris from her uniform.

"I'm fine. Where's Vatarus?"

As he asked the question he turned to his left and saw Vatarus, the medic, and the gun crew still lying on the ground. Martin had seen them first and was already rushing in their direction. Reaching the gun emplacement, Martin looked at the medic and the gun crew. The gun crew was dead and the medic was frantically searching his bag for meds for what remained of his left leg.

Vatarus lay face down in the wreckage. Kneeling next to him, Martin rolled him over and with a sigh gently returned him to his previous position.

“He’s dead,” said Martin as Stone reached them.

“Damn it!” he exclaimed. “That’s it, Captain, We’ve bled enough here. Get me the comm link. We need to get off this rock.”

Martin paused momentarily. She had never seen her mentor accept defeat. She slowly handed the comm link to Stone.

“Lima Charlie, this is Romeo Charlie, over.”

Onboard *Lucius*, Cataline, Admiral Sequentius, and Colonel Neo stood behind the senior watch officer in Combat Control. *Lima Charlie this is Romeo Charlie over* came through the comm lines.

“This is Lima Charlie,” replied the watch officer.

“Lima Charlie, this is Romeo Charlie. Have engaged enemy in force. Estimated Tango strength two or three brigades. Romeo Charlie effective strength five zero percent, no hawks available. Believe large assault is underway. We’re completely defensive and losing ground. Request immediate evac with air cover or support from reserve regiment, over.”

Admiral Sequentius looked toward Cataline. Once the infantry was off his ship, the admiral had no tactical command of army elements. He could not help Stone.

“Sir, shall I prepare my regiment?” asked Neo.

“No, Colonel, the fight is not going well with the main force. If things do not get better, then we will need your men to support withdraw of the main force.”

“Sir, it sounds as though they are in quite a bit of trouble down there,” replied Neo, unsure of himself but compelled to speak. “My regiment can help them establish a safe perimeter and my transports can start evacuations."

"The mission of the 25th was to divert enemy troops from the main force, Colonel," retorted Cataline. "If he is engaging two brigades, then those are two brigades the main force does not have to deal with. In times such as this we must look toward the mission first, Colonel."

"Lieutenant," said Cataline to the watch officer, "inform Romeo Charlie that transports and reserve units are to remain in reserve to support operations of the main force."

"Remain in reserve!" shouted Stone into the comms link when he received the report. "Lima Charlie, place ground force Charlie Oscar on comms link; I know he is there."

"Charlie Oscar," Cataline said dryly.

"Charlie Oscar, this is Colonel Stone commanding what is left of the 25th Air Assault Regiment. We have no air cover, we are running out of ammunition, and have not been resupplied. If my unit is not provided close air support and reserves or immediately withdrawn, we will be destroyed. Is that clear, Charlie Oscar?"

"Your situation is understood, Romeo Charlie. Your orders have not changed. Is that clear, over?"

"I understand you needlessly killed a thousand of your own men, General. We will stand our ground and die, as is our duty, while you cower under the protection of Sequentius's fleet."

"Romeo Charlie, you are breaking protocol and showing disrespect for your commanding officer, over."

The argument was interrupted by Martin grabbing Stone's arm. "Sir, Ters are advancing along our entire front. Major Bruni..." Martin paused.

"Yes, Captain?" asked Stone.

"Major Bruni has been killed."

"Damn it! Emily, take command of the right wing. I will stay here. Make them pay for every centimeter!"

"Yes, sir," replied Martin. She started to turn away but paused. "Sir."

"Yes."

"It has been my greatest honor to serve with you. I will pass into oblivion with the knowledge that I fought and died with one of the bravest men who ever lived."

She paused for a minute and then wrapped her arms around him in a strong embrace. As Martin held him he was sure that if he had survived to have a daughter that was how it would have felt. She quickly regained her composure, saluted, and bounded down the slope in the direction of the right wing, her pony tail bouncing as she ran.

Stone returned his attention to the comms link and Cataline.

"Protocol be damned!" he shouted into the comms link. "As for my disrespect, come down to the surface and I will show you just how much I disrespect you, coward!"

"Romeo Charlie, this communication is ended, you will not be reinforced. You are directed to do your duty."

"Very well! Lima Charlie, this is Romeo Charlie. Request planetary bombardment from all available warships. Target location marked 300 meters in all directions of this communication."

Sequentius quickly stepped forward, almost knocking Cataline over. Stone had finally requested something within his authority.

"Colonel, this is Admiral Sequentius. The damage zone from our main batteries are within your danger close zone. I cannot assure you we will not inflict damage on your position."

"Yes, sir," replied Stone, "I acknowledge proximity. I request danger close support from main batteries."

"Understood, Colonel. I will detach *Intrepid* to provide fire support until we no longer have communications with your unit. Get your heads down, Colonel. You honor your family with your bravery."

"Thank you, Admiral," replied Stone.

Stone opened the comms link so all of his officers could hear.

"All company commanders, this is Romeo Charlie. Standby for danger close fire support from orbital destroyer main batteries. Get your heads down."

***

Onboard *Lucius*, Cataline was fuming.

"Admiral, I am unsure if now is the most prudent time to detach one of our orbital destroyers." said Cataline, questioning the admiral's tactical decision.

"General," replied Sequentius sharply, "I have not interfered with your conduct on the planet. Please do not question my decisions with the fleet. If I can at least give Colonel Lucius a fighting chance, I will do so."

Cataline stared coldly at Sequentius. Knowing he had no authority to counter the admiral, he conceded. "Very well, Admiral," he sneered.

After a slight pause, Cataline turned to Sequentius.

"It seems as though we may have bitten off a bit too much on Juliet 3. I wish to commence withdrawal of the main force and request that your fleet, minus the *Intrepid* of course, support my withdrawal. That is *my* prerogative as ground commander."

"That's it then, General," replied the frustrated admiral. "Captain, pass the word to our transports and fighter cover—commence extraction operations."

***

Back on Juliet 3, Stone watched as Terillian infantry again swarmed over the battlefield. *Let's hope the Intrepid is enough*, Stone thought as he looked skyward.

Finally he saw them. The tell-tale fluorescent blue flashes dotted the night sky.

The *Intrepid* had opened fire.

From the flashes he saw the lines of bright blue light—actually superheated metals turned into plasma in the main battery chambers—streaking toward the ground. The brilliant streaks of light traced their path through the night sky.

Rapidly growing closer, the metallic screeching of the molten metal as it slowed to sub-sonic speeds in the atmosphere overshadowed the other sounds of battle. Stone's ears ached against the pervasive roar of metallic death. As the massive spheres of molten metal hit their targets, the front of his lines burst into a brilliant flash of red and white, killing hundreds with each blast.

The fire was close. Although hundreds of yards away, Stone could feel the searing heat of the explosions against his face as the field in front of him was turned into a burning caldron of destruction.

"The *Intrepid* is doing a number on them," said Martin.

Stone was in agreement. He had read the manuals on the power of a destroyer's main batteries but had never seen it in person.

Stone replied, "This might actually—"

The screeching of the next volley from the *Intrepid* drowned out the rest of the sentence.

The roar was louder than the last volley and continued to grow.

Something isn't right, Stone thought, as he looked into the night sky. The incoming volley was getting closer, too close.

"Take cover!" shouted Stone, but no one could hear him over the roar.

He quickly grabbed Martin and a nearby corporal and threw then to the ground.

When the volley impacted, the landscape was filled with a brilliant white light and a solid high-pitched tone pierced Stone's ears. Simultaneously, a wave of heat radiated over Stone's position.

Stone groaned against the explosion of noise and the almost-unbearable heat surrounding him.

Eventually the heat and roaring dissipated, leaving only the ringing in Stone's ears. As he rose to his feet, Stone felt Martin grab his arm and turn him toward her.

"Sir," huffed Martin, still visibly shaken by the explosion, "a round impacted within 100 meters of Bravo Company!"

"Son of a bitch," replied Stone. "Let's get over there."

Stone, Martin, and a medical crew raced toward the location of Bravo Company. In a few minutes they reached Bravo Company's position.

The entire party stopped simultaneously.

"Shit…" said Martin.

Smoke billowed from where 1st platoon had been, 2nd platoon's position was still a lake of fire, and wounded were streaming from 3rd platoon's location.

"Help those wounded," directed Stone as he motioned for the medical team to aid the survivors.

"This is bad," said Martin. "Those idiot gunnery officers overshot their grid. I'm calling them now."

Stone overheard Martin contacting the *Intrepid.*

India Foxtrot, this is Romeo Charlie. Recalculate firing grid. You're frying our asses down here. Grid 235-59 held friendlies. Repeat, recalculate firing grid. Resending our position coordinates.

Romeo Charlie, this is India Foxtrot, authenticate…

Martin interrupted the comm. *Shift your damn fire, Intrepid, you are hitting friendlies…*

As Martin worked to correct the *Intrepid's* fire, Stone saw a sergeant stumble by.

"Sergeant," called out Stone. "Are you all right?"

The sergeant stopped to report. When the sergeant turned toward his commander, Stone could see his face was severely burned and his left arm—broken and charred—hanging limply at his side.

"Sir," replied the sergeant with a vacant stare, "I don't know what happened."

"That's all right Sergeant," replied Stone, steadying the wounded man to keep him from collapsing. "Who is commanding Bravo Company now?"

"I-I think I am, sir," replied the dazed sergeant.

As he finished the report, the sergeant collapsed into Stone's arms, dead.

***

Throughout the night, the *Intrepid* remained on station raining death down upon the Terillians from orbit, with Martin keeping them on target. By the morning, Stone had 200 men left fit for duty. His lines had collapsed their defensive position on the ridge of the tallest hill. As the light from the suns began to break over the horizon, Jackson approached Stone to make a report.

"I think we might have lasted them out," said Lieutenant Jackson as he applied meds to his injured leg. "The main batteries sure did a number on those Ters."

Bodies dotted the landscape in every direction. The fields that had once brought subsistence to Nero's private empire now gave forth a harvest of death. Stone could not even estimate the dead. Among the bodies were wrecked hover tanks, heavy weapons, and burning hulks of aircraft. Smoke billowed from dozens of burning tanks and fires started by the *Intrepid's* bombardment. The burning sensation of smoke and the acrid smell of molten metal that stung Stone's nostrils were punctuated by the putrid stench of charred flesh.

"We need to contact command and find out the status of the main withdraw. Maybe they could pick us up if it isn't too much trouble," added Martin, still unscathed as usual.

"Very well," replied Stone, coughing against the smoke drifting over the field.

***

Meanwhile, onboard *Lucius,* Cataline and Sequentius were discussing the operation.

"The last transport is off the ground," said Sequentius. "Let's get the fleet above Colonel Stone and pick up any survivors."

"Very well, Admiral. It may have cost me a regiment but we maintained the division intact and inflicted a lot of casualties on the Terillians."

"That we did, General," replied Sequentius dryly. "Perhaps your body count will make up for the mission not going as well as planned. Once we pick up Stone's remnants, I recommend we commence bombardment of the planet and wait for Blue Fleet to arrive with the rest of the Corps to recommence operations on the planet."

"I concur, Admiral. We may have not established a foothold on the planet, but we just may have taken the bite out of their ground forces. Our follow-on landing with the entire corps should go smoothly."

"I hope so, General," said Sequentius. "Captain, inform Colonel Lucius we are in route for extraction."

***

"Sounds like they are coming to get us," reported Martin. "They're in orbit and waiting for reinforcements to try it again."

Stone did not care about the follow-up operations. His thoughts were filled with the decimation of his regiment and his hatred for Cataline.

"I will not serve under General Tacitus," said Stone matter-of-factly to Martin.

"Sir?" she asked. It was out of character for him to speak ill of a superior, even General Tacitus, in front of junior officers but the night had taken its toll on his formality. Stone could tell Martin had not expected his comment and saw that she wasn't sure how to respond.

"He has cost so many lives," continued Stone. "Over 800 men died bravely when we should have waited for reinforcements in the first place. You have served well, Emily, and I will mention that in my report. After this, it might be smart to distance yourself from me. I have openly disrespected a superior officer from a First Family and will not rescind my comments. He will not face me in single combat so he will see that I am relegated to some menial task far from a combat command."

"All of that political crap means nothing, sir," answered Martin. "We are warriors and we play the hand we're dealt. You are my commander and I will follow you…even that means handing out towels at the Humani gymnasium."

"I know you would, Emily. You would hate it, but you would do it."

"You're right," interrupted Martin with a small smile. "I would hate it."

"Emily, I appreciate the—"

"What are those flashes?" interrupted Jackson as he pointed toward the sky.

Stone looked upward into the early morning sky. In the red hue, bright flashes could be seen. It was not the main batteries of an orbital destroyer this time. It was something different…something was not right.

***

"*Lucius*, this is *Intrepid*," broke through the communications link onboard *Lucius*.

"*Lucius,* this is *Intrepid*, several large magnetic concentrations marked. Corresponding increased neutrino levels in…twenty-five locations."

"Is it our fleet?" asked Cataline to Admiral Sequentius.

“There’s no way,” responded Sequentius. “They have to be Terillian ships…Captain, inform Admiral Claudius on the *Arilius*, place all ships at battle stations. Scramble all condor fighters.”

Another officer in the Combat Center interrupted. “Admiral, *Intrepid* reports verification of large Terillian fleet including eight battleships and four carriers. *Intrepid* is currently engaged with several Foxtrot squadrons and two battleships.”

“Son of a bitch!” exclaimed the admiral as he turned toward Cataline. “That has to be a grand fleet. They could be carrying close to 15,000 ground troops.”

“Even with the rest of the corps we could be outnumbered,” replied a surprised Cataline.

“I am not worried about the planet. I only have six ships of the line against at least ten already. We need to prepare to jump and get out of here.”

“What do we do with Colonel Lucius?” asked Cataline, knowing what the answer would be.

“We do not have time to extract his survivors,” replied the admiral as he looked up from a status screen. The green hue of the screen illuminated a calm but determined look.

“He was a brave warrior and shall be honored in the Forum as a hero,” replied Cataline, relieved that Stone would not be around to challenge his handling of the operation or his bravery.

“I am sure you will sing his praises,” replied Sequentius sarcastically.

A watch officer interrupted again.

"Admiral, *Intrepid* had sustained several hits. Captain Ventu reports that he is down to half power and does not have jump capability."

"Admiral!" shouted the now excited watch officer. "Admiral!"

"Report!" ordered Sequentius, himself fighting to maintain his composure.

"Admiral, fifteen Terillian capital ships reported," reported the watch officer.

"I guess we both lose units to this damnable planet, General," commented Sequentius as he turned toward the ship's captain. "Pass jump coordinates to all ships. Recall all condors that can make it in time. Standby to execute jump in two minutes."

***

General Nero, standing in the farmhouse where Stone had held his war conference the day before, turned toward General Fallingrock.

"They are putting up one hell of fight, General Nero," said Fallingrock. "They are making us pay dearly for every inch of ground we gain."

"The fleet has returned," interrupted a Terillian communications officer.

"They will have additional forces and the Xen will either have to retreat or be destroyed," stated Fallingrock.

"We should call in for an orbital bombardment to finish off their last unit," recommended a staff officer standing next to Fallingrock.

"No, General," replied Nero. "They have fought bravely and taken the lives of thousands of my men."

Nero's Humani sense of honor was still intact, even if he was a traitor.

He continued. "We shall take them by assault and offer them as honorable a death as possible. Send one of your reserve regiments supported by a Scout Ranger company."

"But we could limit our own casualties…"

"No, General," interrupted Nero. "We…I owe them the honor of facing their end standing and facing their foe, not vaporized by plasma. I will send my own men forward, just allow me the use of the Scout Rangers."

"So be it," replied the frustrated Fallingrock.

***

On the hilltop, the remnants of Stone's command were making final preparations for withdrawal.

"What is taking them so long?" asked Jackson, rewrapping his wound. "We should have seen some transports by now."

Stone was still mesmerized by the flashes in the sky. She turned toward Martin.

"Martin, contact *Lucius* and find out what's going on."

"Sir, the Terillians are coming again," shouted Jackson, quickly forgetting about his wound, readying his rifle.

Stone quickly grabbed his weapon and looked back toward Martin to get her report. Unless the evacuation forces arrived soon, they would have to make another stand.

As he looked in Martin's direction, he saw her drop the comms link and slowly draw her sword.

"What did they say, Captain?"

No answer.

"Captain...Emily?"

"They are gone," she said dryly, staring past Stone at the oncoming wave of enemy soldiers. "A large Terillian fleet has appeared. *Intrepid* is disabled and will soon be lost. The rest of the fleet has already jumped. They have left us here alone."

Stone suddenly realized the first flashes he saw were the massive bursts of light caused by electron interactions as the magnetic fields were formed by the enemy ships coming out of their jumps. The flashes that he saw now were those of the *Intrepid* in her death throes.

"Very well." Stone paused for a second of contemplation. "This is it then," he said as he looked over the remnants of his regiment.

"Yes, sir," replied Jackson and Martin in unison.

"I will return to my post, sir," said Martin, expressionless.

Stone saw Martin look toward Jackson. He saw their eyes meet. They both stood silently staring at one another for a second that seemed an eternity. Then Martin quickly turned and sprinted back toward the small group of men she now commanded.

It was not long until the enemy was upon them. The majority of survivors had run out of ammunition and those who had not shortly emptied their magazines in the initial rush. The fighting was hand to hand, knife against knife, sword against sword.

In the deadly melee, Stone used his sword masterfully. He quickly moved through the chaotic mass, slicing and thrusting with his sword. A Scout Ranger jumped in front of him, the Ranger's sword drawn and ready. Stone moved quickly. As the Ranger thrust his sword, Stone smoothly blocked his attack and with one stroke removed the man of his lower left leg. As Stone rose another Terillian grabbed him from behind and drove a knife toward his heart. Grasping the man's wrist before he could force the knife into his chest, Stone flung the enemy over his body, dislocating the attacker's shoulder in the process. Stone had placed his foot on the screaming man's throat and was ready to plunge his sword into him when he heard Jackson's voice over the chaos of the battlefield.

"Colonel! It's Emily!"

He turned toward Martin's location. Her position was all but lost but she refused to give any more ground. As she pulled her sword from a dispatched foe, a Terillian round found its mark. Hit in the shoulder, she spun around and fell to her knees, her sword still in her hand.

"Emily!" shouted Jackson as he raced toward her with Stone not far behind.

Stone, running at a full sprint, watched as Martin, from her knees, thrust her sword into the closest Terillian. As she rose, another round hit her stomach and she fell to the ground again.

"No!" shouted Jackson as he rushed in her direction, wading through anyone who stood in his way.

Two more Terillians approached Martin. She quickly raised a rifle taken from a fallen enemy and fired point blank, killing them both. She tried to get up but this time she could not; she could only make it to her knees where she stayed with her sword in one hand, balancing her bloody and wavering torso.

Jackson was only a few meters away when Stone saw a round impact Jackson's body, sending him tumbling to the ground.

Stone quickly dropped the enemy rifleman with a shot from his sidearm as he rushed to his fallen comrades. He was still too far away. All he could do was watch…and continue to run.

***

Jackson slowly rose to his feet and stumbled the final few steps to Martin, still resting on her sword. He fell to his knees beside her.

"Emily," he cried as he lowered his head toward hers. "I'm sorry I didn't make it in time."

He looked into her eyes. They held a far-off stare, struggling to maintain consciousness.

"I never meant to hurt you," Jackson continued. "I tried to make it to you in time…I'm sorry…for everything. I always thought there would be time to prove to you that I was worthy. I just want you to know that I still love you."

Emily slowly focused on Jackson's face and a weak smile started to form. Emily raised her head slightly as a small trail of blood trickled out of her mouth. Her eyes met his briefly then she glanced over Jackson's shoulder. She tried to raise her sword but no longer had the strength. Jackson gasped for breath as a Terillian sword passed through his body.

***

Stone fired his last round but it was too late. The Terillian fell, but left his sword embedded in Jackson's body.

Stone was a few meters from Martin and Jackson when he felt a sharp sting in his right leg and fell to the ground. He quickly regained his footing despite the searing pain in his leg and turned toward the enemy. More rounds went into his arm and shoulder, twisting his body around and again sending him to his knees again.

He looked toward Martin and Jackson. They were still together, unconscious, slouched over one another with their heads resting on each other's shoulders.

Suddenly, an explosion between himself and the two lifted Stone off the ground and knocked him onto his back. From his prone position, he looked toward Martin and Jackson. They had disappeared in the blast.

Using his uninjured arm, he attempted to rise again to look for them. Almost immediately, he felt a crushing blow to his ribs. He rolled over, grasping for his knife.

As he looked up he saw a familiar pair of burning green eyes, then a rifle butt crashed into his forehead and darkness consumed him.

Chapter 9

The visions were continuous. Stone's reoccurring nightmare always ended the same way. As he rushed toward Jackson and Martin, he could see the Terillian thrust his sword into Jackson's back as he held Martin. He tried to raise his weapon in time, but no matter how many times the scene replayed in his head, he was always too slow. Then there were those green eyes again.

As the current nightmare passed, Stone struggled to open his eyes against the brightness of the light overhead. His whole body ached. Coming to his senses he realized he was lying in a bed. Stone tried to raise himself but the wrenching pain pulsating through his arm and shoulder stopped him and reminded him the dreams had been all too real.

"You are finally awake," came a woman's voice from nearby.

"Astra," he replied, thinking for a moment he had been rescued from Juliet 3.

"I'm afraid not, Colonel," responded the voice. "You have been in and out of consciousness for the two days while the genetic patches were repairing your injuries but it seems as though you're well on your way to recovery."

As his eyes finally adjusted to the room things became much clearer. His bed lay in the center of what appeared to be a prison cell. Looking toward the voice, he saw her.

"You!" exclaimed Stone as he recognized the Terillian standing outside the clear cell door. It was the woman from Sierra 7.

"It looks like you are now my prisoner," she replied. "Captain Mori Skye at your service."

"How many…what is the status of my regiment?" asked Stone as worked out the cobwebs.

"Your regiment is destroyed, Colonel. We took five prisoners including yourself. The rest were killed in the final assault."

Stone felt sick. He knew that few would survive but he had hoped more than four were left. Cataline and those fools at High Command had led his men to slaughter.

"Where are they?"

"The other survivors are still on Juliet 3, being held for interrogation and transport to prisoner of war facilities."

"Did any of my officers..."

"No. The other four were enlisted. I do want you to know, Colonel, that your regiment's performance was honorable. I should not tell you this, but as you are our prisoner there is little harm. Your regiment inflicted over three thousand casualties in your defense of the Lunari fields. General Fallingrock has ordered that all of your dead be placed on a morgue barge and transported to Xen territory so that the appropriate honors and burial rites may be administered."

"There'll be no burial rites," shot back an angry Stone. "Once we're dead we pass into nothingness, as does our flesh. All that remains is legacy. Have the general send a report of our deeds and do whatever he wishes with the bodies."

Mori paused.

"I do not understand you Hanmani. We are so similar but you are so aggressive by nature, and there is your unwillingness to acknowledge that there is more to us than flesh and bones."

She was getting to him again. In addition to his emotional response to her questioning, Stone struggled against the pain from his injuries, the haziness of the neuro-meds, and the anger over the death of his men.

"Captain, spiritual beliefs are for people who are afraid to face their mortality and the struggles of life," continued Stone. "We purged our society of the evils of religion after it nearly destroyed our civilization. When we have conquered your people, we will wash away your barbaric notions of spirituality as well."

"Oh yes," replied Mori. "You Hanmani have forgotten your ancestors and taken on the atheistic dogma of your Xen masters. It's a shame."

"You mean our allies," retorted Stone. He could feel his rage growing. "And as for our aggression, your people have tried to cover up your warmongering with propaganda about our civilization for centuries. I have grown numb to your lies."

"Lies!" she shouted. "You are a prisoner of the Terillian Confederation. You no longer have to spin your web of deceit. It sometimes amazes me that we come from common ancestors."

"Never!" shouted Stone. "I have heard that same Ter propaganda before. Your kind used similar lies as one of the pretenses for the First Terillian War and you are doing it again!"

He rose from his bed but was slowed by the pain in his leg.

"It's you that are the propagandists!" screamed Mori as she pounded her fist against the cell door. "That or you are simply fools."

Stone lunged toward his captor but fell to the ground in agony as his pain reminded him of his injuries.

"Your wounds are healing but you are a long way from being fully recovered, Colonel. Perhaps you should lie back down."

"You should have killed me on the battlefield," snapped Stone. Death was a far more attractive option than living out the life of a prisoner or even worse as an adopted family member, which was rumored to be the case with some of the Terillian groups.

"Sorry, Colonel," Mori replied. "A captured Colonel is much better than a dead one. Besides, I guess I owed you an unwelcome rescue from Sierra 7."

"I thought it was you."

"Yes, Colonel. I am a little intrigued about how you went from a major in the Elite Guard to a Colonel of the Line but I'm sure that will come out during your interrogation. I think we have chatted enough today. You should rest."

Mori turned away from Stone. "Sleep well, Colonel."

Stone slowly hobbled back to his bed. Fighting the searing pain in his leg, he climbed into his bed. Once in the bed, he took a deep breath to help the pain subside. Luckily, the meds quickly took effect and Stone soon drifted off to sleep again. As his eyes closed, he was running toward Jackson and Martin. Maybe this time he would be quick enough…

***

The sting of cold rain peppering her face brought Captain Emily Martin out of her semi-conscious stupor. As she slowly regained her senses, Martin noticed the tingling numbness of her extremities and the red-hot burning of her face, which felt raw against the pelting rain. The darkness told her she had been unconscious for at least a day. Martin listened for signs that someone was nearby but all she could hear was the spatter and low rushing roar of the downpour as the drizzle gradually increased in volume and intensity.

Then the pain hit her.

Martin sucked in a deep, loud breath of agony as a wave of pain centered in her stomach rippled throughout her body. Attempting to sit up, the moan was replaced with a loud cry as an intense, sharp pain in her shoulder nearly caused her to lose consciousness again. Breathing heavily through the pain, she closed her eyes tightly then let out another long breath and turned her head toward her right shoulder.

Martin could see the hole in her uniform where the Terillian round had entered her body near where her arm met her shoulder. The smooth circular hole, soaked with blood, gave little indication to the actual damage underneath.

"Shit," declared Martin, as she began to comprehend where she was and what had happened.

Another wave of pain pulsated through her body.

Martin let out a low, guttural moan as she closed her eyes again and felt her muscles spasm against the pain.

Groaning against the throbbing in her right shoulder, Martin pushed her head and left shoulder off the ground to look at her stomach. She could feel the resistance of her left arm to the suction of the mud, which was slowly consuming her body as the rain continued to intensify. Looking down the length of her body, she could see the steam from her open wound drifting upward from her abdomen and the blood that had pooled around her waist and mixed with the muddy water.

At her feet lay what was left of Captain Hugh Jackson. Jackson's body had absorbed most of the blast from the explosion that had blown them apart. Twisted, mangled, and distorted, Jackson's wrecked body had shielded Martin from the full force of the blast.

"No!" she shouted as she saw him lying on the ground.

Jackson's eyes were frozen in death, staring in Martin's direction. His glare was empty and vacant; he was gone.

Unable to endure the pain of seeing Jackson's body or the wound to her shoulder any longer, she let her left arm go limp and her head fell back to the ground. She could feel the splash of the water and the cold mud ooze around the back of her head. As the water settled, the level had increased so that the muddy fluid began to fill her ear canal.

Martin looked up at the night sky. She could feel the tears of anguish and loss run down her face contrast with the burning sensation caused by the near-freezing rain. Slowly closing her eyes, she contemplated her impending death.

As Martin slowly faded into oblivion, thoughts of her father came to her.

In her vision, Martin was still a child and her father in his prime, wearing the uniform of the Praetorian Guard—hand-selected bodyguards of the ProConsul.

"But, Father," the young Martin had asked, "why do you have to be gone tonight?"

"It's my duty, Emily," replied her father. "I have to stand watch at the Eternal Flame tonight, and if I don't go someone else will have to."

"Well, let someone else do it!" pouted the young Martin, wanting her father to stay with her and her mother.

Martin's father looked sternly at her, but after a quick pause and a sigh of understanding he leaned down and put his hand to her cheek. She could feel his calloused, powerful hands against her face, but his touch was gentle and calming.

"Emily," he said softly, "you're a Martin. And Martins are soldiers. Our society has to be able to count on us. Even if it's hard, even if it seems impossible, we do whatever we have to for our people. We can't give up on our duties, no matter how hard it is or how much it hurts."

With that, Martin's father rose and repositioned his belt to align perfectly with the lines of his tunic.

"Can I count on my little soldier?" he asked.

"Yes, father," replied the adult Martin out loud as she began to summon the strength to move. "You can count on me."

Martin clinched her teeth and sucked in a deep breath. With all of her strength, she quickly rolled up onto her knees. Martin's head slumped toward the ground and she let out a piercing scream which echoed across the abandoned battlefield as the pain from her stomach and shoulder enveloped her. Clenching her left fist, she struggled against the almost unbearable pain to raise her head.

There was carnage all around her. Wrecked equipment and torn bodies littered the ground as far as her agony-blurred vision would allow her to see.

The pain in her stomach seemed to subside to a dull ache in her kneeled position but only made the intense pain in her mangled shoulder more prevalent. A slight shift in her position caused her shoulder's position to change. Moaning against what felt like exposed bones and tendons rubbing against her uniform she fell forward, catching herself with her left arm. As she did, the pain from her stomach wound raced up her spine. Her arm gave way and she fell forward. Pain pulsated through her body as her face fell into the deepening mud and muck.

Rolling onto her left side, Martin let out several rapid heavy breaths of agony. Each quick, short breath pushed out muddy water from her mouth as the ever-increasing rain began to turn the battlefield to an even more horrible lake of mud, metal, and flesh.

Slowly focusing her eyes, she saw the body of a medic lying nearby. His hand, half buried in mud, held a medical pack.

Using her left arm and head for leverage, Martin slowly dragged her body forward as she struggled to reach the pack. Every meter felt like a kilometer as she fought to ignore the pain and maintain consciousness. In a few moments, which seemed like an eternity, Martin reached the pack. Rolling unto her back to free up her left arm, she reached blindly into the bag. Feeling a few items in the bag, she pulled them out and held them to her face.

Martin let out a sigh of relief as she read the labels. There was a coagulant to slow the bleeding from her abdomen and shoulder and a few neuro-inhibitors for the pain. Ripping the cover from the coagulant with her teeth, she shook the bag and a small can fell onto her chest. Taking the can, she quickly sprayed the sticky fluid onto her stomach and shoulder. It was ice cold, and she could instantly feel the area around her wounds tighten as the chemicals constricted vessels and slowed the flow of blood to the wounds.

Next she took one of the neuro-meds in her hand; this would not be as easy. Again biting off the protective cap, she exposed a thick metal injection pin. Gripping the back of the tube tightly, she let out a deep breath and then drew in another, holding it. In as powerful a motion as she could muster, Martin rammed the injector into her thigh. She let out a grunt as she felt the sharp sting of the injector followed by the burning hot sensation of the meds entering her body.

Martin felt her breathing slow and the intense pain in her shoulder transition from a searing, stabbing pain into a dull ache. After taking a moment to ready herself, Martin rolled onto her stomach. Her right arm was useless despite the medication; it flopped clumsily by her side as she moved. Spitting out the mud and water that had accumulated in her mouth, she pulled her left arm under her body, gritted her teeth, and pushed herself up to a kneeling position.

Grunting again, she could feel the tightness in her stomach along with a nearly unbearable pain in her gut. On her hand and knees Martin positioned herself beside a dead Humani officer to her left. Another painful repositioning and she rocked back on to her knees so that she could take the pistol from dead man's holster. Reaching backwards, Martin stuck the pistol into her waistbelt. Moving again, she slowly crawled her way to Jackson's body.

Again sitting up on her knees, Martin put her hand on Jackson's head. Through the pain of her wounds, the mud caked on her face, and stinging cold rain, she could feel tears flow down her cheeks.

Sucking in the mucus running from her nose and wiping the tears from her face, Martin struggled with a pain more intense than any bullet could create. Placing her hand on Jackson one last time, she spoke. "They will pay, Hugh. I will make it out of here, and I will make them pay."

***

An explosion and the force of the ship lunging to port startled Stone to consciousness. Another explosion almost knocked him to the floor. Rolling off his bed, Stone let out a loud grunt and cursed as his injured leg bore the full weight of his body for the first time since his injury. His muscles were tight and his vision blurred from the medication and the pain, but he tried to keep his composure. Steadying himself and taking a deep breath, Stone moved toward the door of the cell to try to see what was going on.

Crewmembers ran in all directions. Another explosion rocked the ship and the lights dimmed.

"ALL POWER SHIFTING TO EMERGENCY SOURCES" came across the announcing circuit.

Stone felt his prison door move. The shift of power had caused Stone's door to partially open. He struggled to squeeze his body through the opening. Stone was halfway through the door when another explosion ripped through the ship. He let out a yell as the blast knocked his wounded shoulder into the door. The pain was intense and Stone felt his vision start to grow hazy again. Exhaling heavily, he pushed through the door grunting and grimacing as flashes of pain washed over his body.

"ALL HANDS PREPARE TO ABANDON SHIP. ALL HANDS PREPARE TO ABANDON SHIP. NEAREST FRIENDLY PLANET IS NOVEMBER 5. ALL HANDS PREPARE TO ABANDON SHIP."

Once free of his cell, Stone took a second to recover from the pain and gain his bearings. The emergency lighting eerily lit the passageway in both directions. A repair crew was hard at work fighting an electrical fire and structural damage forward of Stone's position. Their frantic efforts were partially concealed by a smoky haze slowly moving downward from the overhead. Suddenly the panel on which the crew was working exploded in a bright flash of light. Stone's eyes burned from the brightness and his body ached as the concussion from the blast knocked him against the bulkhead. Regaining his senses, Stone looked toward the explosion. The fire engulfed the forward passageway, consuming the repair party. His only choice was to move aft.

Turning the corner of the passageway, Stone crashed into a Terillian marine.

In the collision, both men fell to the ground. The marine quickly recovered and reached for his sidearm. Before the marine could draw his weapon, Stone's foot crashed into the marines jaw, knocking him unconscious. Stone let out a loud moan as the pain pulsated through his wounded leg and throughout his entire body. He pounded his fist on the deck in reaction to the lightning bolt of pain shooting through his leg.

"Damn it," he mumbled to himself as he crawled to the marine.

Taking the pistol from the marine's belt, Stone slowly rose to his feet and hobbled down the passageway.

The ship wouldn't hold together much longer and Stone knew it. His search for an escape pod became more frantic. Turning down another corridor, Stone had only made it a few feet when he stopped. Small fires and debris that littered the passageway were starting to flitter, then die down. Hull breaches and the hunger of the fires onboard were robbing the ship of its oxygen; it wouldn't be long until it could no longer sustain life.

Peering down the passageway Stone saw them—rows of escape pod compartments. Hopefully there was enough air in the passageway. Taking a deep breath, and hoping it would not be his last, he sprinted through the passageway trying his best to ignore the almost unbearable pain from his injuries.

Stone was breathing heavily when he reached the pods. He was becoming light-headed as well; the air was getting worse.

"Empty!" Stone grumbled. "Damn it, this one too," panted Stone as he limped from one empty pod to another, his breathing more labored with every moment.

Finally he found one remaining pod. As he reached up to pull the latch that would open the entrance to the pod he felt someone behind him. He quickly spun around, raising his weapon.

"Where do you think you are going, Colonel?" asked Mori, her sword resting against Stone's chest. He looked down the long blade into those damn green eyes. Looking closer, he also saw the red lines quickly growing darker in the white of her eyes as the remaining oxygen in the space was being consumed by fires and the vacuum of space.

"Looks like...my friends...have come for me," huffed Stone. "You can't escape...escape the reach of the Xen military."

"Apparently a few of your long-range fighters made their way through our lines and got in a lucky shot. They may have destroyed this ship but our fighters are already on their tail. They..." She took a deep breath and put out an arm to balance herself against the cobwebs forming in her head. "...will not escape."

The ship shuddered again with another explosion. Both Stone and Mori quickly regained their balance, neither one gaining an advantage. He saw Mori glance into the escape pod. Stone shifted his stance to allow him to look into the pod and still have an eye on his opponent.

"I...I am taking this pod," stated Stone.

"Both of us are, Colonel," replied Mori. "You're too valuable of an intelligence asset to leave here to die."

Another explosion. This time Stone's weight shifted to his injured leg and he stumbled. Mori rapidly capitalized, striking his wounded shoulder with the hilt of her sword. He recoiled in pain. As he did, she knocked the pistol from his hand and swept his wounded leg, bringing him to the ground. Attempting to prop himself up, he was stopped by Mori's sword against his throat.

"Just finish it," Stone said to her as his focus began to fade and tunnel vision set in.

"You're not getting off that easy, Colonel," said Mori as she looked down at Stone. "Give me your arms," she ordered.

Defeated and injured, Stone complied and Mori quickly tied Stone's hands together. Growing weaker, it was all she could do to lift Stone from the deck.

"Get…in…the…pod," she panted, motioning toward the open hatch with the pistol.

"Not…going to be…easy," stammered Stone as he looked into pod. The last explosion had sent a massive metal shard into one of the seats of the two-man escape pod.

"Damn it!" grumbled Mori as she looked around the compartment at the expended escape pods. Stone could feel her start to stumble, then regain her balance as she held his arm.

After a slight pause and a heavy sigh, she spoke.

"I said g…get in the p…pod," she repeated.

"Where?" asked Stone, now leaning against the pod. "…only holds…one now."

"Both fit in the starboard…" Mori closed her eyes for a second to concentrate. "You can either pledge to remain my prisoner until we reach November 5 or die here."

"I…choose…death…" He was starting to fade.

"Sorry, Colonel," replied Mori. "Not…today."

Summoning what strength she had left, she brought the butt of her sword against the back of Stone's head, knocking him unconscious.

Stone was just coming to as Mori closed the hatch.

"What the hell are you doing?" he demanded as he tried in vain to free himself. Mori had secured Stone in the undamaged hatch and was sitting on top of him.

"Shut up and hold on," she said as she reached for the ejection button.

They were thrown forward and then back into the seat as the thrusters launched the pod away from the crumbling spacecraft. The pod was only a few seconds free from the spacecraft when it finally exploded, showering the pod with shrapnel and causing it to tumble through space. The blast threw Mori's body against Stone's shoulder. As the pain shot through his body he felt his head grow heavy. His vision blurred and he lost consciousness again.

His shoulder was still throbbing when he again opened his eyes. He started to move but felt Mori's weight on him in the confined space. She was fidgeting about and almost yelling.

"Any Terillian ship, this is escape pod 245 from sloop *Lodgehouse* authentication code Golf-Delta-Romeo-3, any Terillian ship respond," pleaded Mori over the long-range communicator. "My navigation computer is damaged. Current trajectory indicates landing on planet November 14. Any Terillian ship, this is escape pod 245 from ...."

Stone contemplated resistance but he did not have the advantage. He was injured and weakened. Perhaps he had better bide his time and try to lull his enemy into complacency, he thought to himself.

"The navigation system is damaged?" asked Stone.

"Yes and the damn impulse engine is damaged as well. It lasted long enough to set us on a trajectory to the closest inhabitable planet. Hopefully there will be enough left to control the landing."

"November 14?"

"Yes, I don't know anything about it other than the data logs say it's populated only by a few isolated settlements."

As she spoke, Stone began to feel the pressure of her body on his. She was thin and muscular, but proportioned in just the right places. Her bottom squirming around in his lap did not help either. He tried to control himself, but his body reacted.

"Could you stop moving around so much? It's bothering my leg," said a frustrated and embarrassed Stone, trying to recover and hoping she hadn't noticed his arousal.

"Sorry. I'll try to be more careful but in these close quarters we both may have to deal with your *leg* until we can land and get out of here," she quipped.

***

After a few awkward and uncomfortable hours, November 14 came into sight. A tiny planet in a forgotten sector, it had no strategic importance nor did it offer much in the way of resources.

"Let's just hope there's enough juice left in this S.O.B to put her down safely," said Mori as she concentrated on the controls.

"Watch your horizon," warned Stone as they entered the atmosphere.

"Don't need any backseat driving," grumbled Mori as she worked to control the damaged pod as it sped through the sky.

Mori peered out the viewing window as the pod rocketed over the terrain. Massive evergreens covered the mountainous land below. The terrain seemed to continue forever, the forest and mountains only broken occasionally by a raging valley river and small openings where the blanket of trees gave way to fields of wildflowers and a few cultivated fields.

Mori worked feverishly at the controls. Slowly, the pod began to steady itself. Stone could not help but be impressed with her skill.

"The thrusters seem to be holding out," she reported. "That looks like a decent spot to put her down over there."

Mori brought the pod to a hover just above a clearing in a patch of evergreen trees.

"I guess this will do," she said, as she set the pod down as if she was returning home from an afternoon drive.

As soon as the pod settled gently to the ground, Mori quickly jumped from the module. In her haste she forgot about Stone's injuries.

"Son of a bitch!" shouted Stone. Mori could see his body tighten as the pain radiated from his leg throughout the rest of his body.

"Sorry," she replied as she quickly turned back toward him, her pistol at her side. "Can you get out?"

Taking a deep breath, Stone placed his bound hands on the lip of the hatch and tried to pull himself out.

"Damn it," Stone cried.

Seeing him struggle, Mori reached into the pod to help him out.

"A little help," she grunted as they both struggled to hoist him from the pod.

Finally, Stone was on his feet. As soon as he had his footing, he quickly landed his elbow against her neck and reached for her sword. The sword slid out of its sheath as she fell to the ground. Stone quickly grabbed the sword and stepped toward her placing the sword to her cheek.

"You bastard!" she yelled.

"I believe circumstances have changed," he said, clearly proud of his victory.

"Not really," replied Mori, recognizing Stone was struggling against the pain and that he did not realize she had the upper hand. "Put the sword down or I'll fire."

Mori could see he was stunned at what he thought was pure audacity.

With a smile, Mori pressed the barrel of her pistol into Stone's groin.

"Since you apparently have trouble controlling it, perhaps I should just remove it for you," she added.

Checkmate.

Stone stared intently at Mori; she could tell he was trying to determine his next move.

"You can put down the sword in your hand and keep the one…"

"If you did fire, I am still close enough to plunge *this* sword into your throat," he replied.

"It seems like we're going to have to come to some agreement. We can kill each other or can both survive."

"I'm listening," grunted Stone.

Mori could tell the pain would soon overcome him.

"There is no use in us waging war with each other as we're the only two combatants on this planet. I suggest we work together to survive until we're found. At that point either one will become the other's prisoner or die."

"As soon as we find a way off this rock, then all bets are off?" asked Stone.

"Agreed, we will try to kill each other then,"replied Mori.

Lowering the sword to his side, Stone conceded.

"Agreed," he said.

Mori slowly lowered her pistol.

Stone dropped the sword and collapsed onto his good knee.

Mori stood over him, her pistol by her side. He was at her mercy and they both knew it.

"You can finish it now," conceded Stone.

Mori paused, conflicted with her promise and self-preservation. After what seemed an eternity, she holstered her pistol.

"My people keep our oaths, Colonel," replied Mori.

"I will honor our agreement," she continued as she leaned over Stone. "Stay there, Colonel. I will get the medipack from the pod."

Chapter 10

Stone spent the next four days in a state of semi-consciousness as the medipacks did their work. He had brokered a good deal with the Terillian captain. She built a makeshift hut, tended to his wounds, and once the ready-meals were gone hunted for food. During his small periods of consciousness, Stone could remember Mori burning incense, singing rhythmic songs, and rubbing some type of substance on his wounds.

On the evening of the fourth day, Stone woke in the middle of his old familiar dream."Who's Emily?" asked Mori as she sat a few feet away eating a soup she had just made from the yesterday's kill. "And you mentioned Astra back on the ship. You must have been pretty busy, Colonel. Sounds like you had problems controlling your *leg* well before the escape pod," she said jokingly.

"No…Astra is…it's complicated."

"I'm sure it is Colonel," she smiled.

"And Emily Martin was one of my company commanders," continued Stone. He paused, concerned about telling too much.

"It's all right, Colonel," said Mori. "I don't think you're going to give away any state secrets."

"She was killed on Juliet 3, when you…" He paused. "…in the attack. She was one of the finest warriors I have ever known."

"I am truly sorry, Colonel," offered Mori, genuinely apologetic. "All of your warriors performed bravely and brought honor to themselves and their unit. In our culture, the status of a warrior is measured by the caliber of our enemy and your men bring honor to both your people and the many lodges of our nations."

"No need to apologize, Captain. Her death was not the fault of any Terillian. Her death is on the hands of coward and a fool that will someday pay for his actions."

"You Hanmani are a complicated civilization."

"Why is it that you call us that?" asked Stone.

"You will not believe it," replied Mori.

"Try me."

"Fine." Mori paused to take a deep breath. "Alpha Humana is the lost colony. Generations ago, your planet was the farthest humanoid settlement of our Confederation. It was colonized by bands from the Akota and a clan from the Iroqua—that is until you fell under control of the Xen. Contact was lost and expeditions failed to return…your people have lost their way and do not understand what they are supposed to d…*Hanmani.* The next contact we had with your people was when we were attacked during the First Tero-Xen war with Humani fighting for their Xen masters."

"Bullshit," replied Stone.

"You asked where the name comes from and I told you. If you don't like the answer, it's not my problem," stated Mori abruptly.

"That's just wrong. Your ancestors have definitely done an excellent job of indoctrinating you into the lie. Our planet was devastated by religious wars and finally by the biological, chemical, and nuclear war between the Eastern and Western Alliances. Only a few hardened military bases survived. Other than that, it was anarchy…until the Xen arrived. A Xen scout ship crashlanded on Alpha Humana, and the recovery effort brought our two species into contact. The Xen took us under their wing and helped restore us and build a new, better civilization—one built on order, structure, and devoid of any religious nonsense that almost destroyed our planet."

"I do not believe I am the one that has been deceived, Colonel."

Mori paused and took a deep breath, her lips curling in slightly on themselves. "I don't think this is going to get us anywhere," she continued. "Why don't you have some soup? You need to get your strength back and start pulling your weight around here."

Stone knew she was right. He had done little but eat and sleep since their arrival.

"Thank you, Captain," he said as he reached for the bowl of soup.

"You're welcome, Colonel. Don't worry, in a few more days you're gonna earn your keep."

***

Martin gently moved a small branch away from her face and peered through the dense underbrush into the small clearing. Her eyes took longer than normal to focus. Although she had been able to stop her bleeding and slow the rate of infection from her wounds, the painkillers, her injuries, and a slowly progressing fever were starting to take their toll. She needed to find a way back to Humani territory soon, and hopefully this was her chance.

Through the thick foliage Martin saw the Terillian transport. A small squad of Terillians had spread out from the transport, no-doubt collecting remains from the battle that had raged weeks ago. Martin quickly sized up the situation; the pilot and navigator were probably still onboard, but otherwise only one soldier remained at the hatch as a guard. As Martin looked on, the soldier paced back and forth around the perimeter of the transport. After a few minutes, the guard propped his rifle against the hull of the transport and walked to a felled tree about five meters from the transport and his weapon. Leaning against the tree, the guard reached into one of his trouser pockets and pulled out a digital pad; he was instantly lost in whatever viewing item he had selected. *This is my chance*, thought Martin.

Martin uncapped the last of her painkillers. She closed her eyes and grimaced as she jabbed the injector into her thigh. After a slow, quiet, long breath, Martin deliberately unsheathed the Terillian sword she had taken from the battlefield and laid it beside her knee. As she set the blade down, she saw a stone on the ground. If only her right arm was not useless from her injuries, she could use it as a distraction. Instead she would have to use surprise, speed, and brute force if necessary to cover the thirty meters of open ground before the guard could warn the crew of the transport.

Picking up the sword in her left hand, Martin balanced herself on her left hand and knee as she brought her right leg up and coiled her body for the rush toward the transport. Focusing on the guard, she sprung from the cover of the brush. The pain from her wounds was excruciating, but there was no choice but to push on. Her legs were still capable, however, and she had covered half the distance before the guard saw her. At a full sprint, Martin's vision tunneled as she zeroed in on her target. Jolted from his distraction, the guard quickly stood erect as he realized he was under attack.

Martin pressed on, grunting against the pain in her gut and shoulder as she pushed her body forward. Martin looked directly at the guard as she sprinted toward him. She could see the shock and fear on his face as he tried to steady himself to react. Finally taking action, the guard made a quick move for his rifle.

By the time the guard grabbed the rifle and swung it upwards toward her, Martin was on him. Martin launched her body toward the guard. Her shoulder crashed into his chest. The blow knocked the guard against the hull of the transport and caused him to drop his rifle.

Martin let out a groan as the pain from the impact sent a shock wave of agony through her body. Staggered from the pain, she fell backwards. As she fell, Martin slashed the guard across the abdomen with her sword. Letting out a moan, the guard fell to his knees grasping at his stomach. Quickly rising to her own knees, Martin thrust the sword forward with all of her strength. The blade passed through the chest of the guard and stopped with a metallic thud as it impacted the hull of the transport.

Martin looked into the eyes of the guard. She could see that last spark fade and his eyes freeze into that too-familiar gaze of death. Grimacing as she rose to her feet, Martin pressed her right foot against the guard's shoulder and with her left hand withdrew the sword from his body. As she did, the man's lifeless body slumped backwards and crumbled to the ground. Martin leaned against the hull and breathed heavily as she fought to gain control of the pain. After a few seconds she stood up straight, sheathed her sword, and withdrew the pistol from her waistband. The confines of the transport would muffle the sound of the gunshots when Martin moved against the crew.

"Time to get off this shithole," Martin said out loud as she stepped through the hatch of the transport.

***

"Don't miss him, Colonel," whispered Mori.

"I *don't* miss," Stone replied. Exhaling slowly, Stone pulled the trigger.

A single shot rang out across the valley. Four hundred meters away a large deer crumpled to the ground.

"Told you," smiled Stone as he stood up from behind the felled tree he had used as a rest.

"I figured you could *hit* it from there," quipped Mori. "Just hope you didn't mess up the meat."

"Let's go see," replied Stone confidently as he shouldered the weapon and headed toward his kill with Mori at his side.

"Since you seem to be doing much better, I believe you should carry it back to the hut."

"I made the kill so you should do the lifting," said Stone, only half-joking.

"Really. What about the last two weeks while you were napping in the hut?"

"I guess I should do the heavy lifting, being the man."

Mori stopped dead in her tracks. "The man?! You know what, I'll get it myself."

"Damn. I was just kidding," said Stone. "I figured we would both share the load."

"Whatever, Colonel," snapped back Mori. "I have not relied on a *man* since my father and have no plans of starting now."

"Well," replied an irritated Stone. "Your father must have done a number on you…"

"Shut your mouth, Humani!" snapped Mori as she turned back toward Stone.

Stone could see her piercing green eyes burn with anger as she struggled to hold back her rage. "You have no right to speak of him. You and your…You know what, never mind. Let's just get the damn deer and get it back to the hut."

"No problem," said Stone, shocked by her response.

"Fine."

Mori moved ahead of Stone by several meters, and the two made their way down the hill and into the valley below without a word.

Stone was the first to break the silence. "I think it's over there," he said, pointing to the location where the deer had fallen.

"If it's not too much trouble," said Mori, "why don't you dress it out while I get some wood down by that stream to carry the meat back to camp?"

"What the hell is your problem, Captain?" asked Stone.

"How about a little gratitude, you Xen pig? *Thawatchin tata husteyA hitunkasan.*"

"What the hell did you say?" asked Stone, even more irritated now that she was speaking Terillian gibberish. "If you want gratitude," replied Stone, "how about I show you just how grateful I am…I am grateful to the Terillians for starting this war, grateful for destroying my unit, for…"

As he spoke he slid his hand to the knife on his waistbelt.

"So, Colonel," replied Mori as she gripped the handle of her sword, "I was wondering how long it would take you to break our agreement."

"I will keep my word, Terillian," he said coldly, "until a passage off the world is found. Then you *will* see my gratitude."

"I will be ready, Xennite slave," spat Mori. "But until then, we need to get the damn meat back to our camp."

Mori stared at Stone for a moment then turned toward the small stream. "Xen asshole," she mumbled in her Akota tongue, still audible to Stone.

"Terillian bitch," said Stone under his breath as he pulled out his knife and began to gut the deer.

***

Stone had just begun his last cuts on the carcass when a thundering crash came from the woods to his right. As he turned toward the noise, a massive bear rushed from the dense undergrowth only feet from Stone's position. Before he could react, a swat from a massive paw sent Stone flying. Crashing to the ground, Stone grabbed the only weapon within reach—a large stick lying on the ground.

Within seconds the massive animal was on top of him. Stone raised the club to fend off the beast but it snapped like a twig in the animal's powerful jaws. *After everything, it ends like this*, Stone thought.

Suddenly Stone heard a dull *thud*, and the bear looked away from him. Then another. This time the beast let out a loud roar, and, turning away from him, it lunged toward the stream. Stone rolled over to see Mori, about fifty meters away, firing at the charging beast with her sidearm.

"Hoka Hay! I'm over here!" she shouted as the bear rushed toward her.

Knowing the pistol would do little but irritate the monster, Stone scrambled to his feet and grabbed the rifle laying nearby. Looking down the sights, the bear and Mori were lined up exactly with one another. He would have to be perfect or he would hit her.

Wounded and enraged, the massive bear roared as it quickly closed the ground between itself and Mori.

Stone saw Mori drop her empty pistol and draw her sword.

***

Standing with her sword by her side, she mumbled a prayer. "Great Spirit, give me the strength to overcome the spirit of my bear brother."

Rushing toward her, the animal eclipsed the landscape in Mori's view. The animal was focused on Mori, his giant paws pounding into the ground and throwing up large clumps of dirt as he launched himself closer to her with each leap.

"Let me show strength and courage and…."

Her prayer was interrupted by three loud percussions from Stone's rifle. The bear stumbled and fell to the ground less than a meter from Mori's feet. She dropped her sword and fell to her knees, trying to regain her breath.

***

"Captain, are you okay?" shouted Stone as he rushed to her.

"Thank you, Great Spirit," said Mori as Stone finally reached her.

"What?" he asked.

"Oh," she replied, regaining her composure. "Thank you, Colonel."

"No, Captain, it's I who should thank you. That bear would have killed me for sure if you had not drawn its attention."

"Well," smiled Mori, "I was counting on your marksmanship. You *don't* miss, right?"

"All the same, thank you."

"And to think, we were ready to kill each other ten minutes ago," said Mori. "It's this way that the Great Spirit directs us in the sacred loop…enemies do not have to always be enemies. We live in a cyclic, fluid universe don't we?"

"I apologize, Captain," replied Stone, confused by Mori's comments but not wanting to start another fight. "I should not pretend to know anything of your culture."

"What do you say we get all this meat back to the hut before it goes bad?"

"Sure. But I'm gonna need a little help. That is if you don't mind helping a man out."

"You men always need help," replied Mori with a big smile. "Let's get to work."

***

That evening they sat beside the fire eating meat from their kill. The light flickered, and the small fire crackled and popped.

"I'm sorry about earlier," said Stone still feeling he had let things get out of control. "I meant no disrespect toward your father."

"It's okay. And I want to say again that I am sorry for the loss of your subordinate Captain Martin. She sounded like brave *blotahonka*...that means war leader."

"Thank you. She was."

Mori rose slightly from her seat to pull another piece of flesh from the roasting meat. As she did, Stone couldn't help notice that the bottom of her shirt rose enough to show her thin, toned waistline. As she turned to sit again, she caught him looking.

"You should be careful, Colonel," she smiled. "We wouldn't want your *leg* to start acting up again."

Stone was sure his face was redder than the fire in front of him. He needed to change the subject...fast.

"I think you can drop the rank stuff. You can call me Tyler."

"What did you say?" asked Mori.

"Tyler."

"Pleased to meet you, Tyler. What does that mean?"

"What does what mean?" asked a still confused Stone. "My name...it means my uncle's name was Tyler and my parents liked it."

"But what is the meaning?"

"I guess there isn't one," replied Stone. "I guess Mori means something?"

"Of course—well, sort of. We're given a Confederation name when we come of age. Part of our education beyond our own language is the Confederation language. It designates me as warrior and means 'stands alone.' My Akota name is Ino'ka–my people's native tongue for badger."

"How many languages to you speak?" asked Stone, feeling linguistically inadequate. He could speak a little of what he now understood to be the Confederation language, but that was it.

"I speak the Confederation Normative Language, Akota, Iroqua, and obviously Hanman...I mean, Humana."

"A warrior and a scholar," declared Stone.

"Shut up," smiled Mori.

Stone could see she had taken the compliment well.

"How did you get your Akota name?" he asked.

"My father gave it to me when I was six. Some boys at the research station we were living on were teasing me and I fought them."

"How many?"

"Three."

"Did you win?" asked Stone.

"Sent them all running and crying to their mothers," she replied with a smile on her face. "My father got a little flak for giving me a warrior name but I guess he had me pegged from the start. Luckily, my nation is one of the few that allows women to be warriors."

"So you're Mori Ino'ka Skye?"

"No," sighed Mori, showing frustration at Stone's lack of knowledge about her culture. "One is a Confederation name and the other is Akota. My nation calls me Ino'ka and anyone outside calls me Mori."

"Your culture seems complicated...and interesting. Without giving up any military secrets, why don't you tell me about your people?"

"Are you trying to start another argument? You don't want to hear truth. Everything I say you will refute as some sinister plot against the Xen Empire."

That's because it is, Stone thought, but he didn't really care. Not only had he been caught peeking, but now he couldn't get the thought out of his head. Better to let her tell some lies to get things back to normal.

"I seriously want to know," pleaded Stone.

"Only if you agree not to challenge everything I say."

"Agreed."

"The people you call Terillians," she said, "are a confederation of free planets, all humanoid, that provide support to one another economically, culturally, and militarily. There is not one 'Terillian' culture but several nations, bands, and clans that share similar, but different, cultures. We also have similar spiritual beliefs as well."

"Spiritual? I have always been fascinated with your civilization's need to hold to archaic beliefs of spirits and an afterlife."

"Yes, spiritual," she replied. "I don't think this is a good..."

"Please, Captain...Ino'ka, continue?" asked Stone.

Mori's eyes opened wide and her jaw dropped slightly. "You can't call me that," she said, an octave higher than her normal voice. "It's not...you're not Akota. I knew I shouldn't have..."

"I'm sorry, Mori," said Stone stressing her name, "I did not mean to offend you. Please continue."

Mori paused. Stone could tell she was trying to decide if this conversation was a huge mistake.

"Very well," she continued after a moment. "Most of us believe there is a Spirit that created everything and if we live good lives and honor the Spirit, as well as its manifestations in nature, we will be rewarded in the afterlife."

"Good life...what is a good life? Invading..." He stopped himself. "Sorry, continue with your story."

"I think we had better stop."

"No, continue," he requested. "I will keep quiet. I promise."

"Okay," she said hesitatingly. "In the afterlife, if you are worthy, the Spirit will let you take on the form of whatever manifestation you choose, such as sable tiger, raven hawk, or that big son-of-a-bitch bear that attacked us today. If you are unworthy, your soul remains in the ether—never finding rest."

"Unworthy? What makes you unworthy?"

"It's easier to explain what makes you worthy. Bravery, endurance, generosity, and wisdom..."

"Part of that sounds a lot like Humani social code to me," replied Stone.

"What is that?"

"It's the basis for our social structure. All Humani are part of the greater society. Depending on your social status, you are required to perform certain tasks."

"Tasks?"

"Yes. If you are from an appropriate family, your duty is to lead and govern. For mid-level families, it's their place to manage and direct commerce and act as junior officers when required. The lower classes provide the labor to support our society and fill the ranks of our military. This provides order and structure to our civilization and has allowed us to flourish."

"That sounds great if you are not in the lower levels of your society. What happens if someone from an inferior family wants to be a leader?"

"Why would they? It's not their duty."

"What about talent, intelligence, motivation?"

"If they are talented they will reflect that talent in the type of service they perform. If they are intelligent they can advise others of higher status. As for motivation, maintaining the natural order and playing their role in supporting the society should be enough."

Stone was surprising even himself. Hearing that from someone else would have made him laugh.

"We're allowed to be judged on our merit, not our family's status," replied Mori. "Obviously the wealthy and influential will always be...well...wealthy and influential, but in our society one can stand on their own accomplishments. Although some of our nations place some importance on inheritance, the majority of our leaders must earn their honors."

"Some of your nations, the majority of your leaders," asked a puzzled Stone. "Does your society have no structure? How does your government and military provide leadership?"

"We have structure, our war council...um, I don't think I'm going to tell you how our military decisions are made, Colonel."

"Of course," he replied. Stone hadn't even realized the question had military implications—he was simply fascinated with the complexity and apparent fluidity of her civilization.

At the same time, Stone was surprised at how much he felt the need to defend his own society. He had started the conversation, though, so he guessed he had brought it on himself.

"Humani can rise in standing," he said, again trying to defend his stance. "A family, over generations, can move up in status if they serve the society well, if their members stay away from scandal, and if they marry accordingly. They will never be a Senator or become the ProConsul, but they will slowly become an acceptable family if their legacy is maintained."

"Generations? What about the individual?"

"The individual does not matter. It's their support of the society that matters. Individual ambition, if not checked by the family or the society, will lead to destruction."

Did I just say that? he thought, realizing the First Families thrived on ambition, and it was ambition that drove everyone in his society to move up the ladder.

"Destruction? Your institutions and caste structure will only lead to stagnation. In our society, a person can rise from obscurity to the highest levels of government, commerce, and the military. It's this avenue for opportunity that stimulates a society to reach its potential. It does not lead to destruction; it leads to advancement. Advancement based on merit."

"Merit?"

"Merit is the measure of a Terillian, not whether you are from a poor family, have a good name, or even if you were an orphan."

"Orphan?" he asked inquisitively. No wonder she had reacted so harshly to Stone's comment about her father. Mori was apparently telling more about herself than he had expected.

"Yes. Orphans."

"What does that have to do with anything? Were you an orphan?" he asked, hoping to get her to open up more but instantly regretting he had dug that deep.

Mori stared blankly into the fire for a moment.

"Yes. I was. My father was a doctor and my mother a musician. When I was eight, my family was onboard the research vessel *Mendelev* where my father was working on a cure for the H3 Virus. He was using microscopic specimens from an asteroid belt near the Neutral Quadrant as hosts for his experiments. Apparently we were close enough for the slavers to attack. When they boarded our ship, my father told me and my sister to hide in one of the specimen cabinets. Through the slit in the door I saw everything."

Stone was so drawn in that it took him a second to notice a tear running down her cheek. Mori continued her story, still staring blankly into the crackling fire. He could sense the pain in her voice as she continued.

"My father tried to stop them but they killed him and left him on the floor like some discarded piece of rubbish. When he fell, my older sister—she was twelve—screamed and gave away her hiding place. The slavers then took my mother and my twelve-year-old sister and they…" She paused for a second that felt like an eternity.

She continued. "When they were done they dragged them away and loaded them onto their ship. I lay there and watched my father's blood drain onto the floor for an hour before other survivors found me. When we reached the nearest Terillian planet, I was sent to my band where my aunt adopted me. My new mother and father, knowing the meaning in the name my father gave me, raised me to be a warrior. When I turned eleven, I joined one of our band's military societies. At fifteen, I was accepted into my nation's military academy and was selected for the Ino'ka or Badger society of the Scout Rangers when I was commissioned."

"That explains why you volunteered for the mission on Sierra 7."

The sound of Stone's voice caused Mori to look up quickly and take in a deep, slow breath. She quickly wiped at the track left by the tear that had fallen down her cheek. She looked back up from the fire with same determination in her eyes he had seen that night they first met.

"Yes. I will kill every slaver I see. I will not stop until there are no more. They are not human. They break families apart, commit atrocities against the innocent, and deserve to have their spirits roam forever, never finding comfort."

Stone did not know what to say. He felt for Mori. Furthermore, he somehow felt responsible. He knew there was nothing he had done himself but knew that it was a damning indictment of the complacent manner his society took toward everything that happened in the Dark Zone. They sat by the fire quietly staring into the flames.

Feeling the tension in the air weighting him down, Stone broke the silence.

"I am sorry for your loss. Despite everything you have become an honorable warrior, and despite what happens in the future between us or our peoples you have gained my respect."

Stone rose from the log where he was sitting and put his hand on her shoulder. She raised her head to look at him, her green eyes still moist from the pain of reliving the loss of her family.

"Thank you. I should not have been so weak. It's not appropriate."

"You have shown no weakness, Mori," consoled Stone. He had gotten much more than he had bargained for when he had tried to distract Mori from his ogling. He felt drained from her story; she had to be exhausted.

"It's late," he conceded. "We should probably call it a night."

Mori nodded her head in agreement.

Stone wasn't sure how it happened, but he felt closer to her than almost anyone he had known in his own society.

Stone extended a hand to her to help her get to her feet. As she stood, she placed her hands around his arms and looked up toward him.

"Tyler."

"Yes?"

She released him and stepped back. "You're right. It is late."

"We should call it a night."

They walked back to the small hut. Stone held open the door for Mori. As she stepped through the door, he placed his hand on her shoulder.

"I'm sorry."

***

For the first time since the battle on Juliet 3, Stone did not dream of the death of his friends. As he slept, he drifted back to the last night he had spent with Astra. He felt the softness of her hair, the moist sweetness of her kiss, and gentle touch of her hand. In his dreams he ran his hand through her hair and moved it from her face. As he did, he realized it was not Astra he was dreaming of but Mori. She looked into his eyes and spoke. "Tyler."

"Wake up! Colonel. Tyler. Wake up!"

He awoke to see Mori knelt down beside him. He raised his hand to her cheek.

"What are you doing?" asked Mori. As he came to, he could tell she was confused by his touch.

Now realizing he was no longer dreaming, Stone attempted to recover. "I was…it…"

"Whatever," she interrupted. "A slaver ship passed overhead. I can't believe you didn't hear it. We have to go."

"Why would slavers be here?"

"There's a small settlement a few kilometers from here. I came across it last week. I'm sure that's where they are going."

"What is your plan?"

"Kill them," answered Mori as she hurriedly strapped her sword to her waist and grabbed the few clips remaining for the assault rifle. "After we kill them then we can use their ship to get out of here."

Stone pondered the situation. Even in her determined quest for vengeance, Mori was right. It probably was the best chance to get off the planet. They would cross the bridge of who was whose prisoner when they came to it.

"Come on!" she shouted as she shot out of the hut.

"I'm coming!" Stone shouted back, half startled, half annoyed by her haste. He quickly picked up the pistol and shoved the extra clips in his pocket as he raced to catch Mori.

It was all he could do to keep her in sight as she sped through the dark forest, ducking limbs and jumping over felled trees. Stone, still trying to catch up, cursed as the branches Mori set in motion whipped him across the face.

Stone could tell he had lost a step while recovering from his injuries. They had only run about five kilometers, and he was starting to feel a burning in his lungs he usually only felt after about ten. Just as he was catching his second wind, Mori came to a sudden stop and knelt down. Stone was quickly at her side.

"There they are," she whispered, pointing to a rundown spacecraft on the outskirts of a small settlement. "Damn it. They have already gone through the houses. It looks like they are taking captives into that building over there."

Stone looked over the scene. There appeared to be ten or twelve slavers. They had already killed a few of the men in the settlement. Their bodies lay in the village square. Near the town square, two slavers held their weapons on a group of men herded from their homes.

"There are only two at the ship," said Stone. "We can take them out and be on the ship before the rest even know..."

He stopped when he saw the emotion on Mori's face. Now aware of her history, he knew that she would not leave the settlement to the mercy of stranded slavers. The old Colonel Lucius Stone would have, but Tyler Stone knew better. "I will take them out and then take up a position at back of the structures."

A woman's scream broke through the night air.

"You get the two at the ship and any that come out of the building," Mori ordered, obviously prompted to action by the scream. "Take the rifle," she said as she grabbed the pistol from Stone's hand and headed off into the darkness.

***

Stone quickly made his way to a group of bushes a few yards away from the ship. Not wanting to use the rifle until Mori had made her move, he placed it on the ground beside him and pulled his knife from his waist belt. Grabbing the knife by the blade, he hurled it toward the guard furthest from his position. The weapon found it target, striking the man in the neck.

The tactic worked. The second guard quickly turned to see his comrade fall. As he did, Stone leapt from the bushes. Hearing the noise, the man spun around to face the threat but was too slow. A solid kick to the side of the knee created a horrible snapping sound. As the man fell Stone grabbed his head and in one violent, rapid motion, snapped his neck. He quickly picked up the rifle and took up a position to cover Mori when she needed it.

***

Mori crouched low, using the shadows for cover as she passed between the small homes in the village. Moving quickly and quietly, she soon reached the building holding the captives. Three slavers stood guard outside. They laughed and joked but it could not drown out the cries from inside the walls. Mori saw a body of one of the men from the settlement just to her left. Placing her pistol in the back waist of her pants and sheathing her sword, she pulled the overcoat off the body.

Mori donned the overcoat. Walking in a slow, disheveled manner, she quietly made her way toward the slavers.

“Sounds like we may have found some good talent on this dust ball,” Mori overheard one of the slavers. The others laughed.

“I wish my watch would be up so I could get a taste before we lift off,” she overheard another say.

Their conversation was cut short by the rustling made by Mori as she approached. Mori noted guards placing their weapons at the ready and spread out in an attempt to encircle her position.

"Who is it? Come out now or I will open fire!" yelled one of the guards.

Mori slowly stepped from the shadows. She held her head down and took quick but uneasy steps, playing every bit the sheepish, frightened villager.

"Looky here, we may have found some entertainment of our own," said one of the guards as he stepped toward Mori and grabbed her by the hair.

"Galdar will want to know about her," said another.

"He will. When we're done with her," said the guard holding Mori's hair.

He pulled her hair backwards, drawing her head up towards the night sky. As he did, Mori quickly threw the overcoat off her shoulders and thrust the sword upward through the man's jaw. The sword penetrated to the hilt. Before the others could react she withdrew the sword and in one rapid swath cut the throats of the others standing next to her. The ground grew damp from their blood as she positioned herself at the window.

Mori wiped the blood from her sword onto her pants and held the blade to the window to see the reflection of the scene inside the room.

There were four slavers. Two were holding weapons on the women and children chained together in the far corner. Another hairy looking man with a large scar on his back was having his way with one of the women. It was her screams that Mori had heard. The fourth—a short, pudgy man—walked over to the group of chained women and children.

Mori felt sick to her stomach as the fourth man walked over to a girl, no more than thirteen, and unchained her. She kicked and screamed as the man pulled her by her hair to a desk near the center of the room.

"She looks a bit young," said one of the monsters.

"Young, but I think willing," said the short man as he pulled her hair, causing the frightened girl to look up at him. "Aren't you, sweetheart?"

The young girl kicked at his feet, but she was too small and weak. The man laughed and slapped her across the face.

"Well…" smiled the slaver. "Maybe not willing but by the time I am done with her she will be begging for more."

Mori wanted to vomit. She would not allow this to happen. Not again.

Mori pulled the pin on a flash grenade and rolled it into the center of the room.

The short slaver was the only one to recognize what had happened but could not cover his eyes in time. The grenade exploded, filling the room with a brilliant flash of light.

Mori rolled into the room and quickly came to her feet. Her first targets were the two men watching the group of captives.

The first slaver, still blinded, raised his rifle to fire blindly. Mori plunged her sword into his neck, severing his spinal cord.

The second guard had fallen to his knees with the explosion and was attempting to find his rifle, which he had dropped on the floor, when Mori struck. One powerful, swift motion separated his head from the rest of his body.

As the screams of the women and children filled the room, the slaver that had been assaulting the woman stood up, his trousers still on the ground. A slash of Mori's sword laid his stomach open and he fell to floor, screaming.

The final slaver released the young girl and reached for his pistol. Holding his other hand over his eyes, still stinging from the flash grenade, he heard Stone open fire in the distance, taking out the other slavers. Mori saw him stumbling clumsily backwards toward the corner of the room, waiving his pistol wildly.

"Marco, Salem, are you there? Who is there?!" he shouted nervously.

As the third slaver lay moaning on the floor, bleeding out, Mori moved to finish her task. She quickly knocked the pistol from his hand with a powerful kick. She then brought the tip of her sword to rest against the slavers throat.

"Your friends aren't here anymore," said Mori in a low steady voice.

Mori saw the slaver's eyes follow the bloody blade to its hilt and into her own gaze. Her green eyes burned through the man. She didn't realize her face was covered with the blood of the men now strewn across the room but it only added to the terror she could see on his face.

"I have money," replied the man, his deep gulp broken up by the pain caused by the tip of Mori's sword slightly puncturing the skin.

"Money," she snapped back. She could feel years of rage and loss well within her as she looked into the slaver's eyes.

"You son of a bitch. What was it you said to that little girl? *Before it's over you will be begging.*"

"No. Wai..."

The plea was cut short as Mori plunged the sword into the man's neck. Focusing her rage into her weapon, she brought the sword downward in on rapid, violent movement. The slaver's insides fell to the floor and blood sprayed over Mori's body as she lowered her sword to her side and stared at the eviscerated body.

***

Stone burst into the room.

"Mori, are you—" His voice froze as he looked over the scene in front of him.

Stone had seen many gruesome sights on the battlefield. He had killed men violently and in anger, but the scene in front of him surprised even the battle-hardened veteran. The men Mori had dispatched had not been killed; they had been butchered. The women, chained together, were silent in shock. The only sound was the victim of the hairy slaver, sobbing as she lay curled up on the floor.

"Are you okay?" Stone asked as he gathered himself.

Mori slowly turned and walked toward him dragging her sword along the floor.

"She was twelve. He was going to take Katalya..."

"Mori, it's over," he said as he walked to her.

He slowly raised his hands to her bloodstained face.

He looked deeply into her eyes. The tears Mori had fought to hold back the night before now began to flow freely. Tears cascaded down her face, creating small trails in the blood on her cheeks.

"She was just like my sister," she sobbed. "It will never stop until they are all dead."

Stone put a hand on the back of her head and pulled her to him. Stone felt Mori rest her face in his chest, her arms tucked between her chest and his. He could feel her taking deep breaths trying to calm herself. In an attempt to help her, he slowly ran his other hand over her hair.

"You've stopped them here, Mori, and saved all of these people. We can help them care for their wounded and leave in the morning. Your father would have been proud of what you've done to protect these people."

Stone felt Mori's breathing slow and her arms slide around his body. He looked down toward Mori. She was looking back toward him. He could see so much in her eyes. Looking back at her, he no longer saw a Terillian officer but a woman. His placed his hands over her face, brushing her hair aside. His eyes remained locked onto hers.

"Thank you! Thank you!" came a voice from behind them.

Stone and Mori, startled out of their embrace, quickly took a step back from each other.

"Thank you!" said the voice again.

Before them stood an older man, apparently the leader of the settlement, standing in the doorway.

"You're welcome," replied Stone. He looked back toward Mori. When he made eye contact with her, she quickly turned her head slightly away from him. He knew she had felt the same thing he felt when they had held each other.

"I am Victor Sinclair, elder of this settlement. You have saved our people," exclaimed the old man. "We will mourn those who the barbarians killed, but without you we all would have perished," he said has he aggressively shook Stone's hand. "All that we have is yours," stated Sinclair. "Just ask of us."

"That is not necessary," replied Stone as he watched Mori help a small child free of her chains. Mori looked back over her shoulder at Stone. This time a small smile came to her face before she turned her attention again to the child.

"If we could stay in your settlement tonight, we will be gone at first light," asked Stone.

"Hank Black's house is empty; he passed away a few months ago. There's not much in it but a bed and a bath. It's yours for the night if you wish," replied the old man.

"That would be more than adequate," replied Stone.

***

"Hank's place is not extravagant, nor is any place here, but it should suffice for the night. I hope it's to your liking," said Sinclair outside the small house as he fumbled nervously with the key card. "Ah, here we go," he said as the door finally slid open.

The main room held a bed, a small fireplace, and a kitchen. A shower and toilet room was connected to the main room. Other than a thin layer of dust, everything appeared to be in order. Mori and Stone both focused on the one bed in the center of the room.

"There is just one bed," replied Stone.

"Well...yes. I had assumed that...If the arrangement does not suit you?"

"This is fine," he replied as he looked toward Mori. "I will take some blankets and sleep on the floor over there."

"As you wish," said the old man, shrugging his shoulders slightly to show his confusion over Mori and Stone's relationship. "I have had a change of clothes placed on the bed for the lady."

Stone looked toward Mori, who had just realized that her clothes were still caked with the dried blood of the men she had slain. She held her hands out slightly from her body, unsettled that she had forgotten about the blood. "Thank you, sir," she said quietly.

"If that is all, I will leave you. Again, we can never repay you for saving our people," said Sinclair as he shook both of their hands again and left the two alone in the small house.

"It's not too bad," said Stone as he walked toward the bed. "Hell of a lot better than our little hut."

"Uh...yes," replied Mori, still distracted by the blood on her clothes.

"I guess we should get settled in," said Stone as he rolled out a small blanket and began to prepare his makeshift bed.

"I need to shower," said Mori as she picked up the clothing from the bed and darted into the bathroom.

Stone continued to work on his bedding as Mori showered. Tomorrow they would board the ship and return to reality. One of them would probably become a prisoner. The other would return to their duties and their lives. Either way, he knew he would never be the same.

Stone had just removed his shirt to lie down when Mori stepped out of the bathroom.

"I can't believe this is all they had for me to wear," stated an exasperated Mori.

Stone was taken aback. Mori was wearing a sand-colored dress that came down to her ankles. The dress was simple, common to women working the hard life on a small settlement such as this one. Her dark hair was still wet as she stood in front of Stone, tucking and pulling at the fabric. She was obviously uncomfortable in the dress. Stone doubted if she had ever worn a dress as an adult. He didn't care; she was beautiful.

"Why did they have to give me a dress?" she said again as she folded her arms over her chest, almost pouting.

"I think you look nice," replied Stone. "It might not be regulation issue, but you wear it well. Very well."

"Shut up," she said. "This is ridiculous. I am a soldier."

"Not in that," he laughed. "Besides, we can be soldiers tomorrow. Tonight let's get some sleep," he said as he fluffed a pile of shirts he had turned into a pillow.

"There is no reason to sleep in the floor. There is room for both of us on the bed. Just make sure you have control of your, ah..."

"I know..." replied Stone, still feeling he would never escape the incident on the pod.

Stone agreed and gathered his blanket off the floor. They both slowly climbed into the bed and lay flat on their backs, afraid to move. Finally Stone turned toward Mori and spoke.

"From the moment I first saw you, there was something about you...something I...I just don't quite understand but I know that the more I learn about you, the harder it is for me to see you as the enemy."

She turned her head toward him. "Thank you, Tyler. You have taught me that all Alpha Humani are not monsters. Whatever happens, at least on this planet, you have gained my respect and I can truly say that you are not my enemy."

As she finished, Mori rose slightly on her arm and leaned toward Stone. She placed her hand on his shoulder and lightly kissed him. She pulled away slightly but still looked into his eyes, her hand moving over his shoulder to his cheek. The touch of her lips was more than he could stand. He ran his hand through her hair.

"I have never met a woman like you before. I can't get you out of my mind."

"I have grown to have feelings for you as well, but..."

She was interrupted by his kiss. His hand held the back of her head, pulling her lips toward his. As he kissed her, he moved his hand down her back and pulled her body to him. She followed his lead, throwing her leg over his and rolling on top of him. She sat up, running her hands over his muscled chest.

"I have thought about this since I first saw you without your shirt in the prison barge," she whispered in his ear as she leaned forward again. She followed up her confession with a nibble on his ear.

Stone grew aroused as she straddled him. He quickly rolled her over and unbuckled his belt. As he did, she unzipped his pants and grabbed him firmly. Stone slid his hand between her thighs, causing her to moan in anticipation.

"Ty, make this night last forever," she said, looking up at him with those beautiful green eyes.

"I don't want to return. I can stay here with you," he said as he thrust his hips forward, entering her.

"Ty," whispered Mori as she wrapped her legs around his waist.

That night Stone slept better than he had in years with Mori's head resting on his chest and the troubles of their two peoples far from his thoughts.

***

Stone's blissful slumber was interrupted by the thundering sound of thrusters engaging. Stone quickly jumped from the bed and pulled on his trousers as Mori slid the dress over her head and shoulders. Grabbing the pistol on the way, Stone ran to the window of the house.

"Who is it?" asked Mori anxiously. "More slavers?"

Stone wiped the fog from the window and peered outside. A group of armed figures were talking to a small group of frightened villagers. As he squinted to focus, the uniform became identifiable through the streaks of the window. They were Xen troops. One of the settlers pointed toward the house where he and Mori were, and the officer directed the men to follow him to the house.

"Who is it?" Mori asked, gripping her sword tightly. Stone paused for a moment. She made the oddest sight—a beautiful woman in a white ruffled dress holding a Terillian Scout Ranger sword.

"Ty!"

"It's Humani regulars," he replied in a low voice, knowing what that meant for Mori.

"Then I am your prisoner," she replied, dropping her sword to the ground and walking toward him. "Do not feel bad, Ty," she said giving him a soft kiss and caressing his arm. "We knew this would happen sooner or later."

"They said it was over here," he heard the Xen officer yell to his men. "Take up positions while I take a look."

A quick look out the window confirmed it. Three soldiers were heading toward the door. Stone turned back toward Mori.

"Get back into bed," he said quickly.

"What?"

"Just do it."

"I don't understand...We agreed."

"Mori, just be quiet," he said as he grabbed her arms, almost shaking her. "Do you trust me?"

"Yes, but—"

"Just be quiet. Get into the bed and don't say anything."

Mori quickly jumped into bed and pulled the covers over her legs. As the soldiers knocked on the door she reached down, grabbing her sword and sliding it under the blankets.

"Open up in there! This is Lieutenant Maximus of the 15th Light Infantry. Open this door or it will be knocked down!"

Mori gripped her sword. She looked at Stone, her eyes screaming with uncertainty. He motioned for her to stay calm and then opened the door as the lieutenant reached to pound on the door once again.

"Yes, Lieutenant," replied Stone as he opened the door. "It's about time you found me."

"Who are you? We had a report of a slave ship and—" The lieutenant noticed the eagle crest tattoo overlaid by the numeral I. It identified him as an Elite Guard officer of the 1st Regiment. "Sorry, sir…I didn't know you…"

"That's okay, Lieutenant," interrupted Stone, ending the confused stumbling of the officer. "I am Colonel Lucius, Commander of the 25th Air Assault Regiment and late battalion commander of the Guard. I was captured when my regiment was overrun on Juliet 3. I escaped from my prison barge and have been living here for the last few weeks."

"Sir," responded the amazed lieutenant. "We heard you were dead. Your regiment's gallant stand was honored in the Senate as one of our people's finest hours. Your defense and General Tacitus's skillful use of manpower resulted in a Terillian Grand Fleet being pulled from the Sierra system, allowing us to take Sierra 7."

Stone felt sick to his stomach. Cataline had escaped justice yet again. He would make sure the coward's crimes were heard. Now was not the time, however.

"Who is the woman?" asked the lieutenant as he looked over Stone's shoulder into the small room. "The settlers tell us she helped save them from slavers. Is she another survivor from your unit?"

Stone looked back at Mori. She said nothing only stared back at him.

"She is a villager from another small settlement. I was injured and she helped me regain my strength."

"The villagers tell me she killed several of the slavers herself. I wouldn't have expected that from a—"

"Lieutenant," snapped Stone, "I am a Colonel of the Line from the Lucius family, soon to be a husband of the Varus line…" He paused, realizing for the first time in weeks that he had a fiancée and had not told this to Mori. He quickly looked in her direction. Mori lowered her head, refusing to look at him. Stone continued, "I do not have time for these questions."

"Yes, sir. I meant no disrespect. I will gather the men and we shall lift off when you are ready. My platoon is detached to the battle frigate *Rubicon* in low orbit. Once aboard, I am sure we will get you back home to the Lady Astra as soon as possible."

The officer saluted and turned toward his men. As Stone shut the door he looked over to Mori.

"Astra…it's complicated," said Mori echoing their discussion in the hut weeks ago.

"I am sorry I never told you about my engagement. I never thought I would fall in…have feelings for you like this…I did not mean to hurt you."

"Ty, I understand. You must return to your world. I cannot expect you to do anything else. At least you didn't have them take me prisoner."

He walked over to the bed and sat beside her. He squeezed her hand hard. "I would not allow that to happen. Mori, I have never felt like this with anyone."

"I know, Ty, but reality has found us. And we must return to it."

As he looked at her, he felt the warmth of his tears as they trickled over his cheeks and fell from his face. How could it be that in a few weeks' time, he had been so completely transformed by a woman he would now never see again unless opposing each other on the battlefield?

"I will make sure the slaver's ship is left so that you can return to your people," he continued as he leaned in and kissed her one last time. "I will always remember you."

With that he rose, wiped his face dry, and walked from the room to return to the society he was no longer sure he understood.

Chapter 11

Sitting in his stateroom onboard the *Rubicon,* Stone looked through the viewing window as the ship made its approach to *Lucius.* Stone looked beyond *Lucius* into the vastness of space and wondered how he had come to this place and pondered his existence in a suddenly confusing world.

Aside from the deeper questions, Stone was beset by ridiculously miniscule items. Astra had bombarded him with comm links. *Father would like you to...Father said it would be good to...There is a ceremony for this...a dinner for that...*

He had replied to most of Astra's communications but he was finding each one more difficult. A loveless marriage was okay when he did not know any better, but now that he had been with Mori the whole idea of his arranged marriage made his stomach turn and his head hurt. As he struggled with his personal demons, he played audio of the last comm link he had received from Astra.

"You are set to arrive on Alpha Humana in one month. Upon arrival you and I will be escorted by my father to the Senate, where the ProConsul is to award you the Imperial Medal of Bravery. Afterwards we will be the guests of honor at a dinner hosted by Field Marshall Maximilus Burto. Things are coming together wonderfully, Tyler. I have also received word that a dinner is being planned for you onboard Lucius when you arrive. I shall be there to greet you and welcome you properly."

Stone shut off the comms link. He realized he now longed for the days when he was a young lieutenant, immersed in a mission and unaware of the duality of the world.

But that time had long passed.

***

When Stone arrived onboard *Lucius* it was a circus.

Given full military honors when his shuttle arrived, Stone passed through a row of sideboys, which lined his path toward the exit of the hangar. At the end of the procession were Admiral Sequentius and Colonel Vatarus. As Stone exited the row of sharply dressed sideboys, Colonel Vatarus stepped forward to greet him.

"I wouldn't have thought it was true," exclaimed Vatarus. "We thought you were dead. I am glad to see you, Stone. Your bravery and sacrifice honors us all."

Stone's thoughts wondered back to Juliet 3 and the death of Martin and Jackson.

"It was my men and their sacrifice that deserve the honor, Vatarus," replied Stone.

"Yes. Of course," responded Vatarus. "But with their bravery under your leadership and General—"

"Where's our brigadier?" blurted Stone, his contempt obvious.

"Well, Colonel," added Vatarus, showing his trepidation. "He thought it best to wait until dinner to greet you. He is attending to some administrative duties currently, but he said he is looking forward to speaking with you tonight."

"I'm sure he is. How did that coward keep his command?"

"Walk with me, Colonel," offered Vatarus as he gently put his hand on Stone's back. "We shouldn't discuss these things in public."

As soon as they cleared the throng of greeters, Vatarus continued.

"You had the worst of it on J3 but it was pretty bad everywhere. As you had feared the Terillians had a full division on the planet, not to mention Nero's men. They were prepared for us. It was a close call."

"A close call! My regiment was destroyed."

"I understand, Colonel," replied Vatarus as he stopped dead in his tracks. "Do not forget I lost my cousin on that damned planet."

Vatarus pulled Stone into a corner of the passageway for more privacy.

"You know how these things work," Vatarus added. "Your unit was destroyed and the entire force suffered heavy casualties but we inflicted even more, mostly due to the bravery and sacrifice of your men. That fleet that arrived while we were being evacuated came from the Sierra system and allowed our forces to gain the edge in that sector, which is more important politically due to its proximity to the Gateway compared to the Juliet system."

"Politically, we could make up for the loss of minerals from the Sierra system a lot easier than we can reroute major trade and transportation lines—"

"I know....and so does every other officer with half a brain. You know as well as I do that politics sometimes drives military decisions in war and sometimes to the detriment of common sense. That is the reason *our brigadier* remains in command. His friends at High Command overlooked the operation since it resulted in us gaining dominance in the Sierra system."

"You know as well as I do that he will cost more lives the next time he leads men into battle. Just like your Atticus."

"That is our fate—and our duty. Atticus understood this. Besides, if you're lucky you will get assigned a new regiment far from Tacitus."

"I hope so. I will not serve under him again," he stated. "You are a good soldier, Vatarus. How do you put up with this political crap?"

"I have to. It may not be a perfect system but our civilization relies on it. Without our system, what would maintain order?"

"What if we valued people only on their merit and not what family they were from?"

"What happened to you on that planet?" asked Vatarus, puzzled by Stone's proposal. "This is the way things have been for generations and our people have made great strides since 'The Meeting.' Would you want us to return to the chaotic and destructive days of religious wars? Our system is necessary."

"I just wonder sometimes."

"You should not speak of this again. It would not be taken well," warned Vatarus as he placed his hands on Stone's arms. "You should just make nice at the dinner tonight and let your people honor you as the hero you are. Besides, I'm sure Lady Astra will take your mind off such silly thoughts," he said with a sly smile as he released Stone and stepped toward the main passageway. "Come on," said Vatarus, motioning for Stone to join him. "One evening with your fiancée and you will forget all of this nonsense."

"My fiancée," sighed Stone as he placed his hand on Vatarus's shoulder. "Just what I need," he said hoping his sarcasm wasn't too obvious. "Thanks for the talk, Colonel," Stone said as he stepped away from a confused Vatarus and headed to his stateroom.

After a short walk, Stone reached his stateroom.

He entered his room and loosened his uniform. It was so confining. Removing it did little good, as it was not the clothing that was suffocating him. With every moment among his people, he felt more isolated.

"The Lady Astra," Stone said out loud. "Well at least she won't be here for a few hours."

Suddenly exhausted from the day, not to mention the upcoming festivities involved with dinner, Stone decided to steal a quick nap. Pulling his shirt the rest of the way off, kicking off his boots, and removing his trousers, he settled in for quick nap.

As he slept, Stone drifted into a dream. He was back in that little house with Mori. Stone remembered the way she smelled, the feel of her hair against his body, the taste of her lips. He felt the weight of her on top of him and sensed her moving in rhythm with him. His pace quickened and he felt the pressure build and the forceful but calming release. Suddenly he awoke to a voice.

"I hope you liked your wakeup call, Colonel."

It was Astra. She had entered his room while he slept. Although dreaming of Mori, he had been with Astra.

"What are you doing in here?" he demanded.

He felt strangely violated and squirmed his way out from under Astra, jumping out of the bed and quickly reaching for his trousers.

"What the hell do you mean?" she snipped. "What is wrong with you?"

"I wasn't even awake and you just took—"

"How dare you!" she shot back before he could finish. "Do you know how many men would kill to be with me?"

"I know one that won't tonight!"

"You son of a bitch!" she retorted as she quickly rose from the bed. "I heard that you were found with a little indigenous slut on that planet. For the good of our families I have decided to overlook your lack of discretion but will not tolerate refusal. No one *has or will* refuse me."

"How do you know of her?" he asked, shocked that anyone knew. He then remembered whom he was talking to. "Never mind. I have a lot of things on my mind and just want to be alone to sort some things out."

"Don't worry, Tyler. You will be left alone...until the dinner tonight. There you will escort me to our table and we will smile and laugh and do everything else that is expected of us. We will marry as arranged also. As for us, our feelings do not matter. I had told my father you were from poor stock but he insisted the marriage would benefit our family. So we will marry, for the family, and I will give birth to a male descendant. Other than social and reproductive requirements, I do not care what you do or whom you do it with. Goodbye for now...*darling*," she snapped as she turned and walked out of his stateroom.

The venom from the word *darling* hung in the air for a few seconds after the door closed. Stone, still wondering exactly what had happened, sat back down on the edge of the bed and took a deep breath. *Dinner is going to be fun*, Stone thought.

***

As Stone walked toward the head table, he could feel Astra squeezing his hand as if she was trying to rip it off. He knew she was angry, but she wouldn't let it show to anyone but him. He expected a long evening of her hiding her anger underneath a cloak of strategic smiles and well-placed compliments.

"Colonel Lucius, Lady Lucius Varus, welcome," said Colonel Vatarus as he rose from his seat. "My wife regrets she could not attend."

"Her company is dearly missed," replied Astra in a blatant lie.

"I am so pleased to see you again, Colonel Lucius," added Colonel Neo.

The beautiful woman standing beside Neo gave him a quick nudge.

"Oh yes," stammered Neo. "You remember the Lady Ophelia. We have recently become engaged."

Ophelia seemed much more polished than the last time Stone had seen her. No longer the wide eyed woman-child of a few months ago, she stood confidently across from Neo, who was still the same nervous boy.

"Lady Astra, what a pleasure to see you again," said Ophelia, taking the conversation over from Neo. "My father was very impressed with Senator Varus's speech before the Forum Thursday last. He was especially moved by his argument for strict adherence to societal systems and structure during the coming conflict."

"Thank you, Ophelia," replied Astra. "It is true that during trying times such as these it is imperative that we hold true to the fundamental beliefs of our society. It is the structure and order of our civilization that will lead us to victory. It is our duty to ensure that everyone knows their duty and their place," said added throwing a cold look at Stone.

"Lady Astra, your seat," replied Stone as he held her chair out for her.

"Of course, *darling*."

Astra positioned herself in front of the chair and pulled the length of her dress in to allow Stone to tuck her into the chair.

"My Lady," said Stone as he pushed the chair forward, almost knocking Astra off balance. She again shot daggers at him with her eyes as he took his seat.

"Oh. Here comes Brigadier Tacitus," exclaimed Ophelia as she again rose to her feet.

Cataline strode toward the table in all of his arrogant glory with his sycophant aide in tow. Astra, already standing, reached back and grabbed at Stone's shoulder in an attempt to make him rise. Another piercing glance and he slowly began to stand.

"Good evening, General," said Vatarus in a flat but not overtly insolent manner.

"Sir," added Neo.

"As always, General, it is a pleasure," included Ophelia with a courtesy.

"General Tacitus," spoke Astra, "my father sends his greetings."

Stone remained silent as he glowered at the general. Astra's fingers digging into his palm did nothing.

"It's good to see you all again," Cataline spoke. "As always the dinner is always much sweeter when we are joined by such beautiful company," he complimented as he looked toward the ladies. "It is also good to have all of my commanders together again." After a slight pause, he continued. "Let the dinner begin."

Cataline took his place and ordered the first course. With his order, several dozen servants entered the room carrying covered dishes. As was customary, the head table received the first plates. Once all attendees had a dish in front of them, Cataline raised his glass—the signal for the servants to remove the covers.

A low rumble came over the banquet hall.

Cataline had spared no expense for the dinner. Nepalan greens, almost more valuable than titanium, made the foundation of the course. Covering the greens were assorted exotic fruits from throughout the Empire, including a few that could only have been obtained through the black market. The entire dish was covered with a brilliant red sauce.

"This is a wonderful setting," spoke Ophelia. "I feel as if I am dining at the 150 Consortium in Mt. Castra. It is marvelous."

"Very well done," added Astra. "Your superb choice of first course has only piqued my interest in the disclosure of the others."

"I am sure you will find the dinner *very* entertaining, to say the least," replied Cataline as he cast another odd glance toward Stone, who was mechanically eating the fruits.

Stone returned the glance as he chewed his food like it was leather.

"Yes, General," added Stone speaking his first words of the dinner. "Perhaps you should have become a chef instead of joining the military."

"General," Astra quickly spoke, "I believe Tyler is trying to say the course is magnificent." Stone felt Astra forcefully kick his shin but he ignored her.

"I am sure that is what he meant," replied Cataline, still smiling at Stone. "Enough about the food. I have a bit of news that may surprise our prodigal son."

Stone had already finished the fruit and was now chewing the greens like a grazing animal in the field. "I would love to hear any news you have, *sir*."

"Thank you, Colonel. I am sure you will find this very interesting. It appears that you were not alone while you were stranded on that desolate planet."

Stone stopped chewing. "What do you mean?"

"It appears a Terillian Scout Ranger was also stranded there."

Stone turned toward Astra, who returned his stare with a false smile. "That is very interesting, General," she added. "Do tell us more," she said, as she delicately placed another piece of fruit in her mouth.

"It appears that she also escaped from the prison barge you were held captive on. I am surprised you did not have contact with her as she was captured in the same area that you were found."

"Captured? How? Where was the enemy captured?" Stone could feel his stomach drop and sweat began to bead on his forehead.

"Oddly enough she was captured just outside the settlement where you were rescued. She apparently was trying to escape in a slaver ship...put up a hell of a fight before she was caught. The report says she killed four of our men and injured several others."

"Where has she been taken?" asked Stone, trying to not give himself away completely.

"No need to worry about her. She has been taken to the prison on Capro. If she has any information, we will find it out."

"Capro," gasped Astra playing up her surprise. "What a horrible place." She placed her hand on Stone's in a feigned attempt at shock.

"What is Capro?" asked an inquisitive and unaware Lady Ophelia.

Colonel Vatarus elaborated. "Capro is where our most dangerous prisoners are sent. Over 95 percent of its surface is covered with a vast ocean of sulfuric acid. The few outcroppings of land are harsh granite plains with high bluffs rising above the acidic water below. The atmosphere is deadly; a few seconds of the toxic air will turn lungs to liquid."

"How awful," said Ophelia. "How does anyone survive?"

"The prison itself is the old battle cruiser *Romulus Nextus*," explained Cataline. "When the Senate passed the Punitive Directive Decree fifty-seven years ago, *Romulus* was decommissioned and configured for use as a special purpose prison. Key military captives are transferred to Capro for interrogation, and other criminals such as rapists, traitors, and high profile murderers, as determined by the regional magistrates, are 'spared' death for a life of punitive rehabilitation at the hands of the highly skilled prison guards."

Stone felt sick. Capro was the worst of the worst of Humani military prisons. Mori would have been better off dead.

"And you say it was a woman," asked Astra again. Stone could see through her façade. He knew she was involved somehow.

"Yes, and apparently a very attractive one," answered Cataline.

"How shocking!" added Ophelia. "Terillians truly are barbarians. A woman, you say."

"Oh, it was no woman," interrupted Astra. "More like a savage beast. The Terillians must be concerned if they are putting females in uniforms. I don't understand why we allow our own lower class women to serve either; it's so ghastly and repulsive."

She took another bite of her fruit and looked at Stone with her galling smile.

"What do you think, darling?" she posed to Stone.

Stone wanted to slap her for the obvious jab at his dead friend Martin. Before he could formulate an answer, Cataline spoke again.

"That is an interesting question," returned Cataline. "There has been some discussion among High Command about that. Even though we need more recruits, the idea of halting female service has been discussed...partially due to the Sierra 7 operation."

"What do you mean?" asked Stone. He was fighting to hold himself together.

"Well some people believe you may have been better served by having a male officer filling Captain Martin's position."

"What the hell does that mean?" shot back Stone.

"Well," replied Cataline as he dabbed his napkin to the side of his mouth. "Perhaps a more skilled operations officer would have provided better communications between your unit and my command on *Lucius*. Actually, Senate has considered lowering the status of her family."

Stone could contain himself no longer. He sprang from his chair. The attention of the entire banquet room focused on Stone as he began to shout.

"Captain Martin was a brave officer and gave her life in service of our people. She died because the idiots at High Command placed an incompetent fool in charge of the brigade. It's your ineptitude that caused the massacre of my regiment."

"Stone, wait!" implored Vatarus.

"No…I can hold my tongue no longer. You, not the Terillians, are the cause for my men's death. Not only did you sign their death warrant by failing to support us but you showed yourself for the coward you are by refusing to come down to the planet!"

"Enough!" yelled Cataline. "You have displayed gross disrespect for your commanding officer for the last time. I order you placed under arrest for disrespect and challenging the honor of a superior officer."

"I have not even begun to disrespect you!" shouted Stone.

Stone moved quickly toward the general. In one swift movement he intertwined his right arm through Cataline's with his hand over his throat—a move that immediately deprived the general of air. Gasps spread through the room. Cataline's aid attempted to draw his weapon on Stone. With his free hand, Stone quickly disarmed him and wrenched his wrist, driving him to his knees. The general's face began to grow red as he struggled for air, his arms uselessly trying to pry loose Stone's death grip.

"Tyler!" shouted Astra. "What are you doing?" She also tried to pull him off Cataline.

The strategic attack on his dead friend and news of Mori's capture had unleashed Stone's demons. Nothing existed for Stone but Cataline's throat and his fingers wrapped around it. The general's face shifted from red to a pale blue as his struggling subsided and his body weakened.

Just as Stone was prepared to see Cataline fade into nothingness, a sudden sting on his back broke his concentration. He recovered quickly but there was another. And another. Security teams had arrived with stun sticks.

"Release the general!" shouted the security team leader over the pleas of Astra and Vatarus and the gasps of other attendees.

Stone tried to maintain his death grip but the shocks took their toll. His hold on Cataline soon weakened and his consciousness faded.

Chapter 12

The hard, cool surface of the cell floor felt soothing to Stone's aching body. His head throbbed and his back burned from the stun stick wounds. Grasping the bars with his hands, he struggled to pull his body erect. His muscles ached from the repetitive shocks. Still hazy, he tried to work out the cobwebs and come to grips with what he had done. As he thought, he rested his head on the bars.

"I cannot believe what you have done!" came a cold voice from the other side of the bars. The comment was followed by a cold burst of fluid splashing over his face as Astra threw a pitcher of water at the bars. As the droplets of water slowly ran down his face, it was as if the splash of water had cleansed him of any illusions about Astra's—and his society's—true character.

"You low-bred animal!" she spat. "You have ruined everything. I cannot recover from this. Our family took a chance on you and you have ruined us. Not only did you betray me with that Terillian bitch, you have ruined yourself and damaged my family's name. I am contacting Father and will see you reduced to private and sent to the most remote post in the Empire, if you are lucky. Better yet, maybe you can join your little whore on Capro."

"That may not be necessary, Lady Astra."

Another voice stopped Astra's tirade. It was Cataline.

"If you agree," he inquired. "I would like to discuss some options with you." As he spoke, he motioned for Astra to move away from Stone's cell.

Stone watched as the two began speaking in hushed voices. At first Astra seemed surprised, but she soon looked deep in thought. Stone overheard only small pieces of the conversation.

"Are you crazy?" asked Astra. "He is an elite guard officer. He would—"

Cataline stopped Astra and whispered into her ear.

"Do you think it will work?" replied Astra. "I will need to inform Father but the proposal makes good political sense."

"Yes, Lady Astra. It would be an excellent political move," said Cataline as he ran his hand over her shoulder and down her arm.

Astra smiled. "I will contact Father. We have an agreement."

Astra walked back Stone's cell. "I can't wait to see you reap the fate you deserve…low class scum."

To make her point she spat into his face.

"Enjoy the final moments of your pathetic existence," she said as she walked out of the brig.

Wiping the spit from his face Stone looked toward Cataline, who was now standing near the bars of his cell.

"You are lucky, coward," said Stone. "A few more seconds and I would have succeeded in squeezing the life from your miserable body."

"You almost succeeded, Stone, but came up a little short. I thought for a minute my plans had been for naught."

"Plans? What are you talking about?"

"No harm in telling you now, now that you have played right into my hands. I knew if I pushed you enough, your self-righteous nature would do you in."

"What the hell are you talking about?" asked Stone as he rubbed his head, still woozy from the shock sticks.

Cataline leaned in toward Stone and in almost a whisper, spoke. "I figured a few comments about your Terillian slut and your dear, dead Captain Martin would force you to make a rash decision."

Stone grabbed for him but the general pulled away just in time.

"Still so aggressive," taunted Cataline. "And foolish. You have openly disrespected a superior officer from a First Family. Regardless of your fame, that will not be tolerated."

"So your plan was to get me to try to kill you?"

"Oh, it is so much more. There will be no relegation to a remote station for you. I intend to challenge you to proporia combata."

"Then you are a fool and I'll have my revenge yet," replied Stone, not believing Cataline would be that stupid.

"Maybe if you were in any condition to fight," replied Cataline as his mouth turned upward in an ambiguous smile.

"You truly are a coward," Stone paused. "If you are the best our society has to offer, the sooner the Terillians conquer us, the better."

"...and traitorous too," replied Cataline. "Maybe I am a coward, but I am not a fool. I will challenge you in public for questioning my honor. Once I have killed you, there will be no more questions of my bravery or skill with a sword and under the code of proporia combata I will have all of your possessions, including the Lady Astra."

"Astra?"

"She has agreed to allow the challenge to include marital rights. It seems the Varus family has grown tired of the novelty of marrying a virtual commoner. Apparently your tendency to not know your place and your dalliances with enemy whores has not endeared you to her."

"She is no whore."

"She really must have been something, Stone. I understand having your way with her. I hear she is quite attractive."

"You are a bastard," replied Stone matter-of-factly.

"Me," laughed Cataline. "Your black sheep branch of the Lucius family tarnished that family for eternity when your ancestor spread her legs for that commoner, and now you have bedded the enemy. It appears treachery and propensity for low-class bloodlines runs in your blood."

"At least we are not a family of cowards and military fools."

"You know," replied Cataline, "I thought about having you shipped to Capro, or even better sent to the Navato System for alteration, but I am going to enjoy gutting you in person."

Cataline had given something up. Stone remembered Mori talking about the Navato System, something was going on there.

"Navato?" asked Stone.

"I had figured your Terillian whore might have mentioned Navato to you. We knew they had found about the operations in the Navato region and our support of the slavers."

"What is going on there?"

The general leaned in again, this time placing his hands over Stone's as he gripped the bars. "Better to have those wretches in the Dark Zone or Terillian religious fanatics be slaves

to the Xen than us. All we need to do is continue to fight and conquer and we will be spared."

"Spared?" asked Stone, his confusion showing.

"Do you think the little problem at Gateway Station was really a Terillian attack? It was all part of our plan to draw Alpha Humana into war," said Cataline. "We needed to start the war in order to increase our number of prisoners and expand the operation of slavers."

Stone stepped back from the bars in shock. Mori was right. It had all been a lie.

"You could have been a part of it too," continued Cataline. "You were set to marry into one of the best families. But now you will die a traitor and a fool and your Terillian bitch will rot in prison, be whored out in the Dark Zone, or maybe even be genetically altered and sent to the Xen."

"Altered?"

"I would love to tell you more, Stone, but I have to prepare for our fight."

Cataline started to walk away, but then turned and walked back to Stone's cell.

"In case you are wondering," added Cataline, "it's true, there's no way I would face you in open combat without a little edge."

"What are you talking about?" asked Stone, still coming to grips with his world being turned upside down.

"That something special I had added to your salad, a little extract from the Hiato leaf, should have you feeling very, very relaxed, when we face each other again," ended Cataline with a treacherous smile. "I will see you soon...Colonel."

***

The banquet hall had been transformed. A large oval area had been cleared in the center of the room. The seating had been reorganized to allow viewing of the individual combat. Word had spread fast, and the hall was filled with the social elite onboard *Lucius.* At one end of the oval stood Cataline, seconded by his aide. The aide held the general's sword in his good hand, Stone having broken the other earlier. Astra sat at a chair midway between the two ends. As part of the property, she would go to the winner. She gave a quick glance and a smile to Cataline and cold glare to Stone, standing across the oval from the general.

Admiral Sequentius stepped to the center of the oval and spoke.

"This proporia combata has been duly called for and accepted. General Cataline Tacitus has challenged Colonel Tyler Lucius for questions of honor. Additionally, the Lady Astra Varus has allowed the proporia to include herself."

After the opening statement, he motioned for the combatants and their seconds to move to the center of the oval.

The men met. Stone stared blankly at Cataline, who, after looking across to Astra, gave a sly smile at Stone. Sequentius continued.

"Colonel Lucius, do you choose to amend your comments or ask for clemency for your actions?"

"I do not. I again state that this man is a coward, a fool, and a traitor to the Humani people."

Cataline's smile disappeared, replaced with an angry scowl. Sequentius sighed and again continued.

"Do you, General Cataline Tacitus, openly and publicly in presence of your peers maintain your challenge to these statements and your request for proporia combata?"

"I do."

"Let it be known that both men—one of the Tacitus lineage, one of the Lucius—do openly agree to proporia combata. Furthermore, let it be understood that no mercy shall be given except at the wishes of the victor."

Both men bowed to Sequentius in acknowledgment. Cataline took his sword from his aide and began swinging it about, testing its balance and feel. He returned it to his aide and began removing his shirt.

Stone did not need to "get a feel" for his sword. It was part of him. Stone removed his shirt, his eyes locked on the general. Once removed, he handed his shirt to Vatarus in exchange for his sword.

"Thank you for agreeing to be my second," said Stone to Vatarus, his gaze still locked on Cataline. "You are a good man and I am sorry you have been deceived just as I have, just as all of us have."

"Do not thank me, Stone," responded Vatarus. "I do not understand any of this. You have broken rules of military etiquette and challenged our social structure. You are a brave soldier, Colonel, but you are a fool. Cataline is an even bigger fool for challenging you. This is all very disturbing."

"Our society is a lie," Stone replied to Vatarus as he walked toward Cataline, already at the center mark of the oval.

Stone stopped a meter away from the general, looked toward Sequentius, and brought his sword out to his side at a 45-degree angle, acknowledging his readiness.

"To the death," spoke Cataline.

"To the death," replied Stone and it began.

Cataline made an instant rush toward Stone, his sword held clumsily over his head. In a giant downward sweeping motion, he brought his sword at Stone. Quickly sidestepping his way clear of the amateur move, Stone grabbed the general's sword hand with his left and brought his other arm, still holding his sword in hand, around Cataline's neck, immobilizing him. He leaned into the general's ear.

As Cataline struggled to break free, Stone spoke.

"Now my turn to tell you a secret, *General.* When my Terillian 'whore' saved me from my injuries, she used hiato leaves to dull my pain. It appears I have gained quite a tolerance."

Stone paused to let those words sink in, then continued. "It's too bad your plate did not have a little, for you will soon be in great pain, but I will also end that for you quickly enough…well, not too quickly."

After his revelation, he gave a quick jerk to Cataline's arm and neck, throwing him to the ground.

Stone circled Cataline, looking toward the audience. They looked as if they were watching a sporting event or an opera. *This is the society I have fought for?* he thought.

Cataline stumbled away from Stone, trying to regain his footing. The fear on his face was evident. He looked around the room as if there was some magical reprieve, if only he could find it.

Stone continued to circle his prey.

"Why do you not attack, coward!" taunted Stone. "These fine citizens and ladies have come to be entertained. Why do you not attack?"

Cataline frantically looked around the hall. A few people began to point and whisper to one another. He looked at Astra. Eagerness and impatience filled her face as she looked toward him and then motioned toward Stone with her head. With nowhere to hide, Cataline finally charged.

Thrashing wildly toward Stone's torso, the general lost his balance. Stone parried the attack, again knocking Cataline's sword to the ground. Stone grasped his opponent's extended arm and brought his elbow against the general's temple. There was no time for Cataline to react to the jarring blow before Stone spun the other direction, bringing his foot against Cataline's jaw. Stone continued forward with the motion of his foot, walking away from his opponent as Cataline crashed to the floor.

Cataline slowly rolled over to his hands and knees. Blood drooled from his mouth as he reached for his sword and regained his feet.

Stone turned back toward his foe and motioned for Cataline to advance again.

"Come on, General. Come win your prize." Stone taunted as he looked directly at Astra. He could see in her eyes she was surprised but was trying to develop contingencies for herself regardless of the winner.

Cataline thrust his sword forward at Stone's waist. Stone again moved out of the way, allowing the general to move past him. As he did, Stone brought his foot against the side of Cataline's knee. The sound of snapping ligaments and tendons was followed by a screech of agony and mumbling of the crowd. As the general grabbed for his knee, Stone again circled.

"Come, General, we must give a better show...Alpha Humana's finest families are here to be entertained."

He looked over to Astra. Things were not going as planned and Stone could see her mind racing, trying to decide how to profit from either the outcome.

"Is the magnificent Lady Astra not worthy of a better match?"

While Stone was taunting the crowd, Cataline had crawled toward his aide. Out of the corner of his eye, Stone saw the aide reach for his pistol.

The aide's pistol was only a few inches out of his holster when before Stone was upon him. His body launched forward as Stone's sword plunged into his abdomen. Letting out a grunt, his pistol dropped to the ground. Stone turned away from the aide, and with a twist withdrew his sword.

Cataline, who was only a few feet away and still on his hands and knees, turned and retreated from Stone.

"Is this how you demonstrate your bravery, General?" asked Stone.

"How awful," said a lady to her husband sitting just outside the oval. "Shouldn't someone stop him?"

Stone overheard the lady and turned toward her. "Stop me?" he asked. "Why, Lady

Vena, is this not what you came to see? The pride of our people locked in honorable

single combat?"

Lady Vena buried her head in her husband's shoulder.

“Colonel Lucius, please,” begged her husband, a senior major. “This has gone on long enough and you have proven yourself.”

“I agree,” spat Stone. “It *has* gone on long enough.”

Stone then turned back toward his advisory. “Where are you going?” taunted Stone again.

Cataline had retreated to the wall at the edge of the oval and pulled himself to his feet. Stone moved over toward the general’s sword, still lying in the center of the oval. A flip of his foot sent the sword skidding across the room to its owner’s feet.

“I submit!” shouted Cataline, refusing to pick up the sword.

“To the death, General. Do you remember? Mercy is at my discretion. Perhaps if the Lady Astra asks for pity.”

He looked toward Astra. Stone knew what her response would be; he only wanted validation. The political wheels turning, she pondered the outcomes.

“Do as you prefer, my affianced,” was her reply.

“So be it, *darling*,” replied Stone, ensuring she saw his disgust before he turned away from her.

“At least die with some honor,” he said as he returned his attention to Cataline, still refusing to wield his sword. “Maybe you will find your courage if I am unarmed.”

Stone tossed his sword toward Colonel Vatarus’s feet.

“Let him live,” pleaded Vatarus. “He is ruined and you are vindicated. Nothing further is to be gained.”

“A family member of yours died because of that bastard, or have you forgotten?” replied Stone.

Vatarus stepped toward Stone. "I have not forgotten, nor will I ever. His shame will be revenge enough."

"Not for me."

Vatarus's attention was drawn to movement behind Stone. "Look out," he warned, as Cataline had found the courage to attack an unarmed man from behind.

Stone pivoted toward the oval and quickly angled his back toward the floor as the general's sword passed by his chest, leaving a small gash.

The slight wound did not distract Stone. Cataline, again off balance and staggering to regain control on one good leg, turned back toward Stone.

As he did, Stone took his opponent's arm and wrenched it upward. In a powerful downward motion, Stone brought his other elbow down against the general's extended arm. Cataline's arm snapped, and Stone snatched the sword from the broken limb. Taking control of the sword, he pivoted his waist and thrust. Cataline let out an ear-piercing shriek as his own sword entered his back and protruded through his chest just below the sternum. Stone drove the sword into him until the hilt pressed against the general's spine.

Stone leaned down toward Cataline.

"You had better hope the Terillians are wrong and there is no afterlife, for if there is I will someday follow you there," Stone whispered into Cataline's ear.

His promise was punctuated by a rapid outward thrust of the sword. The general's scream echoed through the hall as the sword exited his side, laying open his right torso. Stone heard a "Lady" cry out in horror as the general fell to his knees and his bowels spilled onto the floor.

As the sword cut its way free of the body, Stone brought the blade over his shoulder. With a yell of anguish and frustration, he swept the sword back across the general's body, making contact just above his jaw. The blade was strong and Stone's rage provided enough force to pass through the skull in one rapid, violent swath. The audience gasp as Cataline's mangled body fell to the floor.

"Is this not what you came to see?" challenged Stone as he pointed to the decapitated corpse still spilling blood onto the dining hall floor. "Is this not what makes us superior?"

Stone threw the sword to the ground and walked over to Vatarus, who was visibly shaken by the ferocity and brutality he had witnessed.

"Congratulations, uh, General," said the horror-struck colonel.

Stone took his sword from Vatarus's hand. "Our civilization is not structured and ordered," he said quietly to Vatarus as he pointed toward Cataline's corpse. "We, not the Terillians, are the savages."

Once again turning toward the mangled body lying on the floor, he addressed the shocked crowd.

"We are not structured and ordered," he shouted. "*This* is what we are...violent, malicious, and unforgiving."

Stone turned and walked away from the horror he had created.

"Well done, Tyler," said Astra as she stepped in front of Stone, blocking his escape. "You have defended your name and regained my favor. Not only have you gained a generalship through proporia combata, but you now own all of General Tacitus's holdings—his estate, his slaves. Father will be pleased with the new acquisition of…"

Stone stared blankly at Astra and then turned to the audience.

"I wanted nothing from *General* Tacitus other than his life," he snapped. "To all in this room, I renounce *any* rights of property!"

He looked meaningfully toward Astra.

"I want nothing." He stepped in close to her and grabbed her arm. "Nothing."

***

Stone hurriedly ransacked his quarters. The general's death, even though it was moments ago, had already faded from his thoughts. He tossed his sword on his bed and ran to the locker in the corner of the room.

"Damn it!" he cursed out loud as he removed the holster and quickly reached into his closet to pull out an undershirt. Astra burst into the room.

"What are you doing, Tyler? You have lost your mind!" she stormed.

"No, Astra. For the first time in my life I actually see things the way they are," he answered, continuing to button his shirt. "And I have you and Cataline to thank for that."

Astra looked around the cluttered room. "You are going to get her, aren't you? Your little Terillian whore."

Stone paused. After giving Astra an angry glance, he returned to the buttons.

"You bastard!" she yelled. "I will see that she is dead before you get there and you will be arrested as soon as you land," she threatened as she reached for the communicator on the wall. Stone had enough. He brought his fist across her jaw, knocking her unconscious.

"That was a long time coming," he said out loud, realizing how good it felt to finally shut her up.

Stone picked up the unconscious Astra and put her on the bed. He no longer saw any beauty in her. Instead he saw the ugliness of his society; he hated her and himself. His only hope of redemption lay with Mori; he had to get to her. Returning to his locker, he pulled out some rope and bound her feet and hands. Taking a tie from his closet, he placed it over Astra's mouth. Once she was secured, he picked her up and carried her to his closet, sliding her into the back corner.

"Fit for a queen," Stone said as he shut the door.

Having temporarily disposed of Astra, he tucked in his shirt and latched his belt. Reaching back onto the bed, he picked up his holster and locked it into place. Next he grasped his sword and lifted it to his face. Looking at his reflection, he wondered who the man looking back at him was. He exhaled heavily and sprinted from his room. As he exited his quarters he ran into Vatarus.

Catching Stone in his arms, Vatarus spoke. "Sir…I…I just wanted to check on you. After Tacitus I was…"

"I'm fine. I just need a little time to—"

"That's understandable after everything you've—"

Stone interrupted again. "Lady Astra is resting in my room. See to it she is not disturbed for the rest of the night. I will be requisitioning a falcon long-range transport. I need to…I need to get away for a few days."

"Yes, sir. As you wish," said Vatarus as he pulled a small metal container from his pocket. "I have brought your Brigadier insignia. Regardless of your comments in the hall, you have won them rightfully."

Stone took the leaf cluster surrounding three stars from Vatarus's hand. He needed to play along long enough to get to Mori.

"Yes, of course. Thank you, Colonel. I will return in a few days. Until my return, I place you in command of the brigade. Again, make sure Astra is left alone for the evening. It has been a long day for all of us."

"It has sir. I'm glad to see you are more like yourself again."

"More than you know, Colonel, more than you know," said Stone has he placed his hand on Vatarus's shoulder. "Good luck Vatarus, you are a good man. One of the few," he said as he turned down the passageway toward the hangar leaving a confused Vatarus to ponder his last statement.

***

"We're clear of *Lucius* airspace, sir," reported the falcon pilot.

"Shall I plot a jump to Alpha Humana, sir?" asked the navigator.

"No, Lieutenant," replied Stone. "Set a course for Capro."

The pilot and navigator looked at each other, perplexed by the order.

"Do you have a question, Lieutenant?" asked Stone in a stern tone, seeing their confusion.

"No, sir, Capro it is," replied the pilot. "Navigator, set jump coordinates to Capro. Full power set to magnetic coils, acceleration sequence standby."

"Coordinates set," reported the navigator.

"Jump in 3, 2, 1..."

Stone could hear the electromagnetic hum of the coils increase and began to see the blue electron flashes as the heavy metals in the space around them began to magnetize, turning the space in front of the craft into an almost infinite linear accelerator. He was on his way to save Mori and leave everything else he knew behind.

Chapter 13

The bright flashes of blue light alerted Stone that the ship was coming out of the jump. As the ship decelerated, Capro came into view. Even from high orbit, it looked like a hell-hole. It was a perfect place for one of the worst prisons in the Xen Empire.

"General," reported the pilot over the intercom, "making final approach to Capro prison."

As the falcon passed over the sea of acid, Stone could see the prison on the horizon. Billowing plumes of acidic mist rose around the bluff as waste products from the *Romulus* poured into the deadly ocean below. Somewhere inside that hell was Mori.

The five minutes it took to recycle the air in the hangar bay seemed like an eternity.

"Can we exit yet, Lieutenant?" asked Stone anxiously over the intercom.

"Almost finished, sir. Purge complete in three-zero seconds."

Finally, the bay door opened and Stone stepped out. He was surprised by the starkness of the hangar bay. Stripped bare since its days as a capital ship, Stone's footsteps echoed through the vacuous space as he quickly walked across the empty hangar. As Stone peered across the emptiness of the hangar, he saw two men standing by the exit at the far end of the docking area.

Both men looked rough. As he neared them he could make out uniforms. One was wearing the rank of colonel and the other seemed to be a master sergeant.

"Good day, General," reported the pudgy colonel.

The colonel's uniform was wrinkled and soiled and his beard scraggly and ragged. Stone, no slave to uniform regulations, was surprised by his unkempt look.

"Sir," added the master sergeant. He was a massive man. His uniform, much better looking, stretched at the shoulders and sleeves from the bulk of his muscles.

"Colonel, Master Sergeant," replied Stone.

"Surprised to hear we were to be visited by a flag officer," said the colonel as he extended a handshake to Stone. "We don't get many *uninvited* visitors to Capro. I have sent word to High Command regarding your arrival but they take their time to decode our message bursts. We're pretty much a graveyard out here. As far as High Command is concerned, our reports usually go to the bottom of the stack."

This was what Stone had hoped for.

"I am here to see a Terillian Scout Ranger officer," said Stone. "She may have information vital to an upcoming operation."

"She…" smiled the colonel. "He must be talking about our newest guest."

As he spoke he looked back toward the master sergeant, who returned a demented smile.

"She is something else," added the master sergeant. "Stubborn…but nice to look at, or at least she was."

Stone had to control himself. He was in no position to make a scene. "Yes, that sounds like her. I would like to see her."

"I'm sure we can make those arrangements for someone of your stature," replied the colonel as he turned toward his companion. "Master Sergeant," said the colonel, "have our guest brought to interrogation room 1."

"Yes, sir."

"Oh, and freshen her up a bit first," he said with another cold smirk on his face.

"So, General," he said returning his attention to Stone, "shall we have a drink while our prisoner is being made presentable?"

"I really am in a hurry, Colonel."

"You may call me Brutacus if you like. My master sergeant's name is Victor. We really don't place too much stock on ceremony out here. It's not like our careers are in jeopardy...where else are they going to send us? Come on. How about that drink? You can tell me how things are going outside this cage."

"Sorry, Colonel," replied Stone, "but I must insist on seeing the prisoner as soon as possible."

"If you insist, *General*," snapped back the colonel obviously insulted by Stone's response. "I will take you to the prisoner now."

***

The interrogation room was cold and bare. Stone could see his breath as he paced across the small room, waiting for Mori. As Stone paced, Colonel Brutacus sat in the corner leaning his chair against the wall and sipping on a flask he had pulled from the inside pocket of his wrinkled uniform. The door on the opposite side of the room swung open and in stepped the massive master sergeant, followed by two guards dragging a limp body with them.

Stone was horrified. It was Mori, but a hollow, broken version of the woman he had known only weeks ago. Her head was shaved and she wore a grungy half-shirt with a soiled blanket remnant tied around her waist. Her body was covered with bruises and dried blood was crusted on the corner of her mouth.

"As requested, General," laughed the master sergeant as the two men dropped Mori into the chair in center of the room. Too weak to hold herself up, Mori immediately collapsed onto the floor.

Stone quickly kneeled down by her side. Partially opening her eyes, she tried to mumble something to him but did not have the strength.

"Not quite the same wildcat she was when she got here," said Victor. "In the first few days, she put four of my guards and two prisoners in the infirmary. We had to, uh, tame her a bit."

"What have you done with her?" asked Stone, although he dreaded the answer.

"Just the usual for her type," answered the colonel as he stood from his chair. "A few medications and some quality time with our guards seemed to take the bite out of her. To make sure she had learned her lesson we put her in the non-military prisoner bay for a night. After that she didn't fight the meds anymore."

"You threw her in with rapists and murders!" yelled Stone on the verge of losing control.

"What does it matter? She's just a piece of Terillian trash anyway," answered Brutacus suspiciously. "What exactly do you need to know from this prisoner, General?"

Stone quickly gathered his thoughts. "I told you, Colonel. I need information she may have relating to an upcoming mission. She is useless to me in this state. I will have to take her back with me."

Stone noticed a disapproving glance on the master sergeant's face as he looked toward the colonel and shook his head.

"I'm afraid I can't allow that, sir. Even you don't have the authority…"

"The authority!" Stone was taking a huge chance. "You fat, insignificant fool. I am General Lucius, my fiancé is the lady Astra Varus, and I have recently obtained all property of the Tacitus patriarch through proporia combata. You asked earlier what else could be done to you. I will tell you, Colonel. I do not believe you have been isolated on this hole long enough to forget the influence of the Lucius and Varus families. I can have you transferred under my command where I will make sure you see more Terillians than you care to. I *will* take this prisoner with me."

The colonel's face grew a little flushed and he took a quick breath. Although the colonel was an evil, heartless man, Stone knew the colonel also understood he would be a lot safer in seclusion on Capro than in combat.

"If it is that important to the Republic and the Xen Empire, I guess we could forego the usual paperwork," conceded the colonel.

Stone's gamble had worked.

"I want anti-meds administered to revive her and have her brought to my ship in twenty minutes," ordered Stone.

Brutacus alternated his glances from Stone to Victor as he thought over his options. After an awkward silence he spoke.

"Victor, let's get the *general's* prisoner ready for transport. He *is* in a hurry."

"Thank you, Colonel," said Stone. "I will make sure High Command hears of the good work you are doing here. Perhaps there is an administrative role on Alpha Humana that could use your talents."

Brutacus's scowl was replaced by a thin smile as he contemplated his possible reprieve from Capro that didn't involve actual combat.

"Thank you, General. That would be very much appreciated."

***

Stone leaned cross-armed against the falcon as he anxiously waited for Mori. Choosing to wait outside instead of answering questions he did not want to answer from the pilot and navigator, he looked across the vacant hangar bay. The more he examined the hangar, the more evidence of neglect became apparent. The wiring in the hangar was in horrible condition. Frayed cords and loose connections were everywhere. On the forward bulkhead he noticed a slight charring, probably the site of past fire. Stone also sensed a slight hint of sulfur in the air. Looking down at his feet, he saw sulfur residue scattered across the deck. The dusting of tiny yellow particles around the ship indicated the inefficiency of the wash down system at the hangar entrance. In the distance, he could hear the *drip drip* of a leak. Not only was the prison remote and desolate, it was run-down.

The door to the hangar bay opened and Brutacus, with Victor by his side, strode into the bay. Following them were two guards with Mori. The sedatives were starting to wear off as she was at least walking with the aid of the guards. She was shackled at the ankles, the chain running in front of her body and around her waist. The handcuffs were attached to the waist chain, which in turn led to one of the guards' hands. Although slightly more coherent, she still looked beaten and disheveled. Stone walked toward the group, meeting them halfway across the hangar.

"Here she is, all wrapped and ready to go," said Brutacus.

"Thank you, Colonel," he replied as he took the chain from the guard's hand.

Stone felt resistance as Victor placed his hand around the waist chain. "Just a minute, sir. You need to sign for your prisoner and her escorts."

"Escorts, what are you talking about?"

"Even though we can *bend* the rules for flag officers, we can't break them, now can we?" answered Victor with a callous smile. "After you sign for her, she will need to be escorted by myself and one of our guards until she is checked into another military facility. That way we can ensure proper delivery."

"I don't require any assistance in the transport Sergeant Major, but thank you anyway."

"It wasn't a suggestion, General," interrupted Brutacus. "I must insist on these measures. I am willing to turn her over to you, but my men will escort her. I have my superiors as well, General."

Stone, maintaining his grip on the chain, inhaled a deep breath. "Well then, I guess I need to sign for her."

Victor reached the electronic DNA signature pen to Stone. Stone, still holding the chain, took the pen and injected the sharp end into his forearm. Returning a cold smile to Victor, he tossed the pen in Brutacus's direction.

"Is there anything else, Colonel?" said Stone, removing Victor's hand from the waist chain.

"No, sir. I hope you enjoyed your visit to our little oasis. And I look forward to possible openings on Alpha Humana."

He said nothing to Brutacus. Taking Mori by the arm, he led her to the ship.

At the entrance, he stopped to let Victor and the other guards enter the falcon. Victor paused at the hatch. Taking a long deliberate look up and down Mori's body, Victor turned back to Stone with a wicked smile on his face.

"If you need any help interrogating this one, I can give you some pointers."

With a laugh, he entered the ship.

Stone looked to Mori. Still affected by the drugs, her face was vacant of emotion.

His grief for her was overwhelming.

Putting his free hand on the back of her neck, he felt a slight shiver go over her body. He leaned in to her.

"I am so sorry this happened. I will get you out of this."

Mori slowly looked up toward Stone, struggling. Her green eyes no longer sparkled. He placed his forehead against her bald head briefly. "I'm sorry."

Quickly releasing his light embrace, he helped her into the ship. Stone then made his way to the cockpit.

"Sir, do you have a jump location for us?" asked the navigator.

Stone had thought about this question since he left *Lucius* on his rescue mission. The independent moon Port Royal was their best chance. When the first Terillian war started, it was converted into a hardened military base. Several operations against the facility by the Xen military had failed to take the little moon. Undefeated in war, Port Royal had succumbed to the Peace Accords. As with all other known fortifications, it was abandoned by the Terillians as part of the agreements that created the Neutral Quadrant. Almost before the last Terillian warship left the moon, scores of opportunists swarmed to Port Royal.

The founders of the enterprise became known as the Association. They established a corporate-like ruling body for Port Royal. Driven solely by profit, all forms of trade were permitted in the city. To control this "sin city," the Association employed an impressive army of ex-soldiers, mercenaries, and former slavers. In fact, the Association created a military presence formidable enough to give any attacking force fits; both the Terillians and Xen left them alone. The for-profit city was open to all as long as the entry fee was paid. If Stone could make it to Port Royal, he and Mori could fade into the crowd long enough for him to figure out what to do next.

"Oscar system," he replied.

The navigator looked puzzled.

"Oscar, sir?" he asked. "That's in the Dar—"

"I know where it is, Lieutenant," interrupted Stone.

"Aye, sir," replied the navigator.

***

"Oscar," said the pilot to the navigator after Stone left the cockpit. "What the hell is he doing?"

"Beats me," replied the navigator, "but I stopped trying to understand flag officers and First Families in general a long time ago. If he wants to go to Oscar system then that's where we're going."

"First Family bullshit again," mumbled the pilot as he commenced his preflight checks.

***

As the falcon made its way to Port Royal, Stone sat across from a semiconscious Mori, trying to plan his next move. On his left sat Victor. Beads of sweat rolled down his bald head as his shirt sleeves strained against the pressure of his bulging arms. The other guard, a scraggly looking man called Nicholi, sat next to Mori. Nicholi sat with his arm resting on the back of the chair behind Mori's head; he stared at her as if she were a meal he was about to devour.

"Can we adjust the environmentals in this sauna," asked Victor, rubbing the sweat from his head and wiping his hands dry on his pants.

Stone did not reply. Looking across at Mori, he was heartbroken. He could see burn marks on her arms and what looked like ligature marks around her neck. Her left eye was blackened and the entire right side of her head was a dull shade of purple. Although she was starting to regain her senses, her body had been broken. Stone knew her physical wounds would heal, but was not so sure about her emotional scars.

"Looks like the little bitch is coming out of it," said Nicholi as he ran his hand over her bald head.

"Not quite the same as when she came in, is she?" laughed Victor.

Wiping a new accumulation of sweat from his head, he reached over to Mori's cheek. His sweat-drenched hand palmed her jaw as he gave a slight squeeze.

"We just had to teach it some manners. Didn't we, you little whore?"

Mori's eyes turned to Stone. A tear fell down her cheek as a glimpse of the old determination returned to her eyes. As Victor squeezed her jaw, she mouthed something to Stone.

"What's that, honey?" asked Victor as he leaned in closer to her. When he was close enough, she sprung forward, catching Victor's nose in her mouth and biting hard. As Mori made her move Stone pounced on Nicholi, plunging his knife into the guard's chest.

Victor let out a scream as he brought both hands around Mori's neck. He stood up and lifted Mori, still locked onto his nose, off the ground. When he stood, he opened his abdomen up to Stone's knife.

As Stone's blade sunk into his stomach, Victor let out another yell and tossed Mori free of his face. She bounced against the wall and fell to the deck dazed. Rising to her hands and knees, she spit a mouthful of Victor's blood and the tip of his nose onto the floor. Victor fell backward on the seat, Stone's knife embedded in his abdomen and blood pouring from his mutilated nose.

"You traitorous bastard," grunted Victor through the pain. "I'm going to take you apart and then finish off that bitch."

He rose from the seat, drawing his pistol.

Mori, recovering from her jolt, snatched the baton from Nicholi's body. Victor's weapon fell to the ground as the baton slammed against his wrist. Another blow to his chin took Victor down to his knees and Mori's foot against his jaw laid him flat.

Suddenly, Stone felt a presence behind him. Drawing his pistol, he spun around to the find the navigator standing before him.

"What the hell is going on, General?" he asked.

A deafening roar jolted Stone as the navigator fell to the ground, struck by gunfire. Stone again spun around to see Mori move past him, pistol in hand. She moved mechanically past Stone to the navigator, who was writhing in pain on the deck.

Walking straight to him, Mori aimed the pistol and fired two more shots into the man.

Stone watched, frozen, as she turned back toward her former captors.

Victor had removed Stone's knife from his belly and had almost succeeded in pulling himself to his feet.

"You bitch!" he yelled as he pulled himself erect.

He fell to the ground again as a shot from Mori disintegrated his left knee. This time he did not have a chance to recover.

"Tell me how this feels, sweetheart," said Mori coldly as she pressed the barrel of the pistol against Victor's forehead and fired.

Standing over Victor's body, she raised the pistol again, taking aim at his lifeless body. Another shot rang out, then another, and another. Finally, the clicking of the empty pistol stopped her. Throwing the pistol on the ground, she turned toward Stone.

For an awkward moment they both froze. He could only look into her eyes and hope there was still something left. Stone extended his arms. Time stopped. Finally she moved to him, collapsing in his arms, exhausted from her efforts.

“I am sorry, so sorry. I did not know they had captured you. I…”

“You came for me,” she mumbled.

“Of course,” he replied as he gently placed his hand over her bruised cheek.

He felt her legs start to give out again. Supporting her as she collapsed, he helped her into the seat.

“Sepria, come in. What is going on back there?” came across the ship’s intercom. It was the pilot. Now Stone had to deal with him.

Moving toward the front of the spacecraft, Stone opened the door to the cockpit.

“General, what’s going on back there? I heard gunfire. Where’s Lieutenant Sepria?”

“I’m sorry you had to get involved in this,” said Stone as he placed his pistol to the pilot’s temple.

“Sir?” asked the confused pilot.

“Just complete the jump to Port Royal and once I disembark you will be free to go.”

“What about Sepria?”

“He’s dead, Lieutenant.”

“What! I don’t understand. Why did—”

“Lieutenant,” interrupted Stone pressing the barrel into the pilot’s temple, “just make the damn jump.”

The pilot looked coldly at Stone, straining against the pressure of the pistol pressed into his head. “You will be crucified for this.”

“Maybe. But if you want to live, get this ship to Port Royal.”

Chapter 14

The flashing blue light brought the falcon out of the jump. Outside of the cockpit, the massive planet Oscar 1 lay dead ahead. As the ship moved closer the moon, tiny in comparison, came into view. Closer still, and Stone could begin to make out dozens of craft moving all directions. Two of the craft moved quickly toward the falcon, taking up positions on both flanks.

Unidentified Xen warship, this is Port Royal Space Control. State your intentions and cargo, and standby for charge assessment.

The pilot stared at Stone blankly.

"Port Royal, this Falcon 456," answered Stone, picking up the communicator. "Visiting for leisure, three onboard, two will be off loading. Stay indefinite."

Standby Falcon 456.

Falcon 456, this is Port Royal. State name of polis entry.

"All public polis."

Standby.

Another minute passed.

Falcon 456, this is Port Royal. Cost for access is 2000 Humani or acceptable equivalent. What are names of off loaders?

"Undeclared."

Undeclared, over. Cost for undeclared arrival is additional 2000. Do you accept charges, over.

"Port Royal, this is Falcon 456, charges accepted. Request vector for docking."

Escorted by the two fighters until its final approach, the falcon drifted into its mooring amidst the flurry of activity around the port. As the mooring lines locked the ship into place the pilot spoke.

"You will be hunted for the remainder of your days. You will not be able to escape the reach of the Xen military."

"Maybe so, Lieutenant, but they won't find it out from you," said Stone.

A shot from Stone's pistol echoed through the cockpit.

"At least until you reach Humani forces," he added.

The startled pilot relaxed his body. Stone saw him draw in a massive sigh of relief as he realized his target was the ship's communications system.

"Which should take a little while without jump capability."

Another shot and the jump navigation system was disabled.

"You are only slowing the inevitable, traitor."

"This should slow it a little more then," replied Stone as he brought the grip of his pistol against the pilot's temple.

Having incapacitated the pilot long enough to make his escape, Stone returned to Mori. She lay motionless where Stone had placed her after the fight. Stepping over Victor's body, he leaned down and picked her up, cradling her in his arms. As he exited the ship he was stopped by two security guards and a well-dressed man carrying an electronic ledger.

"Welcome to market polis, Mister…oh, I see you are undeclared. That will be 4000 Humani."

Stone reached into his pocket to present a Xen military exchange card. He had several 5000 Humani cards. They were often used to fund expenses on expeditions into the Dark Zone or for high-ranking officials' more discreet activities. Although Port Royal accepted almost all forms of currency, including archaic paper and coin, the Xen military exchange cards could only be purchased by First Family patriarchs, current or former Senators, and through Humani High Command; they were untraceable by design.

"Thank you, sir. Here are your passes and a data chip providing you with our rules and regulations and a map of the authorized polis.

You will be guests A2701 and A2702. Basically, you can do as you please as long as you do not attempt to enter the Administrative polis and follow all orders of security personnel. Enjoy your stay."

***

Carrying Mori through the streets, Stone struggled to operate the electronic pad containing the map of the various polis. Fumbling with the screen pads, he meandered through the crowded streets. Making his way past Recreation Girls, animal traders, and every other sort of panderer and vender one could imagine he searched for someplace to hide for a few days. Finally, he saw a building marked "lodging and recreation rooms."

"I think this will do," Stone whispered to a semi-conscious Mori.

Stone entered the lobby and walked to a beautiful woman behind a large glass desk. "Welcome to the Relaxation Building M-12," said the well-endowed and glamorous looking lady. She took a slight pause as she looked at Mori, half asleep with her arms draped around Stone's shoulders.

"If you would like a little more 'lively' entertainment, I can contact one of our associate recreation houses and have..."

"That will not be necessary. Thank you," interrupted Stone.

"Very well, sir. The room will be 300 per day," replied the woman as she began selecting touch screens on the desk. "May I have your passes please?"

Stone handed over the passes and an exchange card.

"I see you are undeclared, sir. Are you expecting any visitors?"

"No. No visitors."

"Very well, sir. Enjoy your stay," she replied as she returned the passes and handed him a room card.

Stone quickly made his way to the elevator. The elevator dipped slightly as it started its ascent, and Mori looked up toward Stone.

"It's going to be okay," he said in a reassuring voice.

Mori tucked her head back into his shoulder.

After a short elevator ride Stone found the room and, with Mori still in his arms, opened the door. The room was as well kept as was everything else in the city. Stone walked over to the bed and gently laid Mori down. As he did, Mori, still weakened, spoke.

"Ty, where are we?"

"Port Royal. We should be able to lay low here until you are better and give us time to decide what to do next."

"Friends…friends here."

Stone leaned in closer to hear her mumbled words. "What?"

"There are contacts here. They can…help."

"Later. Rest for now," replied Stone as he pulled a blanket over Mori. "I will find us some food."

He leaned in further to place a light kiss on her forehead. She had already drifted back into a deep sleep.

***

When Mori awoke a strange man was looking down at her. Startled, she recoiled away from him.

"It's okay, he's a medical tech," said Stone in a reassuring voice. "He's making sure you are okay."

Finishing up his examination, the medic walked over to Stone and spoke. “She has several bruises and two broken ribs. She’s taken quite a beating. How did this happen?”

“I paid you enough not to ask questions, doc. Just tell me what we need to do to get her better.”

“Well, physically speaking she just needs some rest, but that’s not going to be the hard part.”

“What do you mean?”

“Her hemo-sample analysis shows high level of opia and neuro meds in her system. The next few days are going to be hell for her; if it’s your intention to clean her up. If not, I can direct you to a meds market…”

“No, she needs to be free of the drugs.”

“As you wish. Just be prepared. She will have a violent and painful withdrawal. It will not be pretty. I will give her a detoxification serum that will reduce the recovery period to a few days, but it will be a long couple of days.”

Stone looked at Mori. She had overheard the discussion.

“I can hack it, Ty, as long as you’re with me,” she pledged.

“I’ll be here, Mori. I will always be here for you.”

“All right then,” said the medic as he injected the serum into Mori and gathered his equipment. “You know my price if you need anything else. Enjoy your stay.”

As the medic left, Stone poured a cup of coffee and settled in for what was going to be a long few days.

***

"Ty!" shouted Mori, startled to consciousness by an obvious nightmare.

"What is it, Mori? I'm right here." He placed his hands around her pale, clammy skin. Sweat beaded on her body as she shivered in his hands. She looked up at him, her green eyes dark and sunken.

"I'm cold. And I hurt. I need my medication. Just a little. It hurts so bad."

"I can't," replied Stone. "It will only be a few more days. You can make it."

"Damn you, Hanmani," she snapped as she slapped him across the face. Mori was weakened, but still extremely strong. Although Stone's face instantly reddened where she struck him, he felt no pain; his whole body already hurt to see her like this.

"I should have killed you on J3 like the rest of you animals," she spat at him, but her mouth was too dry.

"You don't mean that."

"I mean it. I wish you were dead—you and your slaver hirelings."

"Mori, I am not giving you meds."

Mori's demeanor suddenly changed. Instead of anger she looked up at him gently.

"I'm sorry, Ty. I didn't mean any of it."

Her words and tone were different but she still shivered and looked around the room, her eyes moving wildly. "I love you. I just need something. Please."

She raised her hand again but this time slowly caressed his cheek.

"Mori, it'll be better soon."

"Please..."

Mori's hand moved from his face slowly down to his buckle.

"No," said Stone backing away from her slightly. "Not like this."

Stone, distracted by Mori's condition, did not realize that while one hand was on his buckle, the other had taken his pistol. He jumped backward as she pointed the weapon at him.

"I'm sorry, Ty, but I need to stop the pain."

Mori could hardly hold the pistol steady but at this range she did not have to aim. Tears filled her eyes as she struggled to hold the gun. "Ty, don't make me do this. Where are the drugs?"

"There are none here."

"Bullshit! There has to be," she said as she rose from the bed, stumbling and almost falling.

Stone took a step toward her, but she regained her footing and pointed the pistol at his face.

"Stop!" she warned. "You don't understand. I need it. I will die without it."

"No. You just think you will. You need to be strong."

"Be strong—like when my family was killed or sold into slavery. Like when I saw entire villages destroyed, young women violated. Like Capro."

The tears that had collected in her eyes now began to flow.

"I am tired of being strong. I am tired of fighting. I just want the pain to stop. *All* of it."

"Mori..."

"Shut up, Ty. If you don't have what I need in here, I will find it elsewhere."

"No, you won't," said Stone as he stepped between her and the door.

"Don't Ty. Don't make me do it."

"If you want to shoot me, then do it. I would rather die than see you give up. I love you."

Mori held the pistol at his chest.

"Just let me go. Please," she begged, her hands trembling.

The pistol began to shake even more as her exhaustion began to take its toll.

"Please," she asked again.

"No, I can't let you go."

"I can't hurt you," she confessed, "but I can't do this anymore."

Stone made a quick move, lunging for the pistol as Mori turned it to her temple. Luckily her reflexes were slowed enough to allow him to direct the barrel away from her as she pulled the trigger. Stone snatched the pistol from Mori's weak hand as the shot echoed through the room.

"I'm so tired," she said as she faded back into unconsciousness.

Stone supported her body as she slumped to the floor. Securing his pistol, he lifted Mori into his arms and carried her to the bed. He had just placed Mori back on the bed when two security guards burst into the room, weapons drawn.

"There was a report of gunfire from this room. What happened?"

"It was accidental, everything is okay."

The lead security guard took a quick look around the room. "Everything seems to be in order. You will be charged 200 Humani for unauthorized discharge and given a warning. Be advised that once you have three warnings, your weapons will be confiscated."

"I understand. It really was an accident. It won't happen again."

"Very well, sir. Enjoy your stay," stated the guard. "And try to not have any more *accidents*."

The next two days were worse than the first. Locking up the weapons and going sleepless, Stone kept vigil on Mori through the nightmares, the breakdowns, and the violent attacks. On the third day, no longer able to fight, he fell asleep on the chair beside her bed.

***

Slowly opening his eyes, Stone realized he had fell asleep and quickly jumped to his feet and glanced toward the bed. She was gone. He began to panic as he looked around the room.

"Damn it!" he said to himself. "Mori!" he shouted. "Where are you?"

"Good morning, Ty."

He spun around to see Mori walking into the room from the shower. The first thing he noticed was the light that had begun to return to her eyes. Covered only in a towel, he saw little trickles of water still flowing down her chest. He also saw beads of water that had collected on the small bristles of hair that had begun to grow on her head. She was still pale and bruised and had a long way to recovery, but she seemed to look like Mori again.

"Mori, your—"

"I still feel like crud but needed a shower. I was—"

She was cut short by Ty's embrace. "I missed you. I didn't know you had been captured. I had…"

"Not now Ty. I just want to rest. And eat. I'm starving."

"Sure. I'll take care of it. I'll go right now and get something," replied Stone quickly. "I'm just glad you're doing better."

Stone quickly picked up an exchange card and turned toward the door. He was stopped by Mori.

She grabbed his arm. "Ty."

"Yes?"

"Thank you. For everything," she said as she rose up on her toes and kissed him lightly. "You saved me."

Stone smiled. "Now let's get you some food."

Chapter 15

"How about blonde?" asked Mori as she looked at the hair growth enhancers Stone had bought at the market.

A few weeks had passed since they had arrived in Port Royal and Mori was getting stronger every day.

"I liked it the way it used to be," replied Stone.

"Bald?"

"No, like when I first saw you."

"Flattery…nice. I think I should change it, though. There will be bounty hunters and spies looking for us if they aren't already. Besides, you get to grow that beard."

"It's not like I have to follow regulations anymore," he said as he rubbed his beard, now about an inch in length.

Stone placed his arms around Mori's waist and kissed her cheek. She returned the kiss and Stone could feel her hands reach up toward his neck and embrace him.

Suddenly, she stopped.

"I'm sorry, Ty," she said, putting her hands over his. "I'm not ready."

"It's okay. I understand."

Stone felt for her. Mori was getting stronger. Her bruises had diminished and her sense of humor returned, but she still had demons that she had to come to terms with.

"I want to be with you. I just..."

"It's okay. Really. Whenever you are ready, I will be here."

"Thank you," she said, pulling his hands to her lips for a kiss. "We're quite a pair."

We really are, Stone thought. So much had happened over the last few weeks.

"We should probably figure out our next move," said Stone as he felt the reality of his situation start to sink in.

"There should still be some agents here that I can contact. They could get us back to Terillian lines."

Stone paused momentarily.

"What is it, Ty?"

"Sorry," he replied. "I knew there would be consequences to my actions but it's just really starting to sink in. I can no longer fight for the Xen war machine, even if I had not left the way I did. At the same time, I have no desire to kill Alpha Humana rank and file. They are only doing their duty."

"We all have to do our duty, Ty," said Mori. "But our duty is to the greater good, not to archaic codes."

"We have to find a way to let the Alpha Humana people know that the Terillians did not start the war."

"So you finally see things for what they are?"

"Yes. I have finally seen the truth and feel like a fool for spending my whole life fighting for a lie."

"How much do you know?"

"I know that the powerful families of Alpha Humana, with Xen support or direction, have instigated this conflict."

"Do you know why?"

"Something about providing slaves for the Xennite home world."

"There's more to it than that, Ty," added Mori. "I am sure the increased raids by slavers over the last two decades and the operations around Navato have something to do with it also."

"What do you think is going on in the Navato system?" asked Stone.

"A few years ago a long-range patrol picked up increased neutrino and electromagnetic readings just outside of the asteroid belt surrounding Venato."

"The asteroids cause that whole area to be electromagnetically unstable though," said Stone. "It's almost impossible to track a ship there."

"The patrol wasn't sure either, but it stayed on station for a few weeks. During that period it picked up signals from Xen warships and dozens of slave transports-all heading into the Navato system. Most likely they were going to Venato. It's the only planet stable to humanoids, so unless they have Dorans running the operation or have environmentally altered another planet, it has to be Venato. Once I return to my unit I will petition for another mission. Maybe there the proof can be found."

"What do you think they are doing there?"

"We don't know. The last two missions have gone missing."

"Maybe we can find support on Alpha Humana?"

"Who will believe you? You undoubtedly have been branded a traitor, and it's not like I could just walk into your Senate and say, 'Look, it's not our fault. Join me in rebellion against your Xen masters.' I don't think that would go over well."

"I know, but there has to be some way."

"Let me know when you come up with a good plan. In the meantime, let's get back to Terillian territory and figure things out where we don't have to avoid Xen hit men and the Elite Guard. There is a recreation center near here where Scout Rangers and spies have set up safe passage in the past. Hopefully we can get lucky. You have made very powerful enemies, Ty, and I am sure they will stop at nothing to get at you."

***

Astra walked into the marbled office of her father. At the end of the room her father sat behind a grand desk surrounded by hanger-ons, advisors, and other cronies.

"Everyone out!" she shouted as she reached her father's desk. The room fell silent and with a cold, concentrated look she stared down the group. Quickly grabbing up their documents, they scurried from the room. As the door shut behind them, Astra sat on the edge of her father's desk and spoke.

"Father, have you found him yet?"

"Not yet, Astra. I have posted the bounty at 100,000 Humani with an additional 50,000 for the Terillian he helped escape. My agents on Port Royal are checking each polis and I have requested the Association council contact me."

"They will not give anyone up. They are too concerned with maintaining their reputation as neutrals. Why do we not just destroy the Association and take the base for ourselves?"

"Our resources are currently stretched too thin. Besides, as you know, the Association is not only useful to our financial endeavors, but vital to the Directive."

"I understand, Father," stated Astra matter-of-factly. "But he must be found. He must be punished for what he has done to me. To us. Increase the bounty as much as you need to catch them," demanded Astra. "Our family has been dishonored and the other families must know you will not stand for it."

She paused for a moment and then leaned down to kiss her father on the forehead.

"I am sure you will do the right thing, as you always do, Father," she smiled.

"I understand, Astra. You mustn't fret. I will find them. Until we have, however, I have arranged for an Elite Guard officer to be assigned to watch over you."

"Do you really think that is necessary? Most of the Elite Guard are from insignificant families and they are so...uncivilized."

"This one is an exception. The newly promoted Major Arilius Tacitus."

"The late General Cataline Tacitus's cousin...Oh. What does he look like?" Astra's face beamed.

"You will find out shortly. I have called for him. He should be here presently. I am sure you will find him satisfactory."

Almost immediately after he spoke, "Senator, Major Arilius Tacitus is waiting outside" was heard over Dominotra's desk intercom.

"Very well, send him in." Looking up toward Astra he smiled. "He is currently unattached as well."

As Arilius Tacitus walked into the room, his tall proportioned stature was the epitome of military bearing and professionalism.

"Major Arilius Tacitus reporting as ordered."

"You may stand at ease, Major. There is no need for military courtesies here."

"Thank you, Senator."

"Arilius Tacitus," said Astra, as she looked him over from head to toe, "it's nice to see that there are a few worthy officers in the Guard."

"Thank you, Lady Astra. I am looking forward to this duty, although I do not think the traitor will bother you again. He is too smart for that, although he is a fool to have left you."

"No need to look at this as duty, Arilius," replied Astra as she looked him over.

"He will do," she said to her father as she turned toward the door.

"Let me show you the grounds," Astra said as she looked playfully at Arilius and extended her left hand for him.

Arilius took her hand and she led—almost pulled—him out of the room.

"Astra, don't worry. I will deal with our problem," promised Senator Varus.

"I am sure you will, Father," replied Astra, her gaze still on Arilius.

"Oh, and, Father," she said, looking over her shoulder, "make sure I see their bodies."

***

Stone and Mori walked into the crowded recreation center. The sound of numerous conversations, loud music, and laughter created a low roar. Scores of Recreation Girls worked the room, looking for the highest bidder. Criminals, smugglers, and renegades all called this and other places like it on Port Royal their temporary home.

They made their way to the main floor, which included two large bars and several gambling tables. A set of stairs in the center of the room led to the second level, where a series of rooms were utilized by the Recreation Girls to make good on the deals negotiated on the lower level.

"What kind of places do you hang out in?" asked Stone, as he smiled at Mori.

"Funny," she replied. "Sometimes you have to get in the muck if you want a dirty job done. Over there," she added. "The Scapi."

Scapi were one of three nonhuman intelligent life forms that were known to the Humani. The Dorans and Xennites were the other two. The Scapi were from the water planet Scapalus. Evolved from sea mammals, they communicated through high-pitched squeaks and squeals. They were also massive. Generally close to three meters tall, they weighed in at over 1000 kilograms. Although very few of them actually left their home planet, those that did were usually pilots, merchants, or mercenaries.

"Good day, Hanagus," said Mori as she bowed toward the Scapi.

The Scapi raised his webbed hand to his massive head and manipulated a device over an ear hole. A series of pitchy squawks and squeaks came from his mouth. A few seconds afterward, the universal translator attached to his ear spoke for him.

"Captain, it took a minute to recognize you. Your hair is a different color. Good to see you. Rumor had it you had been lost in space. Sit, please."

The huge alien rose from the table and extended his arms to invite them to sit. Towering over them, his bluish-gray face and arms glistened from droplets of recycled water that continuously ran through a specialized pack on his suit, creating a slight mist around him.

"I am Hanagus Hanaga Hanagato—Hanagus for short. I manage the entertainment here and am a longtime friend of the Terillians. Who be this?" he asked, turning his massive head back to Mori.

"This is...my friend," answered Mori.

"No need to be secretive with me, Captain. Rumor of a high-ranking Xen officer deserting to the Terillian side has been promulgated in the bounty hunter and mercenary circles. Together, you two are worth more than a million Humani."

"One million," replied a flabbergasted Stone.

"Either you must have some valuable information or pissed off someone very powerful."

"A little bit...well a lot of both," replied Mori. "But that's not important, Hanagus. We just need to get back to Terillian territory."

"I agree. There are a lot of people asking questions and bounty hunters crawling all over Port Royal. Let me have one of my girls help you out."

Hanagus made a motion with his hand and a beautiful, scantily clad woman walked over to the table.

"Hi, Hani," she said in a low, husky voice. "Are these two for me?"

"Yes, Bianca, but these are specials—the ones I have told you about. I recommend you take them to room 5."

"Sure thing, Hani. Come with me, honey," she said to Mori, taking her hand. "Have your man come along too."

"Just a minute, Bianca," interrupted Hanagus. "I am always willing to help, but I am a businessman and Bianca's time is valuable."

"I understand," said Mori as she took one of the exchange cards and tossed it to Hanagus. "This should cover it."

"Thanks, Captain," he replied as he palmed the card with his huge hand. "Enjoy your stay."

"Come with me, guys," teased Bianca as she pulled the two away from the table.

Walking up the stairs to room, Stone took in the scene with a bird's eye view. The bar was full of hundreds of rough-looking sorts, many of whom were no doubt looking to cash in on the bounty on his and Mori's heads.

After the three entered, Bianca punched in the lock code and turned toward Mori and Stone.

"Captain. General. What do you need from me?"

"We need a spacecraft and passage to Terillian lines."

"That will take a couple hours but it can be done for about 2000 Humani. You will meet a man named Tye at launch station 101 at 2200."

"That's it?" asked Stone.

"Pretty much," replied Bianca. "The less you know about the details the better off we all are. That is unless you and your woman had something else in mind. You do have some time to kill and you have paid for me already."

Bianca stepped toward Stone, placing her hand on his stomach and rubbing Mori's arm with the other.

"No, that's okay," answered Stone quickly backing away from Bianca. "Thank you for the offer, but no thanks."

"As you wish," she pouted. "Just be at the launch station on time. He will not wait."

"We will be there," replied Mori. "Thanks again. We should get back to our room to gather our goods."

"Okay, honey." Bianca punched in the code to unlock the door. As they walked past her, she gave a small squeeze to each one's behind. "Enjoy your stay, honeys."

Stone looked at Mori and smiled once they were outside the room.

"You should probably get that thought out of your head for good, Ty," she said with a disapproving glance.

"Come on," he protested. "I was just—"

Stone paused. A man in the background behind Mori drew his attention. The tall, thin, bearded man was looking toward them, but quickly turned away. As he turned, he appeared to be talking into a comms link attached to his wrist.

"Something's up. We should get back to the room and get ready."

Mori slowly turned and walked with Stone.

"The guy over my shoulder?" she asked.

"Yes."

"Over by that table. There's another one," said Mori, slightly tilting her head in that direction.

Stone looked at the table toward the door. Two men sat with their backs to the wall, scanning the room intently. He next looked toward Hanagus. Setting with him was a man wearing a dark cloak. Stone wished it was possible to see emotion on Hanagus's face but the Scapi's flat features made that impossible to a human.

"Excuse me," said a man as he bumped into Mori and Stone. "Too much alcohol, you know," he laughed, holding a drink up to them. "Sorry."

"That's okay," replied Stone as he gently directed the man clear of them.

Mori glanced back at the man. His jovial exterior had changed. Taking a quick, determined look back toward the two, the man raised his hand toward his mouth.

He was speaking into a comms link.

Mori looked toward the man with Hanagus, who quickly placed his hand over one ear and looked toward her and Stone.

"Ty, they got us."

As she spoke, the man that had bumped into them spun around with a pistol in his hand. Dropping to her knees, Mori's pistol rang out over the roar of the bar. The man fell and chaos ensued.

Stone dove over a nearby table. He quickly drew his weapon as he rolled off the table and onto the floor.

The two men at the door jumped to their feet and opened fire. Victims fell in front and behind Mori as their fire tracked her across the room. Mori hurdled a table, dropping the bounty hunter at the bar with two rapid shoots while still airborne. She took two quick steps and dove over the bar as rounds hit all around her.

Amidst the gunfire and scores of fleeing patrons, Stone found a gap in the stampede. Peering down the sight of his pistol, he pulled the trigger. The first man by the door fell. Ducking and sidestepping as the remaining gunman returned fire, he looked for another shot. It was too late, however. Mori had capitalized on the distraction. Leaping on top of the bar, she ran toward the bounty hunter.

Spotting Mori out of the corner of his eye, the gunman turned to react. The blade of Mori's sword shimmered against the multi-colored lights of the bar. The man fired but did not have time to take careful aim. Mori was still a few feet off the floor when she passed the gunman. The reflection of light from her sword flashed bright as the sword passed through the man's body.

Mori and Stone simultaneously pointed their weapons toward Hanagus's table. The man speaking with Hanagus had attempted to open fire when the shooting started.

Although Scapi were slow, they were strong. The final gunman lay sprawled out on Hanagus's table, his neck broken by a twist of Hanagus's powerful hands.

Stone cast a quick glance toward Mori to make sure she was okay then surveyed the carnage. The bar was now empty of patrons, save the dead and wounded randomly strewn on the floor. Stone looked back toward Mori, who was walking toward one of the bounty hunters. Still alive, he was crawling toward the door.

"Mori, you okay?"

"Yeah," she replied. "This one's still alive."

Mori easily caught up with the wounded man. Placing her foot under his belly, she flipped him on his back. He was severely wounded. As Mori looked down on him, he frantically dug through his pockets. Blood collected in his mouth as his eyes moved wildly.

"You won't need that," stated Mori as she knelt down and pulled a medipack from the man's bloody hands. "You're probably too torn up anyway, but tell me who sent you and I might give it back."

The dying man glanced away from Mori as Stone joined her. A wince of pain from Mori's foot pressing on his wound quickly regained his attention. "Who?"

"An open bounty," he answered, spitting blood as he spoke, "from Senator Varus."

"My ex-fiancée's father," Stone informed Mori. "I did not leave on good terms with the Varus family."

"I see," replied Mori as she looked back toward the man, who was now lying motionless on the floor. A quick nudge from her foot then a check of his pulse confirmed his fate.

"He's dead," reported Mori.

"Friends of yours?" Hanagus's voice translator carried across the room.

"No, but I am sure they are the first of many," replied Mori. "We need to get out of here tonight."

Stone was distracted. Looking over the bodies of the bounty hunters, his brow furrowed.

"What is it, Ty?" inquired Mori.

"Sorry. I just had an idea about how to find the information you need about Navato."

"How?" asked Mori.

"Hanagus," said Stone, turning toward the Scapi, "how much will it cost to get us passage to Alpha Humana?"

Chapter 16

"I hope this works," Mori said to Stone as they stood in the landing bay.

"It has to, especially since it pretty much took the rest of our Humani to get this ship and crew," replied Stone.

"Hopefully we get our money's worth."

"Bianca assured me the crew was top-notch."

"I'm sure she did, Ty," scowled Mori as she looked at the antique spacecraft in front of them. The outer hull was pock-marked with welding discolorations, showing dozens of repairs, and rust was visible in a few spots. On the exterior near the control station was a painting of a multi-headed serpent with the word *Hydra* underneath and on the outer blast deflectors read the words *Haulin'Ass.*

"But look at this old falcon," she continued. "I think its 3rd generation, your grandfather would have thought this was a piece of junk."

"It's got character at least," laughed Stone.

"I guess," said Mori.

"Over there—" said Stone as he was distracted by a noise behind them. Four figures were approaching. "I wonder if that's our crew."

"Our crew or more bounty hunters."

Mori drew her weapon and brought it to the ready. Stone followed suit.

As they came closer, Mori could make out their features. "It's your new *friend* Bianca," she said as she lowered her weapon.

"Come on," said Stone as he holstered his pistol.

"Captain. General. Pleased to see you again," said Bianca as she moved closer, much closer to Stone. "Very pleased."

"Thanks," said Stone uncomfortably. "It's not 'gGeneral' anymore—just Tyler."

A seductive smile came to Bianca's face. "Very well, Ty."

"It's Tyler," corrected Mori, irritated that Bianca had used her nickname for Stone. "Is this the crew?" she continued.

"Oh, yes," replied Bianca. "Let me introduce you to the crew."

"Yes, let's do that," demanded Mori as she stepped between Bianca and Stone.

Bianca continued. “This is your pilot, Cassandra Orion. She was a highly decorated Terillian fighter pilot.”

“Was?” asked Mori questioning Orion.

“And a damned good one,” replied Orion, “but I chose retirement over a boring desk job that promotion would have brought. Besides, going into private business has been pretty…well, profitable. So you two are the crazy S.O.B.s?” she continued.

“I wouldn’t call us crazy,” said Stone. “Besides you’re taking this little trip too.”

“I am, but I’m doing it because I’m greedy, not crazy. Big difference. We’ll have time to discuss philosophies on the trip. Meanwhile let me introduce you to the crew. This is my engineer, Rickover Fermi.”

“Good evening. Rest assured you will have no engineering problems on your trip.”

“That’s good to hear—”

“Damn it!” Stone was cut short by the engineer’s explosion. “That freakin’ exhaust panel is loose. It looks like the maintenance crew has dropped the ball again. I had better get to work. Excuse me.”

As Rickover pushed past Stone and Mori and stormed into the ship, Orion continued.

“My navigator is slightly less…uh…high strung. His name is Cavanos Cavanarus Canora, but we call him TC for short; you know, three Cs.”

"Greetings," said the Scapi as he presented his massive hand to Stone.

"Nice to meet you, TC," said Stone as his hand was encompassed by the Scapi's.

"The trip should take a few days, as long as we don't have any jump interruptions. I have just updated the navigation system to GEN4 so hopefully we won't have too many."

"TC is a hell of a navigator," added Orion. "The only problem is his side of the cockpit is always damp," she paused, hoping for a laugh. None came.

"Well, anyway," Orion continued. "It looks like we're ready to get going. Welcome aboard the *Hydra*. TC can help you stow any gear and show you to your bunkroom."

TC led the two into the crew entrance and past the open door to the reactor bay. Rickover's curses echoed through the passageway as they moved aft.

TC stopped outside a small stateroom.

"I hope these quarters will do. If not...well, it's all there is so it will have to do."

"It's fine," said Mori. "Thank you."

"I will let you two get settled while we make preparations for takeoff."

As the massive Scapi ducked to leave the room and closed the door to the stateroom, Mori turned toward Stone.

"At least he didn't say, *Enjoy your stay*."

"It's good to be getting out of here, but we've got a long way to go."

"Do you really think it will work, Ty?" asked Mori.

"I hope so. If anyone knows what is going on in the Navato system, it's Dominotra Varus. If we can capture him, or at least get him to talk, we won't have to go into Navato blindfolded."

"And we can get rid of the bounty hunters too," added Mori.

"Hopefully. If we can make it to his estate we will have to take out his communication center and deal with his security team. Luckily, I know my way around his estate."

"The prodigal son returns, eh."

"Not quite," laughed Stone. "We should get some sleep. We will need the energy when we get to Alpha Humana."

***

The gut-wrenching, nauseating deceleration threw Stone and Mori onto the deck from their slumber. Following them to the ground was everything in the room not tied down.

"What the hell was that?" asked Mori as she struggled to catch her breath and push herself off the ground to her hands and knees. "It-it's too early to come out of a jump."

"I don't know," huffed Stone. "We sh-should check it out."

He tried to stand but was too dizzy and fell back to his knees.

"As s-soon as I can…" He exhaled heavily. "…stand."

In a few seconds he was able to rise to his feet. Taking a deep breath, he turned to help Mori but she was already on her way out the door. They sprinted down the passageway to the cockpit.

"Captain Orion, what happ..." Stone had to take another breath as his stomach was still settling. "What happened?"

"We had a rapid deceleration. Not sure why, yet. It happens sometimes. We'll check our position and reset our course for another jump. Engineering, this is the captain, report status of engineering systems."

Rickover's angry voice came over the intercom. "It wasn't my fault. There is nothing wrong with the reactor or—damn it! Wait a minute. I have a small fire...let me..."

There was a short pause.

"It's out," he continued. "Like I said, it's not engineering. What did that big blue bastard do?"

The squeaks from TC almost conveyed his annoyance before the translator echoed his sentiment. "There's nothing wrong with my NAVSYS, jackass."

"What caused the deceleration, TC?" asked Orion.

"Checking."

TC disconnected his translator. High-pitched squawks filled the cockpit as he worked the navigation system.

Orion looked back toward Mori and Stone. Both were still a little queasy. Their faces were pale and they were breathing heavily.

"It must be your first de-cell," said Orion. "Don't worry, it gets better after about a hundred of them."

"I think one will be enough," replied Mori, exhaling heavily.

After a few moments of squeaks and manipulations of the navigation systems, TC activated the translator again.

"It looks like we're in the Sierra system, about halfway there. Magnetic fields pulled us out of the jump. That's odd," said TC after a slight pause. "The new upgrade should have helped with that. Let me check. These fields are huge and there are a lot of them. There are some neutrino fields too, but weak. Just a minute and we should be in visual range."

"Engineering, make sure we're ready to jump again," said Orion.

"I've been ready the whole time," came back over the intercom.

"I have plotted a quick jump course out of the system if we need to get out of here fast," reported TC.

Outside the cockpit window small specks appeared, then more. A few more seconds and distant objects began to become identifiable.

"That's a Xen battle cruiser," exclaimed Orion. "TC, get ready to jump."

TC reached toward the navigation controls, but Mori stopped him.

"Wait," she said as she placed her hand on his massive shoulder.

"What do you mean wait?" said Orion, as she looked toward the ship. "Oh," she added.

"There's a Terillian battleship right beside it…or part of one," said Mori.

"Son of a bitch," said Stone as the scene became clearer. "There has been a fight here—a big one."

"Great," said Orion. "We have decelerated in the middle of a battlefield."

At first a few, then dozens of abandoned and wrecked ships came into view. A Xen battle cruiser with several hull breaches was visible in the distance. Dozens of massive fires created an orange pulsating glow in the hangar as they burned up any oxygen left onboard. As they passed through the wreckage, each new sight was more shocking than the last.

"Over there," said TC as he pointed toward the forward end of a Terillian battleship that lay behind the Xen battle cruiser hulk. "It has been split in half. And there's a Terillian corvette embedded in its forward end."

"It must have either lost control during the battle and collided with the battleship or drifted into her afterwards," said Orion.

As they moved deeper into the wreckage, more carnage unfolded. Capital ships of the line wasted, Terillian Foxtrots and Alphas drifted past them as did Condor fighters and Eagle bombers. Then there were the bodies. The vacuum of space had horribly distorted the already torn remains.

"The Terillians must have tried to take back the Sierra system," said Stone, his eyes glued to the devastation outside their small ship.

"We won't be able to accelerate for a jump until we get clear of this mess," said Orion. "I have never seen anything like this before. So many dead."

"It looks like at least two grand fleets fought it out here," added Mori. "That's tens of thousands of naval personnel and perhaps a corps of infantry on each side."

"It looks like both sides suffered heavy losses," said Stone in a low voice as his heart sank. "All of these people have died for a lie. On the whim of a few powerful Humani and their Xen masters, an entire generation of two civilizations will be sacrificed."

Mori placed her hand on Stone's arm. "We will find a way to stop this."

As Orion skillfully piloted her way through the minefield of wreckage, Mori pointed out more wreckage to Orion.

"Over there, that orbital destroyer," she said.

In the distance an orbital destroyer, its hull weakened by internal fires, exploded in a brilliant flash of orange and red. The wave of debris from the blast was visible as it radiated outward from the explosion.

"Look at that," Mori continued.

"Crap," exclaimed Orion. "Engineering—I need full power now!"

"What's wrong?" asked Stone.

"That explosion just released enough force to accelerate everything out here." As she spoke a body flew, not drifted, past the cockpit. "TC, keep your eyes open."

The tail section of a condor fighter passed over the ship. A dull but piercing screeching sound could be heard as it grinded over the top of their ship. Another body slammed into the cockpit, disintegrating in a puff of red mist.

"Son of a bitch," said Stone as he and Mori buckled themselves into the chairs behind Orion and TC.

"Damn it!" yelled Orion. "TC, give me a hand with the controls."

As Stone looked up from the clasp on his harness he saw the hulk of Terillian corvette tumbling bow over stern toward them.

"Look out!" he shouted.

Orion and TC pulled hard on the controls to take the ship vertical. Stone felt Mori's hand grip his wrist. They could hear metallic clangs as small pieces of debris whacked against the hull of the ship and the occasional sickening thud as non-metal objects slammed into *Hydra*.

"Did we clear it?" asked Stone.

"I don't..." Orion's response was interrupted by a massive jolt and the deafening sound of metal crunching. Stone felt his stomach do somersaults as the *Hydra* flipped over and spun violently to port.

"Give me thrusters to the port," ordered Orion.

"Not responding," reported TC.

"I'm taking starboard thruster to one-third. Initiating reverse pulse. Stabilizer to full." Orion was not a good pilot—she was a great one. Before long the ship was leveled and righted.

"Navigation, report status."

"Navigation system ready. Jump computer online, still recalculating jump coordinated to Alpha Humani. Short jump programmed for 500,000 kilometers."

"Roger. Engineering, report status."

"Online. Small fire in auxiliary propulsion room. Automatic organic halide flooding system has extinguished Charlie fire. Delta under control. Port thrusters inoperable. No known hull damage. Intermittent warning lights on aft stabilizer and O2 scrubber stations. Recommend putting down for hull inspection. I'm sure something else is f'ed up."

"Roger, Engineering," replied Orion. "Damn it," she continued while contemplating her options.

"To your starboard!" warned TC.

Orion lunged the ship forward and down as she took evasive action against a large chunk of metal that used to be a magnetic main battery.

"We need to get out of this crap," she added.

"I'll turn and try to match our speed with the debris until we reach orbital range of Sierra 7. When we're there, I will slingshot us around on a tangent and take us back around for a landing with the planet covering our approach."

Turning *Hydra*, Orion and TC worked to calculate the speed of the debris and quickly matched it. Once they were in equilibrium with the speed of the system, Orion let out a sigh of relief.

"So have either of you ever been to Sierra 7?" asked Orion. "It's beautiful from the sky."

Stone looked over to Mori, who was smiling. "Sierra 7. I think we may have been there before."

***

"Captain, coming up on Sierra 7 gravitational field in 40 seconds," reported TC.

"Mark the tangent line," ordered Orion.

"30 seconds to mark," reported TC.

"30 seconds, aye. On my mark, standby to initiate full thrusters and hard to starboard. Let's hope she's got enough left in her to make the turn."

"15 seconds to mark…10…5…"

"You two should get ready. This is going to be a bumpy ride," said Orion. "Engineering, standby for acceleration and hard to starboard in 3…2…1…Mark."

Stone could feel the force of the acceleration pushing him into the seat. It was almost as powerful as the initial acceleration into a jump. A powerful force pressing his body outboard told Stone the bank to starboard had started. Turning at full thrusters with the added acceleration of the gravitational pull of Sierra 7 had the *Hydra* at almost jump speed.

"Hold on," said Orion. "Here comes the gut buster."

"Securing thrusters, full port-180 Z-plane-NOW!"

Stone and Mori lost consciousness. Orion grunted as she struggled to keep her focus and control the ship through the maneuver. As the ship rapidly decelerated and full stabilizers placed a downward force on the *Hydra*, Orion shifted the controls downward and quickly pulled back. The maneuver caused the ship to tumble nose over tail. As it completed its revolution, Orion engaged full thrusters and leveled the ship, now traveling at cruising speed and heading inbound to Sierra 7.

"Whew! I wasn't sure that was gonna work," declared Orion. "I guess TC's buying drinks back on Port Royal."

"Maybe," said TC after the squeaking was decoded. "If we make it back alive though, Rickover will owe us a drink so it'll be a wash."

"How are the passengers doing?" asked Orion.

Mori and Stone were slowly coming to. Mori was pale and breathing heavily.

"What the hell did you do?" she asked.

"Looks like they'll make it," laughed TC.

"Sorry for the acrobatics, but we needed a quick way to get out of the debris path and on the safe side of the planet," explained Orion.

"That...was insane," said Stone.

"No," answered Orion. "That was necessary. Your suicide mission to Alpha Humana is insane. Either way the money's still worth it. Besides, it hasn't been boring. And if there's anything I hate...it's boring," she said as she looked back toward the two and smiled. "TC, let's get this bird on the ground so Rickover can work his magic."

Hydra entered the atmosphere over the Great Sea and moved swiftly toward the plains and mining villages. Before the plains came into view on the horizon, large plumes of smoke could be seen in the distance.

"Wonder what that is?" asked TC.

"I'm not sure but it doesn't look good," answered Orion. "We will set down just short of the Red Moss on the other side of the ridge at the end of the plains. That should be the safest place if there are any Terillians or Xen still around."

While the crew was concentrating on the columns of smoke dotting the horizon, Mori was scanning the foreground. A large object appeared near the rapidly approaching shoreline. The mangled steel structure was still recognizable.

"Look at that," she said.

Half-submerged, the wreckage of a Terillian carrier jutted out of the water only a few hundred yards from shore. The massive ship must have been pulled out of the sky by the planet's gravity. *Hydra* passed over the shipwreck seconds later and continued on toward the smoky columns.

"The fighting must have extended to the planet," said Stone. "Terillian carriers don't just fall out of orbit."

"And towns don't just disappear," added Orion as they flew over what had been the trading post town of Farland.

Vaporized by main batteries from either the Terillians or Xen, nothing but ash and debris remained. As *Hydra* sped over one destroyed village after another, the magnitude of the damage began to sink in to the crew. Passing over the remains of Slocum City, the ship pitched upward to clear the volcanic mountain marking the entrance to the Red Moss fields.

"We'll set down as soon as the Red Moss fields come into…."

"I don't believe it…" uttered Stone. "It's gone."

In place of the Red Moss fields lay a blackened wasteland. The bloody confrontation that had taken place in space had been mirrored on the plains and fields of Sierra 7. "Unbelievable," muttered Orion as she settled herself. "We still need to set down and check *Hydra* for external damage. I guess this place is as good as any."

Hydra slowed to make its landing a few hundred yards from where the fields would have begun.

***

"I guess we should go outside and take a look," said Stone as he unlatched himself from his seat.

Orion, Stone, and Mori stood at the outer door of *Hydra* preparing to exit.

As the outer door opened, Mori and Stone quickly moved to the right and left flank, rifles at the ready. Orion moved straight ahead.

The smell of charcoal and death filled the air. As far as Stone could see, everything was dead save the groups of scavenger birds feasting on the carnage. As Orion moved to his right, she choked against the odor.

"It's all gone. Everything," she said, placing her undershirt over her nose and mouth.

"The infantry from the fleet we passed must have fought here," said Mori in a hushed tone. "So many dead. There must be thousands of dead…tens of thousands."

"I knew that both the Xen and Terillian had the power to destroy entire worlds but I never thought I would see it," said Orion, still covering her face from the horrible smell.

As Orion, Mori, and Stone stared emptily across the land, a rustling noise from the burned debris caused them to instinctively react. All three turned and trained their weapons toward the noise.

"It's coming from that foxhole," said Stone.

The butt of his rifle firmly secured against his shoulder, Stone moved toward the sound. His finger rested on the trigger guard as he moved slowly. His body crouched down to present a smaller target and to allow him to stay compact and coiled if he had to react. In his peripheral he saw Mori circling toward to flank the position while Orion took up a defensive stance. When he was close enough, he stood fully erect and leveled his weapon at the source of the noise.

After a quick glance he looked over toward Mori, lowering his rifle to his side and motioning for her to do the same.

"What is it?" she asked as she rushed toward Stone.

"A wounded tiger," he answered.

The tiger looked up at Stone, its mouth open and ears flattened. In a feeble warning, it let out a low growl. The gaping wounds on its thigh and side made it obvious that the growl was only for show.

"Damn," said Mori as she reached the foxhole. "I wonder—"

Stone raised his hand to quiet Mori. "I hear something."

At first the sound was almost inaudible. Stone slightly shifted his position to get a better viewpoint.

"She has cubs," reported Stone. "They must have followed her into the foxhole."

"They will stay there until she dies and then they will starve," added Mori as she stood beside Stone.

Stone did the only humane thing. Taking careful aim, he fired three shots. Lowering his weapon, Stone stepped away from the edge of the foxhole.

"What is it?" shouted Orion as she made her way to the foxhole.

"More victims of Xen deception," replied Stone coldly.

"What is he talking about?" asked Orion as she looked toward Mori.

"Nothing. Nothing is out there," replied Stone. "Maybe that's what it will take to make things right again."

"What are you talking about?" asked Orion again.

"Maybe we all just need to be wiped away," he continued.

Mori responded. "Ty, hold on…"

"I'm going back to the ship," interrupted Stone. "We need to get to Alpha Humana and Dominotra."

Orion stood dumbfounded as Stone walked past her and toward the *Hydra*.

"Is he all right?" Orion asked Mori.

"I think so. He is having a hard time coming to grips with all of this. For years he thought he was doing what was right, just to find out he was a pawn of an evil empire. He will be fine. It will just take him some time. The Great Spirit has a destiny for him—I know it."

"I hope it's sooner rather than later," said Orion. "We don't have a lot of time. It will only be a few days once we get *Hydra* up and running."

"He will be fine," restated Mori. "He will do what is right when the time comes. His spirit is strong; he has powerful medicine but doesn't yet know it. We should get back to the ship and see how the repairs are going."

As the two women reached *Hydra*, Rickover was working feverishly on the externals of the old falcon.

"Where's Ty?" asked Mori.

"How should I know?" snapped Rickover as sparks flew while he secured the last of the hydraulic rods that had been damaged in the debris field. "He's onboard somewhere, I think."

"How much longer, Rick?" asked Orion.

"Not much, if people would stop asking me questions. Leave me alone, and it will be done in an hour."

"No problem. Would you like TC to give you a hand?"

"No!"

"Fine," replied Orion as she held her hands up in the air and backed away from the short-tempered engineer. Orion wasn't too upset, though; Rickover did his best work when he was pissed off. And he was usually pissed off.

Orion and TC were going over their startup checks when Rickover stuck his head into the cockpit. "Everything's fixed. I'll be back in my reactor spaces bringing up the auxiliaries for the jump. By the way, Captain, when are you going to shell out some Humani for me to hire a snipe or two? Unless you enjoy me slaving away down there by myself."

"Sure thing, Rick. We'll look at some assistants for you when we get back to Port Royal."

Orion laughed to herself. She had tried to hire help for Rickover three times but he never found any of them qualified enough.

"Maybe this time I can find one or two that aren't complete idiots," Rickover shouted on the way back to the engineering space.

As he moved aft, Rickover came across Mori.

"Rickover," she asked, "do you know where..."

"Your man was back in the storage bay earlier—if you're still looking for him," stated Rickover as he quickly walked past her, down into his engine room.

When Mori found Stone, he was pacing back and forth in the storage space.

"Ty, are you okay? You seemed a little out of sorts out there."

"I'm fine, Mori. That tiger and her cubs just put things in perspective for me."

"What do you mean?"

"It just helped me come to grips with the truth about the Xen and what I must do."

"What must you do?" Mori asked as she took Stone's hands in hers.

"I must fight them. That includes the Humani, including the innocent that know nothing of the Xen evils. I hate it but I don't think I can do anything else."

"You must look toward the greater good, Ty. The sooner the Xen are defeated, the sooner your people have a chance to see them for what they are and create their own identity."

"I don't know if they are my people anymore. Our whole civilization is based on a lie anyway. Most of them may not know it, but I do and everything about Humana society disgusts me now. I am alone."

"You are not alone, Ty. You have me," said Mori as she placed her arms around Stone. "You are one of the most honorable men I have ever known. You may have been born Hanmani, but you have the heart of a Terillian warrior and if you so desire, you will become one."

"I have lost everything I thought I wanted."

"But you gained everything you need, Ty."

Mori pulled his head down to hers for a slow, tender kiss. "Continue to let your heart and your honor lead you and everything will work out. Your spirit is strong. That is why you have been burdened with so much."

"My spirit?" asked Ty.

"Just because you don't believe doesn't mean it's not real. I felt your spirit the first time I saw you. Someday you will feel it too."

"I don't know about that," said Ty. "I can only handle having one world at a time shattered. Let me deal with the real world before I worry about a spiritual one."

"Okay, Ty." Mori gave him another kiss. "One thing at a time."

Chapter 17

Mori and Stone quickly made their way to the *Hydra's* cockpit.

"We're entering Alpha Humana airspace," reported Orion.

"I can't believe we've actually made it this far," confessed TC.

"I guess those codes we bought on Port Royal have paid off," replied Orion.

"Well," interrupted Mori, "the next test will be getting through Alpha Humana Airspace Control and gaining entrance to the Varus family estate."

"It will work," said Stone. "It has to."

As *Hydra* entered orbit, they were met by two condor fighters.

"*Falcon* vessel, this is CAP 23. You have entered Alpha Humana orbit. State intended destination."

"I hope your plan works," said Orion turning back toward Stone. "If not, we're going to have half the Humani fleet on top of us."

"CAP 23, this is bounty vessel *Hydra*," replied Orion. "Our destination is Estate Varus. Request clearance to deliver bounty A87430. Contractor Senator Varus."

"Standby *Hydra*. Contacting Estate Varus security."

"TC, make sure we have a jump calculated," warned Orion. "If this doesn't work we will only have one chance to get out of here."

"It will work," said Stone. "Astra always gets what she wants."

"*Hydra*, this is CAP 23, Estate Varus requests verification of bounty A87430."

"Roger, CAP 23." Orion turned toward Stone. "Any ideas?"

"Upload this," said Stone as he reached a data chip to Orion. "She will want to see my body. She's thorough."

"Sending data, standby to receive."

"Data received. Transmitting to Estate Varus."

A few moments passed. Then a few more.

"This is taking too long, Ty," said Mori. "I don't think its working."

"TC, double check those jump coordinates," said Orion.

"Roger, checking coor—Captain, picking up Xen frigate at three thousand kilometers, target angle…right in the middle of our jump path."

"Damn it," said Orion. "What is that ship doing there?"

"We're screwed," said Mori. "They are not buying it."

"TC, start a new jump calc."

"Aye, that will take a few minutes."

"We may not have it," warned Orion.

"Everyone relax," said Stone. "It will work. It will."

A few tense seconds passed.

The comm stated, "*Hydra*, this is CAP 23, patching Estate Varus through."

"Ah...Roger, over."

"*Hydra*, this is the Lady Astra Varus. A87430 verification is confirmed. What about A87431. Do you have the whore as well?"

Mori looked at Stone and mouthed the word *whore* to him. "That was your fiancée?"

"Like I told you earlier, she—"

"Never mind. I'm looking forward to meeting this *lady*." She gave another annoyed look at Stone and then spoke into the comms link. "She got away."

"Unfortunate. I would have liked to have had them both. You are authorized for landing. I am sending coordinates. As soon as I see the body, you will have your money."

"We understand," said Orion. "We will be arriving shortly."

The condors withdrew and *Hydra* banked toward the location of the Varus estate. In a few minutes they were overhead.

The estate was larger than most towns. At atmospheric cruising speed Hydra flew over gardens, lakes, servants' quarters, vineyards, stables, and a small military detachment.

"You have got to be kidding," said Mori. "One family lives there?"

"One family, their servants, their assistants, their security, their—"

"I get it."

"Still," added Orion. "It's almost as large as a polis on Port Royal."

"The Varus family is one of the wealthiest and most influential on the planet," said Stone. "They are expected to live like this."

"*Hydra*, this is Varus Estate security. You are cleared to land in bay 3. Vector to hangar is 235; ten kilometers."

"Roger, Varus Estate. We will be on deck in five minutes."

"It's game time," said Stone. "I will get ready. Just remember, you are bounty hunters."

***

A security team awaited the *Hydra* when it docked. Five heavily armed regulars stood on the loading dock as the bay doors opened. Behind them was a hovercraft.

"You must be the bounty hunters," said a sergeant from the security team. "We're here to escort you to Lady Varus and the Senator. Lady Varus insists on seeing the body."

"My crew is bringing it out from storage now," said Orion.

Mori stepped out of the bay behind Orion. The surprise on the sergeant's face was obvious. "Two female bounty hunters. I can only assume how you trap your prey," he smiled. "If all the bounty hunters look like you two," he continued, "being wanted might not be so bad."

The sergeant walked over to Mori. He leaned in close to her, his hand grabbing her bottom. "Maybe you do other 'jobs' for money as well."

Before he knew it, the sergeant was on his knees. Mori had control of his wrist and drove him to the ground. It was her turn to get close.

"There is not enough Humani on this planet, pig."

Mori released the man's wrist and gave him a kick in the rear as he scrambled to his feet.

"Should have known better than to mess with you Dark Zone trash anyway," said the sergeant as he rubbed his wrist.

"Besides," interrupted Orion. "We're the brains. Here comes the brawn."

The entire security team stepped backwards as TC exited the ship. He carried a large box in his massive arms. The soldiers parted as TC walked to the hover craft and dropped the box.

"There he is. Now take us to the money," said Orion.

"If you *women* will get aboard," replied the sergeant sarcastically, "the *Lady* Varus is waiting."

Once everyone was aboard the craft lifted off and headed toward the main estate, gliding over the immaculately landscaped terrain. During the short journey the majority of the security team stared at TC, jumping at his slightest movements. All except for the sergeant, whose ego was damaged; he stared at Mori.

"What's wrong, Sergeant?" asked Orion. "More used to the delicate flowers you call women on this planet?"

"Humani women are respectful...and know their place," he replied as he cast another glare at Mori.

"Oh, I know my place well, Sergeant," Mori shot back. "And it's not cowering to a man."

"You are lucky you are guests of the Senator, you arrogant bitch, or I would show you some manners," he retorted.

"If you do not shut up, Humani, I will show you my blade," warned Mori as her anger grew.

Orion placed her hand on Mori's arm.

"We must remain civil. We are guests of the Senator...the *very wealthy* Senator who is going to pay the bounty."

Mori realized she had almost given them away. Removing her hand from her sword, she put her hand on Orion's.

"You are right," she said. "Sometimes I am impetuous. It is a good thing you are here to provide balance."

"I see why she didn't like you, Sergeant," said one of the men who had taken his attention off of TC long enough to hear the conversation. "You know...maybe men aren't their type," he laughed.

Mori quickly moved her hand from Orion's and cast a cold look at the soldier. "I like men. I just haven't seen any on this planet yet."

"That's enough," said the sergeant. "Let's get them to the Senator, get them their money, and get them the hell off of our planet."

***

Lady Astra and Senator Varus stood beside a grand marble fountain in the center of the quest hall. The sergeant entered the room followed by TC, Mori, and Orion. Behind them four guards flanked a hover board carrying the large box TC had brought off the ship. The sergeant stopped a few paces from Astra and Dominotra, and bowed.

"Senator Varus, sir. Lady Astra. I present the bounty hunters."

"Two females and a Scapi," Astra replied. "What a strange combination for bounty hunters."

"Women are often underestimated," answered Orion. "It usually is an advantage for us."

"Yes. We are. Men are so often too busy being men," Astra smiled.

"Astra, you should view the body so that we can have these people on their way, dear," said the senator, not used to dealing with commoners.

"Yes. Of course, Father," she smiled at Orion. "See what I mean?" she whispered.

Astra looked toward the sergeant. "Sergeant, open the box," she ordered.

"Yes, ma'am."

The sergeant walked over to the hover board and disengaged the gravitational controls, causing the board to slowly drift to the ground. Once on the floor, he unclasped the lock for the box and opened the lid.

"It's him, ma'am," said the sergeant looking toward Astra.

Suddenly a sword sprung from the box and through the sergeant's neck. He fell backwards, dead before he hit the floor. Before they could react, TC wrapped his giant hands around the two guards beside him. In one quick, powerful motion he slammed their skulls together, killing them. Orion drew her pistol on Astra and Dominotra as Mori quickly sliced her way through the two remaining guards.

"What is this?" shouted Astra.

"It's a reunion, *my lady*," mocked Mori as she moved toward Astra, blood-soaked sword in hand. "It's your long-lost ex-fiancé and his Terillian *whore*."

Mori placed her sword against Astra's chest. As the blade pressed against her Astra showed no fear, only hatred. Looking past Mori, she saw Stone climbing out of the box.

"You despicable, low-bred son of a bitch. You have the audacity to attack my soldiers in my house and to bring this bitch with you."

Mori pressed the tip of the sword harder against Astra's skin, making a small cut. "I would watch my tongue, you elitist Xen cow."

Astra winced from the pain but quickly recovered. "Kill me if you like, Terillian slut. I do not fear you. I despise you. You will not make it off this planet alive."

"You were going to marry this viper?" asked Mori. "She does nothing but spew venom."

"It took me a while to see her true colors," replied Stone.

"True colors," snapped Astra. "You betrayed your people and your planet. For this?" She looked back toward Mori, disgust covering her face. "I should have realized it the way you cared about that commoner Martin. You deserve to wallow in filth like this."

"Oh—just shut up," said Mori and she brought her elbow against Astra's temple, knocking her unconscious.

"Ty, seriously, you and her?"

Stone turned toward Mori and shrugged his shoulders as he walked toward Dominotra.

"I will give you whatever you want, Stone. Just do not harm me or my daughter."

"I want the truth, Dominotra."

"The truth?"

Mori now turned her blade on the Senator. He winced as the blade just broke his skin as she slid it against his neck. "Navato. What is going on in Navato?"

"Navato? What do you mean?"

"Senator, do you think we came all this way with a bounty on our heads to have you play games?" warned Stone. "Maybe I should just have the Scapi tear your arms off?"

"Or maybe your enchanting daughter's?" added Mori.

"You truly have turned on your people, Stone. I regret the day I allowed Astra to speak to you."

"That's okay Senator; so do I," replied Stone. "I know the Xen started this war," he continued. "Cataline Tacitus knew what was going on at Navato, so I know you do, too. Now talk, or I will have my big blue friend start ripping things off."

Dominotra paused briefly to look at Astra, then spoke.

"It's the virus."

"The virus?" asked Stone.

Dominotra continued. "The Xen need labor for their home planets. For millennia, humanoids have supplied that labor. They conquer a civilization and take a portion as chattel to maintain the genetic mixing of their slave population. The rest are reorganized and over the years the conquest is covered up by the history links, just like the fairy tale about the war between the Eastern and Western alliances. There was no war except Alpha Humani trying in vain to defend itself against Xen and Doran invaders."

"So it's all true," said Stone.

"Yes," answered Dominotra. "After several generations the conquered worlds, just like ours, become yet another ally to the Xen. These allies supply them resources, military assets to fight their wars, and slaves when necessary in return for nothing other than their word they will not enslave the entire populace. The Dorans were conquered so long ago they no longer need 'advisors.' No one left on their worlds know the truth—"

"That makes perfect sense," interrupted Mori. "What about the virus and the slavers?"

"About three decades ago a virus infected their humanoid slaves. They tried to create vaccines, but all efforts failed. As a result they needed more and more slaves from the Dark Zone to maintain their population."

"Do you mean my sister could be a slave on a Xen home world?" asked Mori as her anger grew.

"She is most likely dead. The virus continued to spread and the slave population declined even with increased shipments. That is when the Xen issued their Directive."

"Directive? What is that?" asked Orion.

"They couldn't kill the virus, but they found a genetic answer. On Venato, they started a genetic testing program trying to alter humans to be immune. Apparently they have had success. The only problem is that only 5 percent of humans are genetically acceptable for the alteration. The rest just die a painful death as their body destroys itself."

"What is the Directive?" demanded Mori again as she pressed the blade against Dominotra's neck once again.

"With only a small percentage viable, the Xen ambassadors proposed an ultimatum which they called the Directive. The relatively small numbers captured by slavers were not enough to meet their demands so we could either attack the Terillians or push into the Dark Zone and hopefully into Terillian worlds to obtain enough genetically acceptable specimens, or face enslavement of our entire civilization. We chose war over enslavement."

"Better poor settlers and Terillians than rich Humani," said Mori as she pressed the sword against his neck a little harder. A small trail of blood rolled down Dominotra's skin.

Gasping against the pressure of Mori's blade, Dominotra continued. "Whether instilled by the Xen or not, it is our way. The strong do what they can and the weak endure what they must. If we stay strong and force our will on lesser peoples, we will stay free."

“Free?” spat Mori. “You are nothing put puppets, lap dogs for a species most of you have never seen. A proud and strong civilization…my ass. You are cowards. In your fear you pretentious self-important bastards will have entire worlds enslaved rather than tell your people the truth. What makes you think you can defeat the Terillians now? You were unable to defeat them before.”

“We supported the last war until the Xen grew tired of fighting. Although we carried a heavy burden, the Xen and Doran worlds bore the bulk of the fighting. They began to negotiate when they felt themselves economically strained. This time it’s different. The Xen will expend more because they need more slaves for their society to function and we will expend everything. If we lose, we will become slaves. Failure is not an option.”

“Why not tell the truth to the people and turn on the Xen?” asked Stone.

“The truth. You are a fool, Stone. Even if we told the commoners and somehow fended off the Xen, the higher classes would lose their power forever. This was deemed the best option by the First Families. Besides, it will not matter soon.”

“What do you mean?” asked Mori.

“I cannot.”

“Forget about the Scapi,” said Mori. “I am going to cut your little bitch’s heart out myself if I can find one in there.” Mori turned toward Astra’s unconscious body.

“Wait…don’t. I will tell you. Just don’t harm her.”

“Talk!” demanded Mori.

"The research on Venato has not only created a viable subspecies, they have almost completed a weaponized version of the virus. Once complete it can be used to decimate populations in the Dark Zone or even Terillian planets if we can reach them, leaving them defenseless. The survivors will already be predisposed to genetic alteration and shipment to Xen worlds. That same virus can be used on us if we fail."

"You bastard. You will kill hundreds of millions," interrupted Orion.

"To keep our civilization strong. It is worth it."

"How do we get on the planet?" asked Mori. "We have to stop them before they complete the research."

"Other than Dorans, Xen, and certain slavers, no one has access."

"How do we get access?" asked Stone.

"The Association. They control the access. They ar—"

From behind the darkness of the columns surrounding the room, a small cloaked figure pounced on top of Dominotra. As the Senator screamed in pain, the hood fell down from the attacker as it sank its teeth into his neck. The creature had brownish-green prickly scales, an angled forehead, and black eyes inlaid in deep sockets. It was a Xennite ambassador.

"Holy shit!" yelled Orion as she fired her pistol.

The creature rolled off of the Senator, blue liquid flowing from the holes Orion had placed in its body. Mortally wounded, the Xen rolled onto its back attempting to draw a small pistol. Another shot from Orion hit the Xen and the pistol fell from its scaly hand. As its long black tongue flicked in and out, the Xen hissed and spat blue liquid from its mouth.

"Human waste. You have killed Batalus." More blue liquid pooled on the floor. "Foolish senator talked too much. I should have taken care of him sooner. If it was up to Batalus, I would let all of you die and find another species of slaves. The virus was a sign. A sign to let your kind perish as is the natural order."

It continued to speak.

"Evolution does not tolerate the weak. Fortunate for your species the Emperors have found your kind interesting over the eons." The creature began to spit blue bodily fluid as it rapidly filled its mouth. "Should have destroyed you interlopers when we found you. It is you who are the virus."

"Father!" screamed Astra as she regained consciousness and saw her mortally wounded father.

The venomous Xen saliva worked quickly on Dominotra. Necrosis rapidly spread over his body as Astra ran toward her father.

"Astra," he coughed as she knelt beside him. "The Varus line now passes to you. Keep it strong and ensure the survival of our people and our way of life."

He reached upward toward her cheek, his arm now blackened by the Xen's poison.

"The Varus family shall prosper, Father, and you will be avenged," Astra promised her father through her tears.

A few meters away, the Xen lay motionless.

"I think it's dead," said Mori, motioning to the creature surrounded by a pool of blue.

"And so is my father, you bitch," interrupted Astra, her eyes filled with tears.

Sadness and anger poured from her entire body. She pounced at Mori, but was no match for her. Another blow sent her back to the ground. She looked up at Mori, her hatred burning strong.

"I will see you suffer if it is the last thing I do," she grumbled. "You will not make it off this planet alive."

"The gunfire could have been heard by someone," interrupted TC. "We need to silence their communications center."

"Where is it?" asked Orion.

"I know where it is," answered Stone. The excitement of the incident had caused him to lose focus. "It's down that corridor and to the left. I will go. As soon as I get back we need to get out of here."

Stone gave a quick glance toward Mori. She was standing over Astra, her weapon drawn. Astra stared back up at Mori. Tears poured down her face, but her eyes showed nothing but rage and a thirst for vengeance. Mori looked to Stone.

"You need to get going, Ty," she said.

"Right," he replied as he quickly turned and ran toward the communications center.

***

Precious moments passed as Mori, Orion, and TC waited for word from Stone.

"What is taking him so long?" asked Mori, her pistol still pointed at Astra.

"TC, maybe you should see if he has had any trouble," added Orion.

"I will see what is keeping him," said TC as he turned and rumbled down the passageway.

"I hope he's dead," said Astra, still huddling over her father's corpse. "I hope you all die."

"You are one evil bitch," said Mori. "It's nice to see the cream of Humani civilization crawling on the floor with the other vermin."

"You are all scum," replied Astra. "Once we have defeated your troublesome race, I will find all of your surviving kin and make them my personal slaves."

Mori raised her pistol to Astra's head. "My family has suffered enough at the hands of your kind," she replied.

"Wait," interrupted Orion. "Don't become like her."

Mori looked down the barrel of her pistol toward Astra's face. She was not human, not really.

"You are lucky, bitch," said Mori. "Watch yourself, or I WILL finish this."

***

Stone rushed out of the control room and turned down the corridor. Taking out the communications center had gone without a hitch and he was returning when he ran headlong into the unexpected. Standing between Stone and escape was Major Arilius Tacitus, sword drawn.

"I did not think you would be stupid enough to come after her," said Arilius Tacitus as he walked toward Stone.

Stone raised his hand in a gesture for Arilius to wait.

"Major Tacitus...Arilius, you don't understand. You...we have been lied to all this time. You think you are doing the right thing but you are not."

"Silence, traitor. I do not wish to hear anything you have to say. You have taken the life of a family member, dishonored the Lady Astra, and killed other fellow Humani, all to help a Terillian. And now you have the audacity to try to attack the Senator and Lady Astra in their home."

"Arilius. I did not come here to fight you," pleaded Stone. Stone stepped backwards, but readied himself.

"That is too bad because I have dreamt of nothing but taking your life for weeks. I once looked up to you as a mentor. Now I despise you for the traitor you are."

"Listen. You have to believe me."

"If you have anything else to say, traitor, say it with your sword."

Arilius swung upwards with his sword, knocking the rifle out of Stone's hand and sending him reeling backwards. Quickly regaining his balance Stone drew his sword, but Arilius was already on him. Bending his body to avoid Arilius's attack, he was just a little too slow. The blade cut across his arm, leaving a gash in his sleeve and sending blood trickling down his arm.

"I don't want to fight you," pleaded Stone.

"Then die!" shouted Arilius as he thrust his sword at Stone.

Stone parried and landed a punch across his opponent's face. Major Tacitus countered quickly, landing a boot behind Stone's knee, flipping him onto his back. Stone brought his sword up just in time to block the next attack. Grabbing his opponent's arm, Stone kicked him in the ribs, causing him to back off momentarily. Both men were immediately on their feet again, circling.

***

In the guest hall, Astra continued her verbal attack against Mori.

"Enjoy this moment, whore. I will have my vengeance. I will see your traitorous lover crucified and you sold to slavers and whored out to the masses."

Astra's threats resulted in a backhand from Orion, trying to act before Mori's anger overflowed.

"You and your slaver accomplices will face justice for your evils—in this life or the next. For now you need to keep your mouth shut," warned Orion.

***

Stone continued his battle with Major Tacitus, slamming him against the wall and landing several elbows to the side of his head. Arilius groaned and responded with a knee to Stone's kidneys. Stone stumbled backwards as the major fell to his knees. They stared at one another, both bleeding from several superficial wounds. Arilius sprung from his coiled position. Stone dropped to the floor as Arilius passed over him. Their swords both hit their marks. Stone stood up, slowed by the new wound across his leg. Major Tacitus stood facing

Stone, one hand holding his sword, the other the gash across his stomach.

"We're going to kill each other," said Stone.

"So be it, traitor. Then I will have done my duty."

As Arilius Tacitus spoke, he did not notice TC approaching him from behind. At the last moment, he sensed a presence behind him. He spun right into TC's fist. The blow knocked Arilius against the wall, unconscious.

TC drew his pistol to finish him off.

"No!" shouted Stone as he placed his hand over TC's weapon. "Let's just get out of here."

***

Astra looked up at Orion, wiping the blood from her lips.

"First of all, there is no 'next' life, you barbaric religious fanatic."

She turned toward Mori.

"Second, I am from a First Family, you ignorant Terillian slut. I am the law. Before I fade into nothingness, I will make sure my progeny hunt down you and your family until none is left. I will erase your line from existence."

"Progeny?" laughed Mori. "I pity any whelp you would birth."

"You shall see soon enough. As you stand there in your misplaced triumph, your lover's seed grows inside my womb."

"Liar!" shouted Mori as she landed another backhand against Astra's face.

"It is true. A son," she continued, smiling through the blood dripping from her face. "He will be raised as the heir to the Varus line. Raised in the seat of power and taught to hate all enemies of the empire, especially the traitor who killed his grandfather and his Terillian concubine."

"Hit her again," said Orion.

Mori obliged.

Spitting blood from her mouth, Astra smiled. Her perfect hair was now a tangled mess, her well-structured checks were soaked with the salty stains of tears, and her once-intoxicating smile was replaced by wells of blood that pooled around her teeth.

"Does it bother you that I carry your man's child? Imagine what it will do to him when he hears the news?"

"He will never know," replied Mori as she slowly raised her pistol.

"Do it!" yelled Orion.

Mori fired. Astra's body slumped limply onto the ground and blood began to pool from the back of her head. Mori, still holding her pistol at Astra's motionless body, looked over toward Orion.

"You probably did more good for the Terillian race and humanoids in general with that one bullet than the millions that have been fired before."

"What happened?" asked Stone, who had turned the corner into the room seconds after Mori's shot rang out.

"Ty…I…"

"She grabbed a weapon," interrupted Orion. "I had to shoot her."

Surprised, Mori looked over to Orion. Orion returned a glance of acknowledgment.

Stone stood silent.

Mori turned back toward Stone and started to speak.

"I—"

"You had no choice," interrupted Stone. "We have to get out of here."

***

The group quickly made their way back to *Hydra*. As the hovercraft came to an abrupt stop, they jumped off and ran toward the ship. Rickover stood at the entrance as Orion and TC raced past him.

"What the hell?" he said. "That took long enough."

"Shut up, Rickover," ordered Orion. "Get below deck and make sure we have full power until we can jump."

Rickover felt the urgency in her voice.

"Aye, Captain. I'll make sure you've got what you need."

Orion and TC jumped into their seats and started bringing the ship to life. Mori and Stone took their places behind them and buckled their straps. Orion's and TC's hands were a blur as they worked the controls. In a few seconds *Hydra* was free of the magnetic mooring and rapidly accelerating upwards toward orbit.

"TC, have us ready to jump as soon as we get out of the atmosphere."

"Roger, where to?"

"Navato system," she replied.

"Roger."

"You don't have to do that," said Stone. "I don't have enough money left to cover you taking us that far."

"Consider this one on the house. After what I heard back there, I'm all in on this one."

"Captain, two condors closing fast. Fire control radar is tracking."

"Son of bitch," replied Orion. "Engineering, remove all safeties."

"Remove safeties, Aye."

Hydra shuddered as Orion took her to full throttle.

"Arilius," said Stone. "He must have had an alternate communication suite installed. I should have thought of that."

"They're firing!" shouted TC.

"Hold on," ordered Orion as she rolled the ship and pulled into a full vertical accent. Explosions rocked the ship as the first salvo barely missed them. "Are the coordinates ready?"

"Thirty seconds. Firing again."

"Release countermeasures. I'm gonna try to get behind one of them."

Before he met Cassandra Orion, Stone would have thought it was suicide for a pilot to engage condors with a thirty-year-old falcon. Ten seconds and a stomach-wrenching maneuver later, she was behind the condors.

"Engaging fire control. Tracking."

The first condor engaged after thrusters and started to pull away, but the second thought himself a worthy opponent. He was not.

"Fire control locked. Firing."

Two plasma pulses traced a line from the falcon to the condor. Both found their mark. The condor disappeared in a white hot explosion as *Hydra* accelerated through the debris. Passing through the explosion, the bluish sky turned dark as the ship sped out of the atmosphere into space.

"Ten condors approaching from Alpha Humana. Picking up a frigate accelerating toward us off the starboard quarter," warned TC. "Jump coordinates locked. The frigate is opening fire."

"Engage jump, now," ordered Orion.

In a bright blue flash, *Hydra* accelerated and then disappeared into the vastness of space.

Chapter 18

A few minutes out of *Hydra's* jump and the massive asteroid belt came into view. Beyond lay Venato and possibly the fate of two civilizations.

"Damn," said Orion as she peered out of the cockpit. "That is a lot of asteroids."

"How are we going to navigate through that?" asked Stone, amazed by the vastness of the field.

"Looks like it's not going to be easy," answered Orion.

"Magnetic fields are disrupting my short range navigation systems," reported TC.

"Not easy at all." Orion reached over to reduce the gain on search radar, which was clouding due to the field. "We're gonna have to do this manually, TC," Orion added as she continued to adjust the radar.

"Is that possible?" asked Mori.

"I don't know," Orion replied, "but there's not really any other choice but to go back."

"Captain," said TC, "picking up comms on Xen frequencies."

"So there is something out here," said Stone.

"Put it through," Orion said to TC, still adjusting the gains.

"*Falcon* vessel, this is Venato Control. Pass identification codes or you will be engaged."

"What codes?" asked Stone. "Aren't we already emitting Xen idents?"

"We are but I have a feeling they want something else."

"Captain," informed TC, "picking up craft off our bow, coming in...*really fast*."

Two fast-moving craft rapidly approached *Hydra*. A few kilometers from the ship, they slowed and took up escort positions. Their silver metallic coating shimmered against the backdrop of space.

"I think those are condors," said Stone. "But none like I have ever seen."

"Daaammn," declared Orion. "That's the sexiest ship I've ever seen."

"I hate to break up the love-fest, but if we don't give them whatever code they want that sexy ship is going to vaporize us," warned Mori.

The group stared at one another, not sure of their next move.

"Might as well give it a shot," said Orion, breaking the silence. "TC, upload that code we purchased on Port Royal...the one you said was a waste of Humani."

"What code?" asked Stone.

"I came across a Xen code in the market polis a few months back. The dealer said it was a code for slaver vessels allowing access to special territory. They were asking a fortune for it but the dealer was reputable and had some connections with the Association so I figured it might come in handy someday...Let's hope today is that day."

"Sending the code," reported TC. "Hopefully it was worth the money."

A few seconds elapsed.

"Confirmed," came through the comms circuit.

"Damn, that was close," exclaimed Orion.

While they were celebrating their minor victory, the two advanced condors cut in front of *Hydra* and, with a flash of silver, were gone, accelerating to near-jump levels in seconds.

"Those condors were something," said Orion, still impressed. "But I don't think we're gonna get through the field as easily as they are."

Falcon vessel vector to 320 relative, maintain current Z position.

"Roger?" answered Orion as she looked toward TC and shrugged.

Following the ordered course, *Hydra* continued on toward the asteroid belt. Soon, two large orbital stations came into view in the distance. Seconds later, an opening began to materialize in the field between the stations. Eventually, a void large enough for *Hydra* to pass was created.

"Those stations are putting out a massive magnetic field," said TC. "It must be acting on the metals in the asteroids."

"I guess they're opening up the doors for us," said Mori. "Better get through before they change their mind."

Hydra drifted through the corridor created by the stations. Massive floating boulders floated in all directions—held back by electro-magnetic force. Those same magnetic fields were also wreaking havoc with ship.

"Thrusters to port," ordered Orion as she struggled against the forces pulling the ship off course. "It might have been easier to navigate the field."

Stone looked over toward Mori and smiled.

"What is it?"

"Your hair."

Mori's hair had returned to its normal length, and the static electricity created inside the ship caused it to expand in all directions. Mori's cheeks grew flush as she felt her hair.

"Shut up, Ty," she replied with a quick jab to Stone's shoulder.

A quick jolt of electricity passed from her hand, giving Stone a little shock and giving Mori obvious satisfaction.

"Looks like we're almost through," said TC. "Systems are returning to normal."

"There it is," said Orion.

Venato lay dead ahead of them.

"Shit!" uttered Orion as an enormous Royal Xen battle cruiser drifted along in high orbit. Noticeably larger than the Humani or Doran versions, the gigantic ship orbited Venato like a small moon, keeping watch on the secret project and ensuring the Directive was being carried out. Several smaller crafts made their way toward the planet—undoubtedly slavers with more specimens for the Gateway.

"All right, Tyler," asked Orion, "where do we go from here?"

Stone froze. He didn't have a plan. He was actually surprised they had made it as far as they had.

"Stone?" asked Orion again.

"I'm thinking."

"You need to come up with something fast. We're entering the atmosphere, and a slaver ship without a cargo of slaves is going to cause some problems."

"We need a way to get on the planet and not have them come after us," said Stone, thinking out loud.

"Oh, that's all," said Orion sarcastically. "Why didn't you say so?"

"Just give me a couple minutes."

"Another couple minutes and we're either gonna be face to face with those reptiles or shot out of the sky."

"Wait," interrupted Mori. "You've got it."

"What the hell are you talking about?" asked Orion.

"We need to crash."

"What?" said Orion as she turned in her cockpit to look at Mori.

"You can do a dead stick entry, right?"

"Like a silent insertion mission?" added Stone, starting to understand Mori's plan.

"Yeah…but…" Orion mouthed the word "Oh" as she grasped Mori's plan.

"TC, kill the sensors…Engineering, standby for deadstick landing. TC, patch in our comms."

"Engineering, standing by," reported Rickover.

"Securing thrusters and stabilizers," warned Orion. "Hold on."

Hydra pitched downward as all electronic power was lost. The familiar floating stomach sensation came to Mori and Stone as the ship plunged downward.

"Time to give 'em a show," said Orion as she activated the comm link. "Venato Control, this is falcon vessel, captives have escaped hold. Electronics damaged, flight control inoperable, losing altitude."

Falcon vessel, this is Venato control. Per Directive instructions, assistance is not authorized.

"I knew they wouldn't give a damn about a single load of captives or the crew," shouted Mori, breathing heavily against the gravitational force exerted during the free fall.

"Venato, falcon vessel, approach too fast...can't maintain control..." Orion looked over toward TC. "I hope they bought it."

Condor CAP 7, this is Venato Control, incoming track 32 experienced power failure, crash imminent, perform visual.

"Are they going to buy this with a flyby?" said Stone as he struggled against the force of the dive.

"They will now," said Orion as she yanked back on the controls.

Stone felt dizzy as the ship tumbled end over end, spinning as it fell. The condors were looking for a ship out of control—Orion would give them one. As the horizon appeared, disappeared, and rolled in the cockpit view, Orion saw two condors flash past *Hydra.*

Venato control this is CAP 7, verified falcon control and power failure. Returning to orbit.

Stone tried to focus on the horizon but had to close his eyes as the spinning a rattling of the ship took its toll on his senses.

"They bought it," huffed Orion. "TC...mark...altitude..."

"One...five...zero...zero...meters."

"Give...me...hydraulics and weapons control," she ordered as Orion's muscles strained against the controls.

"Come on *Hydra*, you bitch!" she yelled. "Work with me!"

Hydra complied and slowly righted itself with a little help from Orion.

"TC, release debris storage. Reverse thrusters, full rudder. Standby to release explosive inventory."

"What kind of explosives are you carrying onboard?" asked Stone.

"I had Rickover make a mod to carry six carriage bombs…never know when you might need to make your own landing zone, or in this case, fake your own crash," smiled Orion.

TC reported he was ready. "Debris hatch open, standing by to release…"

"Release."

With Orion's order, the ship bounced as the weight of the debris and the bombs were released and the thrusters engaged. As *Hydra's* descent slowed, Orion fired the main engine to get forward momentum before the bombs impacted. The explosion pitched *Hydra* forward, but it was nothing Orion could not control. Bringing *Hydra* to the treetops, Orion turned to view the impact area.

"Hopefully this scattered debris and scorch patterns should provide enough evidence to satisfy any follow-up Xen patrols. TC, secure everything except passive search, hydraulics, and weapons. Let's keep as quiet as possible."

She turned back to Stone and Mori. "We're about ten or fifteen kilometers from their main base. Sorry I couldn't get it closer. We'll move parallel until we find a place to sit down and figure out our next move. That should give you more than a 'couple minutes' to get a plan together," she smiled.

"Cassandra," said Mori. "If the Terillian Confederation had more pilots like you, we could deal with the Xen easily."

"I'm not sure about that," answered Orion, "but consider me in the service of the Confederation once again. I can't sit this one out. It's too big…and way too exciting."

In a few minutes, Orion found a small clearing that Stone would never have thought a falcon could land in, until he met Orion. Once on the ground, Orion unbuckled herself from her seat and turned toward Mori and Stone.

"TC, you and Rickover find some camouflage to hide the ship from overhead patrols," said Orion.

She then unbuckled and turned toward Stone and Mori.

"Let's get some fresh air and figure out our next move."

Stone felt the warmth of the sun and the cool breeze on his face; he breathed deeply. The smell of wildflowers, trees, and a nearby stream filled his senses.

"Now that's refreshing after all that time on recycled air," said Orion as she stepped out of *Hydra* and onto the soft ground below.

"It's actually kind of beautiful," said Mori as she looked into the forest surrounding their ship.

"It's hard to believe that amidst all this beauty, such evil is taking place," added Stone, remembering what had brought them to the planet.

"Well, what do we do from here?" asked Orion.

"At first I just wanted to find out what was going on out here, but now we have to find a way to shut down the operation," said Stone.

"Maybe we should just try to get out of here and inform the Terillian military," proposed Orion. "Let them take out the base."

"First," added Mori, "we would have to get out of here without getting killed. Then we would have to get through the asteroid belt, no doubt chased by those badass condors. If we somehow make it past them and get through the Dark Zone to Terillian territory, they would have to redirect at least an entire national or even Confederation fleet and fight their way here. By then they could have the virus weaponized."

"Looks like we will have to do it from here," replied Stone. "Now we just have to figure out how to destroy an entire base with a thirty-year-old falcon and five people."

A report from Rickover came through the short-range comm link.

"Captain, we've got something over here you should see. We're about half a kilometer forward of the ship."

"Roger. We'll be there in a minute," replied Orion.

Thick layers of decomposing plant life, moss, and fallen trees covered the ground in the dense deciduous forest as the group headed toward Rickover and TC. A few yards into the forest, Stone began to feel uneasy; something was not right. He brought his rifle to the ready and motioned to Mori, who had already done the same.

Stone quickly and quietly moved to take a flanking position and faded into the wilderness.

***

"What is it?" asked Orion as she caught her breath after reaching TC and Rickover.

"It looks like an abandoned camp of some sort," said TC, sifting through the grayish black remains of a fire.

"About a day old," stated Mori. "Probably about ten strong."

"Wonder what they're doing out here," added Rickover. "I would have assumed the Xen would have cleared the planet of any indigenous populations."

"They would have," replied Mori as she rummaged through the remnants of the campsite,

moving a small branch with her foot. Seeing a metallic object lying underneath the brush, she knelt down to investigate.

It was a clip for an assault rifle.

Placing the clip in her pocket, Mori quickly scanned the forest and made her way toward a large felled tree to take a defensive position.

"Everyone find a place to take cover."

The rest of the group was looking for adequate cover when Mori heard a noise coming from the dense foliage.

"Get down!" she shouted as she pointed her rifle downfield toward the noise, waiting for something to appear.

Focused on the initial threat, she was slow to hear the noise to her right. Finally, the sound registered and she swung her rifle toward the new threat.

As she turned, a blow to her shoulder knocked the rifle out of her hands and sent her tumbling. Rolling to her left she drew her sword and brought it to bear just as the attacker stepped toward her. A tall, slender man stared down the blade as she looked into the barrel of his pistol.

Her intuition had been right. Several attackers had rushed out of the forest. A quick scan of the situation appraised Mori of the fate of her comrades. Rickover hadn't even moved from his prone position. A woman had a foot placed on his back and a rifle to his head. Orion was wrestling with two attackers, but it appeared they were getting the best of her. TC had one attacker in each hand, dangling them several feet off the ground, but two more had their weapons pointed at him and he was submitting.

Mori was disgusted with herself. How could she have let someone get that close? Had her skills deteriorated that much or were they that good?

"Who are you?" she asked.

"I will ask the questions," snapped the man. "Your friends are captured. Submit or they will be killed."

Mori thought she at least had a chance to take out the man in front of her, but she was less confident about the others. Just as she was about to concede, there was more rustling from the trees.

"Put down your weapons!" came a voice from nearby.

Mori turned toward the noise to see Stone emerge from the forest with a woman in front of him. He held her hair tightly, forcing her head toward the sky. His pistol rested firmly against the base of her skull.

"Drop your weapons or I will scatter her brains across this forest," he warned.

The man in front of Mori looked toward Stone. In doing so, he was distracted just enough to allow Mori to make her move. In a quick, fluid movement Mori grabbed the weapon and twisted it behind the man's back and brought the blade of her sword to his neck.

There was a long silence as each person nervously examined their opponents, playing out options in their minds.

***

Fearing someone would make a hasty and deadly mistake, Stone took action. He twisted the woman's hair, forcing her to her knees. Pressing the pistol to the top of her head he issued the warning again.

"Now!" he ordered.

Stone noticed the rest of the attackers looking toward the man under Mori's blade. Pegging him as the leader, he turned the woman's face toward him.

"Surrender!" he shouted.

"I'm sorry, Horatio," said the woman.

The man's focus remained on Stone's captive. From the look on his face, Stone could tell the two shared deep feelings toward one another. Either way, Stone had the advantage. It was time for him to capitalize on it. He shifted his grip on the pistol from his right to left hand and then, placing his boot on her neck, he forced her to the ground. Once she was pinned, he drew his sword and placed it against her neck.

"Maybe I will take her apart piece by piece."

The sword against her neck had made the difference. After a deep breath, the man conceded. "Release them," he ordered. "Drop your weapons."

The attackers released TC, Orion, and Rickover, who quickly picked up the would-be captors' weapons.

Mori gave the man a shove and pushed him in with the others while her companions corralled the attackers into the center of the old camp. The man snarled, actually snarled, when he turned back toward Mori.

"Release her!" he ordered. "We have surrendered. Do not harm her!"

Stone removed his foot from the woman's back, allowing her to scramble over to the leader. They embraced and then turned back toward Stone and Mori.

"Like I was saying," said Mori. "Who are you?"

The woman looked toward the leader. "Horatio, don't tell them anything."

"I guess the Humani have finally starting helping their Xen masters with the experiments," replied Horatio.

"We're not working with Xen," said Orion in a reassuring voice.

"We're here to stop them," added Mori.

Horatio turned his nose back toward Mori and drew in a deep breath, sniffing the air.

"Kendra, the scent," he said.

"Yes," she replied, "I smell it too."

Pointing to Mori, Horatio asked, "What is that one's name, please?"

"Captain Mori Skye," Mori answered.

Horatio and Kendra looked at one another. Kendra nodded and Horatio looked back toward Mori and slowly stepped forward.

"My name is Horatio. I am the second leader of the wolf clan. This is my mate, Kendra."

"Wolf clan?" asked Orion. "Are you native to this planet?"

"Native!" said Horatio. "I am from Bravo 3 in the Dark Zone. I was captured by slavers when I was ten and transported here. Kendra was a Terillian trader before she was taken. We are a small group of escapees from the Citadel."

"Were you captured for genetic testing?" asked Mori.

"Yes," replied Horatio. "But I do not know to what end. All I know is that we escaped and have fought to survive ever since."

"I assure you we're not your enemy," Mori replied, dropping her weapon to her side.

She motioned for the others to do the same.

"The Xen are experimenting with humans to create a hybrid that is resistant to a virus killing off their slave populations," she continued. "We have come to stop them."

"So they have changed us...done all of this only to *keep* us slaves?" declared Horatio, his anger boiling over. "I thought my hatred for them could grow no more."

He let out a guttural groan.

"Five of you?" asked Kendra. "How will five of you stop the Xen?"

"We're still working on that part," said Orion. "Aren't we, Tyler?"

"How do we know this is not some Humani-Xen trap to get us to give up our location? This one reeks of Humani," asked Horatio cautiously.

"I promise you," replied Mori. "We are no friends of the Xen."

"Horatio," interrupted Kendra, "the female, her scent—we must take them back."

Mori looked puzzled. "What are you talking about?" she asked.

"You are…"

"Not yet," Horatio interrupted Kendra's reply. "We must seek out the elder; he will know what to do."

"Yeah," interjected Orion. "Let's go see the elder."

"We shall," replied Horatio. "He will determine if you are friend or foe."

"You must realize we are friends," said Mori as stepped toward Horatio.

"I am sorry," apologized Horatio, as he quickly backed away from her. "You smell—"

"What are you talking about?" asked Mori, more than a little embarrassed.

"Horatio," said Kendra. "They are not aware of our…differences."

"You're right," he said. "Forgive me. I forgot. The testing…it has created some…well…we must see the elder."

As Horatio spoke, Stone looked closely at his face. His jaw protruded forward more than normal. Behind the thick head of hair that covered his head and his bushy beard, she could make out a slight peak to his ear.

"The genetic alterations?" asked Mori, having noticed the same.

"Yes. But we can talk about that later. Follow me. We shouldn't stay in one place too long."

***

They followed Horatio and his group a few yards into the forest. Coming to sudden stop, Horatio began to sniff the air.

"Here it is," he said as he reached down into the undergrowth. Withdrawing a rope from the undergrowth, he gave it a tug and the ground opened up to expose an underground passage.

"Welcome to our den," he smiled as he motioned for everyone to enter.

Mori felt the dampness of the air as she entered the tunnel. Looking down the long corridor, she saw a series of very dim lights extending into the darkness beyond. A few hundred yards into the tunnel and a voice called out.

"Horatio, is that you? Who are the strangers?"

Horatio again sniffed the air. "Yes, Caliph. It is I. I have brought visitors."

The group continued forward until another man came into view in the poorly lit tunnel. He was a small man, but had fierce eyes that almost glowed in the dim light. As the group approached, he lowered his weapon and sniffed the air, just as Horatio had. "One of them is..."

"Yes, Caliph," interrupted Horatio. "I am taking them to Magnus."

"What are they talking about?" whispered Mori to Stone.

"I'm not sure. Just keep your guard up," replied Stone.

Continuing past the guard, they soon entered a large open area. Slightly better lit than the tunnel itself, a group of about twenty people could be seen scattered throughout the den. All activity ceased as the strangers walked into the room.

Suddenly two young males ran toward them aggressively.

"Caleb! Nathan! Stop!" ordered Horatio.

The youths stopped in their tracks. Still staring at the strangers, they started to circle them, their noses in the air collecting scents. As Horatio walked toward them, they lowered their heads.

"These people are our guests. Return to your parents."

"Yes, Horatio," they answered in unison and scurried back toward the edge of the den. As they retreated a large figure stepped forward. He was older and his jaw jutted awkwardly outward and large canine teeth could be seen as he spoke.

"Horatio, who are these people? And why have you brought them here?" he asked.

"We found them in the forest, Elder. They say they have come to fight the Xen."

"An army of five. I am sure the Xen are shaking in their scaly skins," replied the large man mockingly. After a pause, he stepped toward Mori, moving his head from one side of her face to the next.

"And one of the women, she…"

“Yes,” interrupted the elder. “I see.”

“Yes, Elder, that is why I brought them.”

“Very, well,” replied the elder. “Caleb!” he shouted while still staring at Mori.

The youth came running.

“Yes, Elder.”

“Go get Magnus and his mate. Tell them it is important. We have guests.”

Stone began to feel uneasy. There was something about Mori that had the entire group of mutants on edge. Slowly and quietly, he tilted his rifle to ensure he had plenty of ammo left in his clip.

The others felt it too.

“What the hell is going on, Mori?” asked Orion.

“I don’t know,” she replied, “but it’s starting to freak me out.”

“We’re in a cave surrounded by wolfmen,” added Rickover. “What could go wrong?”

“Just keep quiet and stay alert,” replied Stone.

“Great. Here come some more,” said Orion.

From the darkness two figures came into view. The male was huge by human standards. Well over two meters, his broad shoulders and muscled physique could not be hidden by the thick hair growing on his bare torso. Behind him was a female, standing in his shadow.

“What have you brought us, Horatio?” asked the large man.

“We found them in the forest, Magnus,” replied Horatio, his head looking toward the ground. “This female…her…”

"Her scent," said the woman behind Magnus. "She smells like…"

The woman stepped into the light. She was beautiful with piercing green eyes.

"…like family," concluded the unknown woman.

Stone looked toward Mori. Her jaw dropped as she let her rifle fall to the ground. The two women stepped toward each other.

"Kat…Katalya? Is that you?"

Tears welled in Mori's eyes and she began to tremble.

"Sister!" shouted the woman as she embraced Mori. "I thought I would never see you again."

"I never gave up," sobbed Mori. "I knew in my heart you were alive."

Magnus walked toward the two, towering over them. "Katalya, this woman is your kin?"

Still embracing her sister, she answered.

"Yes, Magnus. My sister. We were separated when I was captured, but now we are…"

"Together," added Mori.

"Yes, together."

"And the others?" asked Magnus.

"We're here to find a way to destroy the base and stop the Xen from weaponizing the virus," answered Stone.

"I did not know if we could trust them," added Horatio as he slightly bowed his head. "I thought it best to bring them to you and the elder."

"Yes," answered Magnus. "Perhaps we should leave the siblings to themselves and we shall talk of the virus."

Running his hand over Katalya's hair, Magnus lowered his head to her ear.

"I am happy for you, mate," Magnus said to Katalya as he motioned toward a separate room in the back of the den. "Come with me, we shall talk. Horatio, Elder, please join us as well."

Placing his head toward the ground, the old man answered, "As you wish, Magnus."

Upon entering the room, Magnus spoke.

"This is probably more to your liking," said Magnus, flipping a switch on the wall. As he did, additional lights illuminated the room to normal levels.

"Sit, please," he continued as he took a seat at the head of a large table, the elder and Horatio standing behind him.

"So how did you get here?" Magnus asked as his guests took their seats.

"It wasn't easy," said Rickover.

"They say the Xen are performing the tests to create hybrids for their slave populations," reported Horatio.

"We recently found out about the Directive and existence of this base," said Stone.

"It must be very secretive if even Alpha Humana officers do not know of it," answered Magnus.

Stone was surprised that Magnus had identified him. "How did you know?"

"Your Humani scent fills the air…and I can see part of your Elite guard marking from your torn shirt."

"I am no longer in service of the Xen Emperor," he said. "I am with your mate's sister."

A series of squeaks came from TC. "What has happened to you?" he asked bluntly.

"All we know is that we're the second in a series of three tests," replied Magnus.

"Magnus, may we join you?" Katalya asked, her head looking toward the ground as she and Mori stood at the doorway.

"Of course, please sit. You as well, Elder, Horatio."

As the others took their seats, Magnus continued.

"How many have there been?" asked Stone. "How many have been part of the experiments?"

"Over the years," said the elder, "millions."

"Millions!" echoed Mori.

"Yes," continued Magnus. "It is a very large operation. At first the Xen used vulpes genes to create the fox clan."

The elder spoke next.

"The testing showed that few survived the alterations and that most that did failed to conform to captivity. The species was then…discontinued."

"That is how Mother died," added Katalya as she placed her hands over Mori's.

"Next was the canis gene," continued the elder. "They created two strands. The familiarious and lupus genomes were tested creating the canine and wolf clans. Ours is the lupus or wolf clan. We adjusted well to the modification, although the first few months are extremely painful as the alterations occur."

"At least the children do not suffer the change like us," added Katalya.

Magnus picked up where the elder had left off. "But we, too, refused to cooperate with our would-be masters. The canines proved much more…loyal. In the canines, they found not only slaves, but subservient ones."

"What of the wolf clan? How did you end up out here?" asked Orion.

"We too were scheduled to be eradicated," said the elder.

"The elder," added Magnus, "led an uprising against the Xen. His leadership and bravery allowed us to escape and survive. He was our leader until he grew too old and I replaced him."

"Thousands died, but a few of us escaped," said the elder. "I only wish more had survived."

"You are all that are left?" asked Mori.

"Out of thousands that resisted, we forty-one remain," said Katalya. "Not quite human, not quite wolf."

"The alterations may look subtle," added Magnus, "but they are significant. As you can tell, our sense of smell is heightened as well as our night vision. Our offspring also mature much more quickly, usually by age twelve. Additionally, we have taken on several mannerisms such as our loyalty to the pack and our hierarchy."

"At least you earn your positions of power," said Stone, thinking back to the social stratification of the Humani.

"Thank you," said Magnus, nodding in recognition of Stone's compliment.

"Can this be reversed?" asked Mori as she looked at her sister.

Magnus's head snapped in the direction of Mori, his teeth showing. "Reversed? Why would we want to change?"

"Magnus, please remember this is new to them. They mean no disrespect," pleaded Katalya.

Regaining his composure, he continued. "Excuse me. I must remember you have only today learned of us. We can never be human again, nor can we have human offspring. Hopefully, we can survive to display the best virtues of each species. We are what we are and would not want to have this as you say…reversed."

"It's okay, Mori," said Katalya. "I still have nightmares about being taken from my family, the testing, and the deaths of so many, but I do not regret what I have become. If only we could escape this planet and find a place of our own."

"And be allowed to fight those reptilian demons on equal terms," added Magnus, "instead of hiding and running. It's not *our* way."

"That is why we're here," said Stone. "We must find a way to destroy this place while allowing us to get out safely…if possible."

"How can so few destroy an entire planet?" asked Magnus.

"You want to destroy the planet?" asked Rickover matter-of-factly.

"Well, to destroy the virus, the base, and the Xen on it, I don't see what else to do," said Stone.

"Again, how the hell are we gonna do it?" posed Orion. "I just don't see..."

"We can do that," interrupted Rickover.

"What the hell are you talking about?" asked a confused Stone.

"It's all about the magnetism."

"What *are* you talking about?" asked Orion. "I think your big brain has finally snapped."

"Funny, Captain. It's not my fault if I understand magnetic forces and you don't."

"I don't understand," said Mori.

Rickover stood up from the table and let out a sigh of disappointment. He was a genius; his biggest problem was in not understanding why everyone else wasn't.

"Look," he said, grabbing a stylus from the desk and writing on its surface, much to Magnus's chagrin. "The asteroid belt circles this planet like this. There's force put on the asteroids by the magnetic field of this planet. The asteroids are polarized against the North and South poles of this planet. If we disrupt either the magnetic field of the planet or the polarity or electron flow patterns through the asteroid, we can allow the planet's gravity to accelerate the asteroid toward the planet. The last time I checked, planets don't like thousands of massive asteroids slamming into them."

"You can cause the asteroids to crash into the planet?" asked Magnus.

"Well, I can't, but the captain can—if she is a good enough pilot and if TC is a good enough navigator. Oh, and if we don't get shot down while trying to do it."

"I still don't understand what you are talking about," said Orion, knowing all too well she was about to get another lecture from Rickover.

"Look," said Rickover as he took a deep breath. "If you make *Hydra* go roundy-roundy fast enough around the asteroid belt," he said as he made funny hand gestures, curling his hand in one direction and sticking his thumb out, "you will create a magnetic field this way, which is opposite of the natural field, hopefully collapsing it momentarily and allowing the new force and gravity to do the rest. You have to rotationally accelerate to a jump and then establish a reoccurring jump to build up the field as you go."

"Will that really work?"

"It should. You just have to get to the asteroid belt and then pull out of the jump just as the asteroids start to accelerate."

"How the hell do we know when to do that?" asked TC.

"If you can get the jump sequence down, I can calculate the hypothetical nominal time."

"Hypothetical?"

"Well, it's hard not to be hypothetical until we actually do it, isn't it?"

"What if we're off a little?" asked Orion.

"We'll either be crushed by the wall of asteroids as they accelerate or decelerate into the waiting arms of Xen condors."

"Nice," replied Orion. "Wonderful options, as always."

"Rickover," asked Stone, "can this work?"

"I wouldn't have mentioned it if it wouldn't."

"I think we should try it," said Mori.

"Me too," said TC.

"What do we have to lose?" asked Orion.

"Everything," added Stone. "But it's the only option on the table."

Mori looked toward her sister. "What about the…"

"You may call us the wolf clan," said Magnus.

"The wolf clan. Can we get them all off the planet with us?"

"It will be a tight fit," said Orion, "but we should be able to squeeze everyone in, especially without the weight of the bombs."

"We accept your offer," said Magnus. "We can be ready by nightfall."

"It's settled then," said Stone. "We go tonight."

***

Martin's dreams were crowded with jumbled distorted flashes of memories of her father, Jackson, and Stone. As her broken body struggled to heal itself physically, her mind raced. As she lay in the infirmary, Martin's visions were interrupted by muffled, far-off voices.

"Shouldn't she be coming out of it soon?" a female voice spoke.

"It might be a while longer," responded a male voice. "She had lost a fair amount of blood, but the infection from her wounds would have killed her if she hadn't gotten aid when she did. Actually, it should have killed her anyway. She must have one hell of a reason to stay alive."

Stimulated by the voices, Martin attempted to move her body but her limbs would not respond. Focusing all of her efforts on her left hand, Martin tried again. *Move*, she thought.

"Doctor," interrupted the female voice. "Her hand."

"I see it," he replied. "hand me the injection. I think we can try to bring her around."

The voices grew clearer.

"This should do it."

Martin felt her arm grow warm, and light began to flood her consciousness.

"She's coming back," exclaimed the woman.

Martin began to realize she was regaining consciousness; her head was foggy and her eyes difficult to open. Struggling to regain her sensing, she first felt a dull ache in her shoulder and her entire body felt as if it had been hit by a hovercraft. Slowly she opened her eyes.

"Welcome back, Captain Martin," said the doctor. "We weren't sure we were going to get you back."

Martin tried to speak but she could not form the words. Her jaw was stiff and her throat was dry and chalky.

"Don't try to speak, Captain," explained the doctor. "It may still be several days before you can speak. But I am sure you have many questions."

Martin nodded her head slightly in acknowledgment.

"Your unit was overwhelmed on Juliet 3. You are the only survivor that we know of."

Martin's mind raced, trying to make sense of the visions and nightmares that had filled her dreams while she was unconscious.

"Jack-son?" asked Martin in a scratchy, distorted voice. As she spoke, pain shot through her throat into her stomach.

"I don't know who that is," responded the doctor. "But as far as the reports have stated you are the sole survivor."

Suddenly she flashed back to the final moments of battle as the Terillian sword passed through Jackson's back and then to her staring into his vacant eyes on the abandoned battlefield.

"That is, except for the Traitor," interrupted the doctor.

Martin looked up toward the doctor, unaware of any of the events that had transpired after the battle.

"Your commander…Tyler Stone, betrayed your positions and then killed Cataline Tacitus and assaulted our ProConsul Astra Varus."

Martin could not comprehend what the doctor had just revealed. All she could do was shake her head slowly in denial.

"I'm afraid it's true, Captain," continued the doctor. "Apparently he came under the influence of a Terillian spy and became her lover, further betraying the Lady Varus and our people."

"No!" choked Martin, even though speaking caused searing pain in her throat.

"The Traitor and his whore attacked the Senator Dominotra and Lady Varus on their estate, killing the Senator and permanently scarring Lady Varus, now our ProConsul."

Martin continued to shake her head, growing more animated.

"It's not possible," replied Martin as blood started to trickle out of her mouth. "No!"

"Captain," warned the nurse, as she placed her hands on Martin's left arm, "you mustn't get too excited. You are still very seriously injured."

Martin pushed against the nurse and attempted to pull herself out of the bed. The pain was agonizing but she wasn't thinking clearly. None of it made sense and she needed to get out of the bed.

"Nurse," shouted the doctor, "we need to sedate her again."

Martin had pulled herself into a sitting position when the doctor injected her. The medication worked quickly; Martin felt her head grow even heavier and her muscles loosen. She fell back into the bed and her vision started to blur. With all of her strength she grasped for the doctor's arm. Grabbing his arm tightly she looked directly into his eyes.

"No. It can't be," she coughed.

Martin's grip on the doctor loosened and her arm fell limply to the side of the bed.

Chapter 19

The wolf clan and their new allies emerged from the trap door just as darkness enveloped the forest. They quietly made their way, single file, toward *Hydra*.

"These guys are natural warriors," Stone whispered to Mori as they crept through the blackness of the forest.

"Even the young ones," added Mori. "It would take months to train men to do what seems to come naturally to them."

"It must be the alterations, but you are right," continued Stone.

Suddenly Magnus stopped, his nose high in the air. He quickly, and quietly, made his way to Stone.

"Xen," he said. "About a hundred meters ahead."

"That's were *Hydra* is," whispered Orion.

"Elder," ordered Magnus, "stay here with the youths. Horatio, take your group to the right. Caliph, move forward and take up positions. I will move to the left."

Magnus looked back toward Stone. "Shall your team join me?"

"I'll help keep an eye on the youths," said Rickover. "Hand-to-hand combat isn't my bag. I'm an engineer, not an infantryman."

Magnus and his men quietly took up positions near the clearing.

Kneeling behind a felled tree, Magnus whispered to Stone. "Do you see them?"

Struggling to focus through the darkness, Stone gave up and donned his night goggles. Adjusting the gain, he saw several Xen troops milling around *Hydra*. One, apparently the officer, was inspecting the bay doors to the ship.

"Are your men in position?" whispered Stone.

"Yes. They are waiting for my signal."

"Wait," added Orion, who had just crawled up beside the two. "I can add a little more distraction. Tyler, you may want to take that off," she said, as she tapped lightly on his goggles.

She reached into her pocket and pulled out a small remote module. "Get ready for the sun to come up," she smiled.

Orion activated the remote and every exterior light on *Hydra* lit up in flash of blinding brightness. The Xen soldiers, startled and partially blinded, staggering in the intense light. Before they could recover, Magnus let out a loud piercing howl and gunfire erupted.

The majority of the Xen fell in the initial salvo. As the survivors attempted to regroup, Magnus leapt from his position, followed by the rest of his clan and the humans. A mixture of guttural howls, hisses, and gunfire echoed through the forest. Magnus dropped the first Xen in front of him with a shot from his pistol. The next Xen, an officer, was waiting for him with his sword drawn and mouth gaping open, venomous saliva dripping from its mouth.

The two collided in a burst of growls and hisses. When they came to rest, Magnus had his hand against the Xen's head, forcing its snapping jaws away from him while he sank his powerful canines into its neck.

The attack was over quickly. As he pulled his sword from the torso of a dead reptile, Stone looked for Mori. He saw her, next to her sister, checking the Xen for survivors.

"That felt good. I haven't tasted Xen blood for quite some time," said Magnus as he walked toward Stone. "Just stay clear of their saliva and they are actually pretty tasty," he added as the blue life-fluid of the Xen officer dripped from his mouth.

Having ensured there were no survivors, the group gathered outside *Hydra* and quickly went about their tasks. Rickover immediately made his way back to the security of his engine room. TC went to work calculating the complex jump sequencing Rickover had recommended. Katalya assisted the young and old onboard the ship while the rest discussed their situation.

"We need some kind of diversion in order to make it to the asteroids," said Orion. "Otherwise, if the land-based condors don't get us, the batteries of the warships in orbit will."

"We won't be able to cause a distraction big enough to draw the attention of every fighter and warship. There's just too many," said Mori.

"We may not need a grand diversion," Magnus postulated. "Slavers are constantly coming and going. Maybe we can just leave."

"They may not be looking for anything leaving the planet since they spend so much time keeping everything out," said Orion. "If it works, that should get us at least close to the asteroids. From that point we'll just have to rely on luck and Rickover's big brain."

"Does anyone have a better plan?" asked Stone.

Silence.

"I guess that settles it," said Orion. "Let's stuff ourselves onboard and wait for Rickover and TC to finish the calcs."

***

Everyone fit onboard. Barely.

Rickover cursed under his breath as he squeezed his way through the crowded compartment to the cockpit. Pushing his way through the hatch he handed a piece of paper full of diagrams and calculations to Orion.

"Forty-five seconds."

"What?" asked Orion, trying to interpret Rickover's calculations.

"Forty-five seconds," repeated Rickover. "That's how long you need to stay at jump speed. Not forty-four, not forty-six...FORTY-FIVE. If you're off one second...we're screwed."

"I got it, Ric. Forty-five seconds."

"TC, do you have the jumps calculated?" Orion asked.

"I think so. I don't think anyone has intentionally, or unintentionally, jumped in a circle before. I had to do some manual overrides but it should work."

"What if it doesn't?"

"If it doesn't, we won't have to worry about condors or battle cruisers. Hydra could tear itself apart, shoot off on some tangent and end up running into a planet or star, or we could just crash into the asteroid belt."

"More good news," puffed Orion. "I'm just gonna go with the glass-half-full look at this one. It's gonna work...It has to."

She paused. After a deep breath, she flipped the switch aligning thrusters to the ship's power.

"Let's get this baby off the ground," Orion added as the ship began to hum and rumble from liftoff.

"My numbers are good," said Rickover. "Just don't screw up your part," he added as he turned and headed back toward the crowd and the safety of the engine room, cursing all the way.

"Bringing up passive search, nav, and weapons," reported TC.

"Bring everything up," ordered Orion. "Remember, we're not trying to hide. We're just another slaver headed off planet."

"Roger," replied TC as he brought all systems online.

Hydra banked to the right and began her ascent through the atmosphere. Orion nervously scanned the sky for condors while TC kept watch on his radar systems. To their amazement, the ship passed through the atmosphere into orbit without a hitch. Passing the massive battle cruiser, the asteroid belt appeared in the distance.

"I don't believe it," said Orion, "but I think its working."

"Are the coordinates set?"

"Set, Captain."

"Roger."

Their small celebration was cut short by a transmission from the planet. *All outbound traffic, this is Venato Control. Return to Venato immediately.*

"Damn it," said Orion. "What is that about?"

"The patrol," mumbled Stone. "They must have found it."

"We're too far gone now," replied Orion.

All outbound traffic, return to Venato immediately.

"Going to full power, standby."

Outbound falcon this is CAP 5. All outbound traffic is to return to Venato. Change course or we will engage.

"Full power, now."

Hydra shuddered and accelerated rapidly toward the asteroid belt.

"Captain, condors are accelerating," warned TC. "They will be in weapons range in...damn, they're fast...twenty seconds."

"How long until jump speed and location?"

"Twenty-one seconds."

"Let's hope it takes more than a second for them to pull the trigger," said Orion, thinking out loud.

Hydra raced toward the jump point with the advanced condors closing quickly.

"Condor fire control radar already has a lock, Captain," reported TC. "They will be able to fire as soon as they are in range."

"How long till jump?" asked a nervous Stone.

"Fifteen seconds. Condors have increased speed," said TC.

"What? They were already at top speed," added Orion. "This is gonna be way too close."

"Weapons range in five seconds," TC continued to report.

"Damn it," said Orion as her fingers turned white gripping the controls.

Her body moved forward as if she was trying to urge *Hydra* on. "Engineering, remove all safeties. Max power," she ordered.

"Weapons range now five seconds. Jump location in eight."

"That didn't help much. How much maneuvering room do I have?" asked Orion.

"Point five degrees, Captain. Anything else will put us off course for jump," replied TC.

"That's useless, TC."

"Condors in weapons range. Three seconds to jump. Two...Condors firing...one...at location."

"Engage jump!" shouted Orion.

Blue light filled the cockpit as *Hydra* initiated the jump. Unlike normal jumps, the blue light flashed bright then disappeared as the ship initiated the same jump coordinates every half cycle. Orion and TC fought off the urge to close their eyes in the ever increasing, wind-milling jumps.

"Time?" asked Orion as she closed her eyes against the brilliant flashes of blue.

"Ten remaining."

"I hope this works," added Mori.

As *Hydra* continued to accelerate around the asteroid belt, the blue light grew more intense. Tracks of lightning began to flash between the ship and the asteroids.

"I hope that means its working!" shouted Orion, still clutching the controls.

"Standby for last jump coordinate," said TC.

"Three…two…one…"

The release from the spiraling centrifugal forces was overwhelming as the ship shot of off on a tangent at incredible speed. *Hydra* began to rattle and Orion noticed the bulkhead buckling inward.

"She won't hold together very long at this speed," warned Orion as she struggled to slow the ship. "Once we slow, we'll turn back to see if it worked."

***

A Royal battle cruiser slowly accelerated from its orbit around Venato as dozens of condors sped past. Onboard, the Xen admiral reported back to Venato.

"A large magnetic disturbance has affected the asteroid belt. The orbital stations have received damage from asteroids deviating from normal orbits. I am ordering the squadron clear of the planet until the disturbance is clear."

"Admiral," reported the watch officer, "the condors are reporting acceleration of the asteroids toward Venato and our positions."

"How many?" hissed the admiral.

"All of them, sir. The magnetic field has collapsed."

"Collapsed. The gravity will...Captain, commence jump preparations," spat the Xen admiral.

"Admiral," replied the Captain, "backup reactors are not online. It will take ten minutes..."

The Admiral turned toward the viewing screen. Dozens of massive rocks grew closer. His tongue flicked and saliva dripped from his mouth.

"Set battle stations. Turn to starboard, open fire with all batteries on the asteroids."

"Sir, batteries will be at full power in three minutes."

"Then we are doomed," replied the admiral. "Watch officer, send a long-range message packet. The Directive operation has been destroyed. Suspected Terillian clandestine operation."

"Roger, sir. Preparing packet."

"Very well," he replied. "Damn humans...they are a weakness we cannot free ourselves from. It is we who are the slaves...they will be the downfall of us all," he said aloud.

As the admiral looked back up toward the view screens a massive asteroid appeared on direct course with the battle cruiser.

"Admiral, constant bearing decreasing range on asteroid at 010, estimated size three kilometers by one kilometer."

"Hard to port, full power…"

Atlantis II was ripped in half as the colossal asteroid passed through the ship on its path toward Venato. Dozens of small craft darted from the planet in vain as the shower of death began to rain down from space. Nothing could escape the wall of metal and stone racing toward the doomed planet.

"Wow," said Orion as she sat in the cockpit watching shock waves ripple across the Venato as hundreds of planet killing asteroids impacted on its surface.

"I would have to call that a success," she added.

"We've done it," said Mori as she leaned over from her seat to give Stone a kiss.

"It's only the beginning," answered Stone as he held Mori's hand in his.

"Where to from here?" asked Orion. "Consider me back on the clock, though," she joked.

"What do we do now, Ty?" echoed Mori.

He looked into her green eyes and thought of the future. There would be many battles and more than enough death in the coming months and years. Once a hero to his home world, he had become a traitor to his own people and found he had more in common with his enemy than his own civilization. A future of darkness and uncertainty lay ahead. But there was hope. At least the immediate threat to the entire human species had been destroyed. In giving up all that he had known before, he had found love and purpose. A purpose he knew was just.

"Port Royal...and then Terillian territory," he replied.

"Sounds good to me," said Orion. "TC, set a course for home."

***

Tens of thousands of Humani soldiers snapped to attention in one crisp, sharp movement on the illuminated grounds of the Procession Field. Regimental and divisional flags rippled in the slight breeze that drifted over the field. The corridor to the Eternal Flame was adorned with marble and lined with fluorescent roses. As the drums beat and the trumpets sounded, the procession began.

An Elite Guard battalion, led by Major Arilius Tacitus, was at the van. Stepping in unison, the polished swords sparkled and flashed as they passed the Eternal Flame and took up positions by company.

Next in line was a single figure on a grand and ornate hovercraft, standing erect and wearing a hooded brilliant-white cloak with crimson trim. Each regiment saluted in unison as the craft passed their positions. Moving slowly past each unit, the craft came to a halt in front of the Eternal Flame. The figure stepped down from the craft and slowly walked down the path to the Forum steps. Members of the First Families bowed their heads as the person passed them. Near the steps, fifty senators rose to their feet. The figure continued on, ascending the steps to the entrance of the Forum.

Reaching the marble parade stand and podium, a subtle hand gesture silenced the drums and trumpets. Stepping up to the audio amplifier, the figure removed the hood and spoke:

"Fellow Humani, I come to you on this day not to celebrate but to caution. We are in dark times. Our forces are engaged throughout the systems to defend against the unwarranted aggression of the Terillian hordes.

"We have also suffered personal loss, all of us. I am no different. Like you, I have felt the pain of the loss of a loved one. My father, Senator Dominotra Varus, was murdered by a man who betrayed not only my family but also our entire civilization. Thanks to the fates, I survived the attempt of this traitor's Terillian concubine to kill me. The attack left my face scarred, but we have all been scarred by his treason. Let these scars be a warning to you all: never grow complacent and never forget the basis of our society. Honor, bravery, and social order are the cornerstones we must rely on. They are the foundation of our strength.

"It is with great reservation and a heavy sense of burden that I accept both the appointment to my father's post and my election to the position of ProConsul. On this day I again caution you not to celebrate but to commiserate, not to play but to plan, not to rejoice but to remember. Remember what it is we are fighting for. For me, my scars remind me of the treachery of the past just as my unborn son gives me hope for the future; a future where the Xen Empire flourishes and Terillian aggression is crushed. Long live the Xen Empire."

The parade field erupted with a roar of applause. ProConsul Astra Varus, leader of the Varus family and the Alpha Humani civilization, pulled the hood over her scarred face and turned to lead the procession into the Forum. Walking ahead of the others, she paused near one of the large columns in the entry and looked into the shadows.

"Well said, ProConsul," hissed a voice from the darkness. "You will serve us well."

Epilogue

Astra sat cross-legged on an ornate chair in the ProConsul receiving chambers. On each side stood a Praetorian guard in pristine black uniforms holding an assault rifle at parade rest, their purple and white shoulder-ropes designating their honored duty. To the left of Astra's throne-like chair stood several high ranking Humani officers, two Senators, and a group of minor hanger-ons and aides.

Astra let out a sigh of boredom as she listened to a captain present the latest casualty reports from the ongoing war with the Terillian Confederacy. The ProConsul wore a knee-high scarlet dress embroidered with rubies along the line of her skirt and the plunging v-neck top. The dress was not too tight but still highlighted her perfect, toned body. Her golden hair was tied into a tight bun as was her typical fashion after receiving the head wound at the hands of Mori. It was her way to show all Humani what Stone and Mori had done to Astra, and through her, to the Humani race.

The new ProConsul had moved quickly to consolidate her power. Astra's first act was to dissolve the Senate-selected council of seniors and create in its place the younger, more easily manipulated patrician council consisting of members hand-picked by the ProConsul herself. Next, she convinced the patrician council that as Stone was her intended husband and had killed Cataline Tacitus in proporia combata, all property of the Tacitus patriarch fell to Stone. And when Stone committed his act of treason Astra, as the victim of his betrayal, naturally had a legal right to Stone's property, including the vast holdings he had won from his defeat of Cataline. In these two moves, Astra had gained almost unchallenged political power and doubled the size of the Varus family holdings, of which she was now the matriarch.

Astra tapped her fingers on the marble arm of her chair, slightly repositioned herself, and gave a slight tug to the skirt of her dress as the captain continued.

Capital ship losses for this quarter: 3 Battlecruisers and 4 Oribital Destroyers

Total Aircraft losses for this quarter: 328 Raven Transports, 401 Condor Fighters, 78 Eagle Bombers, 123 Hawk attack craft

Hover tank and heavy equipment losses: 275

Total KIA: 47,000; WIA: 110,000; MIA: 5,345

First Family KIA: 21; WIA: 145; MIA: 2

Enemy losses—

"Enough," interrupted Astra. She sighed again and looked up toward the captain.

After shooting the man a cold stare, Astra turned toward the group of admirals and generals.

"Gentlemen, I do not need all of this superfluous information. Cut the next report down to the important data—how much territory we have gained, First Family losses, and how many Terillians we have killed. The rest really does not matter."

"Yes, ProConsul," answered a general from the group brave enough to answer.

"Well?" asked Astra looking coldly toward the group.

She could tell they didn't understand what she wanted and she liked it that way. The last thing she needed was a flag officer that felt too comfortable around political leaders. She let out another sigh to show her disappointment.

"General, how many dead Terillians?" she finally relented.

"Yes, ProConsul," answered the General quickly as he motioned for the captain to continue.

Terillian capital ships destroyed—

"Damn it, General!" shouted Astra, causing the entire room to recoil in reaction. "I don't give a shit about the machines. How many Terillians have we *killed* this quarter?"

Astra turned back toward the captain and gave him a look she was sure would chill him to his core.

The rattled captain responded.

Uh... Yes, ProConsul. Terillian dead estimated at 50,000.

"It seems we have always inflicted just a few more casualties than they on us General," asked Astra inquisitively.

"Well, uh, yes—"

"General, I don't really need an answer. What I want is an accurate body count on the Terillians. As I have said, I don't need to know our casualties, so you don't need to inflate Terillian losses to save face. I just want to know how many we kill."

As Astra spoke she saw a light blink on the screen embedded in her chair. After looking down for a moment she spoke.

"My next appointment is here. We're done," directed Astra as she rose from her chair.

The captain quickly disappeared amid the small crowd of flag officers as the door to Astra's chambers opened.

"Enter," ordered Astra.

With Astra's command two officers walked into the room, stopped directly in front of the ProConsul, and quickly snapped to attention. Astra smiled and shook her head in satisfaction as Majors Arilius Tacitus and Emily Martin came to attention.

***

As she popped to attention, Martin felt the dull pain in her shoulder transition to a sharp pain. *Damn it*, she thought to herself as she fought the urge to wince in pain.

"Relax. Please," invited Astra as she stepped closer to the two majors.

Martin fought the effort to relax, even though she had been given permission; Astra had no intension of them actually standing at-ease. Letting out a small, inaudible sigh against the pain, she glanced toward Arilius while holding her head straight ahead. In her peripheral vision she could see Astra move in close to Arilius, brushing her body ever-so-slightly against Arilius.

"Major," Astra spoke gently but loud enough for Martin to hear, "it is very pleasant to see you again. It is unfortunate that you were assigned to other duties after my father's death and my attack at the hands of the Traitor and his whore. It seems you are no worse for the wear, however."

"Yes, ProConsul," replied Arilius in a respectful but emotionless tone.

Martin knew Astra had blamed everyone within a kilometer of her estate at the time for her father's death, and she also had no doubt that Astra had played a part in Arilius's reassignment from that of her bodyguard to a deployed unit. It also didn't hurt to have a well-known member of the Tacitus family solar systems away while Astra was making her play for control of a large portion of the Tacitus family holdings.

Martin had not had much of a chance to speak with Arilius since they had both returned to Alpha Humani. All Martin knew for sure about Arilius was that he felt betrayed by Astra as a First Family member and probably as a lover. She also knew none of it mattered to anyone but Arilius and he was too damn "proper" to show any public disdain for a sitting ProConsul.

"The newly promoted Major Emily Martin…the hero of Juliet 3," said Astra mechanically as Martin readied herself for her turn with the ProConsul.

"Yes, ProConsul," snapped Martin, still at attention. Martin despised Astra but she thought, *the enemy of my enemy is my friend.* And Martin would do anything to get her revenge on both the father-figure that had betrayed her and her people, as well as his Terillian concubine.

Martin gave another quick glance toward Astra and then focused forward as the ProConsul slowly walked in her direction. Martin soon saw Astra come into view. The ProConsul stopped directly in front of Martin and peered into her eyes.

Martin, not knowing how to do anything different, returned Astra's stare.

"You are definitely an arrogant one," said Astra as she leaned toward Martin's ear and continued. "Too bad you aren't a man…and from a better family. Maybe you would have been assigned as my *bodyguard*," she added in a taunting voice.

Fuck you, Martin thought. But at least she had that much self-control.

"Skill breeds confidence, not arrogance," answered Martin out loud.

Martin could hear a rumble in the group of flag officers to her left—no doubt shocked by her response to a ProConsul. Martin saw Astra quickly turn her head toward the group to silence them.

"Yes, it does," smiled Astra, still looking toward the senior officer. "But don't overplay—"

Martin saw Astra pause mid-sentence, and her gaze turn down toward the sword on Martin's belt.

"What is this?" asked Astra, as Martin felt the ProConsul unsheathe the sword. Holding the weapon to her face, Astra continued. "This is not your Guard sword, is it?"

"No ProConsul. It's a Ter Scout Ranger sword."

"Well, why do you have it?" questioned Astra sternly with her head tilted slightly.

"Some Ter bastard has my sword. Captain Hugh Jackson was impaled on the sword you now hold on Juliet 3. I took it from the field and will keep it until I can plant it in the heart of the Traitor or the gut of his whore."

Martin could hear more rumbling from the crowd of senior officers.

"Gentlemen," snapped Astra, "does someone have something to say?"

The group fell silent.

Martin could see Astra's face grow red.

"General," continued Astra as Martin saw her pick out Lieutenant General Leto Vispa, a former rival of her father, "one of you had better say something."

"Yes, ProConsul," answered Vispa grudgingly. "We, that is the High Command, feel it inappropriate to give a commoner such authority."

Martin, still unsure of why she had been called to the ProConsul, turned her head toward the general in surprise.

"Authority," shot back Astra. "I am not asking her to have dinner with us, my dear Leto, I want her to be my wolf-hound…hungry, rabid, and single-minded."

Martin grew more anxious over what Astra had in store for her.

"Yes, ProConsul," replied Vispa, "but—"

"General!" snapped the ProConsul. "Let me tell you…no, let me show you why I don't give a shit about her social status."

Martin, still subconsciously looking toward Astra and the High Command officers, saw Astra turn back toward her.

"Martin!" ordered Astra as she pointed at her side and nodded with her head to let Martin know to approach her.

"Yes, ProConsul," replied Martin as she stepped forward, faced toward Astra, and came to attention again.

"Leto," said Astra as she turned back toward Vispa, "is your son, Leittus, among your little sewing circle?"

"Yes, ProConsul. He is here," answered Vispa. "What—"

"Captain Vispa, come forward," interrupted Astra.

Martin saw Captain Leittus Vispa emerge from the crowd. He stood two meters tall, had massive arms and a perfectly tailored uniform.

Meat, Martin thought.

Captain Vispa stopped in front of Astra and saluted.

"So, Captain," spoke Astra, "where did you receive your commission?"

"The Xenus Military Academy, ProConsul."

"Our best military school," replied Astra, sounding impressed.

"How far back can your lineage be traced to a First Family?" she continued.

"Well," said an obviously puzzled Captain Vispa, "to the beginning, ProConsul."

"A pure-blood, and a graduate of our best military program," added Astra.

"Yes, ProConsul," replied a proud Captain Vispa.

"Excellent," stated Astra. "Now take this sword from my hand and kill Major Martin."

"ProConsul?" asked Captain Vispa uncertainly.

Martin could not help but let an inviting smile come to her face as she looked toward Captain Vispa.

"She is unarmed, correct? You have your sword and hers?"

"Yes, ProConsul," answered Captain Vispa timidly.

"Am I not your ProConsul?" Astra asked mockingly, slightly raising the pitch of her voice.

"Yes—"

"Then kill her," ordered Astra calmly and quietly, as if she was asking to have her wine glass recharged.

"But—"

"Now!" shouted Astra.

Martin could almost sense Captain Vispa's muscles tighten, coiling to rush her.

Martin readied herself as the captain charged. Vispa swung the Terillian sword downward at an angle toward Martin's shoulder. Martin waited until the last second and swiftly ducked under the attack. As the sword passed over her head Martin quickly rose up and brought a knee to the captain's ribcage, causing him to let out a loud grunt. As she brought her knee back down she stepped into her opponent, locked his right arm under hers, and swung her body vertically, wrapping her legs around the captain's neck. Torquing her body, she drove the captain's head backward and downward causing him to lose his balance and fall. As he hit the ground, the captain lost his grip on Martin's sword.

Martin was quickly on her feet, drawing Captain Vispa's sword from his sheath as she rose. Captain Vispa scrambled to his feet and took up a defensive position.

Martin, holding both swords, slowly started walking toward the captain.

"ProConsul," pleaded Lieutenant General Vispa.

Martin looked toward the General with a look of bitter hatred for his entire class. Still looking toward General Vispa, she tossed both swords to the ground.

"I would hate for someone to say it wasn't a fair fight," said Martin loudly in a sarcastic tone.

Captain Vispa looked toward Astra. Martin could see he was too proud or too stupid to concede defeat.

"Continue, Captain," directed Astra with a smile as she motioned for him to attack Martin again.

Captain Vispa moved in quickly and the two collided. The captain, actually no novice at hand-to-hand combat, landed a quick elbow to Martin's shoulder. She let out a grunt of anger and pain as his blow reminded her she was still not fully recovered from her injuries. The captain then moved to land a knee to her midsection, but Martin blocked his attack with her own knee. Having blocked his attempt, she quickly slid her leg between the captain's, locked her right leg behind his left, and pushed him backward onto the floor.

When he impacted the floor again, Martin instantly pulled herself up toward the captain's chest and landed a powerful elbow to his sternum. He let out a moan and quickly tried to push his way up by his elbows. As his head lifted from the floor, Martin pivoted and hopped onto her knees, instantly crashing her fist into the captain's head just above the bridge of his nose. The force from her punch caused the captain's head to crash into the floor and bounce slightly.

Although dazed, the captain rolled to his left side to escape Martin's attack. Martin saw her opening and in one continuous motion landed a blow to his kidneys and fell onto his side, placing him in an arm lock. Although the captain was massive compared to Martin, she had the advantage of leverage and slowly drove the man onto his stomach. Once there, she slacked off her hold slightly to allow him to think he had worked free.

Believing he had overpowered Martin, the captain pressed himself off the ground with both arms but as he did Martin quickly wrapped her legs around his waist, slid her right arm under his chin, and locked in the choke hold with her left. With a groan, Martin clasped down on the captain's neck with all of her strength. After a few seconds she felt him waiver and collapse unto the floor. Feeling his body limp underneath her, she envisioned Stone in her grasp. Rage built of unrequited anger and betrayal shot through her body and she strained to squeeze harder.

"ProConsul!" shouted General Vispa, losing all sense of protocol as he watched Martin choke the life out of his son.

"Very well," replied Astra nonchalantly. "Martin, release him."

Martin had blocked out everything except the tension in her arms and her rage against Stone and Mori.

"Major Martin!" shouted Astra.

Astra's shouting finally brought Martin back to reality. Slowly releasing her grip, Martin rose to her feet and stood over the unconscious Captain Vispa. Expecting retribution from Astra or General Vispa, Martin placed herself at attention and turned to face the ProConsul as she fought to hide the searing pain in her shoulder.

As Martin looked toward Astra, she was surprised to see a look of satisfaction on the ProConsul's face.

"Do you see, Gentlemen?" said Astra in a contented voice toward the group of elites. "Perfection," she stated as she pointed back toward Martin. "Utter perfection. The anger, the hatred, and that beautiful pain...and combine that with her ability to kill. That's why I have chosen *this* commoner, General. She is natural killer and because, unlike all of you, she has nothing to lose, she naturally focuses that wonderful rage into such splendid violence."

Martin felt like a pet on display for Astra and her senior officers but the ProConsul was right. She was angry and hurt and she hated Stone and that Terillian bitch for what they had done. And not a day went by since she had finally accepted Stone's betrayal that she did not want to make them pay. *But what the hell is she talking about*? Martin wondered.

"I think you see things my way now, General," stated Astra.

"Yes, ProConsul," replied the general flatly, obviously concerned for his son, who was slowly regaining consciousness.

"Excellent," declared Astra. "Now I need some time with my thoroughbreds."

Turning back to Martin and Arilius, she continued. "General, you and your staff may leave now...and please collect your son on the way out."

Martin stood like an oak at attention as the officers cleared the room and General Vispa and a colonel helped Captain Vispa to his feet and out of the ProConsul's chambers. She continued to watch the group exit through her peripheral vision. As the last officer left, Martin saw Astra stroll over to her chair and sit. As the ProConsul settled in, Martin performed a crisp right-face movement to face her.

"I knew I could count on you to prove my point," said Astra, breaking the silence.

Martin looked up toward Astra.

"Yes, ProConsul," she replied. "It is my duty to serve my people and the Senate in whatever capacity they require."

"And what of your ProConsul?" inquired Astra.

Martin looked directly into Astra's eyes. "Of course, ProConsul, as the leader of the Senate and our people—"

"That's enough, Martin," interrupted Astra. "I am bored of the games. I don't particularly like you, and I know you do not like me."

Martin's mouth opened slightly in surprise to Astra's candid remark.

"But it doesn't really matter. I don't care what you think of me and the fact that I think you're nothing more than a trained animal doesn't mean I can't appreciate the skills."

Martin's mouth now tightened with obvious anger. How she hated ProConsul Astra Varus and every First Family asshole like her.

"And it's that skill that's brought both of you here. I need your, shall we say, talents."

Martin looked toward Arilius who had stood silent while the dog-and-pony show had played out in front of him. Martin could see he was a defeated man; despite his family name, proper behavior, and unquestionable military record, he was in the same boat as she—a mouthy, bitter commoner. Martin had always respected Arilius despite his family's status, but now she sympathized with him as well. Knowing he would never speak out, Martin looked back toward Astra and spoke.

"ProConsul," she said as respectfully as she could, "I am honored at the opportunity to—"

"Stop," interjected Astra as she leaned forward in her seat. "There's no one else here that matters. So drop the act. I—"

"Fine," replied Martin, interrupting the most powerful person in her society. "Why are we here and what do want from us?"

"Such a rabid, unruly viper," smiled Astra, "and just right for the job. I am giving you and the dear Major Tacitus exactly what you both want—the chance for revenge."

"Ma'am?" asked Arilius, finally breaking his silence.

"I want you to hunt down, capture, and drag the Traitor and his whore back to this very room where I can personally eviscerate them."

Astra paused slightly, then continued, "or just kill them and bring their bodies back for me to display; either will do."

Martin looked at Arilius again. A determined and slightly satisfied look came to his face.

"To support your mission," continued Astra, "you will officially be envoys of the ProConsul and operate outside the authority of Humani military command, the Senate, or even the patrician council. You will only answer to me."

"Only to you?" asked Martin. "And our authority?"

"My dear Major," replied Astra, "you will carry the full authority of my office with you. And no need to get too acquainted with your new rank. Your ranks will be dissolved and the new title of Paladin will be given to you. In pursuit of the Traitor and the whore, you will have unlimited authority and resources."

"Unlimited?" inquired Arilius abruptly.

"You will answer only to me," replied Astra in what Martin thought was a surprisingly reassuring voice.

Despite Martin's hatred for Astra, she couldn't help but smile at the opportunity and the freedom it offered to accomplish her quest for vengeance.

"Well, this has been so very exciting, but I must tend to my son," continued Astra as she stood from her seat and turned slightly toward her personal exit.

After a few steps, she stopped and turned back toward the two.

"You must be on your way, my wolf-hounds. It's time to get hunting," said the ProConsul with a smile before she turned and exited the room.

About the Author

Brian Dorsey is a retired Naval Officer and is currently a Nuclear Test Engineer for a Naval Shipyard. When not spending time with his family, Brian enjoys reading and researching US and Native American history, watching good TV shows or films (anything by Joss Whedon), hunting, teaching the occasional history class, or working on his next writing project.

Credits

This book is a work of art produced by F.W. Fife, an imprint of The Zharmae Publishing Press.

James Crew
Editor-in-Chief

Erin Ormsby
Editor

Benjamin Grundy
Typesetter

Gary Hanna
Artist

Amanda Kreklau
Proofreader

Star Foss
Designer

Dean Taylor
Reviewer

Allyson Schnabel
Managing Editor

Tomiko Breland
Associate Publisher

Travis Robert Grundy
Publisher

August 2014
The Zharmae Publishing Press

33761578R10227

Made in the USA
San Bernardino, CA
11 May 2016